STEVEN GOLDSMITH

Heartlands: Fields Of Gold

BOOK ONE OF THE HEARTLANDS TRILOGY

Esqueva Publishing

*To Keziah, Tiggy, and Gus—my greatest inspirations
. Your joy, curiosity, and love light up every word I write.
This story is for you.*

Contents

Acknowledgments   vii

Introduction   1

   The Wheat belt Awakens   1

   Harding Family   2

   Farmstead   3

   Town and Community   5

1   The Discovery   6

   The Unusual Jolt   6

   The Gold Revealed   11

   Building Tension   14

2   The First Dig   19

   Preliminary Works   19

   Discussing The Find   23

   A Covert Exploration   25

3   A Private Discussion   27

   Weighing Up The Risks   27

   Lucy Comes Clean   29

4   The First Signs Of Trouble   37

   Strangers Approach   37

   A Stranger Raises Concerns   40

5   Lucy's Curiosity   45

   Lucy's Curiosity   45

   Bill's Place   47

   Dig Deeper   48

6 Alternate Plans 51

Conflicting Plans 51

Making Plans 54

Lucy's Future 56

7 Unwanted Attention 61

Unwanted Visitors 61

Emma's Decision 66

University 71

Permits for Mining 74

Securing The Farm 78

8 Hard Determination 83

A Difficult Decision 83

Resembling Normal Life 85

9 Veiled Preparations 89

Threshing Shed 89

10 A Plan In Motion 95

An Active Strategy 95

11 Banks Warning 100

Crucial Correspondence 100

Mr Wilson Pays A Visit 105

The Cost of the Future 109

12 Lucy's Discovery 114

Intruder 114

13 Parcel at the Door 118

A Mysterious package 118

14 Bill's Place 123

A Visit to Bill Turner 123

15 Legal Counsel 128

Legal Counsel 128

16 Unlawful Threat 134

Lucy's Encounter 134

17	Law Enforcement	140
	The Police Call and Sergeant's Visit	140
	Sergeant Harris Arrives	142
18	Trespassers	145
	Strange Tracks	145
19	Conversation Overheard	150
	The Strangers Connection	150
20	Confrontation	154
	Confrontation At The Store	154
	Revelations And Concern	157
21	A Warning	159
	Sullivan's Warning	159
	Property Offer	162
	Workplace Inspection	163
22	The Document	167
	The Hidden Document	167
	Letter of Hope	169
23	Surveillance Begins	171
	Camera Surveillance	171
	Fire Protection	173
24	Reconnecting	175
	A Call For Help	175
25	The Strangers Past	178
	History	178
	The Revelation	180
	The Quiet Concern	182
26	Break In	184
	Sabotage	184
	Repair and Secure	187
27	A Secret Meeting	190
	Following The Stranger	190

The Meeting   191

Reporting The Meeting   192

28   A Confession   194

Bill's Confession   194

29   Lucy's Plan   198

The Design   198

Planning and Preparations   201

30   Threatening Message   206

Daniel And Lucy Strategize   208

31   Community Engagement   211

Rallying The Town   211

32   A Close Call   216

A Close Call   216

Mike's Group Call   218

33   The Proposition   221

McRae's Proposition   221

The Return Call   225

34   Lucy's Secret Project   228

Digging The Tunnel   228

Enlisting The Help Of Friends   230

35   A Desperate Gamble   234

Pursuit   234

Intense Confrontation   236

The Ride Home & Strategic Planning   239

36   Fortifying The Farm   242

The Plan Unfolds   242

Constructing the Safe Room   245

37   Emma's Discovery   248

A Troubling Discovery   248

The Race Against Time   250

38   Unwanted Attention   254

The Courtroom Contest . . . 254

Unravelling McRae's Schemes . . . 257

A Community Celebration . . . 259

39 The Final Warning . . . 264

An Ominous Warning . . . 264

Reporting to the Authorities . . . 267

40 Jame's Battle . . . 270

Tragedy Unfolds . . . 270

Urgent Care . . . 272

Recovery . . . 274

41 Lucy's Strength . . . 277

Descending Together . . . 277

The Golden Breakthrough . . . 280

Farming Fundamentals . . . 282

Fence Mending . . . 285

Water Wisdom . . . 288

Reflections at Dusk . . . 291

42 Underground Operations . . . 294

Expanding the Tunnel . . . 294

A Sapphire Surprise . . . 297

From Ore to Gold . . . 300

Rewarding the team . . . 304

43 Showdown . . . 310

The Attack Begins . . . 310

Confrontation . . . 313

Aftermath . . . 315

44 Resolution . . . 318

Triumph . . . 318

Secret Mission . . . 322

Sunset . . . 325

45 The Storm Unleashed . . . 330

Trapped 330

About the Author 334

Acknowledgments

The creation of "Fields of Gold" has been a journey that reflects not just my own aspirations but the collective spirit and unwavering support of many remarkable individuals. I am deeply grateful for their contributions and encouragement throughout this process.

Firstly, I owe a profound debt of gratitude to Keziah Goldsmith, whose boundless enthusiasm and dedication to constructive criticism have been the bedrock of this project. Keziah, your passion for storytelling and your relentless support have inspired me every step of the way. You are not just the muse behind this work; you are its heartbeat.

Lastly, to you, the reader, who has chosen to embark on this journey through the pages of "Fields of Gold." This story now thrives because you have lent it your imagination and time. Thank you for believing in the world I've created.

"Fields of Gold" is a testament to all who dare to dream and labour to turn those dreams into reality. Thank you for turning this dream into a tangible journey.

Introduction

The Wheat belt Awakens

The first light of dawn spread across the vast plains of Burralyndra, casting a soft, golden hue over the endless fields of wheat that rippled in the early morning breeze. The air was cool, carrying with it the faint scent of earth and eucalyptus. As the sun inched higher above the horizon, the landscape came alive. Sounds of the Australian countryside—a distant crow's caw, the rustling of leaves in the wind, and the soft hum of insects waking with the day.

Burralyndra's time flowed differently to others; nature governed its rhythm. The town itself was little more than a collection of weather-beaten buildings, their white paint peeling under the relentless sun. Main Street, the heart of Burralyndra, was a quiet stretch of road lined with a few essential establishments. A general store where the locals gathered for supplies and gossip, a modest pub where the farmers shared tales and traded advice over cold beers. A post office, also serving as the town's informal meeting hall, and a small schoolhouse, educated the children from the surrounding farms.

Beyond the town, the land stretched out in every direction, flat and unbroken except for the occasional cluster of trees or the distant silhouette of a windmill. This land of wheat, simultaneously blessed and burdened. Every farmer recognised that the hands of nature determined the fragile equilibrium between prosperity and ruin.

For the Harding family, this land was home. It had been for three generations, ever since James Harding's grandfather had arrived from England, seeking a new start after the Great War. He had cleared the land by hand, built a modest homestead from the timber he had felled, and planted the first seeds of what would become the Harding family's legacy. Over the years, the farm had grown, passing from father to son, each generation adding to the homestead, expanding the fields, and deepening their roots in the soil.

Today, the Harding farm was a sprawling 50,000-acre property, a patchwork of golden fields and patches of native bush-land. It was a place where hard work and simple joys intertwined. At sunrise, the land's potential is illuminated, while at sunset, the day's efforts are revealed.

Harding Family

The Harding homestead commanded the heart of the farm, its weathered walls and wide, wraparound verandah bearing the marks of time and history. Though expanded and renovated for a growing family, the house still held the charm of its original construction by James's grandfather. Home's interior: cosy, lived-in, radiating familial warmth and past echoes.

James Harding, family head, was taciturn yet masterful. He had inherited his father's stoic demeanour and his grandfather's relentless work ethic. Years of labour roughened and calloused his hands, and the harsh sun and weight of responsibility etched lines into his face. James, a quintessential farmer, knew his land; he knew his family equally well. He knew the soil, the seasons, and the sky. James knew that the key to a successful farm was a balance of patience, persistence, and respect for the forces beyond his control.

Emma Harding, James's wife, was the heart of the home. Unlike

James's muted and reserved nature, Emma was warm and nurturing, a woman whose strength lay in her ability to keep the family together through the trials of farm life. She managed the household, toiled on the farm, and advised during uncertainty with practicality and keen insight. Emma was the glue that held the Harding's together, her love for her family and her land clear in every action she took.

Then came Lucy, their teenage daughter. At nineteen, Lucy was a mix of youthful energy and emerging maturity. She had inherited her father's determination and her mother's practicality, but she also had a fierce independent streak that set her apart. Lucy loved the farm, but she also dreamed of exploring the world beyond Burralyndra. Of seeing what lay beyond the endless fields of wheat and the dusty roads that led to town. Driven to leave her mark, she had many ideas, some grand, some risky.

Lucy was close to her father, often joining him in the fields, eager to learn the ins and outs of farming. James had always encouraged her, teaching her everything he knew, from how to fix a broken fence to the best time to plant the next crop. His worry stemmed from the possibility of her ambitions leading her away from the farm, leaving him uncertain about his emotions.

Farmstead

As the sun climbed higher in the sky, casting longer shadows across the fields, the Harding farm stirred with activity. Farm work started; there's always plenty to do.

The barn, a large, ageing structure near to the homestead, was the centre of much of the farm's daily activity. Tools, spare parts, and various supplies needed to keep the farm running lined its walls. The air hung heavy with the smell of hay, oil, and diesel; comforting, yet a stark reminder of upcoming toil. Inside, the family stored their equipment: tractors, ploughs, seed drills, and, most importantly, the harvester—a massive machine that played a crucial role during the wheat harvest.

Nearby stood the silo complex, a set of towering structures that stored the harvested grain before its transport to the market. The silos were a prominent feature of the farm, their rust-streaked walls telling stories of past harvests, both bountiful and lean. They recalled the farm's purpose, its past and future labour.

Water scarcity worried this region; thus, the Harding's installed a dependable system for their crops and animals. A tall, creaking windmill pumped water from an underground bore, filling the large tanks that dotted the property. The windmill was a constant presence on the farm, its slow, steady rotation a symbol of the farm's resilience and the constant cycle of life and work.

Vast wheat fields formed the farm's core, extending in all directions. During harvest season, the fields were a sea of gold, the ripe wheat glowing under the intense sunlight. At other times of the year, they ploughed the fields, preparing them for the next crop or leaving them to fallow, to rest and recover. The land was both generous and demanding, giving much, but requiring careful stewardship in return.

The Hardings preserved patches of native bushland on their property, areas where they left the land untouched, a small but important part of the farm's ecosystem. These patches were home to various native animals, from kangaroos that often grazed at the edges of the fields to cockatoos that shrieked from the treetops. The farm thrived; nature and human work harmoniously coexisted.

Town and Community

Burralyndra was more than just a town. It was a tight-knit community where everyone was familiar with each other and where strong, neighbourly connections existed. Wheat belt challenges didn't deter Burralyndra's resilient population. They were farmers, shopkeepers, teachers, and tradespeople, all of whom had carved out a life in this remote corner of Western Australia.

Its small population, barely 500, lacked nothing in spirit. In Burralyndra, a powerful sense of community flourished, highlighting interdependence, especially in times of crisis. When a drought hit, when a storm threatened the crops, or when a farmer needed help, the community rallied together, offering support and help without hesitation.

Main Street was the heart of the town, a peaceful road that was rarely busy but always essential. The general store served as a hub for both commerce and conversation, where locals would shop, collect mail, and stay informed on current events. The pub was the men's evening hangout for stories and unwinding. Wives gathered there, exchanging ideas to improve their farms. Families and friends caught up, and communities formed.

The schoolhouse was a small, single-story building on the edge of town, where the children of Burralyndra received their education. Despite its modesty, dedicated teachers and eager students flourished there, understanding that their futures, like their parents', would likely remain connected to the land.

Despite its remote location and the challenges of farm life, Burralyndra was a place of deep pride and strong connections. This community understood hard work, community bonds, and land respect.

1

The Discovery

The Unusual Jolt

The sunrise had barely kissed the horizon when James Harding fired up the harvester. With a growl, the machine came alive, its engine rumbling steadily, promising another long day of hard work. Crisp air carried the scent of wheat and the distant aroma of damp earth. The wheat field stretched out before him. A sea of gold was ready for the harvest. Each stalk standing tall as if in anticipation of the great machine that would soon sweep through.

Lucy stood nearby, a few meters from the harvester, her boots planted firmly in the soil. She watched her father with a practised eye, her hands idly playing with a piece of straw. This was a familiar scene for her. One that had repeated itself every harvest season. From her earliest memories. The whirr of the harvester. The rhythm of the machine cutting through the wheat. Stalks rustling as they fell in neat rows. All of it was part of the life she had grown up with. But today felt different, although she wasn't sure why.

James, seated in the harvester's cab, gripped the controls with a steady hand. He had been doing this for years, each movement precise, each decision calculated. The farm had always been his life, and every year, the harvest was a make-or-break moment.

He was familiar with the land, the machinery, and the crops. Yet, this season had weighed heavily on him. The pressure from the bank, the uncertainty of the future—it all loomed over him like a dark cloud. But there was work to do, and he was unable to dwell on the what-ifs.

The harvester advanced. Neatly, the rotating reel fed the golden stalks into the machine; the machine then threshed them into grain and chaff. The repetitive process, with the engine's steady hum and rhythmic cutting, was almost hypnotic. It lulled father and daughter into the familiar routine of the harvest.

But then, just as the harvester neared the middle of the field, something unusual happened. There was a sudden jolt, a sharp, unexpected jerk that sent a shudder through the entire machine. James's hands tightened reflexively on the controls, and he quickly brought the harvester to a halt. The engine hummed in idle, but something was clearly amiss.

"What the hell...?" James muttered under his breath, his brow furrowing in confusion. Engineers built the harvester to handle tough conditions; it could plough through stubborn patches of wheat, stray rocks, and even the occasional rogue tree branch. But this jolt had been different, more forceful, almost as if the machine had struck something solid, something that shouldn't have been there.

Lucy, sensing that something was wrong, was already moving toward the harvester. Her father climbed down from the cab, his boots crunching on the dry soil as he made his way to the front of the machine. The field was silent save for the low rumble of the harvester's engine, and Lucy's heart beat a little faster, her curiosity piqued.

"Did we hit something?" Lucy asked as she reached her father's side. Her eyes scanned the ground, searching for the cause of the disturbance.

James didn't answer right away. He focused on the front of the harvester, where the reel met the cutter bar. There, entangled in the machine's teeth, was something small; its gleam surpassed that of wheat. He bent down, squinting in the early morning light as he reached out to dislodge the object.

Lucy watched, her curiosity growing by the second. From where she stood, she saw a glint of something—something that shone like a tiny beacon against the dull metal of the harvester's teeth. Her mind raced through possibilities. Was it a piece of metal? A rock with some kind of mineral in it? Whatever it was, it didn't belong in their wheat field.

James finally pried the object free, holding it up between his fingers. For a moment, he just stared at it, his eyes narrowing as he examined it more closely. It was small, rough around the edges, but undeniably golden. The morning sun caught it just right, and for a split second, the tiny nugget seemed to glow, as if it held a light of its own.

Lucy's breath caught in her throat. "Is that... gold?" she asked, barely able to believe the words as they left her mouth.

James didn't answer immediately. He was too occupied turning the nugget over in his hand, assessing its weight, testing its texture. He had seen gold before, of course—everyone had. But not like this. Not here, in the middle of their wheat field, caught in the teeth of their harvester.

"Perhaps," James finally said, his voice low and tinged with something that might have been awe, or maybe it was fear. He wasn't sure yet. "Looks like it, at least."

Lucy's mind raced. If this was gold, if there was more of it buried beneath their land... She was unable to comprehend the implications. The farm had been struggling for years, barely scraping by, always one poor season away from foreclosure. But gold—real, honest-to-God gold—had the potential to change everything. It might save the farm, pull them out of debt, secure their future. But it was also capable of bringing trouble, more trouble than they were prepared to deal with.

"What do we do?" Lucy asked, her voice trembled with both excitement and anxiety.

James looked up from the nugget, his eyes meeting Lucy's. He saw the same thoughts racing through her mind, the same mix of hope and fear. For a moment, he was at a loss for words. He was a man of the land, a farmer through and through. Gold, wealth, all the things that came with it—those were foreign concepts to him, things that happened to other people in other places.

But this wasn't just about him, or even just about the farm. It was about his family, their future, and if this land would remain their home. And despite his desire to, he was unable to disregard the potential that small detail symbolised.

"First thing," James said slowly, "we keep this between us. It's remaining a secret until we determine the problem.

Lucy nodded, understanding the gravity of the situation. In a small town like Burralyndra, news travelled fast. The wrong person finding out about this nugget might bring a world of trouble down on them. People would come, people who didn't care about the farm, about the wheat, about the Hardings' way of life. They'd come for the gold, and they wouldn't stop until they had it.

"We should dig around here, see if there's more," Lucy suggested, already thinking ahead. "If there's one nugget, there are likely to be others."

James hesitated. The idea of digging up his fields, the fields that had sustained his family for generations, didn't sit right with him. But Lucy was right—if there was more gold to be found, they needed to find out. And they needed to find it before anyone else did.

"Maybe," James said, still cautious. "But we do it carefully. No tearing up the entire field. We need to keep this quiet."

Lucy nodded again, her mind already racing with plans. She'd seen enough movies, read enough stories, to realise that finding gold may be the beginning of something big. But also that it comes with dangers. That people would do anything for wealth. Even if that meant destroying everything in their path.

They stood there for a moment longer, the nugget still gleaming in James's hand. The sun had risen higher now, bathing the field in warm, golden light. It was a beautiful day, the kind of day that made farming feel like the most rewarding job in the world. But now, there was something else, something new and uncertain, hanging in the air.

Finally, James slipped the nugget into his pocket and turned back to the harvester. "We'll finish the harvest first," he said, his voice firm. "Then we'll decide what to do."

Lucy didn't argue. There was work to be done, and as much as she wanted to search for more gold, she saw her father was right. The wheat wouldn't wait, and neither could they. But as she returned to the harvester, she sensed their lives had been irrevocably altered.

The rest of the day passed in a blur of activity. Side by side, father and daughter worked to the rhythm of the harvest. The sun rose higher in the sky. Long shadows stretched across the fields as the harvester moved steadily through the rows of wheat. Despite the familiar routine, there was a tension in the air, an unspoken understanding between them that everything was different now.

Lucy couldn't stop thinking about the gold, about what it meant, about what it means. Her father was worried that he was thinking about the dangers, the risks. But she inevitably felt a thrill of excitement. This was their chance, their chance to save the farm, to secure their future, to have something more than just getting by.

As the sun dipped lower in the sky, casting a warm, golden glow over the fields, James brought the harvester to a stop for the last time that day. James had cut the last of the wheat, safely storing the grain and leaving the chaff to become compost. It had been a good harvest. One of the best they'd had in years. However, it was the small, rough nugget of gold in James's pocket that dominated their thoughts.

James climbed down from the harvester, his body aching from the long day's work. He wiped the sweat from his brow and looked out over the field. Rows of stubble now all that remained of the wheat that had once stood tall. It was a sight he'd seen many times before, but tonight, it was different. The land felt different, as if it was hiding something, something valuable, something dangerous.

Lucy joined him, her hands dirty, her hair tousled from the day's work. She looked up at her father, searching his face for some sign of what he was thinking. But James was hard to read, his expression as steady and unreadable as the land itself.

"Should we go look around now?" Lucy asked, her voice tentative.

James shook his head. "Not tonight. We need to rest, and we need to think about this. We can't rush into anything."

Lucy nodded, though the disappointment was clear in her eyes. She understood her father's caution, but the urge to dig, to search, to find more gold was almost overwhelming. She wisely chose not to push him. No matter how tempting, James Harding's careful and deliberate nature prevented any rushing.

The Gold Revealed

They walked back to the homestead in silence, the soft crunch of their boots on the dry earth the only sound. The sky was a deepening blue, the first stars just beginning to appear, and the air had cooled considerably. It was a peaceful evening, the kind that usually brought a sense of satisfaction after a hard day's work. But tonight, there was something else—a sense of unease, of anticipation, of something waiting just beyond the horizon.

When they reached the house, Emma was waiting for them on the porch, a questioning look on her face. She had noticed the way James and Lucy had been acting, the way they had exchanged glances, the way their conversation had been more subdued than usual. Something was up, and she intended to find out what it was.

"What happened out there?" Emma asked as they climbed the steps to the porch.

James paused, his hand lingering on the railing as he met his wife's gaze. This isn't something he would keep from her, not even for a moment. Emma had been his partner in everything throughout his life, and she was entitled to appreciate what they had found.

"Come inside," James whispered. "We need to talk."

Emma's eyes widened slightly, but she nodded and led the way into the house. Lucy followed, her heart pounding in her chest. This was the moment everything would change, the moment their lives would embark on a fresh path of promise and peril.

They gathered around the kitchen table, the familiar setting suddenly appearing strange, almost foreign. The room was warm, the smell of baked bread and roasting vegetables lingering in the air, but there was an undercurrent of tension, a sense of something about to happen.

James reached into his pocket and pulled out the nugget, placing it carefully on the table. Emma's eyes widened as she stared at the rough, golden object, her mind racing to understand what she was seeing.

"Is that...?" Emma began, her voice trailing off as she struggled to find the words.

"Gold," James confirmed, his voice steady. "We found it in the field. Caught in the harvester."

Emma reached out to touch the nugget, her fingers brushing against the rough surface. It appeared solid, but it also seemed like a dream, like something that shouldn't exist in their world of wheat and soil and hard work.

Lucy watched her mother's reaction, seeing the same mix of emotions that she and her father had felt earlier. Hope, fear, excitement, and dread—all of it mingled together in the small, rough piece of gold that now lay between them.

"What does this mean?" Emma asked, looking up at James with wide eyes.

James shook his head slowly. "I don't know yet. It could mean a lot of things. But what I appreciate is that we can't tell anyone about this. Not until we figure out what we're dealing with."

Emma nodded, understanding the gravity of the situation. In a place like Burralyndra, news of a gold find would spread like wildfire, and it wouldn't be long before people started showing up, looking to claim a piece of the action. They needed to be careful, to be smart, if they were going to protect their home, their family, their way of life.

"What do we do now?" Emma asked, her voice steady but conveying a sense of worry.

James glanced at Lucy, then back at Emma. "We keep quiet. We finish the harvest, we take care of the farm, and we think about our next move. We need to decide whether we want to dig for more, or if it's better to leave it be."

Lucy's heart sank at the thought of leaving the gold where it was, of walking away from the chance to save their farm, their future. But she also understood her father's caution. The farm was their life, and they couldn't afford to risk everything on a gamble, no matter how tempting.

"We'll think about it," James said, his voice firm. "We won't rush into anything. But whatever we decide, we do it together."

Emma nodded, her eyes still on the nugget, her thoughts racing. Lucy remained silent, her mind filled with a whirlwind of possibilities, of what-ifs, of the unknown future that now stretched out before them.

The Harding family sat in silence for a long time, the golden nugget between them a symbol of both hope and danger, of the possibilities and the risks that now lay ahead. Outside, the clear night sky glowed with stars, the only witnesses to their newly discovered secret—a secret that would change their lives forever.

Building Tension

With a clear and bright dawn, the sky was a perfect blue as the sun began its slow ascent over the horizon. The wheat fields, now harvested, lay still and quiet, the stubble casting long shadows in the early light. Although the world appeared calm, the Hardings still felt uneasy, just as they had the previous day.

Early rising, James prepared for work. But today, his mind was not on the tasks at hand. Instead, it was on the gold nugget, safely hidden away in a drawer in their bedroom, and on the implications of what they had found. He knew they needed to move forward, to decide, but he was also painfully aware of the dangers that lay ahead.

Emma joined him in the kitchen, her face drawn with worry. She had slept little the night before, her mind too busy with thoughts of the gold, of what it might signify for their family, for their future. She could see the strain in James's face, the tension in his movements, and she knew he was struggling with the same thoughts.

"James," Emma said quietly as she poured herself a cup of coffee. "What are we going to do?"

James looked up from his breakfast, his expression thoughtful. "I don't know yet," he admitted. "But I know we need to be careful. We can't let this get out of hand. The farm comes first, always."

Emma nodded, understanding. The farm had always been their

priority, their lifeline. It was what had sustained them through good times and bad, through droughts and floods, through years of hard work and sacrifice. But now, the gold presented an opportunity—one that could save the farm, or one that could destroy it.

"We'll figure it out," James said, reaching across the table to take Emma's hand. "But whatever we decide, we do it together."

Emma squeezed his hand, grateful for his steady presence. They had always faced their challenges as a team, and this would be no different. They would make the right decision, even if it wasn't easy.

Lucy joined them a few minutes later, her hair still tousled from sleep. She looked at her parents, sensing the weight of the conversation they had just had. She knew they were worried, that they were thinking about the risks, the dangers. But she also knew that they couldn't afford to ignore the gold, to walk away from the chance it offered them.

"Are we going to look for more today?" Lucy asked, her voice tentative.

James shook his head. "Not today. We need to think about this, plan it out. Rushing into something like this could cause more harm than good."

Lucy's disappointment was obvious, but she nodded, accepting her father's decision. She knew he was right, even if she didn't like it. The gold would wait, and so would they.

The day passed in a flurry of activity, as the Hardings went about their usual chores. But the gold was never far from their minds, a constant presence, a reminder of the uncertainty that now hung over them.

As the sun set, casting a warm, golden glow over the fields, the family gathered on the porch, watching the day fade into night. Orange and pink streaks coloured the sky, a beautiful sight, yet it did little to ease their tension.

"We'll figure it out," James said quietly, his gaze fixed on the horizon. "We'll make the right decision. But for now, we take it one day at a time."

Emma and Lucy nodded, their hearts heavy with the weight of the unknown. The future was uncertain, filled with both promise and peril. But whatever lay ahead, they would face it together, as a family.

And so, as the last light of day faded away, the Hardings sat in silence, the golden nugget hidden away, a secret that would shape their lives in ways they could not yet imagine.

The days that followed were marked by a tense, uneasy routine. The Hardings continued with their usual chores, but the discovery of the gold had changed everything. It was always there, in the back of their minds, a constant reminder of the decisions they would soon have to make.

Lucy found herself drawn to the field where they had found the nugget, her eyes scanning the ground as if she might find another glint of gold hidden among the stubble. She knew it was unlikely, but she couldn't help herself. The possibility was too tantalising, too tempting to ignore.

James was more cautious. He spent his days working the farm, tending to the animals, repairing equipment, and ensuring that everything was running smoothly. But his thoughts were always on the gold, on what it meant, on the risks it posed. He knew they needed to be careful, to make the right decisions, but the pressure was mounting.

Emma did her best to keep the family grounded, to remind them of the importance of the farm, of their life together. She worried about the gold, about the trouble it could bring, but she also knew that it could be their salvation. It was a delicate balance, one that required careful consideration and planning.

As the days turned into weeks, the tension only grew. The Hardings knew they couldn't keep the secret forever, that they would eventually have to decide. But the uncertainty, the fear of the unknown, kept them from taking action.

Finally, one evening, as the sun dipped low in the sky, casting long shadows across the fields, James decided. He gathered the family around the kitchen table, where the gold nugget had first been revealed.

"This can't continue," James said resolutely, his voice steady. "We need to decide. We need to figure out what we're going to do with this gold."

Emma and Lucy nodded, their expressions serious. They knew he was right, that they couldn't keep living in limbo, waiting for something to happen. They needed to take control, to decide their own fate.

"We can't just dig up the fields," James continued. "Not without a plan, not without knowing what we're getting into. But we also can't ignore this. We need to find out if there's more gold out there, if it's worth the risk."

Emma reached across the table, taking James's hand in hers. "We'll do this together," she said. "Whatever we decide, we do it as a family."

Lucy nodded, her heart pounding in her chest. This was it—the moment they had been waiting for, the moment that would set the course for their future.

James looked at each of them, his expression serious. "We're going to do this right," he said firmly. "We'll take our time, we'll be careful, and we'll make the best decision for our family, for our farm. But whatever happens, we stick together. We face this as a family."

Emma and Lucy nodded, their resolve strengthening. They would do this together, as they had always done. The gold was both a blessing and a curse, but they would face it head-on, with the same determination and strength that had carried them through every challenge they had ever faced.

And so, as the sun set on another day, the Hardings made a pact—a pact to face whatever came their way, to protect their family, their farm, and their way of life. The gold was a part of their lives now, a secret that would shape their future in ways they could not yet imagine.

2

The First Dig

Preliminary Works

The Harding family woke early the next morning, the air crisp and cool with the first hints of spring. The wheat fields stretched out before them, a vast expanse of golden stubble gleaming in the dawn light. A sense of anticipation, an underlying tension that had settled into their lives since they found the gold nugget, tainted the morning's usual peace.

James stood on the porch, sipping his coffee and staring out at the fields. The nugget had been a wake-up call, a jolt that had shaken the foundations of their simple life. It was a reminder that the land they worked so hard to cultivate might hold secrets, secrets that could change everything. But as much as the gold had excited him, it also filled him with a deep sense of dread. The land was their livelihood, and he knew that pursuing the gold meant risking everything they had worked for.

Emma joined him on the porch, a gentle hand resting on his arm. She could see the worry etched into his face, the lines of tension that had deepened since their discovery. She shared his concerns, but she also felt a growing determination. The opportunity to secure their future had appeared, and she knew they must explore it despite the risks.

"Are you ready?" Emma asked quietly, her voice soft in the morning's stillness.

James turned to look at her, his eyes heavy with the weight of their decision. "I don't know if I'll ever be ready," he admitted. "But we can't ignore this. We need to know if there's more out there. We need to find out what we're dealing with."

Emma nodded, her resolve firm. "One step at a time, we'll take it slow. We don't have to make any big decisions yet. We just need to know what's out there."

James took a deep breath, the weight of the decision settling over him like a heavy cloak. He knew Emma was right—they couldn't move forward blindly. They needed to be methodical, careful, and, above all, cautious. But the fear of the unknown still gnawed at him, the worry that they might uncover something they couldn't control.

Lucy appeared in the doorway, her eyes bright with excitement. She had been up since before dawn, unable to sleep with the prospect of what lay ahead. The idea of finding more gold had consumed her thoughts, filling her with a mix of anticipation and impatience. She understood her father's caution, but she was eager to start, to dig, to discover what else the land might be hiding.

"Are we going?" Lucy asked, her voice brimming with energy.

James glanced at Emma, who gave him a small nod. The night before, they had discussed their plan and agreed to start with a small area near the nugget discovery site. It would be a simple dig, just to see if there was anything more beneath the surface. If they found nothing, they would reconsider their approach. But if they found something...well, then they would have a fresh set of decisions to make.

"Let's go," James said finally, setting down his coffee cup and turning toward the fields.

They gathered their tools—a few shovels, a pick-axe, and a metal detector James had borrowed from a neighbour several years ago. It was old and slightly rusted, but it still worked, and it would be enough for what they needed today. They weren't professional miners, just a farming family looking for answers.

As they walked toward the field, the tension between them was palpable, a mixture of excitement and fear that hung heavy in the air. The ground crunched beneath their boots, the dry stubble brittle underfoot. The sun was just beginning to rise, casting long shadows across the land, as if the earth itself was reluctant to reveal its secrets.

James paused at the spot where the harvester had caught the nugget, taking a moment to survey the land. The field looked the same as it always had—flat, dry, unremarkable. But now, it felt different. It felt alive with possibilities, with the potential for something greater.

"This is it," James said, his voice low. "We'll start here."

Lucy eagerly dropped to her knees, grabbing a shovel and digging into the soil. Emma and James exchanged a glance, and then joined her, working side by side as they slowly dug into the earth. The soil was dry and hard, packed tightly from years of farming, but they worked methodically, carefully removing layer after layer.

After what felt like hours, the sun now higher in the sky, Lucy struck something solid. She paused, her breath catching in her throat, and then carefully scraped away the remaining dirt. For a moment, she was afraid to look, afraid that it might be nothing more than a rock or a piece of old equipment buried long ago. But as the dirt fell away, the glint of gold caught her eye.

"Dad! Mum! Look!" Lucy's voice was barely a whisper, trembling with excitement and disbelief.

James and Emma knelt beside her, their eyes widening as they saw what she had uncovered. It was another nugget, slightly larger than the first, rough and irregular, but undeniably gold. James's heart pounded in his chest, a mix of excitement and fear flooding through him. This was real—there was more gold here, more than they had ever imagined.

Emma reached out to touch the nugget, her fingers trembling. It felt solid and heavy in her hand, a tangible reminder of the possibilities that lay beneath their land. But it also felt dangerous, like holding a live wire, a connection to something powerful and unpredictable.

James took a deep breath, his mind racing. This changed everything. Finding a second nugget meant there could be more, possibly a lot more. But it also meant they were stepping into uncharted territory, a world they knew little about, filled with risks they couldn't yet comprehend.

"We need to stop," James said suddenly, his voice firm. Lucy looked up at him, confusion and disappointment etched across her face. "But Dad, we just found another one! There could be even more!"

"I know," James replied, his tone gentle but resolute. "But we can't just dig blindly. We need to think this through, figure out what we're dealing with. This isn't a mere chance anymore. We need to be smart about this."

Emma nodded in agreement, though she could see the conflict in James's eyes. The discovery had excited him, but it had also deepened his fears. They were venturing into unknown territory, and the risks were high.

Lucy reluctantly set the nugget aside, her excitement dimming as she realised the gravity of the situation. She understood her father's caution, but the thought of walking away, even temporarily, from the gold was almost unbearable. It felt like turning their backs on a lifeline, a chance to save their farm, their future.

But James was right—they couldn't rush into this. They needed more information, more knowledge, before they took the next step.

The land was their home, their livelihood, and they couldn't afford to risk it all without understanding the full implications.

"We'll take this one back to the house," James said, carefully picking up the nugget. "And then we'll start researching. We need to know what we're dealing with before we make any more decisions."

Emma and Lucy nodded, though the weight of the decision hung heavily over them. The walk home was quieter this time, the excitement tempered by a growing sense of responsibility. They had found more gold, but with it came more questions, more uncertainty. And with that uncertainty came the realisation that their lives were about to change in ways they couldn't yet predict.

Discussing The Find

Back at the house, the family gathered around the kitchen table once again, the second nugget now resting beside the first. The two pieces of gold seemed to glow in the afternoon light, their rough surfaces catching the sun's rays and reflecting them back in a soft, golden hue.

James stared at the nuggets, his mind racing with possibilities and fears. The discovery of the second nugget had confirmed that there was more gold in the land, but it had also confirmed his worst fears—that they were stepping into something much bigger than they had expected. The farm had always been their anchor, their constant, but now it felt like it was slipping away, being replaced by something unpredictable and dangerous.

"We need to figure out what to do next," James said finally, breaking the heavy silence that had settled over the room. "We can't just dig up the entire field. A plan is necessary, and we must grasp the situation."

Emma nodded, her expression serious. "We need to research this, find out what the laws are, what permits we might need, and what risks are involved. We can't afford to get this wrong."

Lucy listened quietly, her earlier excitement now tempered by a growing understanding of the challenges they faced. She had wanted to keep digging, to uncover more gold, but she could see now that her parents were right. They couldn't rush into this. The stakes were too high.

"We also need to be careful who we talk to about this," James continued. "If word gets out that we've found gold, it could bring a lot of unwanted attention. We need to keep this between us for now until we know more."

Emma and Lucy nodded in agreement, the gravity of the situation sinking in. The discovery of the gold had opened up a world of possibilities, but it had also brought with it a host of new challenges and dangers. They needed to move carefully, to safeguard their family and their farm.

"I'll start looking into the legal side of things," Emma said, her voice steady. "We need to know what our rights are, and what we need to do to keep this quiet."

James nodded, grateful for her calm and practical approach. "And I'll start researching mining techniques, see if there's a way we can do this without drawing too much attention. We need to be smart about this."

Lucy felt a surge of pride in her parents, their determination to be open to new ideas and approaches. Giving their farm a future shining through despite the fear and uncertainty. She knew this wouldn't be easy, but she was ready to face whatever came their way. They had always been a strong family, and they would face this challenge together.

As the day wore on, the Hardings pieced together a plan, a tentative pick-axe for navigating the uncertain terrain ahead. They knew there would be obstacles, both legal and practical, but they were determined to move forward with caution and care.

James and Emma spent the next few days poring over books and online resources, learning everything they could about gold mining, land rights, and the potential risks involved. They quickly realised that they were in over their heads, that the world of gold mining was complex and fraught with legal and financial challenges. But they were determined to learn, to understand the full scope of what they were facing.

Lucy, meanwhile, couldn't shake the urge to return to the field, to dig deeper, to uncover more of the treasure that lay beneath their land. But she knew better than to act on impulse. Her parents had clarified that they needed to be cautious, that they couldn't afford to make any mistakes.

A Covert Exploration

Yet, the attraction of the gold was compelling, a persistent presence in her mind. It called to her, urging her to take action, to dig deeper, to find out just how much lay hidden beneath the surface.

And so, late one night, unable to sleep, Lucy slipped out of the house and made her way back to the field. The moon was high in the sky, casting a silvery light over the land, and the air carried a chill. Lucy knew it was risky, that she was breaking her parents' trust by going out on her own, but she couldn't ignore the pull of the gold.

She reached the spot where they had dug earlier, the disturbed soil still soft underfoot. Kneeling down, she dug, her heart pounding in her chest. The soil was cool and damp, and as she worked, she felt a sense of exhilaration, a thrill that came from knowing she was on the brink of discovering something extraordinary.

After what felt like hours, her fingers brushed against something solid, something cold and hard. She paused, her breath catching in her throat, and then carefully scraped away the dirt. Revealing the object made her gasp—a small, rough nugget of gold, even smaller than the first two, but just as beautiful, just as mesmerising.

Lucy's heart raced as she held the nugget in her hand, the thrill of discovery washing over her. But a sense of dread quickly replaced it. What had she done? She had gone against her parents' wishes, had acted on impulse, and now she was holding the proof of her disobedience.

She knew she couldn't keep the nugget a secret. She had to tell her parents, had to confess what she had done. But the thought of facing them, of admitting that she had gone behind their backs, filled her with fear.

With a heavy heart, Lucy slipped the nugget into her pocket and made her way back to the house, the weight of her decision pressing down on her with each step. She knew she had to come clean, to face the consequences of her actions. But as she approached the house, the lights still on in the kitchen, she hesitated. She could see her parents inside, still bent over their research, still trying to protect their family and their farm.

The guilt gnawed at her, but she couldn't bring herself to walk through the door, to confess what she had done. Instead, she turned and walked around to the side of the house, where she carefully hid the nugget under a loose stone in the garden. It would stay there, a secret known only to her, until she could find the courage to tell her parents the truth.

3

A Private Discussion

Weighing Up The Risks

Lucy knew she couldn't keep the nugget a secret forever, but for now, she wasn't ready to face her parents. She tiptoed back to her room, her mind swirling with conflicting emotions—excitement, guilt, fear. The gold was more than just a treasure; it was a symbol of everything that could change their lives, for better or worse.

The next morning, the Harding family gathered around the breakfast table, the tension from the previous day lingering in the air. Emma had barely slept, her mind racing with all the research she had done. James, equally preoccupied, thought about the potential risks and rewards of their discovered gold. Lucy, though quieter than usual, tried to act normal, her secret hidden beneath the surface.

"Let's go over what we've found out so far," Emma said, her tone serious as she pushed her plate aside and laid out a few printouts on the table. "There are a lot of regulations with mining, even on your own land. We'd need to apply for permits, and there's a risk that if the government finds out about the gold, they could claim it as a public resource."

James nodded, rubbing his chin thoughtfully. "That's what worries me. Once we dig in earnest, it won't stay a secret for long. We're going to need help—experts who know what they're doing. But bringing in outsiders could mean losing control over the land."

Lucy's heart pounded in her chest as she listened to her parents discuss the future. The weight of the small nugget she had hidden in the garden pressed down on her conscience. She knew they were right to be cautious, but she couldn't shake the feeling that they were missing an opportunity.

"What if we kept it small?" Lucy suggested, her voice hesitant. "Just... you know, kept digging ourselves. We don't have to tell anyone yet. We could see how much there is before deciding what to do."

James looked at his daughter, seeing the determination in her eyes. He admired her spirit, but he also knew that the path she was suggesting was fraught with danger. "Lucy, I understand why you feel that way, but this isn't something we can handle on our own. There's too much at stake."

Emma reached out and took Lucy's hand, squeezing it gently. "We'll figure this out together, sweetheart. But we have to be smart about it. Rushing in could end up costing us everything."

Lucy nodded, though her heart sank. She knew her parents were right, but it didn't make the waiting any easier. She felt trapped between the desire to act and the fear of making a mistake that could destroy everything they had worked for.

Later that day, while her parents continued their research, Lucy wandered back to the garden where she had hidden the nugget. She crouched down and lifted the loose stone, revealing the small piece of gold beneath it. It gleamed in the sunlight, a tantalising reminder of the possibilities that lay beneath their land.

She sat there for a long time, turning the nugget over in her hand, lost in thought. The gold was more than just a material object; it was a symbol of hope, of a future that could differ from the life they had known. But it was also a burden, a secret she wasn't sure she could carry alone.

As the days passed, the Hardings fell into a routine of sorts. James spent most of his time working the fields, trying to keep up with the demands of the farm while also planning their next steps. Emma continued to dig into the legalities of mining, growing more and more concerned with each new discovery. And Lucy, torn between her desire to help and her guilt over the hidden nugget, retreated more and more into her own thoughts.

As the days turned into weeks, the household grew tense. Despite that, they had made no decisions. The gold was a constant presence in their lives, a shadow hanging over them, but it remained untouched. The small nuggets they had found sat on the kitchen table, a daily reminder of the choices that lay ahead.

Lucy Comes Clean

One evening, as they sat around the dinner table in near silence, Lucy couldn't take it any longer. The secret she had been carrying was too heavy, the burden too great. She looked at her parents, both of them worn down by the weight of their indecision, and knew she had to tell them the truth.

"There's something I need to tell you," Lucy said quietly, her voice shaking slightly.

Emma and James looked up, surprised by the seriousness in their daughter's tone.

"What is it, Lucy?" Emma asked gently, sensing that something was wrong.

Lucy hesitated for a moment, then took a deep breath and reached into her pocket. She pulled out the small nugget she had found and placed it on the table next to the others.

A barely audible whisper escaped her lips as she admitted, "I found this." "I couldn't sleep that night after we found the second nugget. I went back out to the field by myself. I'm sorry, I know I shouldn't have... but I just had to see if there was more."

James stared at the nugget, his expression unreadable. Emma's eyes widened, a mix of surprise and concern crossing her face.

"Lucy..." James began, but he stopped, not knowing what to say. He felt the conflict between anger and understanding, fear, and pride. His daughter had acted on her own, going against everything they had agreed upon, but she had done it out of the same drive that he himself had felt.

Emma reached out and took Lucy's hand again, her grip firm but gentle. "Why didn't you tell us sooner?"

Lucy looked down at the table, unable to meet her mother's gaze. "I was terrified," she admitted. "I didn't want you to be angry. And I didn't want to make things harder for you. But I couldn't keep it a secret anymore."

James finally spoke, his voice calm but stern. "Lucy, understand how dangerous this is. We're not just dealing with gold here. We're dealing with our entire livelihood, our home. I'm glad you told us the truth, but you can't go out there alone again. It's too risky."

"I know, Dad. I'm sorry," Lucy replied, her voice small. She felt the weight of her father's words, the seriousness of the situation pressing down on her.

Emma squeezed her hand once more, then let go. "We're going to have to be even more careful now," she said. "This means there's definitely more gold out there. We need to figure out how to handle this without putting ourselves or the farm at risk."

James nodded in agreement. "We'll have to bring in someone we trust—someone who knows what they're doing and can help us without drawing attention. We can't afford to make any mistakes."

The decision to bring in an expert weighed heavily on them, but they knew it was the only way to move forward. They needed someone who understood mining, who could help them navigate the legalities and logistics without compromising their privacy.

Over the next few days, James made discreet inquiries, reaching out to a few trusted contacts in the region. He didn't give away too much information, only that they were looking for someone with expertise in land surveying and resource extraction. It wasn't long before he received a response from an old acquaintance, a retired geologist named Bill Turner, who lived in a nearby town.

Bill had worked in the mining industry for decades before retiring to the quiet life of the country. Known for his discretion and his deep knowledge of the land, making him the perfect candidate for the Hardings' situation.

When James contacted Bill, he was careful not to reveal too much over the phone. Instead, he invited Bill out to the farm, framing it as a social visit with an old friend. Bill agreed, and a few days later, he arrived at the Harding farm, curious but unsuspecting.

The Hardings greeted Bill warmly, inviting him into their home and offering him a seat at the kitchen table. After catching up on old times and exchanging pleasantries, James finally broached the subject that had brought Bill there.

"There's something we need your help with, Bill," James began, his tone serious. "But before I say anything else, I need your word that this stays between us. It's a matter of great importance to our family."

Bill raised an eyebrow, intrigued but also cautious. "You have my word, James. I've never been one to spread other people's business around."

James nodded, trusting Bill's sincerity. He then carefully explained the situation, starting with the discovery of the first gold nugget and the subsequent finds. He didn't go into too much detail, but he clarified they were dealing with a potentially significant find.

Bill listened intently, his expression growing more serious as James spoke. When James finished, Bill sat back in his chair, rubbing his chin thoughtfully.

"This is quite a situation you've got here, James," Bill said finally. "Gold on your land is both a blessing and a curse. It could bring you great wealth, but it could also bring a lot of trouble if you're not careful."

"We understand that," Emma interjected. "That's why we need your help. We don't want to jump into anything without knowing what we're getting into. We need to figure out what's under our land and how to handle it without attracting too much attention."

Bill nodded slowly. "Well, the first step is to assess what you've got. I can do a preliminary survey of the land, take some samples, and give you an idea of the scale of the deposit. If it's significant, you'll need to think about how you want to proceed. Mining is a big operation, and it's hard to keep something like that quiet."

"We're not looking to start a full-scale operation," James said quickly. "At least, not yet. We just want to know what we're dealing with and how to protect our farm."

"I understand," Bill replied. "But you need to be prepared for the possibility that this could become bigger than you expect. If the gold is as plentiful as it seems, it could change everything for you—both in good ways and bad."

The Hardings exchanged a glance, the weight of Bill's words sinking in. They knew this was a turning point, a moment that could shape their future. But they also knew that they couldn't turn back now. The gold was there, waiting to be discovered, and they had to face whatever came next.

"We're ready to take the next step," James said firmly. "Let's see what we've got."

Bill agreed to start the survey the following morning. He would bring his equipment and spend a few days mapping out the area, taking samples, and assessing the potential of the deposit. It was the beginning of a process that could lead them down a path they had never imagined.

As they prepared for the survey, the Hardings couldn't shake the feeling that they were standing on the edge of something monumental. The gold had already changed their lives in subtle ways, creating tension and uncertainty where there had once been stability. But it had also ignited a spark of hope, a belief that they could overcome the challenges they faced and build a better future.

That night, as Lucy lay in bed, she thought about the nugget she had found, now sitting with the others on the kitchen table. She knew that this was just the beginning, that there was much more to discover beneath the surface of their land. But she also knew that the journey ahead held many risks and unforeseen challenges.

For the first time since they had found the gold, Lucy felt a sense of calm. She had confessed her secret, and her parents had accepted her mistake with understanding and love. They were a family, united in their determination to protect what was theirs, and she knew they would face whatever came next together.

As she drifted off to sleep, Lucy dreamed of the gold, not as a treasure to be hoarded, but as a promise of something greater—a future where the farm, their home, could thrive in ways they had never imagined. It was a future worth fighting for, and she was ready to do whatever it took to make it a reality.

The next morning, the Hardings woke early, eager to begin the survey. Bill arrived with his equipment, and they all headed out to the field where they had found gold. The sky was clear; the sun rising over the horizon, casting a golden light over the land.

Bill set to work quickly, marking out sections of the field and taking soil samples. He explained his process to the Hardings, showing them how he would analyse the samples to determine the concentration of gold in the soil. He also pointed out areas where the ground seemed disturbed, showing possible veins of gold deeper underground.

As the day wore on, Bill moved methodically across the field, his practised eye catching details that the Hardings would have missed. Lucy watched him closely, fascinated by the process. She had seen nothing like it before, and she marvelled at the precision and care with which Bill worked.

By the end of the day, Bill had collected enough samples to begin his analysis. He packed up his equipment and promised to return the next day with preliminary results. The Hardings thanked him, their anticipation growing with each passing hour.

That night, the family gathered in the living room, their thoughts consumed by the day's events. They talked about what they had seen, what it might mean, and how they would move forward if Bill's findings were positive.

"There's a lot to think about," James said, his voice heavy with the weight of responsibility. "But whatever happens, we have to stay grounded. This farm has been in our family for generations, and it's our job to protect it."

Emma nodded in agreement. "We've been through tough times before, and we've always come out stronger. This is just another challenge, and we'll face it together."

Lucy looked at her parents, feeling a deep sense of pride and love for them. They were strong, wise, and resilient, and she knew they would guide the family through whatever came next.

The next morning, Bill returned with his findings. The Hardings gathered around the kitchen table as he laid out his notes and explained what he had discovered.

"The samples show a significant concentration of gold in the soil," Bill said, his tone serious. "It's not just a few small nuggets. There's a good chance that you have a sizeable deposit under your land."

James and Emma exchanged a glance, their hearts racing with both excitement and fear. This was the confirmation they had been waiting for, but it also meant that their lives were about to change in ways they couldn't yet fully understand.

Bill continued, "If you want to move forward with this, you'll need to weigh your options. You could bring in a mining company to extract the gold, but that would mean giving up a lot of control over your land. Alternatively, you could try to do it on a smaller scale, but that comes with its own set of challenges."

James leaned forward, his mind racing. "What would you recommend, Bill? What's the best way to protect our farm while still benefiting from the gold?"

Bill sighed, rubbing his chin thoughtfully. "There's no simple answer, James. It depends on what you're willing to risk and what your long-term goals are. If it were me, I'd start small, keep it quiet, and see how things develop. But that's just one option. Whatever you decide, you need to be prepared for the consequences."

The room fell silent as the Hardings absorbed Bill's words. They knew they had a lot to consider, and that the decisions they made in the coming days would shape the future of their family and their farm.

As they sat together, the weight of the situation pressing down on them, Lucy spoke up, her voice steady and determined.

Looking at her parents with resolve, she declared, "We'll figure it out." "We've always made things work, and this won't be any different. We'll do what we need to do to protect our home."

James and Emma smiled at their daughter, their hearts swelling with pride. They knew that whatever challenges lay ahead, they would face them as a family, united in their love for each other and their determination to protect the land that had been their home for generations.

With Bill's guidance and their own resilience, the Hardings planned their next steps, ready to face the future with courage and hope. The gold beneath their land was a gift, but it was also a test—a test of their strength, their values, and their commitment to each other.

And they were determined to pass that test, no matter what it took.

4

The First Signs Of Trouble

Strangers Approach

The Burralyndra general store was a small, unassuming building that had stood at the heart of the town for decades. Its weathered wooden sign creaked in the wind, and the old bell above the door chimed softly as James Harding pushed it open. The familiar scent of dust, old wood, and a hint of coffee greeted him as he stepped inside, a reminder of countless visits over the years. The store was a lifeline for the small farming community, providing everything from groceries to tools, and it was the place where everyone in Burralyndra eventually passed through.

James hadn't been to town since the day before the survey. The gold, the possibilities it presented, and the risks that came with it had consumed his mind. Today, he needed to restock on a few essentials for the farm, but more than that, he needed a break from the intensity of everything that had happened. As much as he loved his family and his farm, the pressure of their secret was weighing on him.

He walked down the narrow aisles, picking up the items on his list—

flour, sugar, nails, a new pair of gloves. The shelves were sparsely stocked, as they always were, but they had what he needed. James moved methodically, his thoughts only half-focused on the task at hand. His mind kept drifting back to the gold and to the meeting with Bill Turner. The news that their land might hold more gold than they had initially thought was both thrilling and terrifying. They were standing on the edge of something huge, and James knew any misstep could cost them everything.

As James approached the counter, he saw the store owner, Mr. Sullivan, busy organising some cans on a shelf behind the register. Mr. Sullivan was a man in his late sixties, with a full head of silver hair and a face deeply lined from years in the sun. He had lived in Burralyndra his entire life and knew everyone and everything that had happened in the town. A friendly but sharp man, he had a way of knowing more than he let on.

"Morning, James," Mr. Sullivan greeted him with a warm smile as he turned to ring up the items. "Haven't seen you in town for a few days. How's the farm treating you?"

James forced a smile, trying to keep his tone casual. "Morning, Mr. Sullivan. Farm's doing fine. Just needed to pick up a few things."

"Always something that needs fixing or feeding, eh?" Mr. Sullivan chuckled, scanning the items. "Life on the farm never slows down."

"No, it doesn't," James agreed, though his thoughts were miles away, buried deep under the soil of their land, where the gold lay hidden.

As Mr. Sullivan continued ringing up the items, James noticed another presence in the store. A man was standing at the far end of the counter, browsing a display of local maps. James hadn't noticed him when he came in, but now the man's presence seemed to fill the room. He was tall, with dark hair neatly combed back, wearing a well-tailored jacket that seemed out of place in the dusty town of Burralyndra. His face was sharp, his eyes too keen, and something about him set James on edge.

The stranger picked up one map and strolled over to the counter, placing it down with an air of nonchalance. He glanced at James, offering a polite nod before turning his attention to Mr. Sullivan.

"Good morning," the stranger said in a smooth, cultured voice that immediately marked him as an outsider. "I'm new in town, just passing through. Thought I'd pick up a map, get the lay of the land."

"Of course," Mr. Sullivan replied, though James noticed a slight hesitation in his usual calm manner. "We've got a few different maps here—local area, trails, that sort of thing. What are you looking for?"

"Oh, just curious about the countryside," the stranger replied casually. "I like to get to know the places I visit. Beautiful country out here—lots of open land, farms... and who knows what else?"

James tensed at the man's words, a chill running down his spine. He forced himself to keep his expression neutral as he paid for his items, but his mind was racing. The man's interest in the land, the way he spoke—it was too pointed, too deliberate.

"Not much out here but wheat and hard work," James said, his voice steady but guarded.

The stranger smiled, though it didn't reach his eyes. "So I've heard. But you never know what you might find if you look a little deeper."

James didn't respond, but the implication hung heavy in the air. He glanced at Mr. Sullivan, who was watching the exchange with narrowed eyes, clearly sensing the tension. James quickly gathered his purchases, eager to leave before the conversation could go any further.

"Thanks, Mr. Sullivan," James said, forcing a nod to the stranger before heading toward the door.

"Take care, James," Mr. Sullivan called after him, his tone a little too deliberate. "And don't be a stranger."

James pushed the door open, the bell chiming again as he stepped outside into the crisp morning air. The sun was bright, casting long shadows across the main street, but the warmth did nothing to ease the icy knot of anxiety in his chest. As he walked back to his truck, his mind replayed the conversation, analysing every word, every glance.

Who was that man? And what was he really after?

James had lived in Burralyndra his whole life, and he knew everyone in town. This stranger was out of place, his interest in the land too calculated to be innocent. James knew he couldn't dismiss it as mere coincidence. There was too much at stake, and the timing was too suspicious.

As he climbed into his truck, James looked back at the general store. Through the window, he could see the stranger still talking to Mr. Sullivan, though their conversation seemed more relaxed now. James could only imagine what they were discussing, but he had a sinking feeling that it wasn't good.

A Stranger Raises Concerns

The drive back to the farm was long and quiet, the road stretching out before him like a ribbon of uncertainty. James gripped the steering wheel tightly, his thoughts churning. He couldn't shake the feeling that the stranger's presence was a sign that their secret was no longer safe.

When he reached the farm, Lucy was waiting for him in the driveway, her face lighting up as she saw him. James managed a smile, but his heart wasn't in it. He couldn't let Lucy see his worry—not yet. They had enough to deal with already.

"Hey, Dad," Lucy called out as he got out of the truck. "Everything okay? You look... tense."

James forced a chuckle, ruffling her hair as he walked past her. "Just a lot on my mind, kiddo. How's everything here?"

"Same as usual," Lucy replied, though her eyes searched his face for signs of what was really bothering him. "Mum's inside, finishing up the last of the paperwork for the farm. I think she's finally making some progress."

"That's good," James said absently, his mind still on the stranger. He glanced back at the road, half-expecting to see the man's car following him, but the road was empty. "Let's go inside. We need to talk."

Lucy frowned, but she followed her father into the house without question. Inside, they found Emma at the kitchen table, a stack of papers spread out before her. She looked up as they entered, her expression immediately shifting to concern when she saw James's face.

"James? What's wrong?" Emma asked, setting down her pen.

James sighed, running a hand through his hair. He glanced at Lucy, then back at Emma. "I ran into someone in town today. A stranger. He was asking questions—too many questions."

Emma's eyes widened, and Lucy's expression turned serious. "What questions?" Emma asked, her voice tight.

"About the land," James replied, sitting down heavily in a chair. "He was talking to Mr. Sullivan, asking about the farms, what people were up to. He said nothing outright, but I got the feeling he knows something—maybe about the gold."

Lucy's heart skipped a beat, and she exchanged a worried glance with her mother. "Do you think he's here because of the gold?" Lucy asked, her voice barely above a whisper.

"I don't know," James admitted, frustration and fear clear in his tone. "But it's too much of a coincidence for my liking. We've been so careful, but if someone found out—"

"We don't know that for sure," Emma interrupted, trying to calm him down. "It could be nothing, just a curious traveller."

"But what if it isn't?" James shot back. "We can't afford to take that chance. If word gets out, we'll have every prospector and mining company from here to Perth swarming our land."

Emma fell silent, the weight of his words sinking in. They all knew the stakes—they had discussed them endlessly—but now the threat felt more real than ever.

"We need to be even more careful," Emma finally said, her voice firm. "No more talking about the gold, not even here at the farm. And we need to monitor anyone new who comes to town. If this stranger is looking for something, we can't let him find it."

James nodded, though the worry didn't leave his face. "We also need to talk to Bill, make sure he's being discreet. The fewer people who know, the better."

"Agreed," Emma said, glancing at Lucy. "And Lucy, you need to stay close to home for now. No more trips into town unless you're with one of us. We can't take any risks."

Lucy wanted to protest, to argue that she could take care of herself, but the look in her parents' eyes stopped her. She nodded reluctantly, understanding the seriousness of the situation. "Okay, I'll stay here."

James leaned back in his chair, his mind racing with plans and contingencies. The stranger's arrival had thrown everything into uncertainty, but they couldn't let fear dictate their actions. They had come too far, sacrificed too much, to let their dream slip away now.

But as the day wore on, the sense of unease lingered. James glanced out the window more often, watching the road for any sign of the stranger. Every noise, every shadow, seemed to take on a new significance, and he couldn't shake the feeling that they were being watched.

The Hardings went about their daily tasks, but the atmosphere on the farm had changed. There was a tension in the air, a feeling that something was about to happen, though they didn't know what. James tried to keep busy, fixing a fence the last storm damaged, but his mind was elsewhere, replaying the conversation with the stranger over and over.

As the sun set, casting long shadows across the fields, James was in the barn, checking on the equipment. The gold nugget Lucy had found still sat in a locked box in his workshop, hidden away from prying eyes. But even as he tried to focus on the task at hand, his thoughts kept drifting back to the stranger.

Who was he? What was he really after? And how much did he know?

The questions gnawed at James, and he knew he wouldn't find any peace until he had answers. He finished up in the barn and headed back to the house, where Emma and Lucy were preparing dinner. The smell of roasted chicken and vegetables filled the air, a comforting scent that reminded James of simpler times, before the gold had turned their lives upside down.

As they sat down to eat, the conversation was subdued, each of them lost in their own thoughts. But the unease was still there, a constant undercurrent that they couldn't ignore.

After dinner, James stepped outside onto the porch, looking out over the fields. The night was quiet, the stars just beginning to appear in the darkening sky. But even in the stillness, James couldn't shake the feeling that something was wrong.

He heard the door open behind him and turned to see Emma stepping out onto the porch, wrapping a shawl around her shoulders against the cool evening air.

"Couldn't sleep?" she asked softly, coming to stand beside him.

James shook his head. "Just thinking."

Emma leaned against the railing, her gaze following his out over the fields. "I'm worried too, James. But we can't let this consume us. We need to stay strong—for the farm, for Lucy."

"I know," James replied, his voice heavy. "But I can't help feeling like we're in over our heads. We're farmers, not miners. This was never supposed to happen."

Emma placed a hand on his arm, her touch gentle but firm. "We'll make it through this, James. Having faced hard times before, we've always emerged stronger. We just need to be smart, to take things one step at a time."

James looked down at his wife, feeling a surge of gratitude for her strength and support. "You're right. We'll figure it out. But I think we need to talk to Bill tomorrow, make sure he knows what we're dealing with."

Emma nodded in agreement. "We'll go together. And we'll start thinking about how to protect the farm, just in case things get worse."

They stood there in silence for a while, watching the stars appear one by one in the night sky. Despite the uncertainty and fear that had taken hold of them, there was still a sense of resolve, a determination to protect what was theirs.

As they turned to go back inside, James paused, his hand on the door. "Emma... I think we should move the gold. Find a better hiding place. Just to be safe."

Emma hesitated, then nodded. "I'll help you."

They went back inside, their minds already racing with plans and possibilities. The gold had brought them both hope and fear, and they knew that the days ahead would test them in ways they couldn't yet imagine.

But they were a family, and they would face whatever came next together, just as they always had.

5

Lucy's Curiosity

Lucy's Curiosity

A few days after the near-accident with the gold nugget, Lucy's curiosity is getting the better of her. The discovery had already altered her perspective on their quiet wheat farm life, and a nagging feeling had grown deep inside her—the feeling that something bigger was happening and that the gold might only be the beginning.

Lucy trudged along the well-worn path between the farmhouse and the far fields, where the wheat stubble formed a golden grey carpet. Her eyes weren't on the stubble that surrounded her. Instead, she thought about the glimmering piece of gold the harvester had trapped days before.

"What are the odds?" she muttered to herself, kicking a small rock down the path as her boots thudded softly against the dirt. "One tiny nugget, out of nowhere. And why now, of all times?"

The question haunted her, filling her dreams and distracting her from her daily chores. She'd spent the past few nights lying in bed, staring at the ceiling, unable to stop her mind from turning over the possibilities. There had to be more—more gold, or more answers. The nugget couldn't be an isolated occurrence. What else might the earth be hiding beneath the soil, waiting to be unearthed?

James had been cautious, dismissive even, about what the nugget might mean. He was concerned about rumours spreading too quickly, about outsiders sniffing around, just as he had been at the Burralyndra general store when that stranger's words lingered in the air like smoke. But Lucy was different. She wasn't content with her dad's reluctance to dig deeper—both metaphorically and literally.

As she reached the boundary of the property, where the wheat fields kissed the edge of a dusty patch of earth, Lucy paused. Her father had told her to focus on the farm, to stick to the tasks at hand. But curiosity was a powerful thing, and Lucy had never been one to leave a question unanswered.

Bending down, she ran her fingers through the dry soil, her thoughts racing. This spot was a bit of an anomaly—far from the fertile stretches where they planted the wheat. This patch had always been too rocky, too hard to cultivate. James had often shrugged it off, calling it "stubborn land." That was one reason they had left this section of land uncleared. Left it for the wildlife and birds. Now Lucy wondered if it was something more.

She brushed away some loose dirt, revealing small rocks underneath. Her pulse quickened as she imagined what could lie just below the surface.

"There could be more," she thought. "What if it's deeper? What if this is where it's coming from?"

Without wasting another moment, Lucy stood up, dusting her hands off on her jeans. She was going to need some help if she wanted to explore this possibility. But she knew better than to go to her father—he'd tell her to forget it, to stay away from anything that could stir up more trouble.

There was only one person she trusted enough to bring in on this: Bill Turner.

Bill's Place

Lucy immediately headed over to Bill's place. Bill was like an uncle to Lucy—rough around the edges, but always there when the Hardings needed a hand. He had a knack for fixing things, and Lucy had often spent time in his workshop, learning the ins and outs of mechanical repairs and listening to his stories of the old days.

When Lucy walked in to Bills workshop, the smell of engine grease and metal shavings greeted her. Hunched over his workbench, Bill adjusted the parts of an old tractor engine that had given up the ghost years ago.

"Hey there, Lucy," Bill greeted her without looking up. "Come to help me with this heap of junk?"

Lucy smiled, but her mind was elsewhere. "Actually, I came to ask you something."

Bill straightened up, wiping his hands on an old rag. "Oh? Well, ask away. What's on your mind?"

She hesitated for a moment, unsure of how to frame her request without sounding reckless. "You remember that gold nugget we found?" she began.

Bill's eyes narrowed slightly. "Course I do. Caused quite a stir, didn't it? Your dad's been real jumpy since then."

Lucy nodded. "Yeah, he has. But... I can't stop thinking about it, Bill. That nugget didn't just appear out of nowhere. I think there's more. I think it came from the ground out by the far fields—the rocky patch where nothing but scrub and eucalyptus grow."

Bill raised an eyebrow, his curiosity piqued. "That stubborn patch of dirt? You think there's gold under there?"

Lucy shrugged, trying to play it cool. "I don't know for sure, but it's possible, right? And if there is, we need to find it before someone else does. I was hoping you might help me check it out."

Bill leaned against his workbench, crossing his arms. "And what does your dad think about all this?"

"He doesn't want to know," Lucy admitted. "He thinks it's too dangerous, that it'll bring trouble. But if we're careful, if we're quiet about it... we might find something that could save the farm, Bill. We can't just sit on this and hope for the best."

Bill studied her for a moment, then let out a long sigh. "You're a smart girl, Lucy. Always have been. But you're also impulsive—just like your old man used to be when he was your age. You know this could get messy."

"I do," Lucy said firmly. "But we can't ignore it. And I can't do this alone."

Bill glanced at the tractor engine, then back at Lucy. After a moment of silence, he grinned.

"Alright, kid," he said. "I'll help you. But we've gotta be careful. No one else can know about this, you hear? Especially not that nosy stranger lurking around town."

Lucy's heart swelled with a mix of relief and excitement. "I promise, Bill. It'll just be you and me. We'll keep it quiet."

Dig Deeper

In the evening, Lucy and Bill made their way back to the rocky patch, taking advantage of the darkness. They carried shovels, pickaxes, and a small metal detector that Bill had surreptitiously kept in his workshop.

The night air was cool and still, the only sounds coming from the faint rustling of the wheat in the breeze and the occasional call of an owl. Lucy's pulse quickened as they reached the spot she had been examining earlier.

"Here," she whispered, pointing to the patch of disturbed soil. "This is where I found those rocks. I think it's a good place to start."

Bill nodded and switched on the metal detector, slowly sweeping it over the ground. For several minutes, there was nothing but silence and the soft beeping of the machine. Lucy's excitement waned, doubt creeping in as the minutes dragged on.

"Maybe I was wrong," she muttered under her breath.

But just as she was about to suggest they call it a night, the metal detector let out a sharp, high-pitched warble. Bill froze, his eyes widening.

"Hold on now," he said, crouching down to inspect the spot. "We've got something here."

Lucy's heart pounded in her chest as they dug, the rhythmic thud of the shovels breaking through the earth filling the air. The scent of freshly upturned soil mingled with the faint hint of dampness in the breeze. Each shovelful brought up dry soil, the gritty texture slipping through their fingers. Time seemed to slow as they painstakingly removed the dirt, anticipation building with every passing moment. And then, amidst the symphony of digging, Bill's shovel collided with something unyielding, a jarring impact that sent vibrations coursing through their hands.

"There it is," he whispered.

Together, they unearthed a small, shiny object—a third gold nugget, larger than the first two.

Lucy's breath caught in her throat as she held the nugget in her hands, the weight of it sending a surge of excitement through her.

"I knew it," she whispered, her eyes gleaming in the moonlight. "There's more down there, Bill. This could be just the beginning."

Bill nodded, his expression serious. "Looks like you were right, kid. But now we've got a decision to make. We can't let anyone else know about this—not yet. If word gets out..."

Lucy knew exactly what he was thinking. The stranger, the town, maybe even her father—it was all too precarious. For now, this would remain their secret. But in the back of her mind, Lucy knew that secrets this big couldn't stay hidden forever.

The glimmering gold had already transformed their lives, casting a radiant glow upon their fortunes. But amidst the newfound wealth, an undercurrent of trepidation hung in the air, as if a storm was brewing. The distant sound of thunder echoed ominously, a harbinger of the impending danger that loomed ahead. The metallic scent of fear permeated the atmosphere, prickling their senses and causing their hearts to race. They could feel a weight pressing upon them, an invisible force reminding them that the genuine test of their newfound fortune had only just begun.

6

Alternate Plans

Conflicting Plans

It was late afternoon in the Harding barn. The sun hung low in the sky, casting long shadows through the cracks in the barn walls. The air inside is thick with the smell of hay and dust, a familiar scent that usually brings comfort to the family. But today, the barn feels different—charged with tension as an argument is about to erupt.

Lucy knelt in a dim corner of the barn, turning the third piece of gold over in her hand. The weight of it felt solid, promising, like the future of their farm rested in this small, gleaming nugget. She had uncovered it earlier that day, her heart pounding as the shovel hit something hard beneath the dirt once again. Now, as she inspected it under the fading light, the excitement that buzzed through her veins was undeniable. This wasn't just a fluke. There was more gold under their land—possibly a fortune.

But just as she was lost in thought, a voice rang out from the entrance of the barn, sharp and filled with anger.

"What the hell do you think you're doing, Lucy?"

51

Lucy's head snapped up to see her father, James, standing at the barn door. His face was etched with frustration, his jaw clenched tight as he glared at the gold in her hand.

"Dad, I—"

"I told you not to go digging around out here!" James strode into the barn, his heavy boots kicking up dust with each step. "We've already talked about this. You're supposed to be focusing on the wheat, not playing treasure hunter!"

Lucy stood up, her heart racing. She clenched the nugget in her fist, trying to keep her voice steady. "But Dad, there's more! I've found three pieces now—this can't just be a coincidence. We can't ignore it. This could save the farm!"

James shook his head, his expression hardening. "Save the farm? Or destroy it? You think you can just dig up gold without anyone noticing? In order for it to benefit us, we need to sell it! That means we need to tell people where we got it from. Register the find! What happens when word gets out? What happens when the wrong people come sniffing around, ready to take everything we've got?"

Lucy's frustration boiled over. "We can't live in fear forever! I'm trying to help us, Dad! The wheat isn't enough anymore—you know that. We're barely scraping by, and if we don't do something, the bank's going to take this place. What's wrong with trying to fight for our future?"

James stepped closer, his voice low and filled with warning. "What's wrong is that you're risking everything for a few shiny rocks. I'm not going to let this farm be torn apart because of greed. We've worked too hard to build this place up, and I won't see it destroyed by a gold rush that'll leave us with nothing but trouble."

Lucy took a step back, her hands shaking. "It's not greed, Dad! It's survival! This is our chance—our only chance to keep this farm in the family. We could pay off the bank, invest in new equipment, secure our future. Why can't you see that?"

The two stood face to face, their words laced with frustration and hurt. They were both fighting for the same thing—the farm, their home—but their visions of how to protect it were clashing, pushing them further apart.

James's face softened for a moment, a flash of pain in his eyes. "I see it, Lucy. I see what you're trying to do. But you don't understand what kind of danger this brings. Once the word gets out, it won't just be strangers we'll have to worry about. People we thought were our friends will turn on us. I've seen it happen before—good land torn apart because of greed. I won't let that happen here."

Lucy opened her mouth to argue, but before she could respond, another voice cut through the tension.

"ENOUGH! Both of you."

Emma stood at the barn entrance, her hands on her hips, her eyes shifting between her husband and daughter. The weariness in her voice was palpable. She had heard the raised voices from the house and had come to intervene before things spiralled out of control.

"We can't afford to be at each other's throats like this," Emma said, stepping between them. "Arguing isn't going to solve anything. We need to think this through carefully, as a family."

James sighed, running a hand through his greying hair. "Emma, we can't just—"

"I know what you're going to say, James," Emma interrupted, her tone firm but gentle. "And I know you're worried. But Lucy has a point too. We're in a tough spot, and ignoring this won't make it go away. We need to figure out a way to deal with this without tearing each other apart."

Lucy crossed her arms, looking down at the gold nugget in her hand. She felt the weight of it, not just physically, but emotionally. It represented everything she wanted to protect—her family, their home, their legacy. But she also knew her father wasn't entirely wrong. They couldn't just start digging up gold without a plan. There were too many eyes watching, too many people eager to exploit any sign of wealth.

Emma placed a hand on James's arm. "We need a clear plan, James. Rushing into this or avoiding it completely—neither of those options will work. We have to be smart about this."

James looked at his wife, his face softening as he nodded reluctantly. "Alright," he muttered, his voice thick with frustration. "But we're not doing anything reckless. We'll talk about this more. Together."

Lucy exhaled, feeling a small sense of relief. The argument hadn't been resolved, not completely, but at least they were talking. At least they were still a family.

"We need to be careful," James continued, his eyes locking onto Lucy's. "No more secret digging. No more gold hunting without a plan. If we're going to figure this out, we do it together. As a family."

Lucy nodded, though part of her still bristled at the thought of holding back. But she knew her father was right in one sense—if they didn't handle this carefully, everything they had built could come crashing down. She just hoped they could find a way to protect the farm without losing everything—including each other.

Making Plans

Later that evening, in the Harding's kitchen, the family sat down to discuss their next steps.

The dinner table was quieter than usual, the tension from the barn still hanging in the air. Emma had prepared a simple meal—steak and potatoes, with a side of roasted vegetables—but no one seemed to have much of an appetite.

Lucy pushed her food around on her plate, her mind still racing with thoughts of the gold. She had never been one to back down easily, and the prospect of giving up the search gnawed at her. There had to be a way to keep looking for more without endangering the farm.

James cleared his throat, breaking the silence. "We can't ignore what's happening," he said, his voice measured. "But we need to be smart. That stranger in town—he's already asking questions. We can't let him, or anyone else, get wind of this."

Emma nodded in agreement. "We need to keep this quiet. The moment people start suspecting there's gold on our land, we'll have more than just one stranger poking around."

Lucy looked up from her plate, her voice soft but determined. "So what do we do? We can't just leave it all buried. This is our chance to save the farm."

James leaned back in his chair, the lines on his face deepening as he thought. "We start slow. We don't go digging out in the open. If there's more down there, we find it carefully, bit by bit. No one outside this family knows a thing, and we don't risk everything for the sake of a quick payoff."

Emma glanced at Lucy, her expression gentle but firm. "And Lucy, you need to promise us you'll be careful. No more sneaking around. We can't afford any mistakes."

Lucy swallowed hard, her heart pounding with both frustration and resolve. "I promise," she said quietly, though the fire inside her was still burning brightly.

The decision had been made. For now, they would proceed cautiously, as a united front. But deep down, Lucy knew the challenges ahead were only growing. The gold had set something in motion that couldn't be stopped. They would have to navigate the treacherous waters carefully if they wanted to protect their home and their future.

And as much as her father's words rang with caution, Lucy couldn't shake the feeling that bold action would still be necessary. The stakes were high, and they were only going to get higher.

Lucy's Future

Later that evening, after the heated discussion about the gold had died down, Emma and James sat together at the kitchen table. The glow of the lantern flickered across their faces, casting deep shadows as they quietly finished their tea. The day's tensions still hung in the air, but now, a different conversation weighed on their minds—one they had been avoiding for too long.

Emma glanced out the window, where she could just make out the silhouette of Lucy, still outside, gazing out over the fields in the moonlight. She seemed so grown up, so independent, yet so tied to the land.

"We need to talk about Lucy," Emma said quietly, breaking the silence.

James shifted uncomfortably in his seat. "What about her?" he asked, though he already knew what his wife was going to say.

"She's almost 23, James. She's smart, capable... maybe too capable for this place."

James furrowed his brow, leaning back in his chair as if trying to distance himself from the conversation. "She loves this farm, Em. Always has. She's not like the other kids in town who can't wait to get out of here. She wants to stay."

"I know she loves it here," Emma said, her voice soft but firm. "But we can't let that hold her back. With the money from the gold, we could send her to university in Perth. She could have a real future— something bigger than just... this."

She gestured around at the farmhouse, the fields beyond, the world they had built together. It was a good life, but Emma had always wondered if it was enough for their daughter.

James frowned, his fingers drumming on the table. "A future? What's wrong with this future? The farm's been in my family for generations. It's a good life, an honest life. We've always hoped she'd carry it on one day."

"Yes, and part of me still hopes for that," Emma admitted. "But we have to be realistic, James. She's smart enough to do anything she wants. Why not give her the chance to see the world, to meet new people? She could go to university, travel... maybe even meet someone special. She's so young, and she's never really been away from here."

James's expression tightened at the thought. He was a man of the land, deeply rooted in the rhythms of farm life. The idea of Lucy leaving, of her future being anywhere but here, didn't sit well with him. And yet, a part of him knew Emma was right. Lucy was special. She had a spark in her, a drive that went beyond what this farm could offer.

"It's not my intention for her to think we're pushing her away," James said after a long pause. "I don't want her to feel like we don't believe in her dreams here."

Emma reached out, placing a hand on his. "It's not about that. It's about giving her choices. We've done our best to give her a good life here, but we have to be open to the idea that maybe—just maybe— there's more out there for her. With the money from the gold, we could finally give her that chance."

James looked down at their hands, the calluses on his fingers brushing against Emma's softer skin. He sighed, rubbing the back of his neck. "And what if she goes? What if she gets a taste of that other life and doesn't come back? What happens to the farm then?"

Emma's eyes softened with understanding. "We can't hold her back because we're afraid of what might happen. If she comes back, it'll be because she wants to, not because she feels obligated. And if she doesn't..." Emma trailed off for a moment, her voice catching. "If she doesn't, then at least we'll know we did right by her. We can't trap her here, James."

James swallowed hard, his throat tight. He loved his daughter fiercely, and the idea of her leaving, of her life taking her away from the farm, was almost unbearable. But deep down, he knew Emma was right. Lucy had a spark, a fire that deserved to burn as brightly as it could. Whether that fire would keep her here or take her somewhere else was something they couldn't control.

"She's so much like you," James murmured, his voice thick with emotion. "That same stubborn streak. That same sense of adventure. I see it in her every day."

Emma smiled softly. "And that's why we have to give her the freedom to choose her path. Whether it's the farm or something else, we have to trust her."

The kitchen fell silent for a long moment as they sat with the weight of their conversation. Outside, Lucy was still gazing across the fields, her thoughts a million miles away, unaware of the storm of emotions her parents were navigating.

"We'll talk to her," James finally said, his voice resigned but steady. "But we'll let her make the choice. I just hope... I hope she doesn't feel like we're pushing her away."

Emma nodded, squeezing his hand gently. "We're not. We're giving her wings, James. What she does with them is up to her."

Later that night, as James and Emma lay in bed, they continued the conversation in hushed tones, careful not to let their voices carry.

"Do you think she'll go?" James asked, staring up at the ceiling, his heart heavy.

"I don't know," Emma replied honestly. "She loves this place. But I also think there's a part of her that's curious about what's out there. She's never said it, but I can see it in the way she looks when she talks about other places, about things she's read. She's torn between two worlds, James."

James turned onto his side, facing his wife. "What if she meets someone out there? What if she falls in love and decides not to come back?"

Emma smiled softly in the darkness. "Isn't that what we want for her? To be happy? To find love wherever that might be?"

James let out a slow breath. "I just always thought she'd find it here. I imagined her settling down on this land, raising a family like we did."

"Maybe she will," Emma said, her voice filled with hope. "And maybe she won't. But whatever happens, she'll always be our daughter. We'll always have a home for her here, no matter what she chooses."

The silence settled over them again, but this time it was a little less heavy, the weight of their decision starting to lift. They knew they had to trust Lucy, even if it meant letting go of their hopes for her future on the farm.

But deep in both their hearts, they wondered: would the farm be enough to keep her, or was Lucy destined for something bigger, something beyond the boundaries of Burralyndra?

As the days passed, the topic of Lucy's future lingered quietly in the background of every conversation. While the gold and the farm's immediate survival still took centre stage, the question of what lay ahead for Lucy simmered beneath it all. Emma and James kept their concerns to themselves for now, not wanting to overwhelm Lucy as she wrestled with her own plans for the land.

But the time would come when they'd have to tell her their thoughts. About university, about travelling, about the possibility of finding a life beyond the wheat fields. They knew it wouldn't be an easy conversation, especially when Lucy's heart was so tied to the farm.

And yet, as they watched her from a distance, working the fields or tinkering with the equipment, they couldn't help but wonder if their daughter—strong and determined as she was—was destined for more than the life they had built for her.

What if the farm was holding her back from becoming who she was truly meant to be? And what would they do if, when the time came, she chose the world beyond the farm instead of staying to carry on the family legacy?

They would have to wait, and trust that whatever Lucy chose, it would be what was best for her—even if it meant letting go of their dreams for her future on the farm.

7

Unwanted Attention

Unwanted Visitors

The morning sun filtered through the kitchen window, casting a warm, golden hue over the wooden table where James, Emma, and Lucy sat, quietly eating breakfast. The tension from their recent argument still hung in the air like a heavy fog, but it had softened over the past few days. They had reached an uneasy truce, though the uncertainty of their next steps still weighed heavily on them all.

The discovery of the gold had changed everything, and though Lucy was itching to dig deeper—both literally and figuratively—James remained cautious. The family had kept the discovery quiet, and for good reason. The last thing they needed was outsiders sniffing around, especially with the farm already under threat from the bank.

But fate, it seemed, had other plans.

The distant rumble of a car engine echoed through the quiet morning, startling all three of them. Vehicles rarely ventured down their long dirt road, especially uninvited. James's fork clattered onto his plate as he stood and moved to the window, his face darkening as he peered outside.

"Who is it?" Emma asked, her voice a tense whisper.

James didn't answer immediately, squinting at the approaching vehicle. Dust kicked up from the tires, trailing behind the car like a plume of smoke. He watched as it slowed near the house, a sleek, black sedan, out of place against the rugged landscape of their farm. His gut twisted.

"That's the same bloke from town," James said grimly, his eyes narrowing.

Emma rose from her chair, her movements stiff with worry. "The one you mentioned at the store?" She joined him at the window, her expression mirroring his unease.

"Yeah," James muttered, watching as the car came to a stop. "The one who was asking too many damn questions."

Lucy, sensing the shift in her parents' demeanour, stood as well, her gaze following theirs. She hadn't heard about the stranger, but she could feel the sudden tension in the room.

The car door opened, and out stepped the stranger. He was tall and wiry, dressed in a sharp, dark suit that looked entirely out of place on a wheat farm. He took a moment to dust himself off before turning his attention to the house, his gaze sharp and calculating as he started toward the front door.

"Do you think he knows?" Emma whispered, her voice barely audible as she gripped James's arm.

James's jaw tightened. "Let's find out."

He turned and moved toward the front door, his heavy boots thudding against the wooden floorboards. Emma followed close behind, with Lucy trailing, her curiosity piqued. The sense of unease gnawed at them all, a shared anxiety about the stranger's intentions.

As James opened the door, the stranger smiled—a thin, practised smile that didn't reach his eyes.

"Morning," the man said, tipping his hat slightly. "Beautiful property you've got here."

James didn't return the smile. "Can I help you?"

The man's gaze flickered over James, then past him to Emma and Lucy, standing in the doorway. He seemed to take note of everything, his eyes sharp and discerning.

"Name's McRae," he said, holding out a hand. James didn't take it. McRae's smile faltered only slightly before he continued. "I'm a prospector, you see. Been in the area for a bit, looking for potential land investments. Thought I'd stop by and see if you might be interested in selling."

James didn't budge. His body blocked the doorway, his stance unyielding. "This farm's not for sale."

McRae chuckled, though it was more for show than genuine amusement. "Now, now, don't be too hasty. I've heard some interesting things about this area, especially about the land around here. Seems like it might be worth a lot more than just wheat. Wouldn't hurt to have a conversation, would it?"

James's eyes darkened, his hands curling into fists at his sides. "I said, we're not interested."

Behind him, Emma's anxiety grew, her heart pounding in her chest. She glanced at Lucy, who was watching McRae with wide, suspicious eyes. The stranger's words hung in the air like a threat, and though he hadn't said anything outright, there was no mistaking the underlying message: he knew something.

McRae's smile didn't waver, but his gaze grew colder, more focused. "You see, I've got a knack for finding valuable land. And from what I've heard, this place might be sitting on something a bit more... profitable than wheat. Word travels fast in small towns." He paused, letting the implication sink in. "Now, I'm willing to pay a generous price for it. More than any wheat harvest could ever bring in, that's for sure."

James's temper flared, his patience worn thin. "I don't know what you've heard, but there's nothing here for you. We're farmers, not miners. So, if you don't mind, I think it's time for you to leave."

McRae's expression hardened, his smile slipping into something more menacing. "I wouldn't be so quick to turn down an offer, Mr. Harding. Things have a way of changing. And from what I understand, you've got a bit of trouble with the bank. Might be in your best interest to reconsider."

Emma sucked in a sharp breath, her fear spiking at the mention of their financial troubles. How did this man know so much?

Lucy, standing behind her parents, felt her heart race. This was no simple prospector; this man was after something. And he wouldn't stop until he got it.

"The farm's not for sale," James repeated, his voice low and dangerous. "Now get off my property."

McRae's eyes flickered with annoyance, but he didn't push further. Instead, he gave a small shrug, his casual demeanour returning, as if the tense exchange hadn't rattled him at all.

"Suit yourself," he said, turning to leave. "But I'll be around. If you change your mind... well, you know where to find me."

With that, he walked back to his car, his steps unhurried, as if he had all the time in the world. James stood in the doorway, watching him go, his entire body rigid with barely contained fury.

As the car rumbled down the road, kicking up dust in its wake, Emma finally exhaled, the tension in her chest easing only slightly.

"James... what are we going to do?" she whispered, her voice shaky.

James closed the door, his face hard and unreadable. "We're going to be careful. And we're going to keep digging. But from now on, we don't trust anyone. Not even the people in town."

Emma nodded, her heart heavy with dread. They were being watched, and worse, they were being hunted—for the land, for the gold, for whatever secrets lay beneath their feet.

Lucy remained silent, her mind racing. The stranger's visit had rattled her, but it had also solidified something within her. She couldn't sit back and wait for things to unfold. She had to act, to protect the farm, to protect her family.

They had uncovered something valuable—too valuable to keep secret for much longer. And now, it seemed like they weren't the only ones who knew.

The rest of the day passed in a haze of anxiety and whispered conversations. Emma couldn't stop glancing out the window, as if expecting McRae's car to appear again at any moment. Lucy kept herself busy with farm work, though her thoughts were consumed by the stranger's visit and what it meant for their future.

As night fell, the family gathered around the kitchen table, the weight of the day pressing down on them.

"Do you think he'll come back?" Lucy asked, breaking the silence.

James nodded grimly. "I'd bet on it. He's not the kind to give up easily."

"What are we going to do?" Emma asked, her voice edged with fear. "We can't just sit here and wait for him to come after us."

James sighed, running a hand through his hair. "We keep quiet. We don't tell anyone else about the gold, not even Bill. And we stay on guard. If he tries to pull anything, we'll deal with it."

Lucy frowned, her mind already working through possible solutions. "Maybe we should dig deeper," she suggested cautiously. "If there's more gold, maybe we can find enough to pay off the bank and get McRae off our backs."

James shot her a sharp look. "We're not rushing into anything, Lucy. This is bigger than just paying off the bank. We need to be smart about this. One wrong move, and we could lose everything."

Emma nodded in agreement. "We can't let greed cloud our judgment.

We've already seen what it can do to people."

Lucy clenched her fists under the table, frustration bubbling up inside her. She understood the need for caution, but every instinct in her body was screaming at her to take action. The farm was her home, and she couldn't bear the thought of losing it—not to the bank, and certainly not to a stranger like McRae.

She needed to wait. They all would.

As the night wore on, the Hardings retreated to their rooms, each of them grappling with the fear and uncertainty that McRae's visit had stirred. And though the house was quiet, there was no peace to be found—only the growing realisation that their lives were changing no matter what decisions they were to make.

Emma's Decision

The evening air was thick with tension as the Hardings sat around their worn kitchen table, the soft glow of the overhead light casting long shadows across their tired faces. The visit from Mr. McRae had left a weight hanging over the family, an unspoken fear of what might come next. They knew now that their secret wasn't as well kept as they had hoped, and that they were running out of time to figure out a plan.

Lucy leaned back in her chair, her fingers idly tracing the grain of the wooden table. Her mind was racing, filled with thoughts of the stranger's visit, her parents' caution, and the gold they had found beneath their feet. She knew her father was right to be careful, but part of her still itched to take action, to do something before everything spiralled out of control.

Emma, who had been unusually quiet since McRae left, cleared her throat, her eyes flicking to James before settling on Lucy.

"Lucy," she began, her voice soft but steady, "there's something we need to talk about. Something that has been on your father's and my minds for a while now."

Lucy looked up, surprised by the seriousness in her mother's tone. Emma rarely spoke in that way unless it was important.

"What is it?" Lucy asked, glancing between her parents, noticing the way James's jaw tightened as if bracing himself for what Emma was about to say.

Emma folded her hands on the table, leaning slightly toward Lucy. "We've been talking about your future, about what's best for you. You've grown up on this farm, and we know how much you love it, how much you've learned from the land. But..." She hesitated, taking a deep breath. "We don't want you to feel like you're tied down here forever. You've got so much potential, Lucy, and we think you should have the chance to explore that."

Lucy frowned, her confusion deepening. "What do you mean? I want to stay here, on the farm. You both know that."

Emma's expression softened, but her eyes were filled with a mix of love and concern. "I know, sweetheart, and we love that you're so dedicated to this place. But we also don't want to hold you back. There's a whole world out there, beyond Burralyndra, beyond the farm, and we think it's time you saw some of it."

James, who had remained silent up to this point, finally spoke, his voice low and measured. "Your mum and I think you should go to university. In Perth. We've been looking into it, and with the gold we've found, we could afford to send you."

Lucy blinked, stunned by the words. University? In Perth? It felt like a punch to the gut. She never envisioned departing the farm for such a reason. Her dreams had always been rooted in the soil of Burralyndra, in the wheat fields and the dusty roads that led home. The idea of leaving, of stepping into a world so different from the one she knew, filled her with a sense of dread.

"I don't... I don't want to go to university," Lucy said, shaking her head. "I want to stay here. I don't need to leave to know what I want to do. The farm is my future."

Emma reached across the table, taking Lucy's hand in hers. "We know you love it here, Lucy. But we also want to give you the chance to see what else is out there. You're smart, and you've got a good head on your shoulders. We're not saying you have to give up the farm—just that you should have options. Maybe you'll decide that the farm is where you belong, but maybe... maybe you'll find something else that you love just as much."

Lucy pulled her hand back, her heart racing. "This is about the gold, isn't it? You think because we found it, we can just leave everything behind? What if there's more? We could use it to save the farm, to make sure we never lose it to the bank. Why would I leave now, when we're finally so close to making things right?"

James sighed, rubbing a hand over his face. "We're not saying the farm isn't important. But you're nearly twenty-three now, Lucy. You should have the chance to decide what you want your life to look like. We can use the gold to secure the farm's future—and yours. We've thought about it, and we're going to keep the first nugget for sentimental reasons, but we're going to sell the rest."

Lucy stared at him, her mind spinning. "Sell it? To who?"

Emma exchanged a glance with James before answering. "We'll need to do things the right way. We'll have to apply for permits, mining rights. But we know a buyer in Perth who can help us with all of that. The plan is for you and you Mum to take a trip there, visit the university, and while you're there, sell the gold. It'll give us the funds we need to keep the farm afloat and give you the chance to go to school if you want to."

Lucy's chest tightened, the weight of her parents' words pressing down on her. They wanted her to leave, to go to university, to live a life that had never felt like hers. But more than that, they were planning to sell the gold, to turn their quiet discovery into something that would change everything.

"I don't want to go," she breathed, her voice strained. "I'd rather not leave the farm."

Emma's eyes softened, filled with the kind of love only a mother could have. "We know it's hard, Lucy. We're not saying you have to go, not yet. But at least think about it. Think about what a degree could mean for you, for your future. You could study agriculture, business, anything that would help you come back and run this place even better than we ever could."

Lucy stood abruptly, pushing her chair back with more force than she intended. The legs scraped against the floor, the sound harsh in the quiet room. "I don't need a degree to run this farm. I've been learning everything I need right here. I know the land, I know the crops. This is my home."

James stood as well, his expression stern. "We're not trying to take that away from you, Lucy. We just wish for you to receive more than we had. We want you to have choices."

Lucy's frustration boiled over, her voice rising. "But what if I don't want those choices? What if I want to stay here, where I belong? You're acting like I have to leave to find myself, but I already know who I am. I'm a farmer. This is where I belong."

Emma stood, trying to calm the growing tension. "Lucy, we just want what's best for you. We want you to see the world, to meet people, to experience life outside of Burralyndra. There's so much more out there, and you deserve to see it."

Lucy shook her head, tears welling up in her eyes. "I don't care about the world out there. I care about this place, about our farm. I'm not keen about going to Perth. continue as they are.

James's voice softened, though his face remained serious. "Things can't stay the way they are, Lucy. The farm is in trouble, whether we like it or not. The bank won't wait forever. The gold is our way out, but it's also a way for you to have a future beyond this place if you want it."

Lucy looked between her parents, her heart aching with the weight of their words. They weren't trying to push her away, she realised, but they were trying to give her something they never had—a choice. But the thought of leaving the farm, of leaving the life she loved, felt like a betrayal of everything she had ever known.

She turned away, blinking back her tears. "I don't know what I want," she admitted, her voice small. "But I know I'm not ready to leave. Not yet."

Emma stepped forward, wrapping her arms around Lucy in a tight embrace. "That's okay, sweetheart. You don't have to decide anything right now. We'll take things one step at a time."

James came closer, placing a hand on Lucy's shoulder. "We just want you to think about it. When you go to Perth, visit the university, see the city. And while we're there, we'll take care of selling the gold. We'll make sure everything is done properly, with the permits and the mining rights. No one has to know."

Lucy nodded, though her mind was still spinning. She felt torn between the life she had always known and the possibilities her parents were offering her. It was too much to process, too much to decide.

But for now, she had time. Time to think, time to figure out what she really wanted. And maybe, just maybe, time to find a way to protect the farm and her future without losing everything she loved.

As the night deepened, the Hardings sat together in the quiet of their kitchen, the weight of their conversation still hanging in the air.

University

The road to Perth stretched out ahead of them, long and seemingly endless, the landscape slowly transitioning from the familiar golden wheat fields of Burralyndra to the more urban sprawl of the city. Emma's hands were steady on the steering wheel, her gaze focused, but Lucy could sense the undercurrent of tension in the air between them. It had been a quiet journey for most of the way, both of them lost in their thoughts, each contemplating the significance of this trip. For Emma, it was a matter of securing their future—both for the farm and for Lucy. For Lucy, it felt like she was walking into a world she didn't quite understand, one that didn't feel like home.

As the city skyline came into view, Lucy shifted uncomfortably in her seat. She had only been to Perth a handful of times, and never for something this monumental. The city was intimidating in its size and pace, so different from the quiet, slow-moving life she knew back home. She wasn't sure what she was supposed to feel—excitement, maybe? Curiosity? All she felt was uncertainty.

"Are you okay, love?" Emma asked, breaking the silence. Her tone was gentle, laced with the concern of a mother who knew her daughter too well.

Lucy glanced at her, then back out the window. "Yeah, I'm fine. It's just... a lot."

Emma nodded, understanding. "It is a lot. I know this isn't easy for you. But we're just looking, okay? No decisions today. Just... possibilities."

Lucy forced a small smile. "Possibilities. Right."

As they entered the city, the streets became busier, the buildings taller. Emma navigated the unfamiliar roads with the precision of someone determined to stay on course. Both literally and figuratively. They passed through neighbourhoods, filled with shops and cafes. The hum of urban life stark against the quiet that usually enveloped their small farm town. After about twenty minutes of winding through the city streets, they pulled into the parking lot of a modern university campus.

The university stood out immediately—large, sprawling, with modern glass buildings and lush green lawns. A place designed for growth, both intellectual and personal, Lucy imagined. As they parked the car and stepped out, Lucy felt a pang of nerves hit her chest. She wasn't sure what she was expecting, but the idea of walking into a world that wasn't tied to the land she knew so well made her feel out of place.

"This is it," Emma said, trying to sound upbeat as they walked toward the main entrance. "They've got courses in agriculture, mining, environmental sciences... everything you could need to run a farm or work in the industry."

Lucy nodded, though she remained quiet. She didn't doubt that there were things she could learn here. But the thought of sitting in a classroom instead of standing in a field, her boots sinking into the soil, made her stomach twist.

Inside, the university was bustling with student. Groups of people chatting, walking to lectures, or sitting in common areas with their laptops and textbooks. It felt overwhelming to Lucy, the sheer number of people, and the energy of the place. But Emma led the way confidently, already having arranged for them to meet with someone from the agricultural and mining faculties. They found the administration office, where they were greeted by a cheerful woman who introduced herself as one of the program coordinators.

"Welcome! I understand you're interested in both our agriculture and mining programs?" the woman asked, leading them down a brightly lit hallway.

Emma smiled warmly, nodding. "Yes, we're looking at options for Lucy. We run a farm back in Burralyndra, and with recent developments, we're considering some expansions."

Lucy felt herself shrink a little under the weight of the conversation. This was all about the future, a future she wasn't sure she wanted yet.

The coordinator led them into a large, open room lined with displays about various agricultural and mining projects students had worked on. Charts showing crop yields, pictures of farms and mining sites, and interactive screens with data filled the walls. It was clear this university was invested in practical learning, which Lucy found mildly reassuring.

The coordinator smiled at Lucy. "Agriculture and mining often go hand in hand here in Western Australia. We have a unique blend of industries, and our programs reflect that. We focus on sustainable farming practices, resource management, and integrating new technologies into both fields. You'd get hands-on experience, working with real-world scenarios. Have you thought about what specifically you'd like to focus on?"

Lucy hesitated, unsure how to answer. "I... haven't really decided. I've always been focused on the farm, so I guess anything that would help with that."

The coordinator nodded. "That's a great place to start. Our agriculture program is comprehensive, covering everything from crop management to soil health and even emerging technologies like precision farming. And if you're interested in mining, we have courses that focus on mineral extraction, sustainable mining practices, and how to navigate the legal and environmental challenges that come with it."

Emma chimed in, her voice gentle but encouraging. "Lucy's always been a quick learner when it comes to the farm. I think she'd thrive here, don't you, Lucy?"

Lucy forced another smile. "Maybe."

They spent the next hour touring the campus, visiting the agricultural research labs and the mining simulation facilities. Everything was state-of-the-art, designed to give students real-world skills they could apply after graduation. Lucy couldn't deny that it was impressive, and maybe if she had grown up in a different environment, she would have been excited about it. But as they walked through the pristine halls, all she could think about was the farm, the land she knew, and the quiet simplicity of it.

After the tour, they sat down with one of the professors, who explained more about the courses and how Lucy could tailor her studies to fit both agriculture and mining. But by the time they left the university, Lucy felt no clearer about her future than when they had arrived.

As they got back into the car, Emma turned to her with a soft smile. "I know it's a lot to take in. But what did you think? Could you see yourself here?"

Lucy leaned back in her seat, staring out the window. "It's… nice. It's just… I don't know, Mum. It doesn't feel like home."

Emma nodded, her eyes reflecting a mix of understanding and hope. "I get that. You can decide later. I just want you to have options, Lucy. The world is bigger than Burralyndra, and I want you to see it. But we won't push you into anything you're not ready for, okay?"

Lucy nodded, grateful for her mother's patience, even if she still felt lost.

Permits for Mining

In Perth, while Lucy was exploring the university, Emma's time was consumed with a different mission—obtaining the necessary permits and mining rights to legally extract and sell the gold that they had found on the farm. She had done some research before the trip, making appointments with local mining authorities, and knew the process was going to be both bureaucratic and expensive. But it had to be done.

After a morning filled with paperwork, Emma found herself sitting in a small, nondescript government office, waiting for her appointment with a mining official. The walls were lined with maps of Western Australia, marked with existing mining leases, and the quiet hum of fluorescent lights added to the tension she felt. The process of acquiring permits wasn't just about filling out forms—it involved geological surveys, assessments of the environmental impact, and applications for the rights to extract minerals from their own land.

The mining official, a tall man in his late forties with a sun-weathered face, finally greeted her with a firm handshake. He led her into his office, where they got down to business. Emma explained their situation—the discovery of gold on their family farm, the importance of securing the farm's future, and their intention to process the gold quietly without causing disruption to the land or their farming operations.

"It's not a large-scale mining operation we're after," Emma clarified. "We want to do this discreetly and ensure we're following all the legal steps."

The official nodded, scanning through the paperwork she had provided. "That's good to hear, Mrs. Harding. Small-scale mining is definitely an option here, but you'll still need to comply with the regulations. We'll have to conduct a geological assessment of the area first, and you'll need an exploration permit before we can grant any mining rights."

He went on to explain the steps involved: the submission of an exploration application, a waiting period for approval, and then the granting of a small mining lease, which would give them the right to extract and sell the gold.

"It's a bit of a process," he added, with a hint of a smile, "but it sounds like you're determined."

Emma smiled back, trying to remain patient. "We don't have a choice. This gold is our only chance to keep the farm."

While the permits were being processed, Emma turned her attention to the sale of the gold they had already found. She had brought three of the smaller nuggets with her to Perth, including the largest one, which weighed just over three ounces. It was a sizeable find, and she knew it could bring in a significant amount of money.

The current price of gold was hovering around $2,900 per ounce, which meant the largest nugget alone could be worth nearly $8,700. Added to the smaller nuggets, which totalled about another four ounces combined, Emma was looking at a sale that could easily bring them over $20,000.

She had arranged to meet with a reputable gold buyer in the heart of Perth. The shop was tucked away on a quiet street, its modest exterior betraying the riches that lay inside. When Emma entered, she was greeted by a middle-aged man with sharp eyes and a calm demeanour, someone who had clearly seen his fair share of gold deals.

"You've brought something to sell, I assume?" he asked, gesturing for her to take a seat at the counter.

Emma carefully pulled the nuggets from her bag, placing them on a small velvet cloth the man had laid out. His eyes widened slightly at the sight of the largest nugget, but he quickly composed himself, picking it up and examining it under a magnifying glass.

"This is a fine piece," he commented. "You don't often see nuggets this size from private finds."

Emma nodded, her hands clasped tightly in her lap. "It's from our farm. There's more where that came from, but we need the funds to keep things going while we sort out the permits."

The man weighed each nugget carefully, his scales precise. "You've got about seven ounces here in total. At the current market rate, I can offer you $2,850 per ounce. That would put your total around... $19,950. Sound fair?"

Emma knew the price of gold had been fluctuating, but this was close enough to the market rate that she felt comfortable accepting. The nearly $20,000 would go a long way toward covering the upfront costs of the mining permits and the initial equipment they needed to begin the ore processing. It wasn't going to save the farm on its own, but it was a solid start.

"I'll take it," Emma said, feeling a wave of relief wash over her. "But we'll be back soon with more."

The man nodded, pulling out the paperwork for the sale. "You're in a good position. Gold's been strong lately. If you do find more, you could be looking at a very profitable venture."

With the gold sale finalised and the permits in motion, Emma returned to the hotel room that she and Lucy were staying in. She found her daughter sitting at the small desk, poring over brochures from the university.

"Find anything you like?" Emma asked, sitting on the edge of the bed.

Lucy nodded, her face lighting up. "There's a program here that combines agriculture and mining. They teach you how to manage land while also extracting minerals sustainably. It's exactly what we need, Mum. I could help with the farm and with the mining."

Emma smiled, proud of Lucy's enthusiasm. "That sounds perfect. We'll need all the help we can get."

Lucy glanced at her mother, sensing something deeper in her tone. "But you're worried, aren't you?"

Emma sighed. "A little. It's a lot to take on. Your dad and I want you to have options—more than just the farm. With the money from the gold, we can send you to university here, give you a chance to see the world beyond Burralyndra. But part of me... part of me just wants you to stay with us, keep the farm going like we always have."

Lucy frowned. "I don't want to leave the farm, Mum. It's part of me. But there's a way to do both—go to university, learn what I need to help the farm and the mining, and still stay home to help."

Emma nodded, appreciating the compromise Lucy was offering. "Maybe. We'll have to figure it out as we go. But for now, let's focus on the next steps—getting those permits and keeping everything under the radar."

Securing The Farm

While Emma and Lucy were in Perth, James stayed behind, watching over the farm with an ever-present sense of unease. The land had always been his sanctuary, a place where hard work and determination yielded the results you could see and feel. But lately, things had taken a turn. Ever since that stranger, Mr. McRae, had shown up asking too many questions, James had been on edge. He had kept most of his worries to himself, not wanting to alarm Emma or Lucy more than necessary, but he couldn't shake the feeling that they were being watched.

It wasn't just a gut feeling. Over the past few days, he'd noticed small things—footprints along the edge of their fields that didn't belong to him or Bill, strange tire tracks near the entrance to the property, and the subtle movement of figures in the distance that vanished before he could get close enough to confront them. It was enough to set his nerves on high alert.

But it wasn't just the potential intruders that weighed on him. The farm machinery, which had taken a beating during the last harvest season, was now in desperate need of repairs. The harvester, in particular, had been acting up—its engine sputtering and struggling to start, not to mention the conveyor belt that had seen better days. With everything going on, James knew he couldn't afford to have the equipment break down entirely. The farm depended on those machines, and without them, they'd be stuck, vulnerable, and falling behind.

After a frustrating morning spent trying to coax the old harvester to start, James wiped the sweat from his brow and muttered to himself, "Damn things gonna give out any day now if I don't get it fixed."

He decided it was time to make some calls. He rang the local mechanic, explaining the situation and asking for someone to come out and give the machinery a thorough inspection. While waiting for the mechanic to arrive, James realised that fixing the harvester wasn't enough. The farm was a target now, and if strangers were sniffing around, they needed more than just repaired machines—they needed protection.

That's when the idea of setting up security cameras and motion sensors came to mind. The thought hadn't occurred to him before; this was a farm, not a high-tech facility, after all. But now, with the looming threat of thieves or worse, it seemed like a necessary precaution. He picked up the phone again, this time calling a local supplier who specialised in security systems.

"I need some cameras and motion sensors," he said gruffly when the man on the other end of the line answered. "Nothing too fancy, but reliable. I've got a big property, so I'll need coverage for a few key areas—the house, the barn, and especially the fields."

The supplier asked him a few questions, gauging the size of the farm and recommending a discreet setup with wireless cameras that could be linked to his phone. James agreed and arranged for the system to be delivered and installed by the end of the week.

After hanging up, he stood on the porch, looking out over the expansive fields. The wheat swayed in the gentle breeze, golden and serene, but James couldn't shake the feeling that peace was slipping away from them. As much as he wanted to believe the farm could continue as it always had, he knew things were changing. The gold had complicated everything.

In addition to setting up security, James had been thinking about another long-term solution: fencing. Their current perimeter fencing was old and in disrepair in several places. Normally, it was just to keep the livestock in and the occasional curious kangaroo out, but now he needed something sturdier—something that would deter unwanted visitors. He called a local fencing contractor to come out and give him a quote.

When the contractor arrived, they walked the perimeter together, discussing materials, height, and how much land they'd need to secure. "You're lookin' at a pretty decent investment," the contractor had said, running his hand along a rotting wooden post. "But if you want to keep people out, it's gonna be worth it."

James agreed. He couldn't afford to let anyone get too close, especially with the prospect of mining rights and the gold still on their land.

That led to another idea that had been brewing in the back of his mind ever since Emma and Lucy had left for Perth—processing the gold. They had already found more than just the one nugget, and Lucy had hinted there could be even more if they dug deeper. Selling the gold would provide the funds to secure the farm's future, but James knew they couldn't just cart it into town and expect to stay under the radar. They needed a discreet way to process the ore without drawing attention.

After doing some research, James made contact with a company that specialised in small-scale ore processing. It wasn't anything grand— just a basic building that could be used to crush the ore, extract the valuable minerals, and store the processed gold securely until it could be sold. The company rep had explained how they could set up the equipment to be as inconspicuous as possible, blending in with the existing farm structures.

"We'll make it look like any old farm shed," the rep assured him. "No one will know you're running a processing operation unless you tell them."

James liked the sound of that. They needed to keep a low profile, especially with the strangers hanging around. He arranged for a site visit to get a proper estimate on building costs and logistics, making sure it would be hidden away in a back corner of the property where no one would stumble upon it accidentally.

By the time Emma and Lucy returned from Perth, James had already made significant progress. The farm machinery was on the mend, with parts on order and a mechanic scheduled for follow-ups. The security cameras were installed and operational, providing him with a sense of relief, as he could now monitor the key areas of the farm from his phone. The fencing quote was higher than he'd anticipated, but he knew it was worth the investment to protect their land.

But it was the discreet ore processing building that weighed on his mind the most. He hadn't told Emma about it yet, wanting to make sure everything was lined up before bringing her into the conversation. He didn't want to burden her with more worry, but he knew that if they were serious about mining the gold and keeping it quiet, this was the only way to do it.

Sitting on the porch with a cup of coffee in hand, James watched as the sun dipped low on the horizon, painting the fields in a soft, golden glow. He felt a mixture of pride and apprehension. The farm was more than just their livelihood—it was their legacy, a piece of land passed down through generations. But now, that legacy was threatened, not just by the elements or bad harvests, but by people who saw only the gold beneath the soil, not the years of hard work that had gone into keeping the farm alive.

As the shadows lengthened, James resolved that he would do whatever it took to protect their home, even if it meant taking drastic measures. And with Emma and Lucy back from Perth, the time for decisions was drawing near. The gold had set them on a path they couldn't turn back from, and James knew that whatever happened next, they had to be ready.

8

Hard Determination

A Difficult Decision

The warm glow of the living room lamps cast soft shadows across the Harding family's faces as they gathered to discuss the gravity of their situation. Outside, the sun had set, leaving the world dark except for the flickers of light from the fireplace. It was the kind of evening that called for closeness and solemn discussions, and tonight, the topic was more serious than ever: the future of their farm and the hidden gold beneath its soil.

Emma, always the heart of the household, voiced her concerns first, her hands clasped tightly in her lap. "If word gets out, we'll have people coming from all over, trying to take what's ours," she said, her voice thick with worry.

Lucy, who had been a pillar of strength for her family, responded with a fierce determination that brightened her eyes. "We must search for additional gold efficiently. Maybe we could do it secretly," she suggested, leaning forward in her chair, her hands animated as she spoke.

James, sitting at the head of the table, looked between his wife and daughter, feeling the weight of their words. The thought of strangers descending on their land, driven by greed, made his stomach churn. Yet, the potential to secure their family's future with further discoveries of gold was too significant to ignore.

"We've been careful so far," James mused aloud, rubbing his chin thoughtfully. "We can continue to explore, but everything we do has to be under the guise of normal farm operations. No new trails, no unusual activities that might draw attention."

The room hummed with a tense energy as they all considered the implications. The risks were high, but the rewards could be life-changing. The conversation went back and forth, with each family member contributing their thoughts and concerns.

Emma expressed her fears about their safety and the peace of their home. "It's not just about the gold," she said, her voice softening. "It's about keeping this place safe for us, for our friends, and for the future generations of Hardings. Whatever we decide, we can't let greed or fear change who we are or how we live."

Lucy nodded, her resolve hardening. "That's why we need to control the narrative. We keep working the land, maybe expand the areas we normally plow, and explore while we do it. We make it look like we're just being thorough, or improving the farm."

James considered Lucy's plan. It was risky, but it was also strategic. "We could use the cover of repairing old fences or clearing new land for grazing," he suggested, thinking aloud. "That would give us reasons to be moving earth without raising suspicions."

The discussion turned to logistics, timelines, and potential fallback plans if things went awry. They talked about who in the community could be trusted and who they needed to keep at arm's length. The conversation was exhaustive, leaving them mentally drained, but with a plan that felt robust.

As the meeting drew to a close, they each knew the path forward wouldn't be easy. There was a lot at stake, not just their financial stability, but their way of life and the heritage of the land they loved so dearly.

Finally, James summed up their decision, his voice firm with newly forged resolve. "We move forward carefully. We use our farm work as cover, and we stay vigilant. We protect this family and this land, no matter what."

The family nodded in agreement, a silent pact forming in the room, strengthened by their shared resolve and love for each other and their land.

Emma reached out, placing her hand over James's and Lucy's, her touch a reassurance of their unity. "Together, then," she said, a definitive note in her voice.

"Together," James and Lucy echoed, feeling the weight of their decision as a mix of resolve and anxiety settled in their hearts.

As they slowly stood up and started clearing the room, the quiet of the night outside seemed less daunting. Inside, the Hardings felt the strength of their family bond, a beacon that would guide them through the challenges ahead. They knew the journey would be fraught with difficulties, but with careful planning and a strong adherence to discretion, they hoped to navigate through the looming threats. The gold, a blessing and a burden, was now their secret to keep, and they were determined to manage it with wisdom and caution.

Resembling Normal Life

As the morning sun stretched its golden fingers across the Harding farm, James and Lucy prepared for a day's work on the tractor, tilling a section of land that had lain fallow last season. Though their work was ostensibly regular farm maintenance, their true aim lay beneath the freshly turned earth—they hoped to find signs of gold that old tales suggested were hidden beneath their land.

They started early, the tractor humming steadily beneath them as they made pass after pass across the field. The routine was broken only by Lucy's vigilant scanning of the overturned soil, searching not just for gold, but for any anomaly that might suggest they were on the right track.

Several hours into their work, Lucy spotted something glinting in the sunlight. Her heart leapt. But as they stopped to investigate, they found it was only an old iron stake, likely a remnant from a long-forgotten fence line. Though initially disappointed, Lucy collected it anyway. "It's part of the farm's history, at least," she remarked, trying to stay upbeat.

They continued their work, the morning giving way to the heat of the day. Soon, Emma appeared at the edge of the field with a basket and a blanket under her arm, signalling a break for lunch. She spread the blanket under the shade of an old oak at the field's edge and laid out a ploughman's lunch—thick slices of homemade bread, cheese, pickles, and cold slices of ham.

As they ate, the conversation naturally turned to their secret search. Emma, ever practical, voiced a concern. "If we do find something—gold, I mean—we need to think about what comes next. How we handle it, who we tell... if we tell anyone at all."

Lucy nodded, her mind on the possibilities. "We keep it quiet, at first. We need to make sure we know exactly what we're dealing with."

James, chewing thoughtfully, agreed. "We might also need to consider getting some expert advice. Someone who can tell us the situation without exposing us.

Their meal continued with discussions of potential scenarios, each flavoured with cautious optimism and a clear-eyed view of the risks involved.

Resuming their work in the afternoon, their search turned up a few more artefacts—an old coin that James identified as likely being from the early 1900s and a piece of fool's gold that sparked excitement until Lucy identified it. "Pyrite," she explained, her geology classes paying off, though the disappointment was palpable.

As the day wore on, the sun began to dip toward the horizon, painting the sky in hues of orange and pink. They were about to call it quits when Lucy's rake clinked against something hard in the soil. Bending down, she brushed away the dirt, revealing a small rock with a fleck of something... metallic?

Her breath caught as she picked it up, the small rock fitting neatly in the palm of her hand. Embedded in the side was a tiny but unmistakable piece of gold, gleaming in the dying light.

"Look at this," she called to her father, who hurried over, wiping sweat from his brow. He took the rock, examining the gold fleck closely. "Well, I'll be," he murmured, a wide grin spreading across his face. "Lucy, I think you've found it."

Their excitement was a bright flare against the fatigue of the day's labour. They stood in the field, holding the small rock, feeling the weight of their discovery. It wasn't much, but it was enough to confirm the legends—there really was gold on the Harding farm.

As they packed up their tools, their conversation buzzed with renewed energy and plans for the next steps. They would need to continue their search, of course, but now with the knowledge that their hopes were not unfounded. The presence of gold, even in such a small quantity, changed everything.

They returned to the house as the last light faded, their minds alive with possibilities. Over dinner, they discussed their strategy, more determined than ever to explore their land's secrets. They agreed to keep their discovery between themselves for now, the risks of exposure too great until they knew more.

That night, as Lucy lay in bed, the image of the gold fleck embedded in the rock played over in her mind. It was a small find, but its implications were vast, and it felt like a promise of things to come. For now, it was their secret, a spark of hope that lit up the darkness of the unknown. They would proceed with caution, but the path forward was a little brighter now, illuminated by the glint of gold.

9

Veiled Preparations

Threshing Shed

The early morning light stretched across the Harding farm, casting long shadows over the wheat fields as James stood near the front porch, surveying the open land before him. The smell of fresh earth and hay filled the air, mingling with the faint scent of engine oil from the tractor sitting idle near the barn. His hands rested on his hips, eyes fixed on the dirt road that led to their homestead, the one that had seen too many strangers of late.

Today marked the beginning of the new fencing installation, a necessary precaution after the unsettling encounter with Mr. McRae and the increased interest in their land. But it wasn't just about keeping trespassers at bay; the fence would serve as the first line of defence as they moved forward with their hidden mining operations.

The arrival of the contractor was expected soon, and James had taken extra care in planning where everything would go. The fencing would provide security, but equally important was the construction of the new building—officially a "threshing shed" for the farm's equipment.

But in truth, it would serve as their discreet gold ore processing facility. The structure would sit toward the back of the property, hidden from view by a stand of old gum trees. It was the perfect cover, blending in with the day-to-day operations of the farm while concealing the reality of what was to come.

Later in the morning, the sound of a large truck rumbled up the drive, and the contractor stepped out, wiping his brow beneath a wide-brimmed hat. His name was Daryl, a tall, wiry man with the rough hands of someone who had spent his entire life working with his hands. James greeted him with a firm handshake, offering a nod of approval as the man surveyed the land.

"Good day for getting started," Daryl commented, glancing around. "You want me to focus on the fencing first, or should we start marking out the area for the threshing shed?"

James hesitated for a moment, thinking carefully. The fencing was important, but the shed was essential to their real plan. They couldn't afford any delays.

"Let's get the fencing crew started, but I'd like to begin work on the shed today as well," James replied. "We need it up as soon as possible. I want it ready before the harvest, so we can use it for some of the old machinery we've got lying around."

Daryl nodded, not questioning the urgency. To him, it was just another job, another structure for another farmer trying to keep his equipment safe. Little did he know the true purpose of the building.

As the fencing crew set to work along the property's borders, James and Daryl walked over to the area behind the barn where the new shed would be constructed. It was a secluded spot, carefully chosen for its distance from the main road and its natural cover from the surrounding trees. From this vantage point, no one would suspect the dual purpose the building would serve.

"You're sure about the size?" Daryl asked, pulling out the blueprint and double-checking the measurements James had provided.

James gave a tight nod. "Yeah, this'll work. It doesn't need to be anything fancy, just functional. Enough room for a couple of pieces of equipment and a workspace."

Daryl studied the plans for a moment, then gave a satisfied grunt. "Shouldn't take us more than a week to get the frame up, maybe two to finish the inside. You want electricity running through here?"

James considered it for a moment. "Yeah, we'll need some basic power for the equipment."

He didn't elaborate on what kind of equipment that would be, and Daryl didn't ask. From the outside, it would look like any other farm building—a space for the tools and machinery that kept the Harding farm running. But inside, James knew it would be where their future was processed, one load of gold ore at a time.

As the days passed, the fencing went up section by section, the heavy metal posts driven deep into the ground, topped with sturdy wire mesh that could withstand both the elements and unwanted visitors. The work was slow but steady, and James was constantly out there, overseeing every inch of it. He couldn't afford any mistakes—not with the weight of what was coming bearing down on him.

When the sun began to dip below the horizon, casting the sky in shades of red and orange, James would take a moment to catch his breath, leaning against the fence and watching as the workers packed up their gear for the night. He'd glance over at the back of the farm, where the framework of the new shed was beginning to take shape. The beams were up now, skeletal in the fading light, but soon it would be a fully functional building, a key piece of their plan.

Emma had kept him updated on the progress in Perth—permits were moving along, and they had sold the first few gold nuggets, enough to help cover the cost of the fence and the shed construction. But it wasn't enough yet. They would be drawing down on their loan in order to get the shed and fencing completed. They needed more gold, and they needed the right to mine it before anyone else caught wind of what they were up to.

One evening, after the crew had gone home for the day, James stood outside, staring at the nearly completed fence that now encircled their land. The wind had picked up, rustling the leaves of the trees and carrying the scent of dry grass. His mind was racing with a thousand different thoughts—about the farm, the gold, the strangers who had shown too much interest in their land.

He was tired, more exhausted than he could remember being in years. The weight of everything was pressing down on him, and though he tried to push it aside, he couldn't help but feel the creeping sense of paranoia. What if someone knew? What if they weren't as discreet as they thought? He had installed motion sensors and security cameras around the property, hiding them in strategic locations, but even that didn't feel like enough.

James checked the camera feeds constantly, monitoring every flicker of movement, every shift of the wind. He had never been the type to be overly cautious, but now, with so much at stake, he couldn't afford to be anything less. The smallest mistake could cost them everything.

As the fencing neared completion, James turned his attention back to the shed. He had been working closely with Daryl and the crew, ensuring that everything was built according to plan. The interior would be outfitted with the necessary equipment for processing the gold ore they expected to pull from the earth soon. But outwardly, it was nothing more than a threshing shed—a place to store grain or house an old piece of farm machinery.

The key was to keep up appearances, to make sure that anyone who happened to pass by wouldn't give the new building a second glance. To that end, James had ordered a few old pieces of equipment from a nearby farm auction—rusty threshers and seeders that he planned to leave out front as a decoy.

"No one'll think twice about a couple of busted-up machines sitting in front of a threshing shed," James muttered to himself as he placed the order. It was all about playing the long game now—keeping everything above suspicion until the time was right to reveal what they had really been doing.

Inside the house, Emma and James had long discussions every evening about the future of the farm, the mining, and the permits that were still being processed. They knew they had to move carefully, but time wasn't on their side. With the first few nuggets sold, they had bought themselves some breathing room, but not enough to be complacent.

James also started to explore quotes for new fencing materials. He wanted to make sure that the perimeter around their property was reinforced even further in the coming months. It wasn't just the threat of strangers anymore—it was the potential fallout of what they were about to undertake. Protecting their land, their home, and their secret was now the top priority.

At night, after a long day of work, James would sit in his chair by the window, sipping a cold beer and staring out at the farm. The stars above were bright and clear, a stark contrast to the uncertainty that hung over them. Somewhere out there, in the shadows, was the future of the Harding farm—and it was up to them to make sure that the future remained theirs.

By the end of the second week, the shed was nearly complete. The workers had done a fine job—its simple wooden structure blended seamlessly into the landscape, looking every bit like an ordinary outbuilding meant for farming equipment. But James knew that, inside, they were preparing for something much bigger. It was only a matter of time before the first loads of ore were brought in, and from there, they'd begin to see the true fruits of their labour.

Emma and Lucy were still in Perth, finalising the last of the paperwork and permits, and James had sent word that things on the farm were progressing smoothly. They had kept up the pretence well enough so far, but with each passing day, the stakes grew higher. James could feel it in the air—the tension that came with knowing they were balancing on the edge of something enormous, something dangerous.

And as he watched the final pieces of the fence go up, securing their land from the outside world, James couldn't help but wonder how long it would be before someone tried to tear it all down.

10

A Plan In Motion

An Active Strategy

The crisp morning air wrapped around the Harding farm, the golden wheat swaying in the soft breeze, hinting at the coming harvest. From the outside, the farm looked as it always had—peaceful, industrious, a place where hard work sustained life. But inside the barn, hidden beneath the cover of routine, a different work was taking shape.

James stood by the large wooden workbench in the barn, studying a worn-out map of the property. His hands traced the faint lines he had drawn in secret, marking the spots where they believed the gold could be hiding. The barn, now their base of operations, felt cluttered with farm equipment, bags of seed, and the tools of their new trade: pickaxes, shovels, and tarps to cover their tracks. Everything was in place. The plan was simple—search for gold beneath the very soil that had supported them for generations. But it wasn't without its risks.

The barn door creaked open, and Lucy stepped inside, her face flushed from the morning sun. Her hands were dirty, fingernails caked with the soil she had been digging through for days. She gave James a

95

nod, letting him know the latest spot had been checked.

"Anything?" James asked quietly, his voice barely above a whisper. Even here, surrounded by the familiar walls of their barn, he couldn't shake the feeling that they were being watched, that every move they made was under scrutiny.

Lucy shook her head, wiping the sweat from her brow. "Nothing yet. But we're close. I can feel it."

James exhaled, running a hand through his greying hair. They had been careful, blending their search with their regular farming activities, making sure no one would suspect what they were really up to. Each night, they would bury their tools under piles of hay, hide their tracks in the wheat fields, and keep their conversations low, away from prying ears.

But the weight of it all was beginning to take its toll. The strain of balancing the two lives—one above ground, where they were simple wheat farmers, and one below, where they hunted for gold—was starting to show. The tension hung heavy in the air.

Over the next few days, the routine fell into place like clockwork. By daylight, James, Emma, and Lucy tended to the farm. They mended fences, repaired machinery, and prepared for the upcoming harvest. It was hard work, the kind they had known for years, the kind that kept their minds sharp and their bodies strong. But beneath the surface, a new urgency thrummed.

As the sunset and the shadows lengthened, they would slip away to the barn, ready for another night of digging. Lucy had taken the lead, her determination fuelling the search, her instincts guiding them to carefully selected spots. She would map out new areas, using her knowledge of the land and the subtle clues they had picked up to dig in places that seemed promising.

One afternoon, as they rested in the shade near the barn, Lucy leaned against the rough wooden wall and looked at her father. "We need to move faster, Dad. The more we wait, the more we risk someone else finding out. Or worse... the bank comes looking."

James nodded, his face etched with worry. "I know. But we have to be careful. One wrong move, and we could lose everything. The farm, the land—it's all we have."

Lucy's eyes hardened with resolve. "I won't let that happen. I'll find the gold, Dad. I'll save the farm."

The following evening, they worked late into the night. The moon hung low in the sky, casting a pale glow over the fields, but inside the barn, it was dark and quiet. Emma joined them this time, her usually calm demeanour giving way to a quiet intensity. She had always been the one to keep the peace, to offer a steady hand when things felt like they were falling apart. But now, even she couldn't ignore the weight of what they were doing.

"This has to work," Emma said, her voice low as she passed James another tool. "We can't keep living like this—always looking over our shoulders, always wondering who's watching."

James grunted in agreement, his hands moving methodically as he checked their supplies. "It will work. We've just got to keep at it. There's gold here, I know it. We just have to find it."

Lucy was already on her knees in the dirt, digging through the soft soil in one of the spots they had marked. Her heart pounded in her chest, the adrenaline mixing with the exhaustion that came from days of hard labour. She knew they were close. The land had whispered its secrets to her before—this time, she was certain.

Hours passed, and the family worked in near silence, the sound of metal scraping against dirt the only noise in the barn. The tension was palpable, each of them lost in their thoughts, focused on the task at hand. The stakes had never been higher, and every shovelful of dirt felt like a step closer to either salvation or disaster.

Suddenly, Lucy's shovel hit something hard. The sharp clink echoed in the quiet, and she froze, her breath catching in her throat. James and Emma looked up, their eyes wide with anticipation.

"What is it?" Emma whispered, stepping closer.

Lucy knelt down, brushing away the dirt with her hands. Her fingers trembled as she revealed the dull, yellow glint beneath the soil. The small nugget they had discovered was nothing like the first one they found, yet it was undoubtedly gold.

James crouched beside her, his eyes scanning the tiny vein of gold that wound through the earth like a thread of hope. "There's more," he muttered, his voice filled with awe and disbelief.

Lucy nodded, her heart racing. "We've found it. There's more beneath the land. We're sitting on something bigger than we thought."

With every pulse of the discovery, a new wave of fear crashed over them, a palpable tension that hung heavy in the air. Their eyes were locked on the glittering metal, its shine so bright it seemed to blind them momentarily. The realisation gradually seeped into their bones, sending a chill down their spines. Uncovering more only increased the risk's weight, suffocating their hope. The scent of uncertainty wafted around them, mingling with the metallic tang of the findings. Their hearts raced, pounding in their chests like a relentless drumbeat as they grappled with the knowledge that they couldn't keep this hidden forever. Strangers lurked nearby, their presence felt like a shadow creeping closer, threatening to expose their secret. The bank loomed like a sinister giant, its breath hot and heavy on their necks, a constant reminder of the impending danger.

In the days that followed, the family worked tirelessly, digging deeper, expanding their search, and carefully cataloguing every bit of gold they uncovered. They were cautious, always making sure to cover their tracks, always blending their new operations with the farm work.

James became more paranoid with each passing day. He doubled down on the security, checking the cameras, testing the motion sensors, and making sure the fencing around the property was secure. Every creak in the night, every car that passed on the distant road, sent his heart racing.

Lucy, on the other hand, grew more determined. She had tasted success, and now she was driven by the need to protect the farm, to prove to her parents that they could pull this off. But she wasn't naïve. She knew the dangers. Every shovelful of dirt, every nugget of gold they found brought them closer to both salvation and ruin.

Emma, always the voice of reason, tried to keep things in perspective. "We have to be smart about this," she said one evening as they sat around the kitchen table, the small pile of gold they had found glimmering in the candlelight. "We can't rush. If we move too fast, we'll make mistakes. And mistakes will cost us everything."

James nodded in agreement, but Lucy couldn't shake the feeling that time was running out. They had found a vein of gold, but it wasn't enough—not yet. They needed more if they were going to secure the future of the farm.

"We'll make it work," Lucy said quietly, her voice filled with resolve. "We have to."

As the family continued their secret search, the barn became their sanctuary, their refuge from the outside world. It was there, beneath the cover of night, that they dug for gold and planned their next moves. And it was there, in the quiet hours of the early morning, that they realised just how high the stakes had become.

The gold was buried beneath their feet, but danger lurked as well. Every nugget they found and every bit of ore they processed brought them closer to the truth. It also meant they were getting closer to the moment when their secret would be exposed. Lucy stood in the barn, dirt-covered hands and a racing heart. She felt a mixture of fear and excitement, knowing that the hardest part was yet to come.

They had found gold. But could they keep it?

11

Banks Warning

Crucial Correspondence

The early morning sun filtered through the worn lace curtains in the kitchen, casting a soft, golden light over the simple wooden table. The familiar creaks of the house settling into the day were a small comfort in the quiet tension that now gripped the Harding family. The smell of freshly brewed coffee filled the air, but no one moved to pour a cup.

Emma stood at the sink, her fingers resting on the edge of the counter, staring blankly out the window at the vast fields of wheat that stretched as far as the eye could see. Her heart was pounding in her chest, though she tried to keep her face calm, to maintain the sense of normalcy that had long since disappeared. The letter in her hand, crumpled from her grip, was far from normal. It was a warning—a threat that loomed over them, more tangible than the gold they had yet to find.

James sat at the kitchen table, his face set in a grim frown as he rubbed his hands over his tired eyes. Lucy leaned against the doorway, her arms crossed tightly over her chest. The weight of their situation hung heavy in the room.

Emma's voice broke the silence, quiet but tinged with anxiety. "We're running out of time, James." She turned to face him, her blue eyes wide with worry. "This isn't just a reminder. It's a final warning. We need that gold, or we'll lose everything."

James didn't look up, but his jaw tightened. He'd known this moment was coming for months now, and yet it still felt like a blow to the gut. The bank had been patient, more patient than he'd expected. But patience only lasted so long when money was involved. And now, with their payments overdue and no cash to spare, the farm was teetering on the edge of foreclosure.

"I know," he muttered, his voice low and rough. "But we'll find a way. We've come too far to lose it all now."

Lucy pushed off the door frame, stepping into the kitchen. "How long do we have?" she asked, her voice steady, though her eyes betrayed the fear she was trying to suppress.

Emma glanced down at the letter again, reading the words for what felt like the hundredth time. "A month. Maybe less. They want a substantial payment—more than we have right now. If we don't make it..." Her voice trailed off, but the implication was clear. The farm, their home, everything they had worked for, would be gone.

Lucy clenched her fists at her sides, her mind racing. A month wasn't enough. They had barely scratched the surface of what they believed was beneath the land, and even with what they'd found, it wasn't close to being enough to save the farm. But giving up wasn't an option. Not for her.

"Then we have to push harder," Lucy said firmly, stepping closer to her parents. "We don't have time to waste. The bank's not going to wait for us to find gold at our own pace."

James finally looked up at his daughter, his eyes heavy with the same fear that he had tried so hard to bury. He admired Lucy's determination, her willingness to fight for the farm, but he couldn't ignore the risks. They were already pushing the limits of what was safe—digging deeper, taking more risks, hiding their actions from anyone who might be watching.

"We can't just rush in blind, Lucy," James said, his tone stern but soft. "One mistake, and everything we've worked for, could come crashing down. The land, the farm... it's all tied together. If we dig too deep, too fast, we could lose more than just the farm."

Lucy didn't back down, her eyes blazing with frustration. "We don't have a choice, Dad! The bank's already circling. If we don't act now, there won't be anything left to save."

Emma stepped between them, her voice gentle but firm. "We need a clear plan. We can't afford to make any mistakes, not now. If we're going to keep the farm, we have to be smart about this."

James leaned back in his chair, running a hand over his face. The exhaustion was written in every line of his body. He had always been the one to hold the family together, to bear the weight of their struggles in silence, but now that weight felt unbearable. For years, they had fought to keep the farm afloat, to scrape by season after season. But this time, it felt like the fight was slipping out of his grasp.

"Emma's right," James said, his voice steady but tinged with weariness. "We need to make sure we're digging in the right spots, and we need to do it quietly. We can't afford to draw any more attention than we already have."

Lucy nodded, though her heart was pounding in her chest. She understood the risks, but the thought of losing the farm—the place that had been her entire world—was something she couldn't accept.

"I'll find it," Lucy said, her voice quieter now but filled with determination. "We've already found some. There's more out there, I know it. We just need to dig in the right places."

Emma placed a hand on Lucy's shoulder, her eyes filled with a mixture of pride and concern. "We'll do it together. But we need to be careful. The more gold we find, the more dangerous this becomes."

The days that followed were filled with a sense of urgency that none of them could shake. The farm continued to run as it always had, but beneath the surface, the Hardings were working harder than ever to uncover the gold that would save their home.

James began laying the groundwork for their plan in earnest. He contacted a local fencing company for a quote, under the pretence of securing the farm's boundaries from wild animals, but in truth, he needed the new fence to keep out prying eyes. The cameras and motion sensors he had installed weeks ago were a start, but the fencing would be the final line of defence.

"I'll come out and take a look," the contractor had said on the phone. "Shouldn't be too hard to get that land fenced in."

What he didn't know was that James also had other plans in motion. Alongside the fencing project, he was discreetly organising the construction of a new shed—one that would be used to process the gold they uncovered. Officially, it would be a threshing shed, part of their ongoing farm expansion. But its true purpose was far more valuable.

Lucy, meanwhile, spent her nights digging, searching, mapping out new areas of the farm where the gold might be hiding. Every day, she felt the weight of the bank's warning letter pressing down on her, reminding her that time was running out.

One morning, Emma sat at the kitchen table, poring over the paperwork needed for the mining permits and leases. It had been a slow, tedious process, but they were finally getting close. The gold they had found so far wasn't much—just a few small nuggets, the largest weighing three ounces—but it was enough to get things moving. At today's gold price of around $2,000 per ounce, that nugget alone was worth nearly $6,000. It wasn't enough to pay off the bank, but it was a start.

Emma had already reached out to a reputable dealer in Perth who was interested in buying their gold. The sale remained clandestine, avoiding notice.

"We'll keep the first nugget," Emma had said one evening as they discussed their plans. "For sentimental reasons. But the rest... we'll need to sell it, and fast. Once we have the permits in hand, we can start processing everything more efficiently."

James had agreed, though the thought of selling the gold left a bitter taste in his mouth. It wasn't just about the money—it was about what the gold represented. A chance to save the farm, yes, but also a reminder of the immense pressure they were under.

The final piece of the puzzle fell into place when Emma received confirmation from the mining authorities. The permits were approved, and they were officially cleared to extract the gold from their land.

"It's done," Emma said that evening, handing James the paperwork with a mix of relief and trepidation. "We can move forward now. But we need to be smart about it. We can't afford any mistakes."

James looked down at the papers, his mind already turning to the next steps. "We'll do it right," he said firmly. "We'll keep digging, keep building. And we'll keep this farm."

But as they sat around the kitchen table, the letter from the bank still lingered in the back of their minds—a ticking clock, counting down the days until their time ran out.

The gold was their only hope. And now, it was a race against time to find enough before the bank came to collect.

Mr Wilson Pays A Visit

The sun was hanging low in the sky, casting a golden haze across the wheat fields as James Harding spotted a dust cloud forming along the dirt road to the farm. They didn't get much traffic out here, especially not on a day like this. That could only mean one thing: Horace Wilson, or "Wilson," the manager of the Burralyndra bank, was coming up the drive.

Wilson had been more than a bank manager to the Hardings. He had known James' father well and had handled the family's finances for years. Their relationship had always been friendly, though today James felt a weight of anticipation bearing down on him that was different from the usual casual meetings.

James stepped out onto the porch, wiping his hands on his jeans as he watched Wilson's familiar old sedan rumble to a stop in front of the house. The door opened, and the older man stepped out, his suit jacket neatly pressed despite the dusty drive. His face was lined from years spent out in the sun, but his eyes held a sharpness beneath his kind expression—a banker's eyes, calculating and keen.

"Afternoon, Wilson," James called out, offering a handshake as Wilson walked up to him.

"Afternoon, James," Wilson replied, shaking his hand firmly. "Thought it was about time I dropped by to see how things are going."

James forced a smile, knowing full well why Wilson had come. "Busy time of year. We've been getting everything ready for harvest."

"So I've heard," Wilson said with a smile, but there was something more beneath it—a seriousness that James couldn't ignore. "Mind if we sit and have a chat? We have a few things that require discussion.

James led him to the porch, where Emma had already set out a pitcher of iced tea. Lucy joined them as they sat around the weathered wooden table, the tension thick in the air. Emma poured a glass for Wilson, her polite smile masking the nervousness James knew she was feeling.

"Thanks for coming all the way out here, Wilson," Emma said, offering the tea. "It's been busy on the farm, as you can imagine."

"I can imagine," Wilson replied, accepting the glass. "And I'm glad I made it out. Wanted to talk with you face to face about where things stand."

James braced himself. He knew this conversation was inevitable. The letter from the bank had arrived earlier in the week, a stark reminder of just how close they were to losing everything.

"We got your letter," James said, his voice tight. "We know we're behind."

Wilson took a sip of the tea and set the glass down carefully before nodding. "Yes, you are. And I don't want to cause any alarm, but the bank's growing concerned, James. You're overdue on your payments, and we're getting close to the point where something's gotta give."

Emma's fingers clenched slightly around her glass, her composure slipping just a bit. "What are our options, Wilson?" she asked, her voice calm but laced with anxiety.

Wilson leaned back in his chair, his face thoughtful. "Well, you're not without options, but you're running out of time. If things don't turn around, the bank might be forced to take more drastic action. I'm here to help you avoid that, but it's going to take some work on your part."

James hated the feeling of being at the mercy of the bank, but he knew they had no other choice. "What are you suggesting?"

Wilson set his glass down, leaning forward slightly as he spoke. "One option is to remortgage the farm. We could extend your loan and give you some additional funds to help with the overdue payments, as well as anything else you might need—fencing, building projects, even new machinery. I know you've been working on some improvements."

James glanced at Emma, who was listening intently. The idea of remortgaging the farm didn't sit well with either of them, but it was an option they couldn't immediately dismiss. The new fencing and the threshing shed—the one that would also secretly serve as a gold-processing facility—had cost more than they'd anticipated. And then there was the machinery, old and held together with repairs and sheer determination. A loan could make a big difference.

"That's a lot to ask," James said carefully. "Remortgaging the farm puts us deeper into debt, and we don't know what next season's going to bring. What if the weather doesn't hold? What if the wheat prices stay low?"

Wilson sighed and rubbed his forehead. "I know it's a risk, James. And to be honest, the weather's not looking great. We're hearing reports that next season might be tough. The drought's been hard on everyone, and the price of seed is going up. It's not an easy decision, but you've got to start thinking long term. If you want to keep the farm, you'll need to invest in it now, especially if the wheat crop's not going to cut it."

Lucy, who had been quietly listening, spoke up, her voice steady. "What happens if we don't take the loan, Wilson? If we try to make the payment ourselves?"

Wilson turned his gaze to her, his face softening a bit. "You can try, Lucy, but from what I'm seeing, you're going to be cutting it close. You'd need to make a pretty substantial payment soon, and based on what I know of your wheat yields, it's going to be tough without another source of income."

There was a pause as the Hardings exchanged glances. The gold—buried under their land and their secret lifeline—was that other source of income. But they couldn't share that with Wilson, not yet.

"We're looking at our options," Emma said diplomatically, her voice steady despite the unease. "But we'd like to avoid taking on more debt if possible."

Wilson nodded, understanding but still concerned. "I get that. But you've got to be realistic about what's coming. If the weather doesn't improve and the prices don't change, the farm's going to be in trouble. That's why I wanted to give you another option—remortgaging could give you the funds you need to finish your projects and buy new equipment. If your machinery's as old as I think it is, a new harvester or tractor could make a real difference in your yields."

James sighed, rubbing a hand over his face. He hated how close they were to losing the farm. His father had kept this land running for decades, and now it was in danger of slipping through his fingers. But Wilson wasn't wrong—new equipment could help them not only in their farming but also in managing the secret mining operation.

"We'll think about it," James said finally. "We appreciate you coming out to talk to us, Wilson. But we need a little more time."

Wilson stood, offering James and Emma a sympathetic smile. "I understand, James. I've known your family for a long time, and I don't want to see you lose this place. But I can only give you so much time. If you decide to go for the remortgage, I'll make sure you get the best terms possible, and the bank will help cover the new equipment and any fencing or building you need."

James shook Wilson's hand again, and the older man gave him a firm nod before heading back to his car. As he drove away, the dust swirling in the fading light, James felt a heavy weight settle over him. The farm, their legacy, was hanging by a thread.

"What are we going to do, James?" Emma asked quietly, her hand resting on his shoulder.

James watched the car disappear down the road before answering. "We stick to the plan. We keep digging, we finish the fencing, and we build that shed. No one needs to know what we're really doing."

Lucy, standing nearby, nodded, her face set with determination. "We'll make it work," she said softly. "We have to."

But even as they spoke, the letter from the bank remained on the kitchen table—a stark reminder that time was running out. The gold they had found would have to be enough.

The Cost of the Future

James leaned against the kitchen counter, his arms crossed and his expression tense as he stared out the window. The sun was starting to set, casting a warm, orange glow over the fields of wheat that stretched out into the distance. For as long as he could remember, those fields had been his life—his father's life—and now they were hanging by a thread.

Emma sat at the table, the bank's letter spread out in front of her. The words, though plain and formal, carried the weight of their future. If they didn't find a way to make the next payment or remortgage the farm, they could lose everything. The house, the land, the history of the Harding family—all of it could be swept away.

"I don't like this, Emma," James muttered, his voice thick with frustration. "Remortgaging the farm is a huge risk. We're already in trouble, and taking on more debt... It's dangerous."

Emma sighed, rubbing her temples. She had always been the practical one, the one who saw things clearly even when the future looked dark. But today, she was struggling. "I know, James. I hate the thought of it too. But what choice do we have? The bank's not going to wait much longer. If we don't remortgage, we'll lose the farm. And if we lose the farm..."

She trailed off, the words too painful to say. Losing the farm would mean more than just losing their home. It would mean breaking up the family, scattering their lives like dust in the wind. It would tear apart the legacy they had fought so hard to protect.

"If we remortgage," James said slowly, his voice tight, "we're putting everything on the line. What if the wheat crop doesn't come through next season? What if we can't keep up with the payments? The bank won't just let us off the hook."

Emma met his gaze, her eyes filled with worry. "But if we don't, there's no chance at all. We can't just hope for a miracle, James. We have to do something."

James ran a hand through his hair, pacing across the kitchen. "I don't want to give up farming, Emma. This land... It's been in my family for generations. I have no intention of turning it into a mining operation. It's not what we do."

"And I don't want that either," Emma said quickly, her voice softening. "But mining is just... It's a way to keep the farm going. We don't have to become miners, James. We just need enough gold to pay off the mortgage, fix the machinery, get us through a few bad seasons. That's all."

"You think we can control it?" James asked, his voice low, almost a whisper. "Once we start digging, it'll be hard to stop. Gold changes things, Emma. It changes people. I've seen it before. The more we find, the more we'll need to keep digging. And what happens when we run out? We'll be left with nothing but holes in the ground and debts we can't pay off."

Emma stood up, crossing the room to stand beside him. She placed a hand on his arm, squeezing it gently. "We're not those kinds of people, James. We know what's important. This farm is our life, and it always will be. The gold is just a tool to help us survive. That's all."

James didn't respond right away. His eyes were still on the fields, the golden stalks swaying gently in the breeze. He could feel the weight of generations on his shoulders—his father's, his grandfather's, and all the Hardings before them who had worked this land. He didn't want to be the one who lost it all.

The sound of footsteps broke the silence. Lucy appeared in the doorway, her expression serious. She had been listening from the hallway, her face shadowed by the growing darkness outside.

"I know you're worried," she said, stepping into the kitchen. "But I want you to know something. I love this farm, Dad. I love farming. I don't want to be a miner either. I want to keep the farm in the family, just like you do."

James turned to face her, his eyes searching her face for something—reassurance, maybe. "Lucy, this isn't just about you loving the farm. It's about whether we can afford to keep it."

"I know," Lucy said, her voice steady. "That's why I've been thinking. If we remortgage the farm, we can make it work. We just have to be smart about it."

She reached into her back pocket and pulled out a folded piece of paper. "I've been doing some calculations," she said, laying the paper on the table. "I've worked out a plan."

James and Emma exchanged a glance before sitting down at the table. Lucy unfolded the paper, revealing a detailed breakdown of costs, income, and goals.

"If we remortgage the farm," Lucy began, pointing to the top of the sheet, "we can take out enough to cover the overdue payments, finish the new fencing, and build the threshing shed. But we'll also need to invest in new equipment—about $1.5 million for a new harvester, seed, and fertiliser. If we don't upgrade, we're going to fall further behind."

Emma nodded slowly, studying the numbers. "And how do we pay it back?"

"We've got options," Lucy said. "I calculated the wheat yields for the next five years, assuming we have both good and bad seasons. Even in the worst-case scenario, we can meet the payments as long as we get decent prices. But if we do have a bad season—like Wilson said is possible—then that's where the gold comes in."

James leaned forward, his brow furrowed. "What do you mean?"

"I figured out how much gold we'd need to mine to cover any shortfalls in the wheat yields," Lucy explained, pointing to a separate column on the sheet. "Based on current gold prices—about $2,500 per ounce—we'd need to extract about 20 ounces of gold over the next two years to cover any potential shortfalls. That's not a lot, considering the vein we found. We've already pulled out nuggets that total close to 5 ounces. We can do this, Dad."

James stared at the paper, absorbing the numbers. Lucy had clearly put a lot of thought into this. She wasn't just dreaming—she had a plan.

"So, you're saying we use the gold as backup?" James asked slowly. "We only dig when we need to, just to keep the farm running?"

"Exactly," Lucy said, her eyes determined. "The farm comes first. Always. The gold is just there to help us when we need it—like for bad seasons or new equipment. I don't want to be a miner. I aim to be a farmer, just like you and Grandpa. But we can't ignore the fact that we have a resource that could save us."

Emma's eyes flickered towards James, a glimmer of tenderness dancing in her gaze. The room bathed in a soft, golden light, casting a warm glow on their faces. "She's right, James," she murmured, her voice gentle like a soothing melody. The faint scent of brewed coffee wafted through the air, mingling with the earthy aroma of the farm outside. James sank deeper into his chair, the worn leather creaking beneath him, as he ran his calloused fingers over his stubbled face. The weight of their decision pressed upon him, causing a knot to form in the pit of his stomach. The distant sound of chirping birds and the rustle of leaves in the wind seeped through the open window, blending with the murmurs of their conversation. He couldn't help but feel torn, a storm of emotions raging within him. The gold, once a symbol of uncertainty, now held the potential to bridge the gaps that threatened their livelihood.

"Alright," he said finally, his voice quiet. "We'll do it. But we're sticking to the plan. No more digging than we need to. The farm comes first."

Lucy smiled, relief flooding her face. "I promise, Dad. The farm will always come first."

Emma reached over and squeezed James' hand. "We'll get through this, James. Together."

James nodded, though the weight of the decision still pressed heavily on his shoulders. The future was uncertain, but at least now they had a plan. They had a chance.

And, with Lucy's meticulous calculations, they had hope. The decision had been made. They would go and see Wilson in the morning.

The paper lay on the table between them, the numbers spelling out the future of the Harding farm—a future that hung in the balance between the wheat fields they loved and the gold hidden beneath them.

12

Lucy's Discovery

Intruder

The late afternoon sun slanted through the small, grimy window of the farm's old tool shed, casting long shadows over the dust-covered floor. Lucy stood in the doorway, hesitating. The tool shed was rarely used anymore; most of the equipment had been moved to the newer barn. It had become a forgotten place, a relic of the past—until today.

She felt a persistent unease throughout the morning. A vague sense of unease had settled in ever since their decision to remortgage the farm. Even though they had a plan in place, the weight of secrecy and the growing tension with the bank lingered. Lucy's thoughts kept circling back to one question: where was the best place to hide the gold?

They had been careful so far, but she knew they needed to be smarter. The barn was too obvious. It was the hub of their activity, with tools and supplies going in and out constantly. If anyone was watching them—if that stranger, Mr. McRae, or someone else got suspicious—they couldn't risk having the gold anywhere near their usual work. And yet, the gold was their lifeline.

Lucy walked further into the shed, her boots kicking up small clouds of dust with every step. She looked around, taking in the old shelves lined with rusted tools, a forgotten wheelbarrow in the corner, and crates that hadn't been opened in years. It was quiet, abandoned, and the perfect place to hide something. Or at least, it should have been.

But something wasn't right.

She knelt down by the far corner of the shed where the ground was bare. Her fingers brushed against the fine layer of dust that covered everything—everything except for a faint set of footprints leading from the doorway to the back of the shed.

Lucy's heart skipped a beat, her pulse quickening. The footprints were fresh, unmistakably human, and not her own. She swallowed hard, her mind racing. No one had been in this shed for months, maybe even years. No one should have been here.

As she followed the trail of prints, her eyes caught on something else. Hanging from a rusty nail embedded in the wall was a small piece of fabric. She reached out, gently pulling the scrap free. It was torn, dark blue, and slightly frayed around the edges. Lucy recognised the fabric instantly—it was the same kind of material the stranger, Mr. McRae, had been wearing when he came to the farm.

Her chest tightened with fear. What had he been doing here? How long had he been snooping around? And more importantly, had he seen anything?

Lucy clenched the piece of fabric in her hand, her mind whirling. She looked around the shed, trying to see it from an outsider's perspective. The old crates, the tools... nothing about this place would suggest there was gold hidden nearby. But clearly, someone was curious. Someone was watching.

Her instincts told her that McRae was getting closer to uncovering their secret, or at least to realising that the Harding family was hiding something.

She glanced back at the footprints, noticing that they led toward one of the shelves at the back of the shed. Carefully, she approached it, her heart thudding in her chest. There was nothing particularly unusual about the shelf at first glance, but as she knelt down to inspect it, she realised that one of the floorboards underneath was slightly raised—just enough to catch the edge of her boot.

Curiosity and dread gnawed at her as she pulled at the board, lifting it free with a soft creak. Beneath it, there was a small, hollowed-out space, just big enough to stash something small—something valuable.

And it was empty.

Lucy's mind raced. Someone had found this hiding spot—perhaps it had been used years ago, but now it was exposed. Had McRae found it too? Had he taken anything? Or worse, had he seen the signs of their secret digging elsewhere on the farm?

She stood up, wiping her dusty hands on her jeans, and shoved the floorboard back into place. Her fear was slowly turning into anger. This wasn't just a random visitor—this was someone prying into their lives, threatening their future. And she wasn't going to let it happen.

Lucy walked quickly back to the entrance of the shed, her eyes scanning the area outside. Everything seemed quiet, but that didn't reassure her. Someone had been here, and they might come back.

She needed to tell her parents. They needed to know that they weren't safe, that McRae or someone else was watching them. And they needed to come up with a new plan for the gold, fast. There was no room for mistakes now. The stakes had risen, and one misstep could cost them everything.

As Lucy stepped outside into the fading sunlight, she paused, savouring the warm rays that caressed her skin. She cast one final glance at the weathered tool shed, its peeling paint and creaking door creating an aged symphony of sights and sounds. The piece of fabric, clenched tightly in her hand, emitted a faint scent of earth and oil, reminding her of their shared purpose in safeguarding the farm. Her jaw clenched, her determination palpable in the air. The weight of responsibility settled upon her shoulders, a heavy burden that threatened to consume her. The golden hue of the setting sun shimmered upon the fabric, a tangible symbol of their salvation and potential downfall. With a deep breath, she began her journey back to the house, the crunch of gravel under her boots resonating with each determined step. The fragrant scent of freshly cut grass mingled with the distant aroma of farm animals, creating a tapestry of rural life. Lucy's heart raced, her pulse pounding in her ears, as she embarked on a race against time to protect her beloved farm and the family that resided within its walls. An undercurrent of hope mingled with anxicty as she prayed they would be swift enough to outpace the looming threat that hung over their heads like a storm cloud.

13

Parcel at the Door

A Mysterious package

The sun was just beginning to dip behind the hills, casting a golden glow over the Harding farm. It had been a long, tense day. After Lucy's discovery in the tool shed, she had been on edge, constantly glancing over her shoulder and watching for signs of any more intrusions. The unshakeable feeling that they were being watched lingered in the air.

As evening settled in, James and Emma sat at the kitchen table, their hands wrapped around mugs of tea. The silence between them was heavy, filled with the unspoken tension that had been building for weeks. Outside, the soft sound of gravel crunching beneath boots echoed across the yard, and Lucy entered the house, her expression distant and thoughtful.

"Everything alright?" Emma asked, sensing her daughter's mood.

Lucy nodded, but her eyes were filled with something else—an unspoken worry that was hard to miss. She didn't tell them about the footprints in the tool shed or the fabric she had found. She was still trying to figure out what it all meant herself.

James stood up, grabbing his mug. "I'll take a walk around the perimeter, check the fence line again. With everything going on, I don't want to take any chances."

He left the kitchen, disappearing into the fading light as he made his way toward the barn. Lucy watched him go, then turned to Emma, who was staring out the window.

Just then, a sharp knock echoed from the front door, startling them both.

Emma frowned, glancing at Lucy. "Who could that be?"

They weren't expecting anyone. Visitors were rare, especially at this hour, and the unease Lucy had been feeling all day quickly surged back to the surface. Emma rose from her seat and made her way to the door, her fingers gripping the handle just a little too tightly before she pulled it open.

There was no one there.

Instead, a small, unmarked package sat on the porch, wrapped in plain brown paper. No label, no address. Just a small box sitting in the quiet of the evening.

Emma hesitated before stepping out onto the porch, glancing left and right. The dirt road leading to their property stretched out in the distance, empty. Whoever had left the package was long gone. She crouched down and picked it up carefully, her fingers trembling slightly. The weight of the box was light, almost nothing to it.

Lucy joined her in the doorway, her heart pounding in her chest as she looked at the package. "Who would leave something like that out here?"

Emma didn't answer. She brought the package inside, setting it down on the kitchen table. They both stared at it for a long moment, neither wanting to be the first to touch it again.

"I don't like this," Lucy murmured, her voice barely above a whisper.

Emma agreed, her brows furrowed. "Me neither. But we need to see what it is."

After a moment's hesitation, Emma tore away the wrapping paper with slow, deliberate movements, revealing a plain cardboard box beneath. She carefully lifted the lid, and inside was a folded piece of paper. Nothing else.

Emma exchanged a worried glance with Lucy before unfolding the note. The paper was crumpled, the handwriting jagged and hurried. Three simple words were scrawled across the note:

"Stay out of business that isn't yours."

The cryptic message hung in the air like a dark cloud. The words were a warning, plain and simple, but from whom? And what business were they supposed to stay out of?

Lucy's hands clenched into fists. She knew, deep down, that it had to be connected to the gold. Someone had been watching them—probably for a while now. The footprints in the tool shed, the fabric, and now this. Whoever it was, they wanted the Hardings to stop digging, to stay away from whatever secrets lay beneath their land.

Emma's face had gone pale. She set the note down on the table, her fingers trembling. "James needs to see this."

Lucy nodded, but her mind was already racing. The cryptic note didn't just threaten their plan for the gold—it threatened their entire way of life. If they couldn't move forward with mining, they'd lose the farm. But if they pushed forward, someone out there was determined to stop them.

The sound of footsteps on the porch broke the silence as James re-entered the house, wiping the sweat from his brow after his rounds. He looked at Emma and Lucy, sensing the tension in the room immediately.

"What's going on?" he asked, his voice edged with concern.

Emma handed him the note, her eyes wide with worry. "This was left on the porch. No name. Nothing. Just... this."

James unfolded the paper and read it, his jaw tightening with each word. He was quiet for a moment, the weight of the message sinking in. Finally, he looked up at Emma and Lucy, his eyes hard with determination.

"Someone's trying to scare us off," he said, his voice low. "But we're not backing down."

Lucy watched her father carefully. There was a fire in his eyes that she hadn't seen in a long time, the same fire that had kept the farm running through bad seasons and bank threats. But this was different. This was a threat they couldn't see, a warning that could come from anyone.

"We need to be careful," Lucy said softly, voicing the fear that had been gnawing at her all day. "If someone knows about the gold, they could come for it."

James nodded. "I'll install more cameras around the property tomorrow, and motion sensors by the fence line. We're not taking any chances."

Emma, still pale, nodded in agreement. "And what about this person—whoever left the package? What if they come back?"

"They won't find anything," James said firmly. "Not if we're careful."

Lucy swallowed hard. She wanted to believe him, but the knot of anxiety in her stomach told her otherwise. The note had been a warning, yes, but it also felt like a promise. A promise that whoever was watching them wasn't going to stop until they got what they wanted.

The scent of freshly turned earth enveloped the Harding farm, mingling with the heavy fragrance of wildflowers that danced in the gentle breeze. Lucy could almost taste the anticipation in the air, a bitter tang of uncertainty. The weight of their secret burden settled upon her, pressing down like a suffocating blanket. She could hear the distant sounds of chirping birds, their melody drowned out by the deafening silence that hung over the farm. The sight of the vast expanse of land stretched out before her, with its golden fields shimmering under the warm sun, only amplified the magnitude of their predicament. The strangers lurking at the edge of their lives seemed to linger in the shadows, their presence casting a chilling aura. As Lucy traced her fingers over the note on the worn wooden table, its rough texture sent shivers down her spine, while the words etched into her mind like searing flames. Doubt crept into her thoughts, overshadowing her dad's hopeful reassurances.

14

Bill's Place

A Visit to Bill Turner

The sun hung high in the clear blue sky as James and Emma Harding bounced down the gravel road leading toward Bill Turner's workshop. Dust kicked up in their wake, swirling around the old utility truck as they drove deeper into the heart of Burralyndra. It was a slow drive—both due to the rough road and the heavy thoughts weighing on their minds.

The note from the stranger still burned in James' pocket, crumpled but ever-present. It had been days since the cryptic message appeared on their doorstep, but the unease it had caused hadn't gone away. If anything, it had grown. Lucy had been quieter than usual, constantly watching her surroundings, and Emma had barely slept.

Now, heading to see Bill felt like the right move. Bill Turner had been a fixture in their lives for as long as either of them could remember. He was a no-nonsense, salt-of-the-earth kind of man, one of the few people James trusted with anything involving the farm. He'd be able to tell them if their fears about the stranger were grounded or if it was all in their heads.

As they pulled into the yard in front of Bill's workshop, the familiar clank and whirr of metal against metal echoed through the air. Bill was a mechanic by trade, and his shop was littered with half-repaired farm machinery, engines in various states of disrepair, and tools strewn everywhere. It wasn't pretty, but Bill could fix anything, and James knew that better than anyone.

James cut the engine and turned to Emma. "You sure you want to come in?"

Emma nodded firmly. "We need to know what Bill thinks about all this. Maybe he's heard something we haven't."

They stepped out of the truck and made their way toward the workshop. Bill appeared from behind the shed, wiping his greasy hands on an old rag as he spotted them approaching. His weathered face cracked into a grin.

"Well, look who it is," Bill called out in his usual gruff voice. "You two finally come to ask for my help with that old tractor of yours?"

James chuckled, though his heart wasn't in it. "Not quite, Bill. We're here to talk about something else."

Bill's smile faded as he took in the seriousness on their faces. "Come inside, then. I reckon this isn't just a social visit."

Inside the workshop, the air smelled of oil and metal, the usual hum of activity in the background. They settled around a small, cluttered table, Bill leaning forward with his arms crossed as he waited for James to speak.

"So," Bill began, "what's got you two all worked up?"

James glanced at Emma, then pulled the crumpled note from his pocket and slid it across the table toward Bill. The old mechanic unfolded it, his eyes narrowing as he read the message.

Bill grunted, setting the note down. "This some kind of joke?"

"I wish it were," James said, his voice low. "A stranger left that on our porch a few days ago. He's been snooping around, asking questions about the farm. I saw him in town, but I didn't think much of it then. Now, we're not so sure."

Bill scratched his chin thoughtfully. "A stranger, you say? I've heard whispers, too. People have been talking about someone new, asking a lot of questions around here."

Emma leaned forward, her voice laced with concern. "What kind of questions, Bill?"

Bill shook his head. "Mostly about land. Who owns what, who's thinking of selling? But I heard your name come up a couple of times. He's been asking about the Hardings, alright. Heard he's been poking around the old railway tracks, too. It feels wrong, though it might be nothing.

A heavy silence fell over the room. The tension that had been simmering in the Harding household suddenly felt more real, more pressing.

"What do you think he's after?" James asked, even though he suspected the answer.

Bill looked them both in the eyes, his expression serious. "Gold, most likely. The old miners in town still talk about veins running through this land. And you're sitting on one of the best pieces around, or so they say. If this fellas sniffing around, he probably caught wind of something."

James clenched his fists under the table. He had been dreading this. The gold was supposed to be their secret—something to save the farm, not tear it apart. Now, it seemed like someone else had caught the scent, and things were getting dangerous.

"You know how rumours spread around here," Bill continued. "A few words in the wrong ear and someone'll come looking. I don't know who this bloke is, but if he's been snooping around, he knows more than he should."

Emma bit her lip. "We don't want trouble, Bill. We just want to keep the farm going."

Bill nodded solemnly. "I get that, Emma. I do. But you gotta be smart about this. If this stranger's serious, he won't stop with just a warning note. You've got to be prepared."

James sighed. "We've been lying low, working on the farm as usual, but we're starting to set up some security. Cameras, motion sensors. I even got a quote for a new fence."

Bill snorted. "Fences won't stop a man determined to dig up gold. You need to get a handle on this fast."

James felt the weight of Bill's words pressing down on him. He had always prided himself on being able to handle anything the farm threw his way, but this was different. This wasn't a drought or a busted tractor. This was someone trying to take their land, their livelihood, and their future.

Emma broke the silence, her voice soft but resolute. "What do we do, Bill? We can't just wait for him to make the next move."

Bill leaned back in his chair, thinking for a moment. "Keep your eyes open. Lock things down tight. And maybe—just maybe—you ought to think about talking to some legal folks. Get your ducks in a row before this fella tries something more serious."

James nodded slowly. "Thanks, Bill. I knew we could count on you."

Bill stood, clapping James on the shoulder. "You two take care of yourselves. And if you need anything—anything at all—you let me know. We're all neighbours around here."

As James and Emma made their way back to the truck, the weight of what they had learned settled heavily on them both. Bill had confirmed their worst fears: someone was coming for the gold, and they wouldn't stop until they got what they wanted.

James slid into the driver's seat and gripped the steering wheel tightly. Emma sat beside him, her hands clenched in her lap.

"We can't let them take it," Emma whispered, her voice barely audible.

James started the engine, his eyes hard as he looked out over the horizon. "They won't."

As they drove back toward the farm, the sun began to sink lower in the sky, casting long shadows across the fields. The land stretched out before them, golden and endless, but now it felt like a battleground. The Hardings were about to fight for everything they held dear, and the first shots had already been fired.

There was no turning back now.

15

Legal Counsel

Legal Counsel

The morning sun filtered through the dusty windows of Prescott & Dyer Legal Services, casting a soft glow over the stacks of paperwork that littered the small law office. James and Emma sat in the worn leather chairs, their expressions tense but resolute. They had already secured the mining rights for their land, and while that had given them a sense of relief, there were still other looming threats—ones they couldn't ignore.

Alan Prescott, the family's trusted legal adviser, adjusted his glasses as he scanned the document in front of him. He had been the one to guide them through the labyrinth of bureaucracy when it came to the mining permits, and now he was the one they had turned to again.

"Well, I have to say," Prescott began, his tone measured, "it's a good thing you've got the mining rights in order. It gives you a strong legal foothold if anyone tries to challenge your claim. But from what you've told me, this stranger sniffing around doesn't sound like someone who's interested in following the law."

Emma exchanged a glance with James. She could still feel the knot of anxiety tightening in her chest. The mining rights were secured, but the cryptic note left on their porch, and the stranger's probing questions, still lingered like a dark cloud over their thoughts.

"We're more concerned about what this person might try outside of legal channels," James said, his voice steady but laced with tension. "If he's trying to scare us off or intimidate us into selling the farm, those rights won't matter much if he comes after us another way."

Prescott leaned back in his chair, tapping his fingers against the edge of his desk. "Unfortunately, securing the rights doesn't stop someone from using other methods to get what they want. I'm assuming you're not planning on selling?"

James' jaw clenched. "We're not selling. We've already decided that."

Emma nodded, though her worry lines deepened. "We just want to make sure we've done everything we can to protect the farm. The mining's supposed to help us keep the land, not lose it."

Prescott considered their words for a moment, then leaned forward. "Alright. You've got the mining rights, and that's great. But if you're worried about this stranger—whoever he is—you need to start thinking about how to safeguard your property in other ways. First, I'd suggest looking into a security system. It's not uncommon for disputes over land or minerals to escalate into theft or sabotage."

James and Emma exchanged a glance. They had already discussed installing cameras around the farm, but hearing Prescott confirm their fears added an extra layer of urgency.

"We've started installing motion sensors and cameras," James said, his voice low. "And we're putting up new fencing. But we didn't expect things to get this serious so soon."

Prescott nodded approvingly. "Good. That's a start. The other thing you'll want to do is make sure all your documentation is in order.

Land titles, mining permits, and anything else that could be used to challenge your ownership. I know we've covered this before, but it's worth double-checking."

Emma sighed, running a hand through her hair. "It feels like we're constantly playing catch-up. We've been focused on securing the permits and making sure the gold mining is done properly, but now, with the bank pressing us and this stranger lurking around, it's overwhelming."

Prescott's expression softened. "I understand. But from a legal standpoint, you're in a good position. You've done the hard part already. The key now is to stay vigilant. Document everything—every interaction with this stranger, any unusual activity around your property, even suspicious phone calls. If things do escalate, you'll need that evidence to protect yourselves."

James leaned forward, his eyes hard. "And what if he pushes harder? What if he doesn't back off?"

Prescott frowned. "If it comes to that, you can file for a restraining order. It won't stop him from being sneaky, but it'll give you legal grounds to push back if he crosses the line. And if you feel that he's threatening you, don't hesitate to involve the authorities."

Emma shifted in her seat. "We don't want this to turn into a legal battle."

"I get that," Prescott said sympathetically. "But you need to be prepared for the worst. If you've got the mining rights, that land is even more valuable than it was before. And there's a good chance that stranger knows that too."

The tension in the room was palpable. Securing the mining rights had been a victory, but it had also made them a target. The thought of losing the farm now, after all they'd been through, was unbearable.

"We'll do whatever it takes to protect our home," James said firmly.

Prescott nodded. "That's the attitude you need to have. Just keep things legal and above board, and you'll have the upper hand."

As they stood to leave, Emma placed a hand on James' arm. "We've done everything right, haven't we?"

James met her gaze, his eyes softening. "We have. And we'll keep doing everything right."

Scene: Returning Home

The drive back to Burralyndra was silent. Emma stared out the window, watching the familiar landscape of dry wheat fields and gum trees flash by. The weight of the conversation with Prescott lingered between them, but there was also a sense of determination. They had the rights. They had a plan. Now they just needed to keep moving forward.

When they reached the farm, James parked the truck near the tool shed. He glanced at the newly erected fence posts, still waiting for the wire to be strung up. The old fence had been torn down last week, and Bill Turner's crew would be back tomorrow to finish the job.

"We should check the camera feeds," Emma said as she climbed out of the truck. "Make sure everything's working properly."

James nodded, heading inside to access the feed from the new security system. It was rudimentary for now—just a few cameras covering the key entry points to the property, but it was better than nothing.

As he settled into the worn wooden chair at the cluttered kitchen table, scrolling through the grainy footage on the laptop screen, Emma's eyes darted back and forth, absorbing the flickering images. The faint hum of the refrigerator and the distant chirping of birds outside filled the air, mingling with the scent of freshly brewed coffee that lingered in the room. As she meticulously sorted through the permits and documents, their crisp edges whispered against her fingertips, providing a tactile reassurance of progress. Moments later, James broke the silence, his voice cutting through the stillness. "The cameras have captured nothing but empty landscapes, devoid of any human presence," he stated, his words accompanied by a soft sigh. Emma released a pent-up breath, feeling a fraction of the tension dissipate, yet a residual knot remained lodged in her chest. "Well, at least we have that going for us," she murmured, her voice tinged with lingering unease.

James rubbed the back of his neck. "We need to get that shed up soon. Bill said he could start on the framework next week, but we're running out of time."

"We'll manage," Emma said, though she wasn't entirely sure how. "And once the shed's built, we can move the operation in there. Keep everything discreet."

They had decided to build a small processing shed under the guise of expanding their threshing facilities, something they could explain away to any nosy neighbours or visitors. The real purpose, however, was to have a secure place to process the gold they'd been finding. It was risky, but it was the only way to protect their secret while keeping up with their farming duties.

"We're getting there," James said quietly, more to himself than to Emma.

But as they sat together in the quiet kitchen, the enormity of their situation weighed heavily on them. The farm was more than just a home—it was their legacy. The gold had been a godsend, but it had also brought a new kind of danger into their lives.

Scene: A Quiet Evening

That evening, after dinner, Emma sat on the porch, looking out at the horizon. The sun was beginning to set, casting a warm glow over the fields. James joined her, settling into the chair beside hers.

"We've come a long way," she said softly, breaking the silence. "We've secured the mining rights. We've done everything right. But why does it still feel like everything could fall apart?"

James didn't answer right away. He leaned forward, resting his elbows on his knees, staring out at the land they'd worked so hard to protect.

"Because it's possible," he finally said, his voice low. "We're farmers, not miners. We're facing unfamiliar challenges." Emma nodded, feeling burdened. "But we must continue. For Lucy. For the farm." James reached out and gently squeezed her hand. "We will. We'll find a solution." Sitting there, watching the sun set, they realised that they would confront any obstacles together. The farm was their life, their home, and they were determined to defend it at any expense.

16

Unlawful Threat

Lucy's Encounter

The late afternoon sun cast a warm, golden hue over the dirt path that stretched between the Harding farm and the town of Burralyndra. Lucy had walked this route many times, the familiar landscape of dry scrub and swaying wheat calming her on most days. But today, she couldn't shake a gnawing unease, the weight of recent events pressing on her shoulders. Her mind churned with thoughts of the gold, the bank's warnings, and the stranger her father had seen in town.

The road was eerily quiet. Lucy pulled her satchel tighter against her side, her pace quickening as the dirt crunched beneath her boots. She wanted to get to town and back before dusk, but something— something she couldn't quite explain—was making her nervous. The farm felt exposed lately, as if unseen eyes were constantly watching.

She hadn't heard the footsteps.

Before she knew what was happening, a powerful arm wrapped around her from behind, yanking her backwards. The force of it knocked the air from her lungs, and her feet left the ground for a second as she stumbled, trying to regain her balance.

"Going somewhere in a hurry, miss?" came the low, gravelly voice, sending shivers down Lucy's spine. The sound seemed to echo in her ears, drowning out the other noises around her. Lucy gasped, her pulse racing like a stampede of wild horses as she fought to steady herself. The grip tightened, fingers digging into her shoulder, sending a sharp pain shooting through her body. It was him. The stranger.

She froze, her heart pounding wildly in her chest, its rhythmic thumping resonating in her ears. The man released her, and she spun around, trying to back away, but her legs felt like jelly, weak and unsteady beneath her. There he stood, the same man who had appeared at their door not long ago under the guise of being a prospector. The same one her father had warned her about.

His face bore the marks of time, with deep lines etched into weathered skin. His sharp eyes seemed to penetrate her, leaving her feeling exposed and vulnerable. However, there was now an added element in his expression—a cruel and dangerous aura.

"I didn't mean to scare you," the man's voice said. His voice, unnervingly casual, reminiscent of the sound of gravel being scraped underfoot. As if they were two individuals coincidentally crossing paths. Lucy attempted to regulate her breathing, mustering the determination to maintain her composure, but the atmosphere grew heavy and suffocating, hindering her ability to catch her breath.

"You didn't have to grab me." The stranger smiled, though it was anything but friendly. His smile was like a knife, cutting through the tension, revealing his true intentions. "Oh, just didn't want you running off before we had a little chat," he said, his words dripping with menace. The scent of danger hung in the air, a mix of sweat and something metallic, making Lucy's stomach churn. "Figured you'd have some answers I'm looking for."

Lucy clenched her fists, trying to keep her voice steady, but her knuckles ached from the tightness of her grip. "What do you want?" The man's smile widened, his eyes narrowing as he studied her, his gaze like ice piercing her skin. "I've been hearing some interesting things about your family. Big farm, lots of land... and maybe a little something extra beneath the surface, huh?" The words hung in the air, like a dark cloud, casting a shadow over Lucy's thoughts.

Lucy's stomach twisted in knots. He was fishing, but he was close—too close. She forced herself to keep her voice calm. "We're farmers. That's all we are. There's nothing else to talk about."

The man chuckled darkly, stepping closer until they were nearly face-to-face. His voice dropped to a whisper, full of menace. "Now, we both know that ain't true, sweetheart. Word gets around in places like this, especially when people get greedy."

Lucy took a step back, her heart racing faster. She wanted to run, but she knew better than to show fear. "There's nothing for you here."

His expression hardened, the false friendliness evaporating in an instant. He grabbed her again, this time by the wrist, yanking her toward him with enough force to send pain shooting up her arm.

"You listen to me," he growled, his breath hot on her face. "You tell your old man something for me. Tell him he better mind his business and stay out of things that don't concern him. Otherwise, it'd be a shame if something happened to him... or to you."

Lucy's blood ran cold, her breath catching in her throat. She stared at him, horrified, unable to speak as the implications of his words sank in.

"You leave us alone," she finally croaked out, her voice shaking despite her best efforts to sound brave.

The man sneered, his grip tightening painfully. "I'll leave you alone when you stop digging where you don't belong. And if your daddy doesn't back off, well... let's just say he won't be able to farm that land much longer. Accidents happen, you know?"

Lucy's heart pounded so hard she thought it might burst out of her chest. She could feel the threat hanging in the air between them, heavy and oppressive. Her father's life—her family's future—was at stake, and there was no way to talk her way out of this.

The man shoved her away, and she stumbled backward, nearly falling to the ground. He tipped his hat in mock politeness, his eyes cold and unyielding.

"Be a good girl and pass along the message," he said, his voice dripping with malice. "It's for your own good."

Without another word, he turned and sauntered off down the road, leaving Lucy standing there, shaken and terrified, watching as his figure slowly disappeared into the distance.

Lucy cancelled her trip into town and immediately went home. She was panicked and needed to let her dad know what had happened. By the time Lucy reached the farmhouse, her legs felt like they were about to give out beneath her. She stumbled through the front door, slamming it shut behind her, the sound echoing through the quiet house.

Emma stood in the kitchen, the sharp scent of sliced vegetables filling the air as she meticulously diced them for dinner. James sat at the table, the sound of papers shuffling beneath his fingertips echoing faintly in the room. Suddenly, the slam of the door made their heads snap up in unison. Emma's concerned expression was etched on her face as she caught sight of her daughter.

Lucy's pale complexion and trembling hands spoke volumes. The room seemed to hold its breath, anticipating Lucy's response. A dryness settled in Lucy's mouth, her heart still pounding with the remnants of fear from what had just transpired. She leaned against the counter, the cool surface providing a moment of relief as her breaths came in short, gasping bursts.

"Lucy, what's happened?" James' voice cut through the heavy

silence, his footsteps closing the distance between them. His eyes, sharp and attentive, already sensed the weight of the situation. Lucy struggled to find her voice, her whisper barely audible. "He... He grabbed me." James froze, his features twisting into a mask of anger and concern. "Who grabbed you?" he demanded, his voice laced with a fierce protectiveness. Lucy swallowed the lump in her throat, her voice still shaky. "The stranger. The one who came to the house. I ran into him on the road. He wouldn't leave me alone. He... he threatened you, Dad."

James's hands clenched into fists at his sides, his whole body going rigid with anger. "What did he say?"

Lucy took a shaky breath, trying to steady herself. "He said... he said if you didn't back off, if we didn't stop... he'd make sure you wouldn't be able to farm the land anymore. He said something would happen to you."

Emma gasped, her hand flying to her mouth. "My God..."

James's face was a mask of fury. "That bastard."

"We can't let him get away with this," Lucy said, her voice trembling but filled with determination. "He's dangerous, Dad. I don't know what he wants, but he will not stop."

James's jaw tightened, his eyes narrowing as he surveyed the vast expanse of their land, the golden rays of the setting sun casting a warm glow over the rolling hills. The air was thick with tension, the faint scent of earth and freshly cut grass mingling with the crisp autumn breeze. Fury radiated from James, his voice laced with conviction as he spoke.

"We're not backing down," he declared, his words cutting through the stillness of the evening. Emma stepped forward, her footsteps crunching softly on the dry leaves scattered on the ground. She reached out and took Lucy's hand, the touch offering a sense of solace and unity amidst the uncertainty.

A distant sound of chirping birds filled the air, their melodic chorus a stark contrast to the gravity of their situation. Emma spoke, her voice calm but resolute, as if trying to anchor herself and her family in this moment.

"But we need to be smart about this," she said, her words accompanied by the rustle of the wind through the trees. Lucy nodded, her heart pounding in her chest, a mixture of fear and determination coursing through her veins. Her grip tightened on her mother's hand, seeking comfort and strength.

"I won't let him scare us off," Lucy affirmed, her voice determined but tinged with a hint of vulnerability. She could feel the weight of their adversary's gaze, an invisible presence lurking in the shadows. Every rustle of leaves or creak of a branch sent shivers down her spine, a constant reminder of the danger they faced.

With heightened senses, Lucy understood the importance of proceeding with caution. Every step they took had to be calculated. They were prepared to confront their foe, but they knew also that a single wrong move could lead to their downfall.

Amidst his anger, James's face softened as he looked at Lucy. Concern for his daughter tempered his emotions. He assured her, "We will protect what's ours. No one will take this farm from us, and no one will harm my daughter. You can be sure of that."

As the sun set behind the fields, casting long shadows across the land, the Hardings understood that the fight for their farm had just escalated.

17

Law Enforcement

The Police Call and Sergeant's Visit

The kitchen was heavy with tension. Lucy sat at the table, still shaken from her encounter with the stranger, while Emma paced nervously, her hands wringing together as if trying to squeeze out the fear. James stood by the counter, gripping the landline phone in his hand. His knuckles were white, his jaw clenched tightly. He had just finished dialling the local police station, his voice simmering with barely contained fury as he waited for someone to pick up.

"Come on, come on..." he muttered under his breath.

Finally, the phone clicked, and a gruff voice came through on the other end. "Burralyndra Police Station, Sergeant Harris speaking."

James Harding, a distressed father, wasted no time in conveying the urgency of the situation. "Sergeant, it's James Harding. Please come out to the farm immediately. My daughter was just assaulted on the road between here and town—by a man named Michael McRae. He's been lingering around our property lately, and now he's crossed the line and started making threats."

There was a pause on the other end of the line, followed by a weary sigh. "Alright, James, calm down. What exactly happened? " James bristled at the sergeant's calm demeanour, desperate for immediate action. "I just told you—he grabbed my daughter and threatened her and me. I have his business card from when he came to the farm a few days ago, pretending to be some kind of prospector. Now he's following her around, grabbing her, and making threats." The tension in James's voice was palpable, as he expected a more urgent response from law enforcement.

"Alright, alright, James, no need to get worked up. I'll come out this evening, but I can't make any promises about what we can do." James's frustration grew, his anger seeping into his words. His grip on the phone tightened, veins pulsing in his neck. "Arc you serious? The man grabbed my daughter, and you're telling me you don't know what you can do? " Sergeant Harris sighed again, his tone flat, revealing the limitations of their jurisdiction. "Look, I get it. But until he does something more serious, my hands are tied. I'll come by tonight." With that, the line went dead, leaving James feeling helpless and uncertain about the safety of his daughter.

James slammed the phone back onto the wall with a growl of frustration. Emma flinched at the sound, while Lucy kept her eyes down, still shaken by the memory of McRae's grip on her wrist.

"What did he say?" Emma asked, worry creasing her brow.

James shook his head, his eyes wide with disbelief. The sound of his voice carried a tinge of frustration, echoing through the room. "He's coming by later," he said, his words hanging heavy in the air, "but you could hear it in his voice - a sense of indifference that sends chills down my spine. He's not going to do a damn thing until it's too late."

Lucy, her voice barely audible, spoke in a hushed tone, her words quivering with fear. The room was filled with an eerie silence, broken only by the sound of her voice. "They don't believe us, do they?" Her words floated in the air, mingling with the scent of uncertainty that lingered in the room.

James muttered darkly, his voice filled with bitterness. The weight of his words settled like a heavy fog, enveloping the space around them. "They don't care," he said, his tone laced with frustration. The room grew colder, as if reflecting the indifference that filled the air. "But they'll have to care soon enough."

Sergeant Harris Arrives

By the time Sergeant Harris pulled up in his patrol car, the sun had dipped below the horizon, casting long shadows across the farm. The night air was cool, but the tension inside the Harding household was palpable. Lucy, Emma, and James stood on the porch, watching as the car approached. James clenched the card McRae had left with them days earlier, feeling the weight of what that man represented in every word etched on the little rectangle of paper.

Sergeant Harris stepped out of the car, adjusting his belt as he strolled toward the porch. His expression was one of mild annoyance, like this was a nuisance rather than a matter of urgency.

"Evening," he nodded to James, glancing at Emma and tipping his hat slightly. "So, what's this all about?"

James didn't waste any time. He handed the business card to Harris. "The man's name is Michael McRae. Came here a few days ago, said he was a prospector interested in buying land. Now he's stalking my daughter, grabbed her today, and threatened us—said we wouldn't be able to farm this land anymore if we didn't stay out of 'business, that's not ours.' I want him dealt with before he tries anything worse."

Sergeant Harris studied the card for a moment, flipping it over in his hand. "So, you've got a name. That's a start. But what exactly did he say? Did he hurt her?"

Lucy, her face still drained of colour, recounted her harrowing encounter. Every word trembled with fear as she described the unseen force that seized her from behind, abruptly halting her steps. The menacing voice echoed in her ears, threatening to inflict harm upon her father and strip away their cherished farm. As she bravely displayed the evidence, her bruised shoulder and wrists, she implored the officer with urgency, pleading, "What more can you possibly require?"

Harris furrowed his brow, scratching his head as he released a heavy sigh, the weight of the situation palpable in the air. "Look, James," he said, his voice tinged with concern. "I understand you're upset, but the sight of worry etched across your face tells me this guy is just trying to scare you." The distant sound of birds chirping filled the silence, a stark contrast to the tension in the room. "People talk big," Harris continued, his words hanging in the air, "especially if they're desperate for land." The faint scent of coffee lingered, mixing with the faint aroma of anxiety. "But until he performs a verifiable physical act," Harris explained, his words falling like a gentle rain, "something tangible I can act on, I'm limited in what I can do." "You call grabbing my daughter and threatening us nothing?" he exclaimed, the sound echoing through the room. The feeling of helplessness settled in, like a heavy weight on their shoulders. "What more do you need?" James pleaded, his voice trembling. "Her in hospital? Him burning the farm down?"

Harris's eyes shifted uncomfortably as he rubbed the back of his neck. "Look, I didn't mean it like that. I'm just saying, without a formal crime or witnesses, my hands are tied. This fella McRae, he's probably trying to muscle you into selling. It happens. But I don't have enough to arrest him on. Did you get a license plate when he drove off? Anything more?"

"No," James growled, feeling his temper rise. "But he left that card when he visited. Isn't that enough to look into him?"

Harris tucked the card into his breast pocket and shrugged. "I'll keep an eye out. Maybe ask around town if anyone else has had dealings with him. But like I said, unless he crosses a legal line, there's only so much I can do."

James stepped forward, his hands clenched into fists. "So, we're supposed to just wait until he crosses that line? Is that how it works?"

Harris's gaze hardened, and his tone took on a note of finality. "I'll come by and check in over the next few days. But you and your family need to keep your heads down. Don't provoke him. These things settle themselves. Be smart, lock up, and call me immediately if something more serious occurs."

Lucy looked up, her voice shaking with a mixture of fear and frustration. "He said he'd hurt my dad. Isn't that serious enough?"

Harris sighed, already halfway turned toward his car. "People say a lot of things. If he shows up again, call me, but until then, keep out of trouble."

With that, the sergeant tipped his hat once more and walked back to his patrol car. The Hardings watched in silence as the car disappeared down the dirt road; the realisation settling over them like a heavy fog: they were on their own.

James stood there for a long moment, staring into the distance, his face hard with determination. "We'll protect ourselves. No one else is going to do it."

Emma wrapped an arm around Lucy's shoulder, pulling her close. "We'll get through this," she said, though her voice trembled with doubt.

James turned back to them, his voice a low, dangerous growl. "We need to be ready. This isn't over."

18

Trespassers

Strange Tracks

A few days had passed since Lucy's terrifying encounter with McRae, but the unease lingered in the air like the smell of dust before a storm. James was still fuming, but life on the farm didn't wait for anger to subside. The wheat fields needed tending, the land demanding its relentless upkeep, and with the season moving fast, there was no time to lose. He'd put his frustration aside—at least on the surface—trying to focus on what mattered most: keeping the farm going.

He gripped the steering wheel of his tractor, navigating through the golden sea of wheat. The rhythmic hum of the engine did little to calm his nerves. His eyes darted across the horizon, scanning for anything out of the ordinary. Ever since the incident with Lucy, he couldn't shake the feeling that someone was watching, always lurking just out of sight. The land, which had once been his sanctuary, now felt exposed, vulnerable.

He glanced toward the farmhouse in the distance, barely visible against the shimmering wheat. Emma and Lucy were inside, working

145

on the house or preparing lunch, unaware of the undercurrent of tension that was gnawing at him. Or maybe they were just as aware and choosing to ignore it, trying to maintain some sense of normalcy in the face of everything.

But James couldn't ignore it. Not when his family's safety was on the line.

As he drove deeper into the fields, something caught his eye—a break in the neat rows of wheat. He slowed the tractor to a stop and jumped down, his boots crunching against the dry soil. There were tire tracks. Fresh ones.

He frowned, crouching down to inspect them more closely. They didn't belong to any of their vehicles. His truck and tractor left distinct patterns, but these were different—narrower and slicker, as if made by a smaller, faster vehicle. Someone had driven into his wheat fields, and it wasn't him.

Alarm prickled at the back of his neck. He followed the tracks, weaving through the tall stalks, the wind rustling around him. The further he walked, the more disturbed the ground became, as if something—or someone—had been moving back and forth in this area. His gut clenched when he reached a patch of soil that looked recently dug up. The earth was looser here, the surface slightly uneven, as if someone had been digging—searching for something.

James crouched down and ran his hand over the disturbed soil. He could still see faint imprints of a shovel, marks barely visible, but clear enough to send a wave of alarm through him. This wasn't just some random kid messing around. This was deliberate.

His mind raced. Who had been out here? Was it McRae? Had he sent someone else to snoop around, hoping to find the gold they'd so carefully kept hidden? Or was it a warning—another move in the silent game McRae was playing against them?

James stood up slowly, the weight of the situation pressing down on him. His eyes swept across the surrounding fields. There was no sign of anyone now, but whoever had been here was gone, leaving only traces of their presence.

He clenched his fists, his jaw tightening with resolve. This was no longer just about protecting their farm—it was about keeping their secret safe. He had to figure out how to stay one step ahead of whoever was out there. They were being watched, and that meant every move, every decision, had to be calculated carefully.

Turning back toward the house, James moved with purpose. The others needed to know. They couldn't pretend this wasn't happening any longer. They had to face it head-on. The farm wasn't just a place to grow wheat anymore; it was a battlefield, and they were in the middle of a fight for their land, their future, and their lives.

Back at the farmhouse, James walked into the kitchen, his face set with a grim expression. Emma was at the counter, chopping vegetables for lunch, and Lucy was at the table, flipping through some papers. They both looked up when he entered, sensing the shift in his mood.

"Something wrong?" Emma asked, setting down her knife.

James nodded, tossing his hat onto the counter. "We've got more trouble," he said, his voice low and controlled. "I found tire tracks out in the fields—ones that don't belong to us."

Lucy's eyes widened. "What do you mean? Like someone's been out there?"

"Exactly that. And more." He turned toward the sink, washing his hands as he spoke, the water rushing into the basin like a distant roar in the room. "Whoever it was, they were digging. Near the northern end of the fields. They were looking for something—maybe gold, maybe just to send a message. Either way, they weren't supposed to be there."

Emma's hands stilled, the tension in the room thickening. "Do you think it was McRae?" she asked, her voice tight.

"Who else would it be?" James responded, drying his hands and leaning against the counter, his gaze dark and serious. "We've been careful, kept our heads down. But now they're getting bolder. I don't know what they're after, but we can't let them get ahead of us."

Lucy bit her lip, her fingers nervously tapping the edge of the table. "What do we do, Dad?"

"We stay vigilant," James said firmly, his voice laced with a protective resolve. "I've been putting off the cameras and motion sensors long enough. It's time we got them up. And we can't just keep working the fields like nothing's happening. We need to start thinking like them—figure out what they're after and how they're planning to get it."

"But what about the wheat? We've still got the harvest coming up. We can't just stop everything," Emma said, worry creeping into her voice.

"I know," James said, sighing. "But I'm not going to let this farm fall into the hands of some greedy bastard who thinks he can bully us into selling or walking away. We'll keep working, but we've got to be smarter, more cautious. Every move we make from here on out could be the one that saves or loses this farm."

He glanced at Lucy, seeing the worry etched on her face. "You need to be careful too, Lucy. No more walking into town alone. If you see anything strange, anything at all, you let me know immediately."

Lucy nodded, but there was a flash of determination in her eyes. "I will, Dad. But we can't just keep waiting for them to come to us. We need to figure out how to stop them."

James looked at her, his face softening slightly. "I know. And we will. But for now, we need to stay ahead of them, keep the upper hand. This land is ours, and no one's going to take it from us. Not if I have anything to say about it."

Later that day, James and Lucy took their tools and set off toward the fields. They began to install cameras on the outskirts of the farm, hidden discreetly among the trees and high posts, giving them a full view of anyone who dared trespass again. Every step felt like a battle tactic, preparing for the war they were sure was coming. Every turn of a bolt, every piece of equipment secured, brought them one step closer to protecting their home.

As they worked, James couldn't help but glance around constantly, his senses on high alert. He knew they were being watched. But he was ready—ready for whatever came next.

19

Conversation Overheard

The Strangers Connection

The Burralyndra pub was alive with the murmur of conversation and the occasional clink of glasses. It was one of the few places James felt he could keep his ear to the ground without raising suspicion. He hadn't intended to come in tonight, but the weight of recent events pushed him here, hoping for a moment's distraction—or a hint about the strangers lurking around his farm.

James sat at a quiet corner table, nursing a pint and glancing around the room. Familiar faces filled most of the seats, local farmers and townsfolk gathered after long days in the fields. Then he saw him: McRae, the so-called prospector, was standing near the bar, leaning toward a man who had his back to James. The man was hunched over, dressed in an old leather jacket and looking like he hadn't seen a decent night's sleep in days. He wasn't from Burralyndra. James knew that much.

His gut tightened as he caught snippets of their conversation, words that slipped through the thick pub air and settled uneasily in his mind.

McRae's voice was low, but urgent.

"Look, this place is more isolated than I thought," McRae muttered, glancing around as though to make sure no one was listening. "Hardings have put up security cameras, and they're no fools. There's gold under that farm, but getting to it... that's going to take more than a few threats."

The man beside him let out a gravelly chuckle, the sound echoing through the air as he took a swig from his beer, the bottle clinking against his teeth. "You're telling me you're having trouble with a couple of farmers?" he said, his voice rough and slightly hoarse. "Thought you were better than that, McRae." The scent of the beer wafted towards McRae, mingling with the musty smell of the old tavern. McRae scowled, his face contorting with frustration. "Hardings are different," he replied, his voice tinged with irritation. "The daughter's sharp, too, running calculations for gold yields like she's in on the business herself." McRae's fingers clenched into a tight fist, his knuckles turning white as he continued, "They're not just sitting around, and they're not planning to sell anytime soon."

James's fists were also clenched tightly under the worn wooden table, his knuckles also turning white. The dimly lit room was heavy with tension, the air thick with the acrid scent of stale cigarettes and whisky. The low murmur of conversation and clinking of glasses filled the smoky atmosphere, creating a cacophony of sound that threatened to drown out James's racing thoughts. As he glanced across the room, his eyes met McRae's piercing gaze, the intensity of it sending a chill down his spine. A sense of unease settled in, amplified by the presence of the rough-looking stranger who now stood by McRae's side, emanating an aura of danger. James couldn't shake the feeling that things were about to escalate, and that he was caught in a web of deceit from which there might be no escape.

"Then maybe it's time you brought in some real pressure," the stranger said, his voice like gravel scraping over iron. He leaned closer to McRae, his tone darkening. "Make 'em understand that resistance isn't worth it. Could be that an 'accident' or two around the farm will make 'em rethink their plans."

A chill ran down James's spine, dread settling heavily in his stomach. He'd suspected McRae was trouble, but this? This was far more than he'd anticipated. This wasn't just a battle over land; it was something more sinister, with threats of intimidation and force—measures he hadn't imagined McRae would consider. His family was in real danger.

McRae sighed, a hint of frustration slipping into his voice. "I don't want to draw that kind of attention. Last thing I need is the local cops sniffing around."

The stranger shrugged. "Then work fast and quiet. Either they'll hand over the land, or you find a way to get them out of it. I know people who'd be happy to... help the process along." He took another swig from his drink and added, "And don't worry about the money. I've got connections back east who'll pay a pretty penny for what's under that farm."

McRae gave a grim nod, his gaze shifting, unfocused. "It'll be done. The Hardings will have no choice but to sell."

James leaned back, his mind racing. It was no longer just about land or money. This was a coordinated effort, and McRae was willing to cross lines James hadn't expected. He knew now that his family was in the cross-hairs, and the threat was all too real.

He finished his drink quickly, leaving a few coins on the table before slipping out of the pub. The cool night air hit him, but he barely noticed. His mind was consumed with one thought: he needed to protect his family and his farm, no matter what it took. The stranger's threats had crossed a line, and James was ready to do whatever was necessary to keep the Hardings safe.

James arrived home and quietly shut the door behind him, careful not to wake Emma or Lucy. As he stepped into the kitchen, the house creaked, settling into the night, but he felt anything but calm. He was already strategizing, piecing together the ways he could strengthen their defences and keep watch over the property.

The cameras he'd installed weren't enough—not now. He needed something more, something that would send a message to McRae and his associates that the Hardings wouldn't be an easy target. Tomorrow, he would have a talk with Emma and Lucy. They needed to know the extent of the danger they were facing, and together, they'd find a way to push back.

20

Confrontation

Confrontation At The Store

The dusty Burralyndra general store was a staple of the town, its shelves lined with everything from work gloves to canned goods and jars of local honey. James pushed through the door, his gaze immediately landing on the man he'd come looking for. McRae, the so-called prospector, was standing at the counter, leaning against it as if he owned the place. The sight of him here, chatting casually with the store owner, stirred up a simmering anger in James that was impossible to ignore.

McRae turned slightly at the sound of the door, catching sight of James. A faint smirk crossed his face, as though he'd been expecting this confrontation.

"James Harding," McRae greeted, his voice casual but with an undercurrent of smugness. "Small town, isn't it? We keep running into each other."

James ignored the stranger's forced charm. Instead, he took a step closer, eyes fixed on McRae. "I'll get right to the point. Why are you so interested in my farm?"

McRae pretended to be surprised, raising an eyebrow. "Interested? I'm just passing through Harding. Just a prospector looking for land investments." He paused and studied James's face. "Is there something special about your farm that I should know about?"

"Don't play games with me," James shot back, his voice low and steady. "I've seen you around town, asking questions. You've been watching my family, skulking around where you're not welcome. I don't care what you think you'll find. The only thing my land has to offer is hard work and wheat."

McRae chuckled, barely holding back a mocking smile. "I'm just a curious man, Harding. Just a bit of a wanderer, that's all. You don't need to be so defensive."

"Defensive?" James felt his patience wearing thin, his fists clenching involuntarily. "Stay off my land and away from my family. There's nothing for you there, and if you think otherwise, you're making a mistake."

The tension was thick in the air as the two men stared each other down, the small store suddenly feeling like a battleground. The store owner, old Mr. Sullivan, who had been quietly stocking the shelves nearby, straightened and glanced warily between the two men, sensing the brewing storm.

McRae finally straightened up, shrugging nonchalantly. "I didn't mean any offence, Harding. Just a man making small talk and checking out opportunities. You'd understand if you were in my shoes."

James glared at him, his frustration reaching its peak. He didn't trust this man's smooth words or his cryptic smile. "Let me be clear. If I see you anywhere near my family or my land again, you'll regret it."

McRae's eyes flashed with something—annoyance, perhaps, or even a hint of menace. But he didn't lose his calm demeanour. Instead, he simply leaned forward, lowering his voice so only James could hear.

"You should be careful, Harding. Sometimes, the more you push, the harder things get for you. And sometimes, you find out that what you think belongs to you... might not."

A chill ran down James's spine at the veiled threat, but he refused to back down. He held McRae's gaze, matching his calm facade with a defiant glower.

Without another word, McRae turned and walked past James, tipping his hat slightly as he brushed by, as if dismissing their encounter as nothing more than a passing conversation. The bell above the door chimed as he stepped outside, leaving James standing in the middle of the store, seething.

Old Mr. Sullivan approached cautiously, placing a hand on James's shoulder. "James, everything alright there?"

James took a deep breath, forcing himself to steady his voice. "No, Sullivan. But I think it will be, as long as McRae knows he's not welcome around my family."

Sullivan nodded, concern creasing his brow. "You keep your guard up, James. That fellow's been coming in here, asking questions about your farm. Didn't sit right with me either."

James thanked him, a new resolve taking shape. He'd warned McRae, but something told him this was far from over. This man was here for a reason, and it was no harmless curiosity or casual prospecting venture. James left the store with a last look over his shoulder, watching as McRae's figure faded down the street, a predator masked by a casual stride.

But James knew the truth: he had to be ready.

Revelations And Concern

James looked back at Mr. Sullivan, who hesitated, his brows knitting together in a look of genuine concern. The old store owner seemed to weigh his words, finally deciding to speak.

"James," he began cautiously, glancing toward the door McRae had just left through. "That man... he's been in here a few times now. And not just asking questions about you and your family, mind you. He's been buying supplies, too. Supplies that could be... troubling."

James frowned, his mind racing as Sullivan continued.

"He's picked up rope. A lot of it, and not the kind you'd use for casual work around the place. This is thick, reinforced rope—stuff you'd use to tow a heavy load or to tie something down securely."

James crossed his arms, his expression darkening. "What else?"

Sullivan lowered his voice, leaning in closer. "Last time, he bought a stack of fuel cans, and I don't mean the small ones. Big, industrial-size cans. He said he was fuelling up for a long trip, but most people around here don't go through fuel like that, especially if they're 'just passing through.' And he picked up some flares, too. Said he needed them for emergencies." Sullivan hesitated, glancing around as though he feared McRae might still be lurking nearby. "But... you know how it is, James. With the dry season, a single flare can set half a field ablaze."

The hairs on the back of James's neck prickled. He could feel his pulse pounding harder with each detail, piecing together a picture he didn't like. "Anything else?"

"Yeah. This might not mean much, but he's also bought wire cutters and a whole bundle of spools of wire, along with pliers, bolts, and metal stakes," Sullivan added, rubbing his hands together anxiously. "People don't normally buy all that in one go. Looked to me like he's setting up for something... serious."

James clenched his jaw, feeling a surge of anger mixed with dread.

The purchases alone weren't illegal, but the combination was more than unsettling. Rope, fuel, flares, and tools that could easily be used to sabotage their fencing, break equipment, or even start a fire on his land. He could imagine the scenarios playing out in his mind—accidents that could ruin a year's worth of work, destroy their crops, or worse, put his family's lives at risk.

"Thank you for telling me, Sullivan," he said grimly, looking out the store window, catching the last glimpse of McRae's silhouette as he disappeared down the road. "I need to get back. Can't leave Emma and Lucy out there alone."

Sullivan nodded, a hard look in his eyes. "You be careful, James. That man's trouble, plain as day. And don't hesitate to let me know if there's anything I can do. I'll keep an eye out around here, too, just in case."

James gave a firm nod and left the store, his mind now focused with a new urgency. Back at the farm, he'd check every fence line, lock up the fuel shed, and ensure that any equipment vulnerable to tampering was secure. He'd install the new cameras he'd ordered around the property and double-check the ones already up. This stranger thought he could come here and push them off their own land, using whatever means he had to hand. But James had no intention of letting McRae—or anyone else—lay a single finger on his family or his farm.

21

A Warning

Sullivan's Warning

The late afternoon sun cast a warm, amber glow over the Harding's kitchen as James and Emma sat at the table, taking a rare moment to enjoy a quiet cup of tea. They were both tired, lines of worry etched into their faces, but James felt somewhat reassured by the security measures he'd put in place since his conversation with Mr. Sullivan at the general store.

A knock at the door jolted them from their thoughts. James stood, glancing through the window to see Sullivan's familiar silhouette. A wave of apprehension passed over him as he crossed to the door and opened it.

"Sullivan," he greeted, a forced calmness in his tone. "Everything alright?"

Sullivan stepped in, nodding a greeting to Emma. His usually easygoing expression was replaced by a look of deep concern. "I won't take too much of your time," he said, lowering his voice as though even the walls had ears. "But I had to come and tell you what I heard."

James and Emma exchanged a tense glance, and Emma pulled out a chair for Sullivan. He took it, resting his hands on the table. "That stranger—McRae, right?—he's been poking around town, asking questions about you and your land. But it's more than curiosity, James. The way he's going about it, it's like he's trying to dig up whatever he can use against you."

Emma frowned, her gaze fixed on Sullivan. "What did he ask?"

Sullivan sighed. "He's asked about your finances, whether you've been up-to-date with the bank, and even questioned some of the other locals about your father's land records. It's all anyone can talk about. Folks are starting to wonder what he's really up to."

James felt a surge of anger. "What does he think he's going to find?"

"Don't know," Sullivan replied, his brow creased. "But from the way he's acting, it sounds like he's trying to stir up some trouble, maybe to put some pressure on you. He even tried talking to the real estate agent in town, poking around about sales and land values."

Emma's hand clenched around her teacup. "What can we do, Sullivan? If he's as intent on this as he seems, there's no telling how far he might go."

Sullivan looked at her with a grave expression. "I wish I had better advice for you. But I'm telling you this because it's clear he's not going to back down on his own. I've known folks like him in my time—people who think they can push others off their land with intimidation and force."

James leaned forward, his voice low and resolved. "I'll do whatever it takes to protect my family and my land. We've come too far to let someone like McRae walk in and take it from us."

Sullivan nodded, respect in his eyes. "That's the spirit, James. But just be cautious. If he's already snooping around about your finances, he might try to make it even harder for you to get by. And if he has any connections that can cause you trouble, he won't hesitate to use them."

The room fell into a tense silence as Sullivan's words sank in. The stakes were clearer than ever now; it wasn't just McRae's snooping or his unwelcome presence—it was the threat that he could dismantle everything they'd worked for, simply by leveraging the smallest vulnerabilities.

Finally, Sullivan stood up, adjusting his hat. "I'll keep my ears open and let you know if anything else comes up. But for now, just stay vigilant. Lock things up tight and don't leave anything to chance."

Emma got up and put a gentle hand on Sullivan's shoulder, gratitude and worry in her eyes. "Thank you for coming, Sullivan. It means a lot that you'd look out for us like this."

"Anything for a friend," he said, giving a warm but weary smile. "Just take care of yourselves."

As Sullivan left, James locked the door firmly behind him. He returned to Emma, their unspoken fears hanging heavily in the air.

"We'll need to keep a closer watch than ever," James said quietly. "Every time we turn our backs, he's finding another way to come at us."

Emma reached for his hand. "We'll face this together, James. We have to hold on, for Lucy, for the farm. We'll show him we're stronger than he thinks."

With their hands clasped tightly, James felt a renewed sense of determination. Sullivan's warning had only solidified his resolve— whatever McRae had planned, James would be ready for it. The Hardings weren't just fighting for their land; they were fighting for the legacy they'd built, and they weren't about to give it up without a battle.

Property Offer

Just as the kitchen settled back into a tense silence after Sullivan's departure, the phone rang, slicing through the quiet. James exchanged a wary glance with Emma, feeling an uneasy prickle at the back of his neck. He picked up the receiver.

"James Harding here," he said, his voice gruff.

"Mr. Harding! This is Claire from Burralyndra Real Estate. I hope I'm not catching you at a bad time," the agent's voice chirped with a rehearsed cheerfulness, though it didn't mask the probing tone underneath.

James furrowed his brow. "Afternoon, Claire. What can I do for you?"

There was a brief pause, a hesitation before Claire continued, "I'll just get right to it. I had a gentleman come into the office this week, asking about properties in the area, specifically yours. He seemed very interested and wondered if you were considering selling."

James felt his grip tighten on the receiver. "I'm not planning on selling the farm, Claire. Don't think I've ever given that impression."

"No, of course not, Mr. Harding! I assured him as much. But... well, he was rather persistent. Asked if I could reach out to you directly, see if you might consider an offer if it was high enough. Said he thought it'd be a shame to 'miss out on a lucrative opportunity.'"

James's jaw clenched, and he could feel Emma's eyes on him, sensing his frustration. "Did he give his name?" James asked, though he had a pretty good guess.

"McRae," Claire replied with a sigh. "He left his card here with me, just in case. Seemed like he was trying to get his foot in the door, so to speak. Offered to buy lunch if you were open to a conversation."

James let out a humourless chuckle. "I appreciate the call, Claire, but you can let him know the farm isn't for sale. Not now, not ever."

"Of course, Mr. Harding. I'll make it clear," Claire said quickly. But then she added in a lower tone, "Just... be careful with this one. He's got a way about him, you know? Some folks in town are saying he's not one to take 'no' for an answer."

James sighed, the weight of the day pressing on him even more heavily. "Thanks for the heads-up, Claire. We'll be careful."

As he hung up, James turned back to Emma, who looked at him with wide, worried eyes. "That was Claire. McRae's trying to buy us out. Going through the real estate office, hoping I'll bite on some big offer."

Emma's face paled, her mouth set in a firm line. "He really won't stop, will he?"

"No," James said, his voice hard. "He's got his sights set on this land, and he'll do anything to get it. But I'm not letting him take what my father worked for, what we've poured our lives into."

Emma stepped closer, laying a comforting hand on his arm. "We've got to be smart, James. We know what he's after now, and we know he's willing to use anyone and anything to get it. If he thinks a little money will change our minds, he's got another thing coming."

James nodded, feeling the swell of anger give way to a steely resolve. "Let him try his tricks. We'll be ready."

Their home and livelihood were at stake, and the Hardings would fight, together, every step of the way.

Workplace Inspection

The morning after Claire's call, James was out in the wheat fields, mulling over the idea of installing more cameras along the property line, when he heard the crunch of tires on gravel. Squinting through the early sunlight, he saw a white truck emblazoned with the "WorkSafe WA" logo rumbling up the drive.

"Now what?" he muttered, wiping his hands on his jeans as the truck rolled to a stop near the house. Two inspectors stepped out—a man and a woman, both wearing high-visibility vests and hard hats clipped to their belts. Their expressions were neutral but professionally curt, the way inspectors always seemed to be.

Emma stepped out onto the porch, shielding her eyes as they approached. James joined her, crossing his arms tightly. He could feel the tension radiate from her as well.

The male inspector extended his hand first, introducing himself as Peter Howard, while his colleague, Sarah Lynn, offered a polite nod. "Mr. Harding, Mrs. Harding, we're here for a standard inspection, just a routine check to ensure that your farming operations meet safety regulations."

James raised an eyebrow. "Routine, huh? We've never had an inspection before. What brings you out here now?"

Howard cleared his throat, glancing at his clipboard. "We received an anonymous tip that some of your machinery might be outdated, and that your safety protocols weren't up to standard."

James's jaw tightened. "Anonymous tip, you say?"

Emma gave him a sidelong glance, her brow knitting in concern. James had a sinking feeling in his gut about where that "tip" might've come from. McRae was clearly not one to sit idle when his plans were thwarted.

"Mind if we take a look at your equipment?" Sarah asked, gesturing to the barns and sheds scattered across the property.

"Of course," Emma said, trying to sound accommodating. "We're happy to comply."

Howard and Sarah started their inspection, taking their time to examine every piece of machinery, from the tractors to the old combine harvester that had been in the family since James's father ran the place. They checked guards, examined fire extinguishers, and measured noise levels, jotting down notes and occasionally whispering to each other. They even inspected the grain silo's access ladders and harnesses, things that hardly anyone had used since the last big harvest.

James's irritation simmered as they poked around in the old shed near the barn, the one where they had started storing some of their mining supplies under the guise of farming equipment. He silently thanked his luck that he'd kept things relatively inconspicuous, but the prying eyes and scribbled notes made him uneasy.

After nearly two hours, the inspectors returned to the house, looking thoroughly professional yet slightly troubled.

"Mr. Harding," Peter said, glancing at his clipboard, "while most of your equipment meets baseline safety requirements, there are a few areas that need immediate addressing. For instance, the guard on the threshing machine needs to be replaced, and a fire extinguisher near the fuel storage area is past its expiration date."

Emma, trying to keep the mood light, gave a polite nod. "We'll make sure to address those right away. Anything else we should be aware of?"

Peter hesitated. "There's also the matter of fencing around some of the equipment near the barn and the storage areas. Under new regulations, anything that poses a potential hazard to visitors or workers requires proper demarcation and warning signs."

James clenched his fists, struggling to keep his temper in check. The fencing they were talking about was part of the new boundary markers he'd set up to protect the area around the barn and the shed from anyone snooping. They were hardly necessary for typical farming operations, but with everything going on, it was a precaution he wasn't willing to compromise on.

"We'll handle it," James replied tersely, sensing a lecture coming on.

Sarah gave a small, understanding smile. "Mr. Harding, we know it can be challenging to keep up with every regulation, especially on family-run farms. But we'd strongly recommend making these updates sooner rather than later. There's been a bit of a crackdown recently on compliance for properties like yours."

James exhaled sharply, nodding as the two inspectors wrapped up and left. As soon as they were out of earshot, he turned to Emma, his voice low and laced with frustration.

"That 'anonymous tip' was no accident, Emma. I'd bet my last dollar that McRae's behind it, trying to rattle us."

Emma's face softened in understanding, her voice calm but firm. "It's just another way to pressure us, James. He wants us to feel cornered, to make it easier for him to swoop in and take the farm."

"Well, it's not going to work." He shook his head, resolute. "We'll fix up the things they mentioned, but I'll be damned if I'm going to let him chase us off with a few safety violations."

Emma placed a comforting hand on his arm. "We've handled worse. We'll get through this too."

James nodded, feeling his resolve tighten. They'd jump through whatever bureaucratic hoops were necessary to stay compliant, but McRae would soon learn that the Hardings wouldn't be intimidated that easily. And if he tried to push any further, James would be ready. Every inch of the farm fortified and watched.

As they watched the WorkSafe truck disappear down the drive, both James and Emma silently vowed that McRae wouldn't be getting his way anytime soon.

22

The Document

The Hidden Document

The attic was a dusty maze of old furniture, boxes, and family heirlooms that had collected there over generations. Sunlight streamed through a small, grimy window, casting a dim glow over the old wooden beams and casting shadows over Emma as she rummaged through a chest her father-in-law had kept. She hadn't been up here in years, but a feeling, perhaps desperation, had urged her to dig through their past, hoping it might offer some clue on how to save their future.

She lifted a pile of yellowed papers bound with twine and unfolded them carefully, her fingers trembling. Some of it was mundane—old letters, land assessments, receipts for supplies. But then, as she peeled back the layers, she spotted a worn piece of parchment tucked within a bundle of notebooks. She unfolded it slowly, realising it was a map. It showed the layout of the farm, but with certain areas marked that she'd never seen referenced before.

One spot, in particular, was marked with a small "X" deep in the north end of their property, near a rocky outcrop. Her pulse quickened as she traced her finger over the area, feeling a strange sense of recognition. She recalled her father-in-law mentioning an abandoned shaft long ago, dismissing it as something from the past that held no value. But this map suggested otherwise.

Emma's eyes widened as she noticed faint handwriting along the edges. It was almost too faded to read, but she could make out a few words: "...the vein... untapped... but costly." Her breath hitched. If there was truly more gold on their land, this might be the key to keeping the farm afloat.

A thrill ran through her, quickly tempered by a growing dread. If they weren't the only ones who knew about this map, it explained why McRae had been so interested in their land. He must've learned somehow, maybe through town rumours or by prying into local archives. If McRae had an idea of the potential wealth here, that made him more dangerous than she'd thought.

Just then, footsteps echoed up the ladder to the attic. It was James, a slight look of impatience and worry on his face as he ducked under the low beams.

"Emma, I was wondering where you'd gone off to," he murmured. "Everything all right?"

Without a word, she handed him the map, her eyes wide with excitement and fear. He glanced at it, his face hardening as he took in the details.

"James," she said softly, her voice barely above a whisper. "This might be what he's after. And if it's true... it could mean everything to us."

He stared at the map, then back at her, his expression unreadable. "So he knows, or at least he suspects," he said grimly, folding the map with care. "That means we have to be more careful than ever. But if there's more to find, then maybe... just maybe, we'll have what we need to keep him at bay."

A mixture of excitement and trepidation simmered between them. The discovery had given them a renewed sense of hope, but the stakes had risen higher than ever.

Letter of Hope

As Emma and James descended from the attic, their minds raced with the weight of the discovery and its implications. They found Lucy in the kitchen, poring over farm accounts and her meticulous calculations for paying off the mortgage. Seeing the intensity of her focus, Emma hesitated, unsure how their revelation might affect her. But James, resolute, nodded, silently urging Emma to continue. They had kept enough from Lucy, and now, with all their futures intertwined in this secret, it was time to bring her fully into the fold.

"Lucy," Emma began, carefully setting the old map on the table in front of her. "We found something in the attic—something that changes everything."

Lucy looked up, her brow furrowing as she took in the worn paper. She leaned closer, her fingers tracing the faded lines of the old map. As she noticed the marked area and the small "X" on their land, a spark of recognition and thrill lit up her eyes. "Is this... another gold site?"

Emma nodded, her voice low. "This map shows a section of the farm that your grandfather thought was untapped but promising. If it's right, there might be more than just what we've already found."

Lucy's excitement was palpable, her hands gripping the map tightly as if it might slip away. "This could mean we'd have enough to cover everything—more than enough. We could expand and finally bring the farm up to what it deserves to be."

James's expression grew serious, pulling Lucy back from her daydream. "This isn't just about expanding. If we start another operation, we'll need new mining permits, rights to dig deeper, and ventilation equipment to make sure it's safe. It won't be as simple as pulling a nugget out of the ground anymore."

Lucy looked between them, her mind already processing what this would entail. "Then we'll need to apply for permits to mine lower levels, right? And we'll have to add enough ventilation for safety if we're going underground."

Emma nodded. "Yes, and those permits and rights aren't cheap. But without them, we'd be working illegally, and if someone like McRae finds out about this map... well, he could use that against us."

A look of determination settled over Lucy's face as the full scope of their undertaking dawned on her. "We can figure this out. We'll need to budget for ventilation equipment, support beams, everything to make this safe and legitimate." She pulled out her notebook, jotting down figures and calculations, her focus sharp as ever.

James placed a hand on her shoulder. "There's a real risk here, Lucy. Expanding the operation will attract more attention, and we'll need to be cautious at every step. This map might save us, but it could also bring more trouble than we're ready for."

Lucy looked up, her eyes shining with both excitement and a sense of resolve. "I understand, Dad. But we've come this far. We can't let fear hold us back now."

The family exchanged a weighted glance, the realisation of their unity settling in. They would pursue the promise of this map together, prepared to face whatever challenges might arise. The stakes had never been higher, but with this newfound purpose, they felt a fresh resolve—the hope that perhaps, with hard work and caution, they might just secure their farm's future.

23

Surveillance Begins

Camera Surveillance

As dusk settled over the Harding farm, James and Lucy worked quietly along the outskirts, carefully positioning a series of high-definition cameras and motion detection sensors along key entry points and hidden trails leading into their land. Each motion-activated device had been chosen specifically for this purpose—night vision, wide-angle lenses, and long battery life. They knew that anything less sophisticated might tip off anyone who was snooping, so they kept the equipment as discreet as possible, blending it into the natural environment.

Lucy crouched near a fence post, attaching a hidden bracket for one of the cameras. She felt her father's intense gaze fixed on the edge of their property. He looked determined to protect their hard work. "Dad," Lucy whispered, "will this catch anyone?" James nodded, his focus unbroken. "It must. We can't risk anything. McRae is more than a drifter. If he's as dangerous as he seems, we need every angle covered."

They moved along the fence, setting up another camera at a high vantage point with a direct view of the main road. James checked the feed on his phone, adjusting the lens slightly to get a clear shot of anyone approaching.

"Good angle here," he said, satisfied. "If McRae or anyone else comes through, we'll know." He paused, a flicker of worry crossing his face. "And if something happens while we're not around..."

Lucy understood the unspoken words. She pressed her hand reassuringly against his shoulder. "We'll get an alert if anything trips the sensors. We'll know in real-time, and we can decide what to do from there."

They continued placing equipment, each piece of technology becoming a layer of defence around their land. Every camera, every sensor, felt like an invisible boundary against the unseen threats that seemed to be closing in. For Lucy, the installation wasn't just about surveillance—it was a declaration of protection, a quiet vow that they would not be driven away from their home.

As they set up the last camera, James straightened, scanning the horizon. The evening shadows had deepened, painting the fields in soft hues of blue and grey, but there was an undeniable sense of vigilance in his stance.

"Whomever has been messing around on our land," he muttered, his voice hard with conviction, "they'll soon realise they're not welcome here."

Lucy nodded, her expression mirroring his steely resolve. "And if they don't," she replied, her voice steady, "we'll make them understand."

Fire Protection

The next day, James and Lucy prepared to test the final part of their newly installed security system: an Artificial Intelligence (AI) enhanced fire detection link designed to automatically trigger the sprinklers if any flames were detected on their land. With McRae's recent purchases—including suspicious items like accelerants and ignition tools—they couldn't take any chances. James was keenly aware that if someone were desperate enough to set their fields ablaze, they'd need to be ready to defend against that possibility.

"Alright," James said, running his hand along the screen of his phone where the live feed from the cameras displayed. "Each camera's AI should pick up the slightest sign of smoke or a flame and send a signal to the sprinklers along the fields. We'll run this as a controlled test. You ready with the lighter, Luce?"

Lucy nodded, holding a small bundle of dry sticks she'd gathered specifically for the test. They walked to a clear, safe area at the edge of the wheat fields, where they'd set up a patch away from the crop for the trial. James gave her a reassuring nod as she knelt, struck the lighter, and set the small pile alight. They both stepped back, watching the wispy smoke begin to rise, small but unmistakable against the midday sky.

The reaction was almost immediate. Within seconds, one of the cameras nearest to them flashed a detection alert on James's phone screen. "Fire detected," the app reported, and James's thumb hovered anxiously as they waited. A second later, the field sprinklers roared to life, sending water cascading over the patch in swift arcs, dousing the small fire almost instantly. The AI's accuracy was unmistakable; it had even accounted for the wind's direction and adjusted the sprinklers accordingly.

Lucy couldn't help but grin. "That worked better than I thought," she said, her voice tinged with relief. "Imagine if McRae or anyone else tried to pull something on the farm—it'd be over before they knew what hit them."

James nodded, the tension he'd carried easing for a moment as he surveyed the sprinklers, still spraying in their programmed area. "It's a good start," he replied. "This way, even if we're not around, we'll have a response ready." He couldn't shake the nagging fear, though, that with each added layer of security, they were admitting just how close the threat had come.

They ran the test once more, this time triggering the system remotely to make sure the sprinklers would respond if either of them weren't nearby. Once again, the system worked flawlessly. James and Lucy shared a look—pride, determination, and a mutual understanding of what this meant. They were taking every precaution to protect the farm, their family, and their future.

James switched off the sprinklers, but the quiet whirr of the cameras continued in the background, a silent yet constant guardian watching over them. As they walked back toward the house, Lucy turned to her dad with a new resolve. "We've done everything we can to protect what's ours. Whatever McRae has planned, we'll be ready for it."

James nodded, but his face was sober. "Let's hope it doesn't come to that," he replied, his gaze settling on the golden fields that stretched out before them.

24

Reconnecting

A Call For Help

In the quiet of the Harding's living room, Lucy sat cross-legged on the couch, her phone pressed to her ear. The sun streamed in through the window, casting a warm light in the room, but a sense of urgency pulsed beneath the surface. She had been thinking about the stranger's unsettling behaviour and her own tense encounter with him. It was time to seek help from someone who understood the intricacies of law enforcement without the threat of drawing attention to their situation.

"Hey, Daniel, it's Lucy Harding," she said as the line connected. "How are you?" She listened for a moment, nodding along as he responded. Daniel's father worked as a sergeant in the nearby town of Amberley, and Lucy remembered how close she and Daniel had been back in school. "I could really use your advice on something... It's kind of serious."

As she explained the situation—the strange occurrences around their farm, the unsettling encounter with the man named McRae, and the growing concern about their safety—Lucy felt the weight of the world lifting a little. Daniel's calm voice on the other end reassured her that they weren't alone in this.

"Lucy, it sounds like you guys are in a tight spot," Daniel replied, his tone shifting to one of seriousness. "Have you reported any of this to the police yet?"

"We did, but it felt like they weren't taking it seriously," she admitted, biting her lip. "The officer didn't seem to think it was a big deal. We're trying to be cautious, but I'm worried that if we make too much noise, it could put my family at greater risk."

"I get that," Daniel said. "You don't want to escalate things if you can help it. Maybe I could talk to my dad, see if he has any advice on how to handle this without making it public knowledge. He's been around a lot of small-town politics, so he might have some ideas about keeping things low-key."

"That would be amazing," Lucy replied, her heart lifting. "We just need some guidance. I'm worried about my dad, especially with all the pressure from the bank and everything."

"I'll call you back as soon as I know more," Daniel promised. "Stay safe, alright? And keep your eyes open."

After they hung up, Lucy set her phone down on the coffee table, a mix of hope and cautious optimism blooming within her. She glanced around the familiar room—pictures of their family on the walls, mementos of farm life scattered about—and felt a renewed determination to protect it all.

Just then, Emma walked in, her arms full of laundry. "Who were you talking to?" she asked, her brow furrowing slightly.

"Daniel. I just reached out for some advice about... everything that's been going on," Lucy replied, trying to sound casual but knowing her mother would pick up on her underlying tension.

Emma paused, setting the laundry down on the couch. "Good idea, honey. Sometimes it helps to have an outside perspective." Emma liked Daniel and knew how close Lucy and he were at school and how much she missed him. Maybe an upside to all of this extra pressure would be the rekindling of that relationship for Lucy.

Lucy nodded. "He said he'd talk to his dad, the Sergeant, about what we can do without attracting too much attention. I feel like we're doing everything we can, but it still feels so... overwhelming."

Emma walked over and sat beside her, giving her a reassuring pat on the back. "You're doing great, Lucy. We'll figure this out together, I promise. Just remember, no matter what happens, we're a team."

With her mother's words echoing in her mind, Lucy felt a surge of courage. They were in this together, and she was ready to face whatever came next. As they sat in the living room, the sunlight filtering through the curtains, Lucy couldn't shake the feeling that something was about to change. They were drawing closer to the storm, and she hoped they were prepared for whatever lay ahead.

25

The Strangers Past

History

Lucy's mind was ablaze with suspicion and determination as she entered the Burralyndra library, a modest building nestled near the town's centre. The library was usually a muted haven, but today it felt like the command centre of her investigative efforts. She was there on a mission—to dig into the mysterious stranger, McRae, who had unsettled their lives so profoundly.

Greeted by the familiar musty scent of old books, Lucy approached the main desk where Mrs. Whitmore, the elderly librarian, was sorting through a stack of returned literature. "Afternoon, Lucy," she greeted with a soft smile, adjusting her glasses. "What can I help you find today?"

Lucy returned the smile, though hers was tinged with the gravity of her purpose. "I need to look up some public records and newspaper archives, Mrs. Whitmore. It's about a person who might not be who they claim to be."

Mrs. Whitmore's brow furrowed in concern, but she nodded,

understanding the seriousness of Lucy's tone. "Right this way, dear. Our archives are not as modern as the city's, but we have a comprehensive collection of local newspapers and some access to public record databases."

Lucy followed the librarian to the back of the library. They entered a small room with old microfilm machines and computers. The room had shelves lined with film canisters and dusty reference books. The air smelled strongly of paper and time.

Mrs. Whitmore showed Lucy how to operate the microfilm reader and logged her into a computer that had database access. "If you need any more help, just let me know," she said, leaving Lucy to her research.

Lucy started with the local newspaper archives, searching for any mentions of McRae. She typed his name into the database, her heart pounding as she hit 'enter'. The machine whirred, and soon, images of old newspaper pages appeared on the screen. As she read through the articles, a picture of McRae's past began to emerge, each detail adding weight to her dread.

McRae had been involved in several mining operations across the state, and almost each had ended under dubious circumstances. Several articles detailed legal battles over land rights, disputes with co-investors, and allegations of environmental violations. One particularly damning article from a few years ago covered a court case where McRae was sued by a group of small landholders. They accused him of fraudulent practices and attempting to force them off their land to expand his mining operations. The case was settled out of court, the details sealed, leaving a cloud of suspicion hanging over McRae's business dealings.

Lucy's hands trembled slightly as she scrolled through the articles. The pattern was clear and deeply unsettling. McRae was not just a businessman; he was a predator, using his resources and knowledge of the law to outmanoeuvre those who stood in his way. The realisation that her family was his latest target filled her with a cold fury.

Armed with this new information, Lucy knew she had to warn her family and prepare them for what might be a prolonged fight. McRae wouldn't back down easily, not when his past was riddled with similar conflicts.

Gathering copies of the most relevant articles, Lucy thanked Mrs. Whitmore and left the library. Her walk back to the farm was brisk, each step fuelled by a mix of fear and resolve. She was no longer just a farmer's daughter; she was a defender of her family's legacy against a known threat. The battle lines were drawn, and Lucy felt the weight of the coming conflict settle on her shoulders. But she also felt a spark of defiance; they had right and history on their side, and now, they had knowledge too. With this information, they could form a better strategy, anticipate McRae's moves, and protect their home.

As the farm came into view, with the sun setting behind it, casting a golden glow over the fields, Lucy felt a surge of love and protectiveness for this land and her family. McRae had chosen the wrong property to mess with, and Lucy was ready to stand firm. Come what may.

The Revelation

Lucy arrived home just as the sun began to set, casting long shadows across the Harding farm. The information she had uncovered at the library about McRae weighed heavily on her mind as she walked into the house. The atmosphere in the living room, where her parents waited, felt thick with anticipation. She could tell they were anxious to hear about her findings.

"Mum, Dad," Lucy began, her voice steady despite the turmoil inside her. "I found quite a bit at the library. It's... it's not good."

Emma looked up sharply, concern etching her features. "What is it,

Lucy?"

Taking a deep breath, Lucy laid out the documents she had photo-copied. "McRae has a history of exploiting landowners. He's been involved in multiple legal disputes where he's either tried to force people off their land or manipulated laws to his benefit. There are accusations of fraud and coercion..." Lucy's voice trailed off as she spread the papers on the coffee table for her parents to see.

Emma reached for the documents, her eyes scanning the headlines as Lucy continued. "In one case, he pushed a family in South Mills to sell their land for a mining operation by poisoning their livestock and sabotaging their water supply. The case went to court, but McRae settled out of court under confidential terms."

Emma gasped, her hand flying to her mouth. "That's monstrous," she murmured, horror reflected in her eyes. "Lucy, this man is dangerous."

Lucy nodded, her jaw set. "There's more. He's known in several communities for these tactics. It seems his interest in our land isn't just business—it's predatory."

Adding to the troubling pattern, Lucy pulled out another document. "Here's another instance where McRae was implicated in the sudden bankruptcy of a small farming operation in Westridge. The owners were in the way of a proposed pipeline. Witnesses later testified that McRae used shell companies to hike up the farm's debt, forcing them to sell at a loss. No charges stuck, but the pattern is clear."

She shuffled the papers, finding a third example. "And here, in Creekston, McRae reportedly funded a campaign to rezone agricultural land for industrial use. The local farmers opposed it fiercely, fearing pollution and land degradation. McRae's lobbyists swarmed the town meetings, and suddenly, those farmers faced anonymous complaints being made about them to various regulatory agencies. Most of them spent so much on fines and legal fees that they had little fight left in them. A year later, the rezoning of the land was passed through council."

Emma shook her head, each new revelation adding layers to her disgust and fear. "This man... he destroys lives. And he does it without a second thought."

The Quiet Concern

James had been listening intently, his expression unreadable as he absorbed the information. Unlike Emma's vocal shock, James's reaction was subdued; he sat back, his fingers steepled in front of his mouth, a deep furrow creasing his brow. After a long moment of silence, he finally spoke, his voice low.

"We need to be very careful about how we handle this. McRae isn't just a businessman—he's a predator, as Lucy said. We're not just dealing with a corporate takeover; it's almost like... personal warfare."

Emma looked between Lucy and James, her fear morphing into a fierce protectiveness. "What do we do, then? How do we protect ourselves against a man who plays by such ruthless rules?"

James's gaze was fixed on the documents scattered across the table. "First, we don't let on that we know about his past. If he believes we're unaware, it might give us an advantage. We'll need to strengthen our security, keep a closer watch around the farm, and maybe it's time to reach out to some old friends for support."

Lucy watched her father, seeing the wheels turning in his mind, planning, strategizing. It was in moments like these she was reminded of his strength, his ability to carry the family through crisis with quiet resolve.

"We also keep documenting everything," James continued. "Any interaction with McRae, anything out of the ordinary—it all gets written down. If it comes to a legal battle, we'll need all the evidence we can get."

Emma nodded, her resolve hardening. "We'll stand our ground, then. We won't be bullied or scared off our own land."

James finally turned to Lucy, a subtle nod of appreciation. "Good work, Lucy. This information is invaluable. It's going to be a tough road ahead, but now we know exactly what we're up against."

The room settled into a determined silence, each member of the Harding family processing the weight of the challenge ahead. They were united, bonded even more tightly by the threat against their home. As night fell outside, the documents on the table glowed under the lamplight, symbols of the battle to come. They were no longer just a family bound by blood and love, but comrades in arms against a known enemy, ready to defend their legacy and their future.

26

Break In

Sabotage

The sun had barely crested the horizon when James Harding stepped out onto the porch, coffee in hand, to greet the day. The serenity of the morning was a stark contrast to the turmoil churning inside him, fuelled by the discoveries Lucy had made the previous day about McRae's dubious past. As he walked towards the barn to start the day's work, he noticed something off—a disquiet that seeped through the cool morning air.

Reaching the barn, James found the door slightly ajar. A frown creased his forehead; he was certain he had locked it the night before. The padlock lay on the ground, cut clean through. Alarm shot through him as he pushed the door open and stepped inside. The dim interior slowly came into focus as his eyes adjusted to the light, revealing a scene of calculated sabotage.

The air was heavy with the smell of gasoline. James's heart sank as he took in the sight: wires dangled from the dashboard of his tractor, cleanly severed. The fuel tank was open, a small puddle of diesel staining the dirt floor beneath it—clear signs that someone had siphoned off the fuel. His tools scattered, some missing, others deliberately damaged. It was a clear and menacing message—they were being targeted.

Anger surged through James's veins, hot and quick. He clenched his fists, his initial shock giving way to a fierce protectiveness. He stormed back to the house to alert the family.

Emma was in the kitchen preparing breakfast when James burst through the door, his face grim. "The barn," he said, voice tight with anger. "Someone's tampered with everything. Cut the wires, stole the fuel. It's McRae, it has to be."

Lucy, who had just come downstairs, overhearing the conversation, felt a cold dread settle in her stomach. "He's escalating," she said quietly. "This isn't just a warning anymore. He's trying to cripple us."

"Why didn't the alarms go off when they entered the property?" James exclaimed.

"We don't have money to waste on technology that doesn't work!"

Lucy accessed the camera system to review the footage, where she observed two individuals wearing dark clothing heading towards the barn after crossing the yard. Regrettably, both of them had their faces concealed behind black masks. Interestingly, one of them had a physique that closely resembled McRae's.

Further review of the recorded footage showed the second person tampering with the fence sensors. These people were no amateur vandals. They knew exactly what they were doing and how to do it!

The family gathered around the kitchen table, the morning's tranquillity shattered by the intrusion. Emma's hands shook slightly as she poured more coffee, her eyes worried. "What do we do, James? Should we call the police again?"

James nodded, his jaw set. "Yes, we'll report it. But last time, they did little. We need to be prepared to handle this ourselves."

Lucy pulled out her phone, her fingers tapping rapidly as she contacted the local police station. They promised to send someone over to investigate, but Lucy had little hope that it would cause any immediate action.

After the call ended, the family checked the rest of the property. They inspected the fences, outbuildings, and fields to make sure nothing else was damaged. They felt anxious about what else they might discover.

Fortunately, no other sabotage was discovered, but the damage to their trust and sense of security was done. The realisation that someone had been on their property, tampering with their livelihood, was deeply unsettling.

Back in the house, they discussed their next steps. "We need to tighten security around here," James said. "Maybe install more cameras, better locks, anything that will help protect us."

The Hardings put their plan into action. They installed extra security measures. James reached out to neighbours. Emma documented the damage to the police and the insurance company. As a result, they felt a grim determination settle among them. They were under siege, but they were not helpless. Each new lock installed, each camera mounted, was a testament to their resolve to fight back, to protect their home and each other.

The police Sargent arrived late in the afternoon, taking statements and photos of the damage. He was sympathetic but offered little in the way of reassurances that they could catch the perpetrator. "We'll do what we can, but without witnesses or clear evidence pointing to a suspect, it's tough," he admitted.

After the Sargent left, the family gathered again in the living room. The day's events had taken a toll, leaving them exhausted but more united than ever.

"We're not just going to roll over," James declared, looking at each of his family members. "This farm is our home. It's been in our family for generations. We're going to stand our ground."

Emma nodded, her expression resolute. "We've faced challenges before. We'll get through this, together."

Lucy, though shaken by the day's events, felt a renewed sense of purpose. "He thinks he can scare us off," she said, her voice steady. "But he doesn't know who he's dealing with. We're Hardings. We don't back down."

The family's resolve was a bright flame in the gathering dusk, their shared determination forging an even stronger bond among them. They were more than just a family; they were a force to be reckoned with, and they would meet this challenge head-on, whatever it took.

Repair and Secure

The aftermath of the sabotage weighed heavily on the Harding family, but they channelled their frustration and fear into action. Over the next few days, they set about repairing the damage to their equipment and securing the barn to prevent future incidents. Each task was undertaken with a renewed sense of urgency and determination.

The first order of business was addressing the immediate damage. James and Lucy assessed the tractor and other machinery to determine what needed fixing. The severed wires on the tractor's dashboard were a critical concern; without the tractor, their ability to manage the farm was severely compromised.

James, who had some electrical knowledge from years of maintaining old farm equipment, took the lead. He painstakingly reconnected each wire, double-checking diagrams he downloaded to ensure everything was correctly wired. The work was meticulous and slow, demanding a steady hand and a great deal of patience.

"Good as new," James declared several hours later, wiping grease and sweat from his brow as he turned the key in the tractor's ignition. The engine roared to life, a small victory that brought a relieved smile to his face.

Lucy, meanwhile, took an inventory of the stolen fuel and other supplies. She calculated what they needed to replace and organised a trip to town to restock. The theft had been a setback, but it was one they could recover from financially, thanks to their careful management of the farm's resources.

With the immediate repairs underway, the Hardings turned their attention to securing the barn. The broken padlock was a stark reminder of their vulnerability. James decided that upgrading their security was essential.

He and Lucy installed new, high-security locks on the barn doors and added additional locks to the windows. They didn't stop there; James purchased a state-of-the-art alarm system that included motion sensors and cameras that could be monitored via their smartphones. The system was an investment, but the peace of mind it offered was worth the cost.

Over the next day, Eric, Lucy's tech-savvy friend, came over to help install the new security cameras around the perimeter of the barn and other strategic points around the farm. The cameras were capable of night vision and would send an alert to their phones if they detected movement after hours.

"Anyone tries to sneak around here again, we'll know about it immediately," Eric assured them as he tested the system, showing them how to monitor the feeds and review recordings.

Lucy took to the system quickly, setting up alerts and checking the camera feeds periodically to ensure everything was working as expected. The digital map of their property, now dotted with camera icons, gave her a sense of control over their domain.

Aware of the need for more than just technological solutions, James reached out to neighbours to let them know about the break in. He didn't go into a large amount of detail, but let them know that fuel had been stolen and machinery damaged.

"We need to look out for each other," James told those he ran into, his voice carrying a mix of earnestness and command. "What happened to us could happen to you. We have to be vigilant."

The process of repairing the damage and fortifying their farm brought the Harding family closer together. Each night, after the day's work was done, they sat together at the kitchen table, discussing their progress and planning for the future.

"We're making the farm stronger than it ever was," Emma commented one evening, a note of pride in her voice. "Not just in terms of security, but as a community. We're turning something terrible into something that strengthens our bonds with our neighbours."

James nodded, looking around at his family with a fierce sense of pride. "We're doing more than just surviving this. We're growing from it. And no matter what comes our way, we'll be ready."

As they moved forward, the Hardings knew that the threat might still be out there, but they also knew they weren't facing it alone. With each new lock installed, each camera set up, they were not just protecting their farm; they were fortifying their way of life and ensuring the legacy of the Harding family for generations to come.

27

A Secret Meeting

Following The Stranger

James had spent the morning in town, picking up supplies and keeping an uneasy eye on McRae, who had been frequenting the local hardware store more often than seemed necessary. His suspicions grew each time he saw McRae interact with townsfolk, always with a smile that didn't quite reach his eyes. Today, James's intuition told him not to head straight home after finishing his errands. Instead, he lingered, watching McRae from across the street as he left the hardware store.

McRae glanced around casually before he started walking. His pace was brisk, purposeful, and he took a route that led away from the main street of Burralyndra toward the outskirts of town. James waited a few moments before following, keeping his distance, using his knowledge of the local streets to stay out of sight while maintaining McRae in view.

The route was familiar, one that skirted the edge of town where the residential area thinned into open fields and sparse woodlands. James's truck was nondescript enough, but he was careful to hang back, occasionally pulling over as if to check his phone to avoid drawing attention. As he drove, his mind raced with possibilities of what McRae might be up to. His gut churned with a mix of suspicion and anxiety, each mile adding weight to his worry.

McRae eventually turned off the main road onto a dirt track that wound through a densely wooded area. The track was less travelled, marked with the overgrowth of untended nature. James parked his truck a safe distance away and continued on foot, moving silently between the trees, using his skills as a lifelong hunter to navigate quietly.

The woods were thick here, the sounds of nature masking his movements. James moved with careful steps, keeping his eyes on the faint path McRae had taken. The foliage was dense, but occasional breaks allowed him glimpses of McRae up ahead, who seemed oblivious to being followed.

After a tense twenty-minute trek, James saw McRae stop. He crouched behind a large oak, peering through the underbrush. Up ahead, a small clearing opened, and McRae was not alone. Several men, four or five, James couldn't be sure, were gathered. They greeted McRae with handshakes that were too firm, too quick to be friendly. James's heart pounded in his chest as he realised this was no casual meeting.

The Meeting

From his hidden vantage point, James watched as McRae and the men began to talk. He was too far to catch their words clearly without revealing his position, but their body language was enough to tell him this was serious. One of the men, large and imposing, gestured aggressively as he spoke. McRae nodded, pulling out what looked like maps or plans, spreading them on a makeshift table made from a fallen log.

The group leaned in, pointing at various sections of the document. McRae's voice occasionally reached James. Phrases like "next phase" and "ensure they comply" floated through the air, chilling James to his core. It was clear they were planning something—something that went beyond simple threats or intimidation.

The discussion seemed to turn more intense. A man, younger and less imposing, showed something on his phone. It made the group laugh, but it sounded harsh and grating, lacking humour and carrying a sense of shared malice. James felt a surge of frustration at not being able to hear their plans clearly. He needed more information, but getting closer was too risky.

After some time, the men shook hands again, this time with a sense of conclusion to their meeting. They dispersed, disappearing through the trees in different directions, while McRae stayed behind, gathering the documents with a satisfied smirk on his face.

James waited until McRae had left, taking a different path back to the main road before he dared to move. He retraced his steps back to where he had parked his truck, his mind racing with the snippets of conversation he had overheard. James knew he needed to share this with the family and the authorities, but what could he say? He had seen a meeting, yes, but had no concrete evidence of their plans.

Reporting The Meeting

Driving back felt longer than it should have. James's mind was a whirl of anxiety and resolve. As soon as he reached home, he called a family meeting, gathering Emma and Lucy in the living room, where he recounted everything he had witnessed.

Emma's face grew pale as she listened, and Lucy's fists clenched in anger. "We need to go to the police," Lucy said firmly once James had finished. "This isn't just a threat anymore. It's a conspiracy against us."

James nodded. "I'll head over now. They need to know what's going on, even if we don't have all the details."

At the police station, James spoke with Sargent Collins, who had taken their previous reports. He listened intently, his expression growing increasingly grave. "I'll file a report, James, and we'll start an investigation, but without physical evidence or more to go on, it might be hard to take immediate action."

Frustrated but not deterred, James returned home, where the family discussed increasing their own security measures and staying vigilant. They agreed to keep a close watch on their land and maintain communication with their neighbours, who were also uneasy about the recent developments.

As the days passed, the Hardings implemented new security protocols, including surveillance cameras and regular patrols around their property. Though they felt isolated in their struggle, their determination to protect their home and each other only strengthened. The secret meeting James had witnessed was a stark reminder of the lengths McRae and his associates were willing to go. But it also solidified the Harding family's resolve to stand against whatever might come their way. They were ready to defend their farm, united in their cause and unwavering in their commitment to see it through.

28

A Confession

Bill's Confession

As James took a seat on the worn metal stool in Bill's workshop, he couldn't help but feel a heavy weight in his heart. The fear of the unknown loomed over him, intensified by the foreboding atmosphere of the cluttered space surrounding them. Bill, a strong and weathered man whose hands bore the marks of years of mechanical labour, emanated a palpable sense of regret.

"James, about that night at the bar—it was just after your father passed," Bill began, his voice tinged with remorse. "It was one of those evenings where the past felt close, you know? We were talking about the old days, the land, and the legends of gold." He paused; the memory clearly pained. "McRae was there, seemed like just another drifter, curious about local tales. I never imagined..."

Bill's admission that he had unintentionally shared potentially lucrative information with McRae was a significant blow. James valued loyalty and trust above all, principles instilled in him by his father and reinforced by his own experiences running the family farm. This revelation tested those values deeply, but it also underscored the complex nature of human relationships and the mistakes that come from misplaced trust.

"I didn't see the harm then, talking about old legends in a public place. I thought they were just stories," Bill added, his gaze meeting James's with earnest sincerity. "But when I saw him asking around, showing too much interest in the land, I realised he might be after something more. I should have warned you sooner."

James absorbed Bill's words, the complexity of his emotions swirling inside him. Anger, betrayal, but also an understanding of human fallibility. His response would set the tone for their next steps.

James rubbed his temples, taking a moment to compose his thoughts. "Bill, you've been a friend of the family for as long as I can remember. My father trusted you, and so have I," James said slowly, his voice firm despite the turmoil inside. "This... this is a hard pill to swallow, but I know you didn't mean for any of this to happen."

Bill nodded, visibly relieved by James's response but still burdened by his mistake. "I want to make this right, James. Let me help you protect your land. I've got tools, cameras, we can set up something that'll keep McRae at bay."

James's sense of loyalty—to his land, his family, and his friends—was central to his character. It compelled him to see beyond Bill's mistake to the intention behind it. This capacity for forgiveness and strategic thinking in the face of betrayal had made him a respected figure in the community.

"Alright, we'll do it together," James decided, extending his hand to Bill in a gesture of renewed trust. "We've got a lot of work ahead of us. Let's start by securing the farm. Any edge we can get over McRae is crucial."

As James and Bill leaned over the weathered map spread across the workbench, they zeroed in on the various access points to the Harding farm. Bill, with his intimate knowledge of the land's layout, pointed to several critical areas that could be potential vulnerabilities.

"Here, the back road leading up to the north field, it's secluded and lightly travelled. Perfect for someone trying to slip in unnoticed," Bill noted, his finger tracing the dusty road on the map. James nodded, his mind processing the strategic implications.

"For the back road, let's install a heavy-duty padlock on the gate. It's seldom used, so keeping it locked won't disrupt our operations," James suggested. Bill agreed, making a note beside the road on the map.

"Good idea. And what about the main entrance? It's more visible, but we should secure it after hours," Bill added.

James considered for a moment before responding. "Let's install removable bollards at the main entrance. During the day, we can keep them aside to allow for farm traffic. At night, or when we're not expecting anyone, we can block the path. It'll add an extra layer of security without being too conspicuous."

Bill nodded in approval, jotting down the suggestion. He then pointed to another area on the map, a narrow path leading through a dense copse of trees near the creek. "This path here, it's another weak spot. Not many know about it, but I'd bet McRae has done his homework."

James agreed, recognising the potential threat. "Let's reinforce that area. Maybe set up a few trail cameras hidden in the trees. If anyone tries to sneak through, we'll have them on camera. We can also put up more 'No Trespassing' signs as a deterrent."

"Right," Bill said, marking the spot for cameras. "And for added security, how about some motion-sensor lights? If someone is prowling around at night, the lights could scare them off, or at least alert us."

"Perfect. Let's do that. I'll order the lights and cameras this week,"

James confirmed, feeling a sense of proactive control as they fortified the farm's defences.

As they continued their planning, James and Bill also discussed routine checks of the security measures. They decided to conduct weekly inspections of the locks, bollards, and surveillance equipment to ensure everything was in working order and no tampering had occurred.

Bill pulled out a small notebook and created a maintenance schedule. "I'll take the first round of checks. We'll look over everything, make sure the locks aren't rusted, and that the bollards move freely. Maintenance is key with this kind of setup."

James appreciated Bill's thoroughness. "Thanks, Bill. I'm glad you're on top of this. It's a lot to manage, but with your help, I'm confident we can keep the farm safe."

As they wrapped up their session, they reviewed their notes, ensuring no detail was overlooked. The map was dotted with their annotations, a testament to their meticulous planning. They agreed to meet again the following week to implement the measures they had discussed.

Feeling fortified by their strategic planning, James left Bill's workshop with a renewed sense of partnership and purpose. The challenges ahead were daunting, but with their combined efforts, the Harding farm would be a stronghold, safeguarding its secrets against any threats that loomed on the horizon.

29

Lucy's Plan

The Design

Inside the Harding's weather-beaten barn, the air held the musky scent of hay and the aged wood creaked gently underfoot. Sunlight filtered through gaps in the wooden slats, creating streaks of light that danced across the dusty floor. Against this backdrop, Lucy stood ready, a set of rolled-up blueprints clutched firmly in her hands, her face set with a mixture of resolve and anticipation.

As James and Emma entered the barn, they found Lucy standing beside an old workbench, which had been cleared to make room for the discussion. They could feel the seriousness of the moment as they approached, noting the determined glint in their daughter's eyes.

"Mum, Dad," Lucy started, her voice echoing slightly in the spacious barn, "I've been doing a lot of thinking and research about how we can protect our find and possibly discover more without attracting unwanted attention." She unrolled the blueprint across the workbench, revealing a detailed map and cross-sectional drawings of underground structures.

Emma leaned over the blueprints, her brow furrowed in concentration as she tried to make sense of the diagrams. "Lucy, this looks incredibly detailed. What exactly are we looking at?"

Lucy pointed to a section of the blueprint labelled 'Main Access Shaft.' "This is the central point of our new underground system. It's designed to be discreet yet functional, providing us secure storage for our gold and a potential to explore deeper for more deposits."

James, who had been quietly observing the plans, chimed in, his voice tinged with a mix of scepticism and interest. "You're talking about building a mine under our farm? That's a major undertaking, Lucy. It's not just about digging a hole; it's about doing it safely and secretly. How do you propose we manage that?"

Lucy's preparation shone through as she addressed her father's concerns. "We start with a vertical shaft, right beneath the old tool shed. It's remote enough to avoid casual observation and has easy access from the house without being too obvious." She then traced her finger along a drawn line leading away from the shaft. "From this main shaft, we can branch out into smaller tunnels. These will follow the natural lay of the land and take advantage of existing geological features to minimise our need for extensive digging."

Emma interjected, her practical nature coming to the forefront. "And what about safety? Digging tunnels isn't something we've ever tackled. How do we ensure it doesn't collapse on us?"

Lucy nodded, expecting this question. "That's where proper shoring comes in. We'll use timber framing techniques—like the ones used in early mining operations. Each section we dig will be reinforced before we proceed to the next. For ventilation, we'll install discreet air shafts that can also handle any water drainage issues, camouflaging them as part of the natural landscape or integrating them into our existing farm structures."

James, looking slightly reassured but still cautious, asked another critical question. "And the equipment needed for such an operation—how do we get our hands on it without drawing attention?"

"That's covered too," Lucy responded confidently. "We can order a small excavator and a motorised conveyor for dirt removal, justifying them as necessary for pond digging and other land management tasks we publicly plan around the farm. This way, everything appears above board, and the actual use remains hidden."

The trio discussed various aspects of the operation, from the procurement of materials under the guise of regular farm upgrades to the scheduling of construction phases to coincide with less busy periods on the farm to avoid suspicion.

As the meeting drew to a close, the initial shock and scepticism had given way to a cautious hope. Emma and James were impressed by Lucy's thoroughness and her ability to foresee potential challenges. The proposal was ambitious and fraught with risks, but it was clear Lucy had considered these angles deeply.

"Alright, Lucy," James finally said, a slight smile breaking through his apprehensive demeanour. "Let's take tonight to think this over. We need to sleep on it, weigh our options, and look at this plan with fresh eyes in the morning."

Lucy nodded, pleased with her parents' response. "Thank you both. I know it's a lot to consider, but I truly believe this is our best shot at keeping what we've found safe and potentially finding more."

As they left the barn, the setting sun cast long shadows over the farm, and the Harding family felt a renewed sense of purpose. The challenge ahead was daunting, yet the possibility of securing their family's future invigorated them with a determination to proceed cautiously yet boldly.

Planning and Preparations

Under the heavy wooden beams of the Harding farm's oldest barn, Lucy laid out her comprehensive plans for a secret underground storage and mine entrance. With her parents watching closely, she unfolded detailed blueprints that illustrated an innovative approach to concealing their newly discovered gold.

"Here's the main idea," Lucy explained, pointing to a section of the blueprint designated as the 'Main Access Shaft.' "This will serve as both a secure storage area for our gold and the primary entrance to further explore the mineral veins beneath our farm."

James studied the design, his brow furrowed in concentration. "This is going to require careful execution. We can't just start digging without considering every possible outcome," he noted, echoing the strategic caution necessary for their operation.

Lucy nodded in agreement, her mind racing with logistics. "Absolutely, which is why our first step is acquiring the right equipment under the guise of standard farm upgrades. We need machinery that won't raise eyebrows but will be capable of eventually handling the tasks we have planned."

The list of necessary equipment was extensive, but justified by the farm's legitimate needs. Lucy had identified several key pieces of equipment that would be essential for the project and had placed them on a list:

"Each piece will be brought in slowly, under the cover of these projects, which will also be real. That way, there's nothing out of the ordinary going on here, just usual farm work," Lucy explained, detailing her strategy to avoid suspicion.

To ensure that no one would suspect the true purpose of their acquisitions, Lucy devised a plan to involve only the most trusted individuals in the actual project. Hank, their longtime contractor and family friend, would assist in acquiring and delivering the equipment discreetly.

"We'll store everything here in the back of the old barn until we're ready to begin. Hank can help us set up a false partition inside to hide the equipment from anyone who might wander in," Lucy suggested, her mind meticulous in covering all angles of security.

James was impressed with the thoroughness of the plan. "Good. Let's also make sure we have a secure communication plan in place. If anything goes sideways during this setup phase, we need to know immediately."

Understanding the importance of community perception, Lucy also planned to enhance their cover story by engaging in visible and viable farm improvements that would benefit the land and the community. "I'll schedule a series of soil health workshops here at the farm. It'll provide perfect cover for the increased activity and new equipment coming in," she proposed, knowing this would also solidify their standing in the community as progressive and responsible landowners.

Emma, always concerned with the finer details, added, "Make sure you document everything, Lucy. Take photos, keep receipts, and maybe even invite the local paper to do a feature on our conservation efforts. The more visible our reasons are, the fewer people will question our actions."

As they wrapped up their meeting, the family felt a renewed sense of purpose and unity. Their plan was bold and fraught with risks, but with meticulous planning and careful execution, they were ready to take on the challenge. The blueprint was rolled up, the meeting adjourned, and each member of the Harding family went about their tasks with a determined spirit, knowing well what was at stake.

Community Engagement

In the days following their strategic planning meeting, Lucy took the lead in orchestrating a series of highly visible activities that aligned perfectly with the cover stories for their equipment acquisition. The first order of business was the soil health workshops she had proposed. Lucy reached out to local agricultural experts and invited them to lead sessions, which were scheduled to take place right on the Harding farm.

The announcement of these workshops was well-received by the community. Lucy advertised them in the local paper and on community bulletin boards, highlighting them as a way to combat soil erosion and improve crop yields. The positive attention not only bolstered their standing in the community but also provided a perfect diversion for the influx of new equipment and supplies.

While Lucy handled the public-facing aspects of their plan, James and Hank focused on the groundwork. The first piece of equipment to arrive was the compact excavator. It was delivered early one morning, cloaked in the mundane routine of farm deliveries. Hank was there to receive it, directing the delivery to the rear of the old barn where it was carefully concealed behind the new partition Lucy had suggested.

Next to arrive was the motorised dirt conveyor. It came under the guise of aiding in a new project to level out several uneven sections of pastureland, which would supposedly help with water management and reduce the risk of flooding—a plausible explanation that fit well with the farm's operational needs.

James took personal charge of organising the storage and mainte-nance of these tools. He documented their arrival as part of the farm's asset management records, ensuring everything appeared standard and above board.

With the equipment securely in place, the next step was to tighten security around the farm without making it appear fortress-like. James installed new locks on the barn doors and updated the farm's existing surveillance system, adding a few more cameras under the pretence of deterring theft, which he casually mentioned had been a minor issue in the past.

Lucy and Emma worked together to prepare the paperwork and permissions allegedly needed for the upcoming construction projects. They created a detailed log of activities, which included fake invoices and work orders that Hank helped to fabricate. These documents would serve to justify the movement and use of the excavation equipment should anyone from the local council or community inquire.

As the date of the first soil health workshop approached, Lucy spent her days preparing the farm for visitors. She set up signs directing attendees to the workshop areas, arranged for seating and refreshments, and prepared informational packets that highlighted the Harding farm's commitment to sustainable practices.

The workshop proved to be a great success, drawing a good number of local farmers and several members of the agricultural extension office. The discussions were lively and productive, with plenty of attention focused on the techniques and equipment being showcased, exactly as Lucy had hoped.

In the midst of these public engagements, Lucy, James, and Emma held private meetings to refine the details of their tunnel and storage facility. They went over the blueprints again, discussing everything from the depth and diameter of the proposed shaft to the best methods for disposing of or re-purposing the excavated soil in a way that wouldn't arouse suspicion.

One evening, after the guests had left, and the farm had settled back into its routine quiet, Lucy stood on the porch looking out over the fields bathed in the soft light of the setting sun. Her mind replayed the events of the past few weeks—the planning, the community engagement, the covert preparations.

"This land is ours, and its secrets are ours to keep," she thought, a fierce sense of protection swelling in her chest. Her family had laid the groundwork for what would be their most daring endeavour yet. As she watched the dusk envelop her family's land, her resolve hardened.

"We're doing more than just farming here," she whispered to the evening breeze. "We're protecting a legacy." Lucy knew the road ahead would be fraught with challenges, but she felt ready to lead her family through whatever lay ahead, safeguarding not just the land, but the hidden treasures it held.

30

Threatening Message

A Threatening Message

James's morning started as usual; he headed to the mailbox with a steaming cup of coffee, just as the sun was coming up. Today, however, was unique. A simple, unlabelled envelope unexpectedly drew his attention from the regular mail. The insufficient postage and careless placement triggered immediate alarm.

Back in the kitchen, he slit the envelope open with a knife, his hands steady despite the unease brewing inside him. Emma and Lucy, noticing the tension in his posture, watched silently from across the table.

With the letter open, James' eyes darted over the scribbled words. His expression turned stern as he read aloud, "'Sell the farm and leave, or face the consequences of staying.'" This is your last warning." The words hung heavy in the air, a tangible cloud of threat.

Emma covered her mouth with a trembling hand, her eyes wide with shock. Lucy's face flushed with anger, her fists clenched tightly at her sides.

"It's McRae," Lucy spat out, the name like venom on her tongue. "It has to be. Who else would go this far?"

James nodded grimly, his jaw set. "He's desperate, and that makes him dangerous. We need to be more vigilant than ever now."

Just then, a car pulled up the driveway, the sound of gravel crunching under tires drawing their attention. Daniel stepped out, his arrival unannounced but timely. His expression was serious as he approached the front door, having seen the anxiety etched on Lucy's face through the window.

Lucy opened the door before he could knock, a mix of relief and worry in her eyes. "Daniel," she greeted, her voice a mix of emotions.

"I got here as soon as I could," Daniel said, stepping inside. He glanced at James and Emma, acknowledging the gravity of the situation. "I talked to my dad. He's concerned about the escalation and suggested a few precautionary measures. He's also willing to come by and offer some advice in person if you think it would help."

James appreciated the offer, nodding in gratitude. "Thank you, Daniel. Right now, any help is good help."

Turning their attention back to the letter, Daniel furrowed his brow. "This threat... it's blatant and direct. Let's revisit police involvement, regardless of prior unsuccessful attempts. Putting the threat in writing may make them take it more seriously.

Lucy was quick to agree. "Let's do it. Let's not take any chances."

Emma, however, seemed more introspective, her gaze drifting toward the window overlooking their sprawling lands. "We can call the police, yes, but we also need to protect ourselves. James, maybe it's time to reach out to some security companies. Professional surveillance, patrols... perhaps even a security consultant."

Their determination led them to formulate a plan. James was to contact a security firm; meanwhile, Daniel and Lucy would take the letter to the police, hoping for a quicker response with physical evidence. Emma stayed behind, her thoughts focused on safeguarding her home and family.

As they split up to tackle the tasks, the air was thick with a cocktail of defiance and fear. They were united, stronger together, but the threat had shaken the very foundations of their peace. The Hardings knew they were in for a fight to protect their legacy, a fight they were now fully prepared to take on. The stakes were clear, and they were ready to defend their home, come what may.

Daniel And Lucy Strategize

As Daniel drove Lucy to the police station, his mind raced with strategies to enhance the Hardings' safety beyond what law enforcement could offer. He recognised the limits of the police's involvement from his father's experiences in law enforcement and knew that community support could be just as crucial in situations like this.

"Lucy," Daniel began, breaking the silence in the car, "have you thought about rallying the town? Maybe setting up something like a neighbourhood watch? It could be a way to monitor things more continuously."

Lucy turned to look at him, considering the idea. "That's actually a really valuable idea," she admitted. "McRae might think twice if he knows the entire community is watching and ready to back us up."

Daniel nodded. "Exactly. And it's not just about watching out for trouble. It's about showing that you're not alone in this. My dad always says that there's strength in numbers. If McRae sees that the whole community supports you, it might deter him from doing anything drastic."

Lucy felt a spark of hope. "I think you're right. Dad and Mum have been so focused on securing the farm itself, we didn't really think about mobilising the community. But I know many of our neighbours would stand with us if they knew what was going on."

As they pulled into the police station parking lot, Daniel touched

Lucy's arm lightly, reinforcing his support. "When we get back, let's talk to your parents about it. I can help organise a meeting, maybe at the community centre. We can invite everyone, explain the situation, and see how they want to help. We could set up patrols, have people on lookout, anything that makes you all feel safer."

Lucy smiled, feeling genuinely relieved for the first time in days. "Thank you, Daniel. Having you here already makes a huge difference."

Back at the farm, after their visit to the police station, Lucy and Daniel presented the idea to Emma and James. Initially surprised, they quickly saw the potential benefits of having the community involved. James, who had always been a respected figure in the area, knew they could rally the support of their neighbours.

"That's an excellent idea," James agreed heartily. "We've been here for generations. People know us, they trust us. If we explain what's been happening, I'm sure they'll come together to help keep an eye out."

Emma, always the organiser, immediately began thinking about logistics. "We could host a community meeting this weekend," she suggested. "Invite everyone to the farm or maybe to the hall, maybe have a barbecue. Make it a community event, not just a security meeting. It'll be less intimidating that way."

Lucy and Daniel nodded, and with that, the plan was set into motion. They drafted invitations that afternoon, planning to distribute them around town the following day. The idea of a community gathering sparked a sense of unity and purpose, transforming their fear into a proactive mission.

As the plans for the community's support coalesced, the Hardings felt bolstered not just by the potential increased security but by the palpable sense of solidarity from their neighbours. The threat to their farm could become a unifying issue for the town, and with each passing day, McRae's shadow over their lives seemed a little less threatening.

The neighbourhood watch wouldn't just be about keeping the farm safe; it was about preserving the heart and soul of their community.

31

Community Engagement

Rallying The Town

The Burralyndra town hall, usually a place for local dances and bake sales, was tonight filled with a different kind of community spirit. Chairs were arranged in a semi-circle, fostering a sense of openness and unity, as the townsfolk of Burralyndra trickled in under the bright lights of the hall. Emma and James stood at the front, their faces a mix of determination and nervous anticipation.

James cleared his throat as the murmuring settled down, and he began to address the gathered crowd. "Thank you all for coming tonight," he started, his voice steady but carrying an undercurrent of urgency. "We're here because our family is facing a situation that could affect the whole community."

Emma took over, her tone sincere and appealing. "As many of you know, our farm has been in James's family for generations. Recently, we've encountered some... challenges. Some threats to our safety and to our land." She paused, choosing her words carefully, mindful not to reveal too much about the gold but to convey the seriousness of their plight. "We've found some small gold nuggets on our property—nothing major, but it's not uncommon around here, as you know."

Nods and murmurs of agreement rippled through the crowd; gold finds were part of the local lore, a spark of excitement in an otherwise quiet rural life.

"But," James continued, "since the discovery, we've been harassed by an individual who's trying to intimidate us into selling our land. We believe this is not just about us—it's about setting a precedent that could affect any one of us here."

The room tensed, with some attendees exchanging uneasy glances. The idea of being coerced or threatened hit close to home for many of the townsfolk.

Lucy, standing slightly behind her parents, stepped forward, her voice ringing clear in the suddenly quiet hall. "I've been personally threatened by this individual," she disclosed, her honesty and vulnerability cutting through the room's growing anxiety. "If we don't stand together, who knows who might be next?"

Daniel, standing beside her, added his voice to hers. "That's why we're asking for your help—not just to watch over the Harding farm but to come together as a community. To look out for each other. We're proposing setting up a community watch. Not just for our sake, but for the safety and security of all of us in Burralyndra."

A silence followed, heavy with consideration and the weight of decision. Then, from the back of the hall, old Mr. Thompson stood up. He was a long-time resident and a respected figure in the town. "I've known the Harding family all my life," he declared, his voice gruff but supportive. "They've been good neighbours, good citizens. If they say there's trouble, then we need to help 'em out. I don't want to live in a town where folks can be bullied off their land."

His words seemed to break the dam, and one by one, other community members began to voice their support. "We can take turns patrolling," suggested one farmer. "Keep an eye out, especially at night."

"I can set up some cameras around the main roads," offered another, a young, tech-savvy man who ran the local computer shop.

However, a few were still hesitant, their worries about retribution palpable. "What if this puts a target on our backs?" one woman asked, her voice shaking slightly.

Emma responded, her expression empathetic but firm. "We understand the fear. But we believe there's strength in numbers. If this person sees that we're united, that we're looking out for each other, it might deter further trouble."

The meeting concluded with plans to organise the first community watch schedule, and a committee was formed to handle logistics and communications. As people slowly dispersed, many stayed behind to offer personal assurances to the Hardings or to volunteer specific help.

As the crowd began to disperse after the meeting in the town hall, a small group of local farmers and residents lingered behind, their conversation turning to more personal observations that echoed the concerns the Hardings had raised. Among them was Mike Jenkins, a middle-aged farmer who lived on a property adjacent to the Hardings.

"I've been meaning to mention something," Mike said, drawing the group closer with his lowered voice. "Last week, I found some strange tire marks in my paddocks. Not from any vehicle I own, and they were too heavy to be from anything other than a large truck or something similar."

Sarah Bennett, another farmer whose land bordered the other side of the Harding's property, chimed in. "That's not all. Some of my cattle have been acting up, spooked like. I thought it was dingoes at first, but I haven't seen hide nor hair of them. Something else is making them jittery, and it's been happening late at night."

The group exchanged uneasy glances, the implications of their observations slowly sinking in. Hank Morrison, who ran a small orchard nearby, added his own experience. "I've heard noises at night, thought I was imagining things. But now, hearing you folks, it sounds like whoever is bothering the Hardings might be scoping out the rest of us, too."

Lucy, who had stayed back to speak with some of the attendees, overheard the conversation and approached the group. "You've all seen these things happening too?" she asked, her concern evident. "This is exactly why we need this watch. It's not just our farm at risk. We're dealing with someone who's not afraid to push boundaries, literally."

The group nodded in agreement, their earlier hesitation replaced by a shared resolve. "What do you think we should do, Lucy?" Mike asked, looking at her as a newfound leader in this collective struggle.

Lucy considered for a moment, her mind racing. "First, we need to document everything. Every tire mark, every instance of spooked animals. We can use the cameras we discussed setting up to monitor not just the roads but the fields as well. Anything out of the ordinary needs to be logged and shared among us."

"Maybe we could set up a communication network, a quick way to alert each other if something's amiss," suggested Sarah. "Like a phone tree or even a group chat for those of us who are tech-savvy."

Hank nodded. "I can help set that up. We need to be able to act fast if we're going to catch whoever is doing this."

As the group dispersed, a renewed sense of urgency propelled them into action. They were no longer just neighbours; they were allies, bound by the shared threat to their livelihoods and safety. Lucy watched them go, feeling the weight of their collective hope and fear. She knew the road ahead would be challenging, but with the community's support, they stood a chance of protecting not just the Harding farm but all of Burralyndra.

Walking back to their car under the starry night sky, the Harding family felt a renewed sense of belonging and strength. They knew the road ahead might still hold challenges, but with the town behind them, those challenges seemed a little less daunting. The unity and tension of the evening had forged something new in Burralyndra—a communal resolve to protect their own.

32

A Close Call

A Close Call

The moon cast a pale light over the Harding farm, throwing long shadows across the fields that swayed gently in the cool night breeze. Inside the farmhouse, the family had settled down for the night, but James found himself unable to sleep. His mind was on high alert, replaying the meeting's discussions and the community's shared concerns. He decided to check the surveillance feeds, just in case.

As he scanned through the live feeds displayed on his computer screen, his eyes narrowed. There was a flicker of movement near the edge of the north field, close to where the new cameras had been installed. Squinting, he leaned closer, toggling the controls to zoom in on the area. There was someone there, a shadowy figure moving stealthily along the perimeter fence.

Without hesitation, James grabbed his flashlight and headed outside, his heart pounding in his chest. He moved quickly but quietly, approaching the area where he'd seen the figure. The cool night air was sharp in his lungs as he reached the fence, his eyes scanning the darkness.

Suddenly, there was a rustle to his right. James turned just in time to see the figure darting through the field, disturbing the crops as they fled. He set off in pursuit, his flashlight beam cutting through the night, illuminating fleeting glimpses of the intruder.

The chase was brief; the figure was fast and knew how to navigate the terrain in the darkness. Despite James's efforts, the intruder reached the far end of the field and disappeared into the tree line that bordered their property. James stopped, panting, at the edge of the field, his hands on his knees as he tried to catch his breath. He shone his flashlight into the trees, but it was no use—the intruder was gone.

A mix of fear and frustration surged through him. He was relieved that the intruder had fled, but worried they would come back. It was a stark reminder that the threats they faced were not just words on paper or distant possibilities. They were real, and they were here, now, threatening the safety of his family.

Determined, James returned to the house. His resolve hardened. "We need to step up our security," he told Emma, recounting what had happened. "We can't let our guard down, not for a moment."

Emma nodded, her expression set in a grim line. "I'll contact the security firm first thing in the morning. We'll get more lights out there, maybe even some alarms."

Lucy, who had been awakened by the commotion, listened intently. "We should also tell the community watch about this," she suggested. "If they're trying to get to us, they might try the same with our neighbours. We need to be prepared."

James agreed. "I'll call Mike and Sarah in the morning. We'll set up a meeting. Everyone needs to be on alert."

The family spent the rest of the night in the living room, too on edge to sleep. They discussed plans and precautions, each of them more determined than ever to protect their home and each other. The close call had shaken them, but it had also steeled their resolve. They would not be intimidated, and they would not be caught off guard again.

Mike's Group Call

Dawn was still a couple of hours away and with the Harding family still gathered in their living room, the alert on Lucy's phone shattered the tense silence. It was a message from Mike Jenkins on the community watch group chat:

"Alert: Someone's running through my field right now. Heading east towards the Larson's place. Everyone, be on the lookout!"

James was on his feet in an instant, grabbing his coat. "Let's go," he said, determination etching his features. Emma and Lucy followed suit, gearing up quickly.

The community's response was immediate and overwhelming. As James, Emma, and Lucy drove towards Mike's property, they saw other vehicles—pickups, ATVs, even people on horseback—converging from various parts of the township. The early morning quiet was soon filled with the sound of engines and barking dogs as the neighbours came together, their vehicles' headlights cutting through the darkness.

Mike was waiting at his gate when James pulled up, a flashlight in one hand and his phone in the other. "He went through there." Mike pointed towards a break in his fence line where the crops were visibly trampled. "Headed towards the Larson's. We can cut him off if we hurry."

The convoy of trucks and ATVs split up, with some heading deeper into the field and others taking the perimeter roads to flank the intruder. The sound of whistles and shouts filled the air, a cacophony meant to intimidate and corral the trespasser.

Lucy, alongside Daniel, who had joined in with his own truck, coordinated through the group chat, updating positions and sightings. The community moved like a well-organised unit, their familiarity with the land giving them a distinct advantage.

Suddenly, a shout went up from one of the eastern flanks. "There he is! Heading for the road!" It was followed by the high-pitched baying of dogs that had picked up the scent.

The chase was chaotic, the intruder darting desperately for an escape route. But with every turn, he found his path blocked by a truck or a shouting local. Finally, as he neared the main road, a black sports utility vehicle (SUV) screeched to a halt, its doors flung open. The man dove inside, and the vehicle sped off, tires throwing up gravel and dirt as it went.

The community members, though unable to catch the man, had succeeded in driving him off. They gathered back at Mike's field, their breath visible in the cool morning air, faces flushed with the rush of adrenaline and communal spirit.

James looked around at his neighbours, his heart full of gratitude. "Thank you, everyone," he called out over the murmur of conversation. "We didn't catch him, but we sure as hell made it clear he's not welcome here."

Cheers and nods met his words. The group united in their resolve. Emma and Lucy joined him, their presence a clear sign of the family's appreciation.

Mike clapped James on the back. "We look out for each other here," he said. "Let that fella think twice before he tries something like that again."

As the sun rose higher, painting the sky in hues of orange and pink, the group slowly disbanded, heading back to their homes but promising to keep watch and stay alert. The incident had not only thwarted a potential threat but had strengthened the bonds within the community, everyone feeling a renewed sense of security and belonging.

The Harding family drove home, their spirits lifted by the display of solidarity. Though the threat remained, they knew they weren't facing it alone. Burralyndra had shown its true colours, a community that stood strong against adversity, ready to protect its own at a moment's notice.

33

The Proposition

McRae's Proposition

In the quiet lull of the afternoon, James visited the Burralyndra general store to pick up some supplies. The store was a familiar place, a hub where townsfolk gathered to share news and buy necessities. However, today's visit was interrupted by an unexpected and unwelcome presence.

As James was loading a bag of feed into his cart, he sensed someone approaching him from behind. Turning, he found himself face to face with McRae, the very man who had caused so much unrest in his life. The stranger wore a thin smile, his eyes cold and calculating.

"James Harding," McRae began, his voice smooth and unnervingly calm. "I believe it's time we had a proper conversation."

James stiffened, immediately on guard. "I have nothing to say to you," he replied curtly, trying to move past him.

McRae stepped to the side, blocking James's path. "I think you'll want to hear what I have to offer," he insisted, pulling an envelope from his coat. "It's a generous offer for your land—one that would ensure your family's comfort for generations."

James eyed the envelope but made no move to take it. "We're not selling," he stated firmly.

"The sum I'm proposing is substantial," McRae pressed on, attempting to hand the envelope to James. "More than enough to move, start anew with no financial worries. Consider it a... peace offering."

James's gaze hardened. He felt a twinge of temptation at the mention of security for his family, but his resolve quickly snuffed it out. "And what's in it for you? Why such interest in our land?"

McRae's smile faltered slightly. "Let's just say I have plans that require more... discretion than your current activities allow."

Feeling a mix of anger and defiance, James pushed the envelope back towards McRae. "Your plans don't concern me. We're not going anywhere."

McRae's eyes narrowed, the facade of cordiality slipping. "Think it over, James. It's not just about what you want. It's about what's best for your family." He left the envelope on a nearby shelf and walked out of the store, leaving James to ponder the gravity of his words.

Shaken, James picked up the envelope, tucking it into his jacket without opening it. The weight of the decision pressed heavily on him as he left the store. The offer, however tempting, was a reminder of the threat that McRae posed. It wasn't just about money; it was about their freedom and their legacy.

James' encounter with McRae at the general store lingered in his mind as he drove home, the unopened envelope burning a hole in his jacket pocket. The short drive felt longer than usual, the rolling fields of the farm blurring past as his thoughts churned with the implications of McRae's offer. The man's presence in Burralyndra had always been an ominous cloud over the Harding family, but now it cast a darker shadow than ever.

Arriving home, James found the farmhouse muted, Emma in the

garden and Lucy presumably upstairs. He decided to walk the property, needing the open space to think before bringing the matter to his family. As he wandered past the barn and through the fields, the envelope weighed heavily against his chest, each step a reminder of the decision that loomed over him.

James' thoughts were a torrent. The sum of money McRae offered was enough to solve all their financial worries, to start anew far from the troubles that plagued them here. But leaving meant giving up more than just land; it was surrendering a part of themselves, the very essence of what made them a family tied to this land through generations.

As he reached the back edge of the property, James stopped and looked out over the land that his family had tended for decades. The golden hue of the late afternoon sun bathed the fields, highlighting the undulating waves of grain. It was more than just beauty; it was a legacy, a testament to the hard work and love poured into the soil by his father, himself, and now Lucy.

With a deep sigh, James pulled the envelope from his pocket and finally tore it open. He unfolded the check and the contract; the numbers glaring back at him coldly. The figures were more than he had ever imagined seeing in his lifetime. McRae was serious, and his resources were substantial. The contract was straightforward: transfer of ownership for financial security.

James folded the documents and tucked them back into the envelope. He needed to talk this through with Emma and Lucy. This wasn't a decision he could or should make alone. As he made his way back to the house, his resolve hardened. McRae's money could buy their land but not their principles.

Entering the kitchen, he found Emma coming in from the garden, her arms full of vegetables. Her brow furrowed in concern at the sight of James's solemn face.

"What's wrong?" she asked immediately.

James didn't answer at first. He placed the envelope on the kitchen table and helped her set down the vegetables. "McRae made an offer on the farm today," he began, watching her reaction closely.

Emma's eyes widened, and she instinctively reached for the envelope, pulling out the contents. As she scanned the documents, her expression shifted from surprise to dismay. "This... this is a lot of money, James."

"It is," James acknowledged, his voice thick with unspoken tension.

"But what he's asking..." Emma looked up from the contract, her eyes searching James's. "We'd have to leave everything. Our home, our land, our history."

James nodded, feeling the weight of her words. "I know. It's not just a simple transaction. It's giving up everything we stand for. But I wanted us to decide together."

Emma took a deep breath, setting the papers down. "We need to talk with Lucy. She deserves to be part of this decision."

Just then, Lucy walked into the kitchen, sensing the serious atmosphere. "What's going on?" she asked, noticing the papers on the table.

James and Emma exchanged a glance before James explained the situation to Lucy, who listened intently, her face a mask of concentration. When he finished, Lucy's initial shock gave way to a steely resolve.

"We can't let him do this," she stated firmly. "This farm is more than just land to us. It's our family's legacy. How can we just hand it over to someone like McRae?"

James felt a surge of pride at Lucy's words, her passion echoing his own feelings. "That's exactly how your mother and I feel," he said. "But we wanted to discuss it with you before making any decisions."

The three of them sat down at the kitchen table, the contract and check lying forgotten as they talked. They discussed all their options, the pros and cons, the potential outcomes of each choice. The conversation stretched into the evening, each voicing their fears and hopes, their commitment to what the farm represented.

As night fell, a decision emerged from their lengthy discussions. They would reject McRae's offer. Together, they crafted a response to McRae, one that echoed their unity and their refusal to be intimidated or bought off.

The Return Call

James gripped the phone as he dialled McRae's number, the early morning light casting long shadows across the kitchen floor. Emma and Lucy sat at the table, watching him with a mixture of anxiety and determination etched on their faces. The decision made last night hung heavily in the air. It was time to face the consequences, no matter what they were.

The line clicked, and after a couple of rings, McRae's voice came through, smooth and expectant. "James Harding," he greeted, "I was hoping we could complete our discussions today."

James took a deep breath, steadying himself against the kitchen counter. "McRae," he started, his voice unwavering, "I'm calling to let you know that we've made our decision. The Harding farm isn't for sale at any price. We're staying put."

There was a pause on the line, and James could almost picture McRae's surprise, his calculated demeanour slipping for a moment. "I think you're making a mistake, James," McRae finally replied, his tone turning colder. "This is a very generous offer I'm making. It's more than what your land is worth, and I'm offering it in good faith."

James's grip on the phone tightened. "It's not about the money, McRae. It never was. This land is our home. It's where we belong, and no amount of money can change that. We won't be intimidated or bought off."

McRae's voice was slick as he tried a different angle. "Think about your family, James. Are you willing to put them through what's coming? I can assure you this won't end here. I have plans for this area, and your farm is in the way."

The threat was obvious, and it chilled James to the bone, but he stood his ground. "We're prepared to defend our property," James responded, a defiant edge to his tone. "You won't find us easy to push around. And you should know, the entire community stands with us. You're not just up against me, you're up against all of Burralyndra."

There was a sharp intake of breath on the other end, then a curt laugh. "Very well, Mr. Harding. But remember, I gave you a chance to walk away comfortably. You made this difficult."

"And you underestimated us," James shot back, ready to end the conversation. "Goodbye, McRae."

As he hung up the phone, James felt a surge of adrenaline mixed with a profound sense of relief. He turned to face Emma and Lucy, who had been listening intently to every word exchanged. The fear was still there, in their eyes, but so was something fiercer—pride and resolve.

"We did it," James said simply, letting out a long breath.

Emma stood, coming over to wrap her arms around him. "We did," she affirmed, her voice strong. "Whatever comes next, we face it together, as a family."

Lucy joined them, her presence reinforcing their unity. "He's going to push back, isn't he?" she asked, not quite wanting to hear the answer.

"He might," James admitted, his arm around each of the most important people in his life. "But we're ready for him. We've shown we won't be bullied or bought. We're here to stay, come what may."

Their embrace in the quiet kitchen was a silent vow, a moment of shared strength. They had faced down temptation and threats with a united front. McRae and others couldn't shake the Hardings. They stood strong with deep roots in their beloved land, backed by a respected and valued community. The fight might not be over, but they were ready—together.

34

Lucy's Secret Project

Digging The Tunnel

Lucy stood at the edge of the wheat fields, her eyes scanning the horizon as the last of the day's light faded into a soft twilight. Behind her, hidden beneath an old, disused barn, was the entrance to a tunnel—a project she had kept secret from everyone but her closest and most trusted friends. The decision to start this project was not made lightly, but Lucy saw it as a necessity, a way to ensure her family's security no matter what McRae or anyone else tried to throw at them.

The barn was old, its wood weathered and grey, but it was perfect for concealing their activities. Inside, under the floorboards, Lucy had discovered an old cellar hole that led into a natural underground passage. Her father had once mentioned that the land was riddled with mining tunnels from the gold rush days, but this one seemed forgotten, uncharted in any of their land deeds or maps.

Equipped with hard hats, headlamps, and heavy-duty gloves, Lucy and her three friends—Mia, Jon, and Eric—gathered at the barn as dusk settled. They were all locals, raised in Burralyndra, and fiercely loyal to Lucy and her family. Each understood the risks involved and the need for secrecy.

"Are we all clear on what needs to be done?" Lucy asked, her voice echoing slightly in the barn's stillness. She had laid out maps and plans on an old wooden table, detailing the extent of the tunnel and where they suspected more gold veins might be found.

Mia, who had experience in geological surveys, nodded. "We'll start by reinforcing the existing passage. There's been no maintenance, so we need to ensure it's safe before we go any deeper."

Jon, equipped with a background in construction, had brought along wooden beams and metal braces. "I'll focus on shoring up the tunnel walls and ceiling as we go. Don't want anything collapsing on us."

Eric, the tech savvy one of the group, had set up a series of wireless sensors along the tunnel to monitor for any shifts or collapses. "These will alert us to our phones if there's any movement in the tunnel structure. Safety first, always."

With their roles defined, the group began the arduous task of digging and reinforcing the tunnel. The work was gruelling, with each shovel of dirt and rock adding to their exhaustion. They worked in shifts, one group digging while the other installed supports, then rotating to manage fatigue.

Lucy often paused to wipe sweat from her brow, her muscles aching from the effort. Despite the physical toll, her resolve never wavered. Each bucket of earth removed was a step closer to securing her family's future. As they progressed, the tunnel slowly took shape, the light from their headlamps casting long shadows against the raw earth walls.

After several hours, as their shift ended, and they prepared to cover their tracks for the night, Lucy looked back at the tunnel. Pride swelling in her chest despite the fatigue that pulled at her limbs. "Successful work today, everyone," she said, her voice strong despite the weariness. "Let's keep this momentum going."

Her friends nodded, equally determined, their faces grimy but their spirits unbroken. They covered the entrance, camouflaging it with old hay and tools, then dispersed into the night, each taking a separate route home to avoid suspicion.

As Lucy made her way back to the farmhouse, the stars overhead were bright, her path lit by their distant, twinkling light. The night was peaceful, an almost stark contrast to the day's labour. But beneath that peace was a fierce determination, a silent promise to protect her family's legacy at all costs.

Enlisting The Help Of Friends

The following weeks saw Lucy and her team deepen their efforts in the tunnel. The initial phase of securing the tunnel structure had been exhausting but successful, and now they were ready to begin the actual mining process. Lucy had been researching old mining techniques and consulting with Mia about geological formations to ensure they targeted the most promising areas.

Mia had mapped out veins of quartz that were historically known to contain gold, using a combination of modern technology and old miner's knowledge. "The veins run deeper than we initially thought," she explained one evening as they prepared their equipment. "If we follow them carefully, there's a good chance we'll find what we're looking for."

Jon had crafted a makeshift cart system to help transport the removed earth and rocks out of the tunnel. "This should save us some time and backache," he said as he showed the pulley system they had rigged up. The cart clanked along the old tracks they had laid down, a sound that quickly became a regular rhythm in their nightly work.

Eric, meanwhile, continued to refine the sensor network. "I've linked the sensors to a better notification system. If anything shifts, we'll know immediately on our phones and here on this monitor," he said, pointing to a small laptop set up on a rickety table near the tunnel entrance. "Plus, I've set up a camera system. We'll have eyes inside 24/7."

Each night, after the sunset and the town of Burralyndra quieted down, they would gather in the barn and descend into the earth below. The work was hard and the progress slow, but bit by bit, they chipped away at the rock, following the promising veins Mia had identified.

Lucy often took the lead, her pick axe swinging steadily as she broke through the rock face. The sound of metal against stone echoed through the tunnel, a testament to their determination. Her friends worked alongside her, shovelling debris into the cart, reinforcing the tunnel structure, and scanning the walls for signs of gold.

Their efforts eventually paid off. One night, as Lucy struck a stubborn piece of quartz, a glint of something unmistakable caught her eye. She paused, breath held, then reached out to clear the dust. There, embedded in the rock, was a streak of gold, shining dully in the light of her headlamp.

"Hey, look at this," she called out, her voice echoing down the tunnel. Her friends crowded around, their headlamps illuminating the find.

"That's it, Lucy," Mia confirmed, a grin spreading across her face. "You found it."

The discovery reinvigorated them, pushing their fatigue aside as they realised the potential of what lay beneath their feet. Over the next several hours, they carefully extracted the gold-laden rock, their spirits lifted by the tangible results of their hard labour.

As dawn approached, they covered their tracks, hiding the entrance to the tunnel once more and leaving the barn as undisturbed as they had found it. They walked back to their cars parked a safe distance away, their bodies weary but their hearts light.

"We're really doing this," Jon said, a tone of disbelief in his voice.

"Yes, we are," Lucy affirmed, her exhaustion overshadowed by a profound sense of accomplishment. "We're going to keep this farm safe. For my family, for all of us."

With the gold safely stored and their tools cleaned and hidden away, they parted ways, each carrying with them the secret of the night's success. The work was far from over, but now more than ever, Lucy knew they could do it. They had the will, the means, and, most importantly, each other.

Processing Ore

The successful extraction of gold from the tunnel marked a turning point for Lucy and her friends. They now had tangible proof of the wealth beneath the Harding farm, but extracting the gold was only part of the challenge. The next step was to process the ore to extract the gold efficiently and safely, a task that required precision and careful planning.

In the old barn, Lucy and her friends set up a makeshift processing station. They had gained some basic ore processing equipment on the quiet market, including a small, portable smelter and chemical baths designed to separate gold from the surrounding rock and minerals.

Eric took the lead in setting up the equipment, his technical expertise crucial in ensuring everything operated correctly. "We need to be careful with the smelting process," he cautioned as he calibrated the smelter. "It's not just about melting the rock. We have to capture the gold without losing too much to slag."

Lucy watched closely, taking notes and asking questions. Her role had evolved from merely leading the project to understanding each step deeply, ensuring she could manage any part of the process if needed.

Mia handled the chemical separation using a carefully measured solution to dissolve the remaining ore. "The acid will eat away at the base metals," Mia explained, goggles perched on her forehead as she prepared the bath. "What we want should sink to the bottom, and we can collect it from there."

Jon, meanwhile, built a ventilation system to clear the fumes produced by smelting and chemical processing. "Don't need anyone getting sick from this," he muttered as he worked, his hands skilled and sure.

Night after night, they processed the ore, refining their techniques and improving their yield. After each session, they carefully cleaned up, leaving no trace of their work. The gold they collected was small in quantity but high in quality, each nugget a symbol of their hard work and secrecy.

As the weeks passed, the small pile of gold grew, stored in a locked box hidden beneath the barn's floorboards. Lucy often sat beside the box after their sessions, the cool metal of the nuggets pressing into her palm, a reminder of what they were fighting to protect.

One evening, as they cleaned up after another successful processing session, Lucy gathered her friends together. "I can't thank you enough for all this," she began, her voice thick with emotion. "We've done more than just mine gold. We've ensured the farm's safety, and maybe even its future."

Her friends smiled, clapping her on the back and exchanging tired but satisfied glances. "We're in this together," Mia said. "All the way."

Lucy nodded, her heart full. "Let's keep going," she said. "Let's make sure this farm stays in the family, no matter what."

With renewed determination, they continued their work, the barn a silent witness to their resolve. Each nugget, processed and stored, was a victory, each day's end a step closer to securing their peace. The road ahead was still uncertain, but Lucy and her friends faced it together, united by their secret project and their commitment to protecting the Harding legacy.

35

A Desperate Gamble

Pursuit

As the sun dipped below the horizon, staining the sky with streaks of orange and red, James Harding sat in his weathered pickup truck, the engine idling softly. From his vantage point near the edge of Burralyndra, he watched the black SUV that belonged to McRae pull out from the local inn's parking lot. His hands tightened around the steering wheel, a mix of determination and apprehension coursing through him as he prepared to follow.

McRae's vehicle turned onto the main road, heading towards the less populated outskirts of the town. James waited a few moments, maintaining a safe distance before easing his truck into the flow of traffic. He knew this part of the town well, each turn and landmark familiar from years of traversing these roads, yet tonight, each seemed cloaked in a new, ominous light.

The route led them away from the heart of Burralyndra, past the softly lit windows of cosy homes, and gradually into the darker, more isolated stretches where streetlights were few. James kept his eyes fixed on the taillights of McRae's SUV, the red glow a beacon in the growing dusk.

As they passed the last of the small town's shops and cafes, the road wound through denser foliage. The trees, silhouetted against the twilight sky, loomed over the road, their branches swaying gently in the evening breeze. James's grip on the steering wheel tightened as he navigated the curves, his truck's headlights cutting through the darkness.

The black SUV suddenly slowed and turned off the main road onto a narrow dirt track that was easy to miss if one wasn't looking for it. James hesitated only a moment before turning to follow. Ruts scarred the dirt track, bordered on both sides by thick underbrush and overhanging trees. It was a place forgotten by time, secluded and silent except for the sounds of wildlife settling for the night.

James reduced his speed, careful to maintain a distance that would prevent McRae from noticing him in his rear-view mirror. The track twisted and turned, the SUV's brake lights occasionally flickering through the trees as it navigated a sharp bend or dip in the road.

After several tense minutes, the SUV pulled into a small clearing; the area opening up to reveal a patch of ground surrounded by dense woods. James parked his truck a suitable distance back along the track, cutting the engine and lights. He sat for a moment, collecting his thoughts, his heart pounding in his chest.

With cautious movements, James exited the truck, closing the door gently behind him. The evening was cool, and the air carried the scent of pine and earth. He moved towards the clearing with deliberate, quiet steps, using the skills he had honed growing up in the countryside to keep his presence undetected.

As he neared the edge of the clearing, he could see McRae and another figure standing beside the SUV, engaged in what appeared to be a serious conversation. James found a spot behind a thick tree, its trunk wide enough to conceal his frame. From here, he could observe the men without being seen.

McRae was speaking animatedly, his gestures sharp and commanding. The other man, his back to James, listened intently, occasionally nodding. James strained to catch their words, the distance and a gentle wind carrying their voices away.

Frustration knotted in James's stomach as he realised he wouldn't be able to hear their conversation from this distance. However, the very fact of this meeting, secretive and remote, was enough to confirm his suspicions about McRae's intentions. Whatever was being planned, it was clear McRae was not acting alone.

After a few more minutes of watching, James decided it was time to face McRae, despite the others there and the risk that posed. James quietly retraced his steps back to the truck and drove to park next to McRae's' SUV. Taking a deep breath, James got out of his truck, his every movement deliberate.

Intense Confrontation

The air was cool and the coming dusk cast long shadows on the ground as James approached. McRae turned to face him, a sly smile playing on his lips.

"James Harding," McRae began, his voice smooth and confident. "I was wondering when you'd come for a chat."

James's voice was steady, his anger controlled. "You know why I'm here, McRae. Your plans for our land, the threats... they end now."

As the shadows lengthened and the air grew cooler in the secluded clearing, James squared his shoulders and met McRae's gaze unflinchingly. McRae's smile was thin, his eyes calculating as he assessed James's resolve.

"James, let's not mince words," McRae began, his tone casual yet laced with venom. "You think you're protecting your farm, your family's legacy. But you're actually standing in the way of progress—my progress."

James's voice was firm, his stance resolute. "This 'progress' you speak of, it destroys lives, McRae. You prey on people who are tied to their land, their homes. You won't find us so compliant."

McRae chuckled, a sound devoid of true amusement. "Compliant? No, I didn't expect that. But I do expect rationality. Let me lay it out for you." He stepped closer, and his voice dropped to a conspiratorial whisper. "Your farm sits on a gold mine, quite literally. You could profit from this, James. We could partner."

"Partner?" James scoffed. "With a man who threatens families? Who uses fear as a business tool? No, that's not partnership, that's extortion."

McRae's eyes narrowed slightly, his demeanour cooling. "You're a small-town farmer, James. What do you know about business? I'm offering you a way out before things get... unpleasant."

James felt a surge of anger at the thinly veiled threat. "And what if I refuse? What then? You'll poison our water? Burn our fields?"

"James, I'm a businessman," McRae replied smoothly. "I take necessary actions to secure my investments. If that means pushing a little harder against those who won't see reason, so be it."

"Pushing harder?" James echoed, his tone rising slightly. "Is that what you call your tactics? Because where I stand, it looks a lot like criminal activity."

McRae smiled again, but there was no warmth in it. "Call it what you will. I do what is needed. And right now, I need your land. You can make this easy, sell to me, live comfortably somewhere else without the burden of this... endless farming."

"And if I say no?" James's stance was as solid as the earth beneath his feet.

"If you say no," McRae's voice was icy, "then I suppose I'll need to convince you otherwise. Maybe I start by showing you how vulnerable you are. How exposed your precious daughter is when she's out there in the fields."

James felt a chill despite his rising anger. "You leave my daughter out of this," he warned, his voice a dangerous low growl.

"Oh, it's all fair in love and war, James," McRae taunted. "And this is a bit of both, isn't it? You love your land; I love my projects. We're at war over who gets to hold onto this piece of earth."

"I'm not at war, not yet. You go anywhere near my daughter however... War you shall have!" James replied, his voice steady despite the turmoil inside. "I'm standing my ground. This is my family's home, our livelihood. I won't let you or anyone else take that away from us."

McRae studied James for a long moment, then shrugged. "Have it your way, farmer. But remember, I offered you a peaceful solution. What comes next will be on your head."

As he turned to leave, McRae called over his shoulder, "Think about my offer, James. And watch the fields at night. You never know who might drop by."

With that, McRae walked back to his SUV and drove away, leaving a cloud of dust and a heavy silence. James stood alone in the clearing, his heart pounding, his mind racing with what had just transpired. He knew he had to prepare, to protect his family and his farm from whatever McRae planned next. The game had changed, and it was indeed desperate.

Returning to his truck, James's thoughts were on fortifications, on rallying the community, on ways to keep Lucy safe. The drive back home was grim, the weight of the impending struggle, settling around him like a cloak. He was ready to fight, but at what cost? The question lingered, unanswered as the landscape blurred past.

The Ride Home & Strategic Planning

James left the clearing with his heart pounding against his ribs like a drum. The evening had swiftly transitioned into night, and as he walked back to his truck, the surrounding shadows seemed to press in with tangible weight. He was acutely aware of every crackling leaf and whispering wind, each sound magnifying his tension.

As he started the engine, the familiar rumble of the truck was a small comfort. The road ahead was dimly lit by his headlights, winding back through the dense woods towards Burralyndra. James drove slowly, his mind replaying every moment of the confrontation with McRae. The threats against Lucy were forefront in his thoughts, chilling him with fear yet burning him with a fierce protectiveness.

Driving through the quiet streets of Burralyndra, James felt a stark disconnect between the peaceful exterior of the town and the turmoil brewing just beneath its surface. The soft glow of streetlights passed overhead, casting pools of light that flickered across his face. He knew the real dangers lay hidden in the shadows, in the intentions of men like McRae who manoeuvred in the dark corners of greed and power.

The need to protect Lucy from potential harm became a singular focus. James thought about the layout of their farm, the daily routines that might leave Lucy vulnerable, and how he could alter them to ensure her safety. He considered the practicality of modifying the comprehensive security system, more cameras to monitor the perimeter of their property, and more motion sensors near the entrances of their home and outbuildings.

But technology was only part of the solution. James knew the importance of community in rural areas like theirs—neighbours looking out for each other was often the best security system. He resolved to talk more with his neighbours, to subtly build the network of watchful eyes without causing alarm or revealing too much about their fears.

Furthermore, James contemplated emergency protocols—plans for Lucy to follow if she ever felt threatened. He thought about safe rooms, communication strategies, and even self-defence training. Each scenario played out in his mind as he navigated the familiar roads home.

Upon reaching their property, the sight of the farmhouse bathed in porch light was a beacon of safety that eased his tense shoulders slightly. But as he parked the truck and stepped out, the crisp night air reminded him of the fragility of this peace.

Inside, he found Emma waiting up for him, her expression anxious. She stood from the couch as he entered, her eyes searching his for signs of how the confrontation had gone.

"We need to talk," James said gravely, leading her into the kitchen to speak privately before involving Lucy. He shared everything—McRae's threats, his plans, and his fears for Lucy's safety.

Emma listened intently, her face growing pale with each word. When James finished, she reached out to steady herself against the back of a chair. "This is worse than we thought," she murmured, her voice shaky.

"We're going to increase security," James assured her, his voice firm with resolve. "Cameras, alarms, everything. And I'm going to reach back out to Bill and a few other folks tomorrow. We'll set up a watch system. I won't let anything happen to Lucy."

Emma nodded, her eyes reflecting the firelight. "And I'll talk to Lucy in the morning. She needs to be aware, to be careful."

They decided to tell Lucy everything the next day, to prepare her but not alarm her unduly. That night, as James lay in bed beside Emma, his mind raced with plans and contingencies. The weight of his responsibility as a father and a husband pressed heavily upon him, but alongside it was a steely determination.

Protecting his family wasn't just about securing their land or their finances—it was about safeguarding their very lives. And James Harding was prepared to do whatever it took to keep them safe. As sleep finally claimed him, his last thoughts were strategic, his resolve unwavering in the face of the darkness that threatened his family.

36

Fortifying The Farm

The Plan Unfolds

The sun poured its gentle morning light through the kitchen windows, casting long beams across the worn wooden table where the Harding family gathered. Despite the beauty of the dawn, a heavy air hung over the room, filled with the weight of impending decisions.

James cleared his throat, breaking the silence as he addressed his daughter, Lucy. His face was lined with worry, his eyes reflecting the gravity of their situation. "Lucy, we need to have a serious talk," he began, his voice low and steady. Emma reached out, her hand finding Lucy's, giving it a reassuring squeeze.

"We've had a direct confrontation with McRae," James continued, watching Lucy's reaction closely. Her brow furrowed, a flicker of concern flashing in her eyes.

"He made threats, Lucy, not just against the farm but directly aimed at you," James said, his voice tinged with a mix of anger and fear. The weight of his words hung heavily in the room.

Lucy's posture stiffened, her initial shock giving way to a rising tide of determination. "What exactly did he say?" she asked, her voice steady yet tinged with apprehension.

James recounted the confrontation, detailing McRae's every word and the chilling implications behind them. "He implied he might resort to harming you if we don't comply with his demands to take over our land," James explained grimly.

The revelation sent an icy shiver down Lucy's spine, but her response was fierce. "We can't let him intimidate us like this. What's our plan?"

Emma, ever the nurturer, tightened her grip on Lucy's hand, her other hand reaching across to touch James's arm. "We've enhanced our security, starting with building a safe room connected to the main shaft of the mine. It'll be hidden and stocked with supplies, just in case."

Lucy nodded, her mind racing through various scenarios. "And what about Bill? He's been helping us too. We need to ensure his safety as well," she added, concern for their family friend clear in her voice.

James had already considered this. "I'll talk to Bill today. I plan to make sure he's aware and prepared for any potential threats. And I'm reaching out to our local shop owners too, especially those who sell agricultural chemicals. We need to monitor any purchases that could be used against us, like poisons."

"Good thinking," Lucy agreed. "Keeping track of who buys what could give us a heads up if McRae or his people try to buy anything suspicious."

The discussion moved to emergency procedures. James outlined a comprehensive plan that included safe signals, communication strategies in case of separation, and detailed escape routes should they need to evacuate quickly.

Lucy was actively involved in the planning. She suggested realigning the state-of-the-art surveillance system. The system covered both the immediate vicinity of their home and the more remote areas of their property. "I want to catch McRae in the act," she said firmly.

Emma, while supportive, voiced her concerns about their emotional well-being through such a tense time. "We need to be careful not to let this situation consume us. For our health, we can't live in fear. We have to maintain some sense of normalcy for our own sanity," she cautioned, her eyes scanning the faces of her loved ones.

They agreed to keep their daily routines as normal as possible for the sake of appearance and to prevent McRae from seeing how deeply his threats had affected them. However, beneath the surface, they would be vigilant and prepared, ready to protect their home and each other at a moment's notice.

As the meeting drew to a close, the family felt a renewed sense of unity and purpose. They were in this together—stronger and more determined than ever. The challenges ahead were daunting, but the Hardings were no strangers to hardship. They had weathered many storms together, and this one would be no different.

Lucy stood up from the table, her eyes sweeping over the farm visible through the kitchen window. The land that had nurtured her family for generations was now under threat and so was she, but she was ready to fight for it. With the plans laid out and everyone's roles defined, she felt a powerful surge of determination.

"We're ready," she declared, her voice echoing the resolve that filled the room. "Let him come. We'll be waiting."

James and Emma exchanged a look of pride and determination, tinged with a sense of fear. Their daughter was standing tall, ready to defend her heritage. Together, they would face whatever McRae threw their way, their bonds of family and love providing the strength they needed to overcome the darkness looming on their horizon.

Constructing the Safe Room

The construction of the safe room began with the urgency and secrecy it demanded. James had enlisted the help of Hank, a trusted contractor who had worked with the Harding family for years. Under the pretence of building fire shelters, which had recently gained popularity in the area due to a series of wildfires, they started the ambitious project.

The site chosen for the safe room was strategically beneath an old barn that was seldom used. This barn was closer to the house, but isolated enough to not draw unnecessary attention. The entrance to the safe room was cleverly designed to be accessed through what would appear to be a routine cellar door under the barn.

James and Hank, along with a small crew of trusted workers, began by excavating the earth beneath the barn. They used a combination of manual digging and small machinery that wouldn't attract attention or cause too much noise. As they dug, Lucy was often there, observing and offering her input, ensuring that every aspect of the plan was executed perfectly.

The tunnel from the house to the safe room was the most critical part of the project. It had to be both discreet and easily accessible. They routed it from the basement of the farmhouse, through a hidden door behind a false cabinet. The path would then wind its way underground, emerging into the back of the safe room. This route was chosen for its directness, and because it utilised natural land inclines, minimising the need for extensive excavation.

The safe room itself was constructed with reinforced concrete walls and a steel door, designed to withstand both natural and man-made disasters. Inside, the space was divided into several areas: a small living area with fold-down beds, a storage area for food and water, and a basic but functional sanitation facility.

Lucy took the lead in stocking the safe room. She meticulously calculated the amount of food and water needed to sustain her family for at least a month. The supplies were carefully chosen for their longevity and nutritional content: canned goods, dried foods, bottled water, and some comfort foods that would help them maintain morale should they need to stay hidden for an extended period.

Fresh air and ventilation were critical, so a concealed air filtration system was installed. It was manually operated, if needed, to avoid drawing power that could be traced or cut off. Lucy also included a small, hand-cranked generator for minimal electricity needs, such as lighting and to power the air system if prolonged use became necessary.

To cover up the excavation and construction activities, James staged a series of community fire safety meetings. He openly discussed the importance of fire shelters and even offered to show his neighbours the "demo" shelters he was constructing. This initiative not only masked their activities but also positioned the Hardings as community leaders in fire safety, deflecting any possible suspicions about their real intentions.

Throughout the construction, Hank kept a close eye on the workers, ensuring that no one discussed their work outside of the farm. He understood the stakes as much as James did and was fully committed to maintaining secrecy.

As the project neared completion, Lucy took one last inspection of the safe room. She walked through the space, checking each shelf of supplies, testing the beds, and running her hand along the cold, smooth surface of the concrete walls. Everything was in place, each item carefully chosen and organised for maximum efficiency and comfort.

Outside, as the final patches of disturbed earth were smoothed over and covered with fresh sod, Lucy stood beside her father, watching Hank and his crew finish up. James put his arm around her shoulders, a silent gesture of appreciation and reassurance.

"We've done everything we can to prepare," James said quietly, his gaze scanning the landscape as dusk began to settle over the farm.

Lucy nodded, her eyes reflecting a mix of determination and a trace of lingering worry. "We're ready," she replied, her voice steady. "Whatever McRae brings, we'll face it. Together."

As Hank and his team packed up their tools and left, the Harding family stood together, watching the sun dip below the horizon. The farm was quiet, peaceful even, but beneath the tranquillity, it was now a fortress, a stronghold prepared to protect its inhabitants against any threat.

37

Emma's Discovery

A Troubling Discovery

As Emma Harding pushed open the heavy glass door of the local records office that crisp morning, a familiar chime greeted her entry. A sound that usually came with a more leisurely pace and casual intent. Today, however, her steps were quick and purposeful. The musty smell of aged paper and laminate that filled the small building was as comforting as it was foreboding, given her reason for visiting.

"Good morning, Marjorie," Emma greeted the clerk, who looked up from her desk cluttered with files and paperwork. Marjorie, with her perennial cardigan and spectacles slipping down her nose, was a staple in this little bureau.

"Morning, Emma! What can I help you with today?" Marjorie asked, her voice as warm as the room was stuffy.

Emma approached the counter, her demeanour serious. "I need to see recent filings for land use, particularly anything to do with mineral rights or mining claims."

Marjorie nodded, understanding the urgency in Emma's request without knowing the specifics. "Right away," she said, turning to the tall filing cabinets that lined the back wall of the office.

As Emma followed Marjorie through the narrow aisles between cabinets, she couldn't help but feel a twinge of anxiety. Each step seemed to echo louder than usual in the quiet space. Marjorie pulled open a drawer labelled 'Recent Land Claims' and began sifting through folders filled with paperwork.

"Here we are," Marjorie said, pulling out a thick folder stuffed with documents. "There's been a claim filed just last week that might interest you. It's quite unusual."

Emma took the folder, her hands slightly trembling as she opened it to find a series of documents stamped with official seals. The top document was a mineral rights claim, and it didn't take long for Emma to spot the name that turned her stomach: Michael McRae.

"This claim here," Emma pointed, reading more closely, "it states that the land is uninhabited? That's not possible. It's our land, our home." Her voice was a mix of confusion and rising anger.

Marjorie peered over her glasses, equally puzzled. "That's the paperwork, I'm afraid. It's filed as a Section 17 Mining Claim, which grants the claimant exclusive rights to the minerals on the land, assuming it's uninhabited and unused for agriculture. It's rare we see these claims, especially declared on land that's clearly occupied."

Emma's mind raced as she absorbed the implications. A Section 17 claim was particularly aggressive. It not only sought rights to underground minerals but also implied that the surface was unused and could be commandeered for mining operations with minimal compensation or resistance from the landowner. If McRae succeeded, it could mean they would be forcibly removed from their farm.

"But how can he claim it's uninhabited? We live there, we work there every day," Emma reiterated, her confusion turning to a deep worry.

Marjorie sighed, offering a sympathetic frown. "These claims, they go through checks, but sometimes things slip through, especially if no one contests them early on. You'll need to challenge this, Emma. Quickly."

Emma nodded, her resolve hardening. "We will challenge it," she assured Marjorie, her mind already turning to the steps she would need to take. "Is there a copy of the specific boundaries he's claiming? And any additional filings that might be related?"

Marjorie dove back into the cabinet, emerging moments later with a map and additional paperwork that detailed the geographical coordinates of the claim. It encompassed a significant portion of the Harding land, much more than Emma had feared.

Armed with the documents, Emma thanked Marjorie and hurried out of the records office. Each step back to her car was heavy with the gravity of McRae's audacity and the battle that lay ahead. The drive back home was a blur, her mind occupied with the strategy they would need to employ.

Emma understood that this was not just a legal battle; it was a fight for their home, their heritage, and their future. The documents clutched in her hand were not just papers; they were a direct threat to everything the Harding family held dear. As the records office disappeared in her rear-view mirror, Emma felt a surge of anger. This was a challenge they had not expected, but it was one she would certainly meet head-on.

The Race Against Time

As Emma sped back to the farm, her mind raced with the steps they would need to take to challenge McRae's claim. Upon arriving, she found James and Bill discussing the new security installations in the barn. She interrupted them, her voice urgent as she explained her discovery.

"We need to act now," Emma said, spreading the documents on a makeshift table made of old crates. James and Bill leaned in, listening intently as Emma outlined the situation.

James wasted no time. He picked up his phone and called their family lawyer, David Marks, a seasoned attorney who had helped navigate the Hardings through various farm-related legal issues over the years. David answered after a few rings, and James quickly briefed him on the situation.

"David, McRae has filed a claim stating our land is uninhabited and abandoned. We need to contest this immediately. What are our first steps?" James's tone was firm, underscored by the gravity of their predicament.

David's response was swift and precise. "First, you'll need to file an official objection with the state. I'll send you the objection form right away. Fill it out, stating clearly that the land is neither uninhabited nor abandoned. You'll need to provide evidence supporting your claim—photos, sales receipts, any recent contracts or documents that show active use of the land."

Emma took charge of gathering the evidence. She pulled out her digital camera and began photographing various aspects of the farm operations. She captured images of the lush wheat fields, the modern irrigation systems, and the livestock areas. Each photo served as a testament to the active and productive use of the land.

Meanwhile, James headed to the farmhouse to retrieve financial records and receipts. He collected sale receipts from recent wheat harvests, contracts with local grain distributors, and tax documents that reflected the farm's ongoing economic activities. James was glad he had kept these records going back over seven years, including all the council rates notices and water lease notices. These had been in his name for over 15 years and should show the courts a continued ownership and lad use. Each piece of paper was a crucial part of their defence, proving that the land was far from abandoned.

Emma also gathered historical records from the local farming association, which documented years of continuous agricultural use of the property. These records included past awards the Hardings had received for their sustainable farming practices and contributions to local agrimarkets.

Back in the barn, the trio sat down with the objection form David had emailed. The form required them to describe the nature of their objection and provide a detailed account of their land's usage.

James filled in the form, his handwriting steady despite the turmoil within. He described the various crops grown on the farm, the active and ongoing maintenance of the land, and permanent structures and machinery that were critical to their farming operations. He attached the photos Emma had taken and prepared a packet that included the financial and historical documents they had gathered.

With the form completed and their evidence packet in order, the Hardings gathered around the old kitchen table to discuss their next move. David had advised them to deliver the documents in person to ensure they were received and processed without delay.

"I'll take these to the records office first thing tomorrow," James declared, organising the documents into a neat folder. "Bill, could you come with me? Your testimony as a long-time friend and neighbour could be very influential."

Bill nodded, a resolute look crossing his features. "Of course, James. I'll do whatever it takes to help you keep the farm."

Emma, meanwhile, planned to reach out to the local community. "I'll start calling our neighbours and other local farmers," she said. "If we can get them to support our claim, perhaps with letters vouching for the farm's activity, it might strengthen our case."

As they sat there, surrounded by years of memories and the tangible evidence of their hard work, the Hardings felt a collective sense of resolve. The task ahead was daunting, and the opponent they faced was formidable, but they were grounded by their deep connection to the land and each other.

James looked at Emma and Lucy, his eyes conveying a silent message of gratitude and determination. Together, they had built a life here, nurturing the soil and tending to their crops. The farm was more than just a piece of land; it was a member of the family, and they would protect it at all costs.

As the sun set outside, casting long shadows across the fields they loved so dearly, the Hardings prepared for the legal battle ahead. With their documents ready and their community behind them, they were not just defending their property; they were standing up for their heritage, their livelihood, and their future.

38

Unwanted Attention

The Courtroom Contest

The day was tinged with a crisp autumn chill as the residents of Burralyndra filed into the small, somewhat worn-down courthouse. This was a place usually quiet, reserved for minor legal disputes and routine bureaucratic tasks, not the scene of intense community drama. Today, however, it was the epicentre of a significant legal battle involving the Harding family and Michael McRae. A man whose recent actions had sent shock waves through the small farming community.

As Emma, James, and Lucy Harding took their seats near the front, they could feel the weight of the townspeople's stares—some sympathetic, others merely curious. The wooden pews creaked under the shifting weight of the crowd. James's hands were clenched in his lap, his jaw set firm in a mask of determination and controlled anger.

Across the aisle, Michael McRae sat surrounded by a group of slick-looking associates, likely lawyers and financial backers from the city. They whispered amongst themselves, casting occasional, confident glances around the room. McRae's posture was relaxed, an irritating smirk playing at the corner of his mouth as he occasionally nodded in greeting to acquaintances in the crowd.

The sharp rap of the judge's gavel called the room to order. Judge Helen Baxter, a woman known for her no-nonsense approach to the law and a deep commitment to justice, surveyed the courtroom with a stern gaze. "This court is now in session. We are here to discuss the matter of the land claim dispute brought by Mr. Michael McRae against the Harding family," she announced, her voice echoing off the high, panelled walls of the courtroom.

David Marks, the Harding family's lawyer, rose first, adjusting his glasses as he prepared to present his case. "Your Honour, ladies and gentlemen of the court, we are here today to contest an egregious and wholly unfounded claim made by Mr. McRae on land that has been owned and diligently farmed by the Harding family for generations."

David proceeded to lay out the facts. He presented deeds and land records dating back over a hundred years, demonstrating the Harding family's long-standing ownership and active use of the land. Photographs of the sprawling wheat fields, the modern irrigation systems, and the well-maintained farm equipment were displayed on a projector, each image a testament to the Hardings' stewardship of their land.

"Furthermore," David continued, his voice gaining intensity, "Mr. McRae's claim that the land is uninhabited and unused is not only false—it is a deliberate attempt to mislead and manipulate the legal system for his own gain. Here are sales receipts, agricultural reports, and tax documents proving the land's ongoing productivity and habitation."

The courtroom was silent, the gravity of the evidence weighing heavily in the air. David then turned to witness testimonies, calling forward several local farmers and business associates who attested to the Hardings' active role in the community and their continuous work on the farm.

When it was McRae's turn to defend his claim, his lawyer, a smooth-talking city attorney, argued that the land was not being utilised to its "full economic potential" and that McRae's proposed mining operations would bring jobs and increased revenue to the community. McRae himself took the stand, speaking of the economic benefits, his tone rehearsed and persuasive.

However, the community's support for the Hardings was palpable. Whispers of dissent rippled through the courtroom as McRae spoke, his words doing little to sway the public opinion.

After both sides had presented, Judge Baxter took a moment to review the notes she had made during the proceedings. The tension in the room was thick as everyone awaited her decision. Finally, she looked up from her papers, her expression unreadable.

"Having reviewed the evidence and testimonies presented here today, it is clear to the court that the land in question has been and continues to be inhabited and actively used by the Harding family," she declared, her voice firm and authoritative. "Mr. McRae's claim is therefore dismissed."

A wave of relief washed over the Harding family, their hands clasping each other tightly. Around them, the courtroom erupted into subdued cheers and claps from the community members who had come out in support. McRae's face turned an angry shade of red, and he muttered something under his breath to his attorney, his composure finally cracking.

As the Hardings left the courtroom, their steps were light, buoyed by the victory. They exchanged smiles and heartfelt thanks with their neighbours and friends who congratulated them on their win. The fight had been hard-won, but justice had prevailed, reinforcing the community's faith in the legal system and in each other.

Unravelling McRae's Schemes

Following the courtroom victory, Emma Harding's sense of justice was galvanised, but she knew that their fight might not be over. Driven by a mixture of relief and lingering concern, she decided to dig deeper into Michael McRae's activities around Burralyndra. Her determination led to a broader investigation that would soon impact the entire community.

After the trial, while the rest of the family celebrated, Emma returned to her home office, a small, well-organised space where she kept detailed records of all their farm activities. She sat down at her computer and began to search for any other land claims McRae had made in the region. Her research uncovered a disturbing pattern: McRae had filed multiple dubious claims on lands that were clearly occupied and being actively used, much like their own.

Realising the potential impact of this discovery, Emma reached out to other landowners she suspected might be affected. She spent hours on the phone, explaining her findings and encouraging her neighbours to check their land status. Many were unaware of the claims McRae had placed against their properties. The sense of betrayal and outrage grew as more people became aware of the situation.

Emma organised a meeting at the local community centre, inviting all affected landowners and other members of the community. The meeting room was packed, the air thick with tension and concern as Emma presented her findings.

"Michael McRae has been claiming our lands as uninhabited and underutilised," Emma revealed, pointing to a map pinned on the wall behind her that highlighted all the claims McRae had made. "These are not just pieces of land; they are our homes, our livelihoods. We need to stand together to challenge these claims, just as we did for our farm."

The response was a unified resolve to fight back. The group discussed their options, and a good deal of expressed gratitude to Emma for her leadership and diligence. The meeting ended with a commitment from several landowners to challenge the claims legally, each agreeing to share the cost of hiring legal representation.

Over the next few weeks, the community's efforts began to take shape. Emma worked closely with David Marks, who agreed to represent the group of landowners. They prepared a series of legal challenges, systematically contesting each of McRae's claims with evidence similar to what the Hardings had collected: photos, financial records, and personal testimonies.

As the cases went to court, McRae's pattern of deceit became evident to the judges, and one by one, his claims were dismissed. The courtroom losses piled up, severely damaging McRae's credibility and his financial standing, as he had invested heavily in potential mining operations he expected to launch.

During one particularly tense court session, as yet another of his claims was dismissed, McRae's frustration boiled over. He stood abruptly, his chair clattering to the floor, and shouted accusations at the judge and the landowners, claiming he was the victim of a conspiracy to deny the community economic growth. His outburst led to him being escorted from the courtroom by security, a moment that symbolised his complete downfall in the eyes of Burralyndra's residence.

The legal victories had a ripple effect throughout Burralyndra, strengthening community bonds and reinforcing a collective commitment to vigilance against such predatory practices. Emma became a respected figure in the town, her efforts not only saving her family's farm but also protecting many others in the area from McRae's greed.

The experience transformed the community, making it clear that unity and mutual support were essential for their survival and prosperity. People who had once felt isolated in their struggles now knew they had neighbours who would stand with them, a powerful realisation that changed the social fabric of Burralyndra.

In the wake of these victories, Emma felt a deep sense of accomplishment and relief. Her actions had not only safeguarded her family's legacy, but had also ignited a spirit of activism and cooperation in Burralyndra that would endure for years to come. As she prepared to leave the courthouse after the final dismissed claim, Emma looked around at the faces of her neighbours and friends, knowing they had all come through this challenge stronger and more united than ever.

A Community Celebration

The Burralyndra Pub, usually a quiet locale for the town's modest population, was alive with an unprecedented buzz of activity. It was the chosen venue for the celebration after the series of courtroom victories against Michael McRae's spurious claims. The interior of the pub, with its wooden beams and rustic McRae's, glowed warmly under the light of hanging lanterns, providing a cosy backdrop to the night's festivities.

The townspeople gathered in clusters, their faces animated with laughter and relief. There was Bill Turner, his weathered face split by a grin as he recounted tales of past community triumphs to a captivated audience. Near the fireplace, Marjorie, the clerk who first helped Emma uncover the dubious claims, sipped her cider quietly, her eyes twinkling with satisfaction at the outcome.

Behind the bar, Tom, the pub owner, was busier than ever. He poured pints with a steady hand and exchanged jokes with his regulars, pleased by the turnout and the boost in business. Every so often, he glanced over at Emma Harding, who was the unofficial guest of honour for the evening, and raised his glass in a silent toast of gratitude.

Emma, feeling both exhilarated and exhausted from the day's events, moved through the pub, greeting her neighbours. Her efforts had not only saved her family's farm but had also galvanised the community to protect their rights and land. The respect she received from her fellow townspeople was palpable; many approached her to shake hands or offer a warm embrace.

Daniel, who had been by Emma's side throughout the legal battles, watched her with admiration from across the room. He had been instrumental in helping gather much of the evidence needed for the court cases, his background in local history and research proving invaluable. The bond that had formed between them, built on shared goals and mutual respect, was deepening into something more profound. Emma was glad that Lucy and Daniel had maintained a close friendship. She was sure that without the help provided by Lucy and Daniel, she wouldn't have been able to finish what she had started.

As Emma made her way toward Daniel, the chatter seemed to fade. He greeted her with a smile that spoke volumes, and they found a quiet spot near the old jukebox, which played a soft melody that added to the evening's nostalgia.

"Quite the turnout, isn't it?" Daniel remarked, gesturing around the room.

Emma laughed softly, her eyes scanning the faces of those who had come to celebrate. "It's incredible. I had no idea what we started would end up here. It feels like we've not just won a legal battle but revived the heart of this community."

Around them, other stories unfolded. There was young Lucy, Emma's vibrant daughter, who was eagerly discussing future projects with some of her friends from the university. They planned to start a community garden project that would use sustainable farming practices, inspired by the struggle to maintain their agricultural heritage. This community garden project would also count towards their studies, which motivated them even more. Daniel, of course, would be involved in any project of Lucy's. All she had to do was flash one of those smiles and he would do just about anything.

Nearby, old Mr. Jacobs, the town historian, regaled a group of newcomers with stories of Burralyndra's founding days. His tales were a mix of fact and embellished folklore, but tonight, no one seemed to mind the extra flair.

In another corner, Sarah and Mike Johnson, owners of the neighbouring farm, shared their plans to implement some of the security measures that the Hardings had introduced during their fight. Their farm had also been targeted by McRae, and they felt a renewed sense of security knowing the community stood with them.

Quiet Conversations

In the lively atmosphere of the Burralyndra Pub, where the townspeople gathered to revel in their collective victory, a quieter, more intimate dialogue unfolded in a cosy booth tucked away in a quieter corner of the pub. Here, Lucy Harding and Daniel Thompson sat together, their conversation a stark contrast to the boisterous celebrations echoing around them.

Lucy, with her youthful enthusiasm tempered slightly by the seriousness of recent events, turned to Daniel with a grateful smile. "I really can't thank you enough for all the help you've given us, especially helping Mum through all the research and legal stuff. It's been incredible having you with us during all this."

Daniel, whose admiration for Lucy had deepened through their collaboration, returned her smile. "It was my pleasure, Lucy. Honestly, seeing your family fight with such determination—it's inspiring. And working closely with your mum, getting to know all of you better, it's been one of the highlights of my year."

The pub buzzed with laughter and music, yet within their little sanctuary, a palpable warmth grew. Lucy sipped her drink, her gaze thoughtful. "It's funny, isn't it? How tough times bring people together. I feel like I've gotten to know you so much better these past few months."

Daniel nodded, his expression earnest. "Me too. I've always known you were incredible, Lucy, but seeing you in action, standing up for your family's legacy—it's made me see you in a new light."

Lucy blushed slightly at the compliment, then grew more serious. "You know, Daniel, it's not just about understanding each other better. It's about seeing potential for the future, too." She paused, gauging his reaction as she ventured further. "And, well, it's great that you get along with my parents so well. You know, in case... we ever decided to get more serious."

Daniel's heart quickened at her words, sensing the shift in their relationship dynamic. "I've thought about that too," he admitted. "I care about you a lot, Lucy. And being accepted by your family means everything to me, especially considering how close you all are."

Lucy leaned forward, her voice dropping to a whisper as if to share a secret. "I think they like you more than you know. Dad respects how much you've helped us, and Mum thinks you're wonderful. And I... I'm really glad you're in my life, Daniel."

Their conversation drifted to their shared experiences over the past weeks. They reminisced about the late nights spent poring over land records and legal documents, the tense moments waiting in courtrooms, and the relief and joy of each victory. With each memory, the bond between them seemed to grow stronger, their mutual respect and affection deepening.

As the evening wore on, the topic of conversation shifted towards the future. Lucy, inspired by their recent struggles and triumphs, shared her dreams of what lay ahead. "I've been thinking about what else we can do with the farm. There's so much potential, not just for agriculture but as a centre for the community, maybe even an educational resource.”

Daniel listened intently, impressed by her vision. “That sounds amazing, Lucy. And I want to help make that happen. Whatever you need, I’m here. We can work on it together, build something lasting.”

Lucy’s eyes lit up with excitement. “Really? You’d want to be a part of this? Not just as… well, not just as my boyfriend, but as a partner in this venture?”

“Yes, absolutely,” Daniel affirmed, his commitment clear. “I believe in this, in us. And who knows? If things go well, this farm isn’t just where we work, it could be where we build our future, where we raise a family.”

The idea of their shared future, intertwined with the fate of the Harding farm, filled them both with a profound sense of purpose and hope. They discussed ideas for sustainable practices, community engagement, and ways to innovate traditional farming operations.

As the night drew to a close, Daniel reached across the table, taking Lucy’s hands in his. “Lucy, whatever comes next, I’m in this with you. For the long haul. Here’s to future victories, to us, and to Harding farm.”

Lucy squeezed his hands, her heart full. “To us,” she echoed, her voice steady with resolve and promise.

In the soft glow of the pub’s lantern light, they sat together, planning, dreaming, a young couple on the brink of a new chapter in their lives. The challenges they had faced had only strengthened their resolve to stand together, to build a life not just alongside each other but with one another, deeply entwined with the land they both had come to love.

39

The Final Warning

An Ominous Warning

The night had been one of revelry and community spirit at the Burra-lyndra Pub. As the celebrations wound down, the atmosphere shifted subtly from warmth to a chill that had little to do with the autumn air. Lucy and Daniel, still buoyed by the camaraderie and support of their neighbours, lingered outside the pub, reluctant to end the evening.

Lucy leaned against Daniel's car, her breath visible in the crisp night air. Daniel stood close, his presence reassuring. He brushed a stray lock of hair from her face, his touch gentle, sparking a warmth that contrasted with the evening's chill.

"Tonight was amazing, wasn't it?" Lucy mused, her voice tinged with fatigue but filled with satisfaction. "It feels like we really turned a corner with the whole McRae situation."

Daniel nodded, his hand resting lightly on her shoulder. "It was incredible. Seeing everyone come together like that it makes you realise how strong this community really is. And how strong you are," he added, his tone admiring.

Lucy smiled, feeling a flush of pleasure at his words. "We're all stronger together," she replied. "And I couldn't have done any of this without you."

They shared a quiet moment, the distant sounds of laughter and music from inside the pub reaching them like echoes of the night's joy. It was Daniel who broke the silence, his voice a soft rumble in the cool air. "Let's head home, Lucy. It's been a long day, and you look like you could use some rest."

Lucy agreed, pushing herself off from the car. They rounded the vehicle to the driver's side, their steps slow, neither eager to end the night. That's when they saw it—a piece of paper roughly taped to the windshield.

Frowning, Lucy reached out and peeled the tape back, her fingers trembling slightly as she unfolded the note. The message was crudely scrawled, its letters jagged and uneven: "Watch your backs. This isn't over."

The warmth of the night evaporated as if doused by cold water. Lucy felt a knot form in her stomach, and she handed the note to Daniel, her hands shaking. "What is this?" she asked, her voice barely above a whisper.

Daniel's eyes scanned the message, and his jaw tightened. He wrapped an arm around her shoulders, pulling her close. "It's a threat, Lucy. Someone isn't happy about how things turned out tonight."

Lucy leaned into his embrace, seeking comfort in his proximity. "But who? McRae? One of his associates?"

"It's hard to say," Daniel replied, his gaze scanning the parking lot as if the perpetrator might still be lurking nearby. "But we're going to take this seriously. Let's get you home, and we'll start figuring out what to do about this."

They climbed into the car, the note lying between them on the console, a stark reminder of the night's sudden turn. As Daniel drove, his hand found Lucy's, squeezing it reassuringly. The drive was quiet, each lost in their thoughts about what the threat might mean for their future.

Back at the Harding farm, they found Emma and James in the living room, discussing the evening's successes. The mood was light until Lucy showed them the note. Emma's face blanched, and James's expression turned grim.

"We need to report this to the police first thing tomorrow," James said, his voice firm. "And maybe it's time to consider more security around here."

Emma nodded in agreement, her eyes worried as she looked at Lucy. "Are you okay, sweetheart?"

Lucy tried to muster a reassuring smile. "I will be. It's just a bit shocking, that's all. Daniel's going to stay over tonight, just in case."

James approved, nodding at Daniel, grateful for his presence and the comfort he clearly provided for Lucy. "Good. And tomorrow, we'll figure out our next steps. For tonight, let's try to get some rest and not let this... this cowardly act spoil what was otherwise a wonderful night."

The family agreed, dispersing to their respective rooms, but sleep was slow to come for all of them, especially Lucy. She lay in her bed, Daniel beside her, his presence a solid reassurance. He held her close, his hand stroking her arm in a soothing rhythm, his quiet breathing a counterpoint to the racing of her own heart.

"Lucy," Daniel whispered into the darkness, his voice low and serious. "Whatever happens, I'm here. We'll face this together, okay?"

Lucy turned to face him, finding comfort in his resolve. "Together," she echoed, her voice steady despite the turmoil inside. The promise of his support helped ease her into a restless sleep, the note's ominous message a shadow at the edge of her dreams.

Reporting to the Authorities

The morning after the chilling discovery of the threatening note, the Hardings, accompanied by Daniel, made their way to the local police office. The building, a modest structure in the heart of Burralyndra, was quiet in the early hours, the only sounds the occasional shuffle of papers and the distant murmur of morning radio chatter.

Sargent Walters, a stout man with decades of experience, greeted them with a mixture of concern and professionalism as they presented the note. He studied the jagged handwriting carefully, his brow furrowed in concentration.

"Have you had any recent conflicts or disputes that might lead to this kind of threat?" Sargent Walters asked, his pen poised above his notepad.

James spoke up, recounting the recent legal battle with Michael McRae over the false land claims. "We can't be sure it's him behind this note," he explained, "but given the timing and the context, it's a strong possibility."

The Sargent nodded, understanding the gravity of the situation. "While we can't prove it was McRae without further evidence, taking precautions is wise. I'll file a report and start an investigation. We'll also increase patrols around your farm."

Lucy, feeling a mix of relief and lingering anxiety, thanked the Sargent. "What about a restraining order?" she inquired. "Is that possible to keep McRae away from the farm and from me?"

"It's definitely an option," the officer replied. "You'll need to file a petition at the courthouse. Given the circumstances, the judge might well grant it as a precautionary measure."

The conversation turned to the specifics of obtaining the restraining order. Sargent Walters provided them with the necessary forms and detailed the process. He expressed his commitment to ensuring their safety, promising that the threat would be taken seriously.

After leaving the police station, the family felt a cautious sense of security. The legal system's wheels were in motion, providing a protective barrier they hoped would deter any further intimidation.

At the courthouse, Lucy, supported by her family and Daniel, filled out the petition for a restraining order. The document required them to detail the threat, provide any evidence of harassment, and explain why they felt endangered.

Lucy described the note, the recent victory in court against McRae, and her genuine fear of her safety. Daniel provided his statement as well, corroborating Lucy's concerns and emphasising the tension and hostility displayed by McRae during the court proceedings.

The clerk accepted their petition and scheduled a hearing. The judge, aware of the Hardings' recent legal confrontations, agreed to expedite the process given the potential risk to their safety.

In the courtroom, the family presented their case. Lucy spoke eloquently about her fear, the previous attack, the confrontation in the lane, and the impact the threat had on her sense of security. James and Emma testified about the history of disputes with McRae, painting a picture of a man willing to go to great lengths to achieve his ends.

The judge listened attentively, nodding along with their testimonies. After a brief deliberation, he granted the temporary restraining order against Michael McRae, citing the "clear and present threat to the petitioners' safety."

Relieved, Lucy and her family left the courthouse feeling a weight lift from their shoulders, though they knew this was perhaps only a temporary reprieve. Still, the legal system's recognition of the danger they faced reinforced their resolve to protect their home and each other.

Back at the Harding farm, the family discussed the new living arrangements. With the restraining order in place, they felt more secure, but the presence of Daniel at the farm added another layer of safety—and comfort.

James and Emma gave their blessing for Daniel to stay at the farm. They trusted him and appreciated his dedication to Lucy and her safety. "We're happy to have you here, Daniel," James said warmly. "Not just as a protector, but as part of our family."

Daniel was touched by their acceptance and reiterated his commitment to Lucy and her family. "Thank you, James, Emma. I care deeply for Lucy, and I'll do everything I can to keep her, and all of you, safe," he assured them.

That evening, as the sun set over the fields, Lucy and Daniel took a walk around the farm, discussing their plans for the future. They talked about sustainable farming techniques they hoped to implement and community outreach programs they wanted to start.

Lucy leaned into Daniel, her head resting on his shoulder as they walked. "I'm glad you're here," she whispered. "With you, I feel like we can handle anything."

Daniel squeezed her hand, his heart full. "I'm not going anywhere, Lucy. We'll face whatever comes together."

Their steps matched in rhythm, a physical manifestation of their growing bond. As they walked, they envisioned a future where the farm not only survived but thrived—a future they would build together, fortified by love and a shared commitment to safeguarding their piece of Burralyndra.

40

Jame's Battle

Tragedy Unfolds

As the Harding family returned home from their neighbour's dinner that night, James suddenly clutched his chest in intense pain and stumbled. Against the backdrop of a clear, starry sky, the sudden transition from joy to distress was striking. Rushing to James's aid, Lucy and Daniel gently helped him sit on the low farmhouse fence; his breathing was heavy and painful.

Emma, who had been following behind with some of the evening's leftovers, dropped everything when she saw her husband's condition. Her face blanched with fear as she rushed to his side. "James, oh no, please hold on," she murmured, her voice thick with panic, her hands trembling as she touched his face, trying to comfort him.

Lucy quickly pulled out her phone to dial emergency services. The operator responded promptly, asking for symptoms and their location. Lucy described her father's condition with as much clarity as she could muster—his chest pain, the radiating discomfort, his shortness of breath—and the operator confirmed that a medical helicopter would be dispatched immediately. It would take about 35 minutes to reach them, as it was already airborne nearby on a training exercise. Along with this, they would send the local volunteer ambulance.

As they awaited help, the paramedics on the line instructed Lucy to keep her father calm and still, asking if they had aspirin available— a standard preliminary treatment for suspected heart attacks. Lucy found some in their first aid kit, and carefully, she helped her father chew and swallow the pill, which could help prevent further blood clotting.

When the helicopter arrived, the whirl of the blades seemed to cut through the tense silence of the night. The paramedics, with practised speed and efficiency, came equipped with a portable ECG machine and a medical bag. They quickly assessed James's condition, confirming the signs of a myocardial infarction. They administered oxygen to help ease his breathing and provided nitroglycerine to help widen his blood vessels, alleviating some of the strain on his heart.

Emma watched, her hands clasped tightly together, her eyes wide with fear as she observed the paramedics' every move. One of them, noticing her distress, reassured her, "We're doing everything we can right now. The best place for him will be the hospital where they can provide comprehensive care."

They prepared James for immediate evacuation, securing him on a stretcher. Lucy, trying to remain composed, explained to her mother that she would follow by car. Emma, barely able to nod her understanding, stayed by James's side until the moment they had to load him into the helicopter. "I love you, James. You fight through this," she whispered, her voice breaking as she kissed his forehead, a tear trailing down her cheek.

As the helicopter took off, its lights fading into the distance towards Perth, Lucy and Daniel quickly gathered some overnight bags. Despite her own swirling fears, Lucy took a moment to embrace her mother.

"He's strong, Mum. He'll get through this," she assured her, though her own heart was heavy with worry.

The drive to Perth was quiet, each lost in their own thoughts—Lucy fretting over her father's health and the responsibilities now weighing squarely on her shoulders, Daniel worried for the entire Harding family and particularly for Lucy, and Emma tormented by the sudden threat to her husband's life and the implications for their future.

Urgent Care

After the tense drive to Perth, Lucy, Emma, and Daniel arrived at Perth Royal Hospital, their hearts heavy with concern. The bustling atmosphere of the hospital was a stark contrast to the quiet anxiety that enveloped the Harding family. They were quickly ushered into the cardiology unit where James had been taken directly for immediate care.

Upon arrival, the family was met by Dr. Helen Saunders, the lead cardiologist, who was overseeing James's case. Dr. Saunders explained the situation with a calm and reassuring professionalism. "Mr. Harding is in a critical but stable condition," she began, guiding them to a private consultation room away from the bustling corridors. "The tests we've conducted confirm that he has suffered a significant myocardial infarction. There are two main blockages in his coronary arteries that are restricting blood flow to his heart."

Emma listened, grasping Lucy's hand tightly, her other hand pressed to her mouth in worry. Lucy, ever the one to seek details, asked, "What are the next steps, Doctor?"

"We need to perform coronary artery bypass surgery as soon as possible," Dr. Saunders replied. "It's a procedure where we'll create new pathways around the blocked arteries to restore blood flow to the heart. This should significantly reduce the risk of another heart attack and improve his overall heart function."

Daniel, trying to take in the technical explanation amidst his concern, asked, "How serious is the surgery?"

"It's major surgery, but it's also a routine procedure for us," Dr. Saunders reassured. "We have an excellent team here, and Mr. Harding is in good hands. We'll do everything we can to ensure the best outcome."

The discussion moved to the specifics of the surgery and the recovery process, which included a stay in the intensive care unit followed by several days in the hospital for initial recovery. The doctor also outlined the rehabilitation process, which would involve lifestyle changes and regular cardiac therapy sessions.

After their meeting with Dr. Saunders, the family was allowed to visit James briefly in the ICU, where he was being prepped for surgery. Tubes and monitors connected him to the various machines that beeped rhythmically, echoing through the sterile room. James, though pale and clearly tired, managed a weak smile when he saw his family.

"Hey there," he murmured, his voice soft and hoarse.

Emma leaned over, gently squeezing his hand. "We're all here, James. You just focus on getting better."

James's eyes filled with a mix of gratitude and fear as he looked at his family. "I will. You're stuck with me a bit longer," he joked weakly, trying to lighten the mood despite the gravity of the situation.

Lucy and Daniel stood by, offering smiles of encouragement. After a few moments, a nurse gently ushered them out, as they needed to prepare James further for the early morning surgery.

The night was long and sleepless for Lucy, Emma, and Daniel as they waited in the family lounge. Hospital nights were always peculiar. Time seemed to stretch and compress in odd ways. They spoke little, each lost in their thoughts, their silent vigil punctuated only by the occasional updates from the nursing staff.

As dawn approached, the doctors had James stable enough for surgery. As the surgical team arrived and began the final preparations for the procedure. Dr. Saunders met briefly with the family again to reassure them that everything was ready. "We're about to start," she informed them. "I'll update you as soon as the surgery is completed."

With heavy hearts, they watched as James was wheeled away to the operating room, his life quite literally in the hands of the surgeons. Emma, steadfast in her faith, whispered a prayer, her words a soft echo in the sterile hospital corridor. Lucy stood close, her resolve fortified by the need to be strong for her father, while Daniel provided silent support, his presence a comfort to both women in his life.

As they returned to the waiting area, the first rays of sunlight filtered through the windows. Casting a new light on what they hoped was the path to recovery for James. The wait during the surgery was agonising, each minute stretching endlessly. But this family, forged in the hardships of farm life and recently tested by threats and crises, was no stranger to facing challenges together. Now, more than ever, they clung to the hope that the dawn would bring good news.

Recovery

The surgery had been a success, and the relief that washed over Lucy, Emma, and Daniel was palpable when Dr. Saunders approached them with a smile in the waiting area. "The bypass went very well," she announced, her voice reassuring. "We were able to bypass the blockages in James's arteries effectively, which should improve blood flow to his heart and overall heart function."

The family listened intently as Dr. Saunders detailed the next steps. "We will move James to the ICU for close monitoring over the next 24 hours, and if everything goes as planned, we'll transfer him to a regular cardiac recovery ward. He's not out of the woods yet, but the hardest part is over."

"What comes next?" Lucy asked, her mind already racing ahead to the recovery phase.

"Rehabilitation," Dr. Saunders explained. "James will need to take part in a cardiac rehabilitation program, which includes physical therapy, lifestyle education, and counselling. It's crucial for his recovery and for preventing potential complications. We have an excellent team here who will guide him through the process."

Emma nodded, absorbing the information with a mixture of gratitude and concern. "And his work? James is very active on our farm."

Dr. Saunders gave a gentle, understanding smile. "He'll need to limit his physical activities, especially in the first few months. As his strength and stamina increase, he can gradually handle more, but strenuous activities should be avoided for at least six months. It's important that he focuses on his health above all else."

The conversation was sobering, a stark reminder of how life on Harding Farm would need to change. As they discussed the practicalities of James's recovery, Daniel looked for the right moment to speak with James alone, knowing that they needed to address the future of the farm and its management.

Later that day, when James was settled in his recovery room, looking much more himself though still visibly tired, Daniel found his moment. He approached James's bedside while Lucy and Emma stepped out to speak with the rehabilitation coordinator.

"James," Daniel began, his tone respectful and sincere, "I just wanted to say... I know the farm is a huge part of your life, and I promise to help look after it while you recover. But I want you to know Lucy will be running things. She's more than capable, and I'll be supporting her."

James looked up at Daniel, a mix of emotions crossing his weary features. After a moment, he nodded slowly, a gesture of acceptance and trust. "I know, Daniel. I've seen how she handles everything—how you both handle everything. I can't think of anyone better to take the reins."

"It means a lot to hear you say that," Daniel replied, relief evident in his expression. "And don't worry, we'll make sure everything runs smoothly. Plus, this might give you a chance to boss us around from a comfortable chair for a change."

James chuckled, the sound raspy but genuine. "I might take you up on that. Just make sure you keep an eye on the new irrigation system, and don't let Lucy work too hard."

"I will," Daniel assured him. "And Lucy... she's got a good head on her shoulders. We'll handle it together."

As Emma and Lucy returned, the conversation shifted towards James's upcoming discharge and the details of his home care. The family felt a collective sense of duty to support James, each in their own way, ready to adapt to their new roles with determination and love.

The days that followed were a blend of challenges and milestones as James began his rehabilitation program. Emma stayed at the hospital with James, and the others returned home. Lucy called daily to report on how things were going and to check up and ensure her dad's health was stable at least. Their bonds strengthened by the shared experience. Each small progress James made was celebrated, each setback met with renewed resolve. The Harding family, resilient and united, faced the future with optimism, knowing they could rely on each other no matter what lay ahead.

41

Lucy's Strength

Descending Together

The morning air was crisp and carried the faint scent of eucalyptus as Lucy and Daniel prepared for another descent into the small underground mine that had become the centre of their latest project together. The sun was just peering over the horizon, casting a golden glow that illuminated the dew-drenched fields surrounding them. They met by the shed where the mining gear was stored, their breath visible in the cool air.

"Morning," Lucy greeted with a smile, pulling her hair back into a tight ponytail as she approached Daniel, who was already checking the equipment they would need underground.

"Morning," Daniel replied, returning her smile. He handed her a headlamp. "All charged up. I checked the batteries last night."

"Thanks," Lucy said as she secured the headlamp around her forehead. She began inspecting the harnesses and ropes, ensuring everything was in order for their descent. "I think we should focus on the northern vein today. The samples we took last time were promising, and it might widen out further along."

Daniel nodded, his eyes following her hands as she expertly checked their gear. "Sounds good. I've brought the new ultrasonic drill. It should give us a cleaner cut and better samples without too much disturbance."

Lucy looked up, interest piqued. "Perfect. I'm eager to see it in action. Last week's manual samples were a bit too fragmented."

With their gear checked and backpacks loaded with water, protein bars, and sample bags, they walked together toward the mine entrance. The path was now familiar, a narrow trail bordered by wild grass that whispered softly as they passed. The entrance of the mine, a reinforced tunnel that sloped into the darkness, awaited them, its mouth agape like the entry to another world.

Lucy paused at the entrance, turning to Daniel. "Remember, keep close and watch your step on the third section of the descent. The new supports are holding up well, but I want to double-check them as we go down."

Daniel appreciated her thoroughness, nodding in agreement. "Will do. Lead the way."

Clicking on their headlamps, they watched as the world around them faded into darkness. The narrow beam of light from their lamps cut through the black, illuminating their path as they started their descent. With each step, the air grew cooler, and the silence of the underground wrapped around them. The only sounds that broke the stillness were their steady footsteps and the occasional drip of water, echoing through the tunnel.

Once they reached the section Lucy had mentioned, she inspected the supports. They were new, installed after they had noticed some slight shifting in the tunnel walls the previous month. Daniel watched her as she methodically checked each beam and bolt, her focus absolute.

"All good," Lucy finally announced, dusting her hands off on her pants. "Let's keep going. We're close to the northern vein."

As they resumed their trek, Lucy shared her thoughts on the geological formations they were encountering. "This part of the mine cuts through the early Jurassic layers. If my hunch is right, the hydrothermal fluids that formed these quartz veins might have carried more than just gold. We might find traces of other minerals—possibly even silver."

Daniel, ever eager to learn from her extensive knowledge, listened intently, asking questions that sparked brief but insightful discussions about the geology of the region. It was during these conversations that Daniel realised how much he admired Lucy—not just for her determination and strength but for her intellect and passion for her heritage.

Reaching the northern vein, they set up their equipment. The ultrasonic drill whirred to life, its sound a harsh contrast to the stillness of the deep earth. Lucy handled the machine with ease, guided by Daniel's steady hands as they aimed for precise points along the exposed vein.

The first core sample they extracted was promising. Lucy held it up to the light of her headlamp, examining the cross-section. The vein of gold, though narrow, was distinctly visible against the darker surrounding rock.

"Look at that," she exclaimed, a triumphant smile spreading across her face. "That's beautiful. Let's get more samples. I think we're on the right track."

As they worked, moving along the vein and collecting samples, the camaraderie and trust between them deepened. Each core sample, each new discovery, added a layer to their bond. They moved in a comfortable rhythm, their actions synchronised, a dance of exploration and anticipation.

Hours later, as they made their way back to the surface, their backpacks heavier with rock samples, Lucy and Daniel felt a shared sense of accomplishment. Emerging into the daylight, the coolness of the mine replaced by the warmth of the sun, they looked at each other with tired but exhilarated eyes.

"We make a good team, don't we?" Daniel said, his voice rich with admiration and something deeper, a hint of the affection that had been growing between them.

Lucy nodded, her heart light and full. "The best," she agreed, feeling that with Daniel by her side, they could face not just the challenges of the mine but whatever else the world might throw their way.

The Golden Breakthrough

The morning after their successful descent into the mine, Lucy and Daniel sat at a makeshift lab table set up in the corner of the farm's spacious barn, surrounded by the cores they had extracted the day before. The air inside the barn was cool and smelled of hay and earth — a stark contrast to the damp, enclosed atmosphere of the mine.

Lucy, wearing a magnifying headlamp, carefully inspected each core, looking for signs of gold and other minerals. Daniel, meanwhile, meticulously documented their findings, recording measurements and observations in a detailed logbook. The morning light streamed through the high windows, casting long beams across their workspace, illuminating the rock samples with natural light.

"Look at this one, Daniel," Lucy said, her voice tinged with excitement. She held up a core sample, pointing to a section where tiny flecks of gold shimmered subtly under her lamp. "We missed this last night. The natural light really brings out the colour."

Daniel leaned in, his eyes following her finger. "That's a good sign, Lucy. This vein might be richer than we thought."

Encouraged, they continued their examination, each sample providing more clues about the geological story beneath their farm. Lucy's current studies in geology shone as she explained the formation processes to Daniel, who absorbed every word, eager to learn more about the science behind their search.

As they worked, their conversation drifted to the implications of their find. "If the vein extends as I think it might, we could be looking at a significant yield," Lucy speculated, her mind racing with the possibilities. "It's not just about the gold, either. There's potential here for a sustainable mining operation that could support the farm financially without harming the environment."

Daniel nodded, his admiration for Lucy growing. He loved how she always thought about the bigger picture, her commitment to sustainability influencing every decision. "I like that vision," he said. "Your approach could set a new standard for small-scale mining operations. It's innovative and responsible."

Feeling buoyant about their prospects, they decided to send selected samples to an independent laboratory for professional assay testing to confirm their preliminary findings. Packing the samples carefully, they filled out the submission forms with precision, ensuring every detail was correct to avoid any mix-ups.

With the samples ready to send off, they took a short break, stepping outside the barn to enjoy a brief walk around the farm. The fresh air was invigorating, and the sprawling fields of wheat waved gently in the breeze—a golden sea under the bright sun.

As they walked, Lucy shared more about her family's history with the land. "My great-grandfather started mining here, you know. But he was more of a prospector, really—nothing on the scale of what we're planning. He believed this land was special, not just for farming but for what lay beneath."

Daniel listened intently, linking her stories to the physical landscape around them. "It's like you're completing something he started," he observed. "Bringing full circle a family legacy."

Lucy smiled, her eyes reflecting a mix of pride and resolve. "I hope so. I want to honour that legacy by doing this the right way."

Their walk took them to the edge of one of the property's small lakes, a natural reservoir used for irrigation. They paused, looking out over the water, reflecting on what the future might hold.

"Whatever comes from those assay results," Daniel said, turning to face Lucy, "I'm here for the long haul. This project, the farm—it feels right, like I'm exactly where I'm supposed to be."

Lucy's heart swelled with emotion. Daniel's support meant everything to her, and his words reinforced her own commitment to their shared goals. "Thank you, Daniel. Knowing I have you by my side makes all the difference."

They returned to the barn, hand in hand, ready to face whatever challenges lay ahead. With the samples sent off for testing, all they could do was wait. But they were optimistic, buoyed by the preliminary results and their shared vision for a sustainable future.

The next few weeks would be a test of patience and resilience, but together, Lucy and Daniel were prepared. They had each other, a promising gold vein, and a deepening love that was becoming the bedrock of their partnership.

Farming Fundamentals

As they awaited the assay results, Lucy decided it was the perfect time to immerse Daniel deeper into the day-to-day operations of the Harding farm. The wheat fields, ripe and waving under the late summer sun, would soon need to be harvested, and the vegetable garden required daily attention to flourish.

Early one morning, just after dawn, Lucy led Daniel out to the fields.

The air was cool, filled with the fresh scent of earth and growing things. She wore her usual work attire—a faded denim shirt, sturdy jeans, and boots, her hair pulled back in a practical ponytail.

"Today, I'll show you the basics of wheat farming—from soil preparation to what signs to look for when the wheat is ready to harvest," Lucy explained as they walked along the edge of the nearest field. She stopped and bent down, plucking a few stalks of wheat. "Feel this," she said, handing them to Daniel. "The texture and the colour can tell you a lot about the plant's health and maturity."

Daniel took the stalks, rubbing the grains between his fingers, feeling their hardness and noting their golden hue. "So, what are we looking for exactly?"

Lucy took the stalks back and pointed to the heads of the wheat. "See how these are bending slightly and the colour is uniformly golden? That means they're approaching the perfect time for harvesting. We want to make sure we start combining at the right time to maximise yield and minimise loss."

As they walked back towards the barn, Lucy explained the importance of crop rotation and soil management. "We rotate wheat with legumes and other cover crops," she said. "It helps maintain soil health, prevents erosion, and naturally reduces pest cycles. Sustainable farming is all about understanding and working with nature, not against it."

Reaching the barn, Lucy showed Daniel the farm's old but reliable combine harvester. "This old girl needs a bit of a tune-up before harvest next week," she remarked. "I'll show you how to do basic maintenance and checks."

They spent the morning servicing the combine, with Lucy teaching Daniel how to clean filters, check fluid levels, and inspect belts and chains. The physical work was interspersed with laughter and light-hearted banter, making the tasks feel less like chores and more like shared adventures.

In the afternoon, they headed to the vegetable garden, a large plot behind the farmhouse filled with an assortment of plants: tomatoes, peppers, zucchinis, and herbs, all thriving under Lucy's attentive care.

"Vegetable gardening is more of a passion project," Lucy confessed as they kneeled side by side, weeding around the tomato plants. "It's smaller scale compared to the wheat, but it's gratifying in a different way. There's something about eating food you've grown yourself that just feels right."

Daniel nodded, pulling a weed and tossing it into a bucket beside him. "I can see why. There's a tangible result to your efforts. And it tastes better, too."

They spent several hours in the garden, Lucy explaining companion planting and organic pest control methods. As they worked, Daniel felt a deep sense of connection not just to the land but also to Lucy. Her passion for her work, her deep knowledge of the land and its cycles, was inspiring.

As the sun began to set, casting long shadows over the farm, Lucy and Daniel cleaned up their tools and headed back to the house. They were tired but satisfied with the day's accomplishments.

"We've done a lot today," Lucy said as they stored the last of the tools in the shed. "Thanks for being such a great student."

Daniel chuckled, wiping his brow. "Thanks for being a great teacher. I've learned more about farming today than I ever thought I would."

They walked towards the house, their shadows merging on the ground as they moved. The evening was quiet, peaceful, and as they reached the porch, Daniel turned to Lucy.

"This... all of this," he gestured broadly to the surrounding farm, "it's more than just land and crops, isn't it? It's a legacy."

Lucy looked out over the fields, her expression thoughtful. "Yes, it's a legacy. And it's our future, too. One I hope we can build on together."

Daniel reached for her hand, holding it tightly. "I have no doubts about that, Lucy. "

Under the fading light, they stood together in silence, each contemplating the future they were starting to build.

Fence Mending

Lucy and Daniel started their day early, just after sunrise, with a walk along the perimeter of the Harding farm. The morning was brisk, the air filled with the scent of damp grass and earth, signalling a typical morning on the farm. Their task for the day was to inspect and repair a section of fencing that marked the farm's boundaries—a practical job that Lucy was eager to use as a teaching moment for Daniel.

"Good fences make good neighbours," Lucy quipped as they approached the first post, her voice cheerful despite the chill in the air. She handed Daniel a heavy-duty pair of gloves and a wire cutter. "And good fences also keep our wheat and livestock safe from wandering too far."

Daniel laughed, slipping on the gloves. "I guess Robert Frost knew a thing or two about farming, huh?"

"Exactly," Lucy responded with a smile. She grabbed a heavy hammer and a bag of nails from the toolbox and then pointed to the first fence post. "We'll start here. First, we need to check each post for signs of rot or damage. If the wood feels soft or crumbly, it needs to be replaced."

Together, they examined each post methodically. Lucy demonstrated how to prod the wood with a small awl to test its integrity. When they found a post that was damaged, she showed Daniel how to carefully remove it from the ground, ensuring not to disturb the surrounding area more than necessary.

"Maintaining a fence isn't just about keeping things in or out; it's about maintaining the health of the land it encloses," Lucy explained as they worked. "Erosion, animal damage, even weather can turn a small fence issue into a big problem if not checked regularly."

Daniel followed her instructions, removing a rotted post and replacing it with a new one. He found the physicality of the work satisfying, feeling the muscles in his arms work as he dug a hole for the new post.

"Next, we check the fencing wire," Lucy continued, moving to the next phase of their repair. She showed Daniel how to tension the wire correctly, ensuring it was taut but not overly strained. "If the wire's too tight, it can snap under pressure from wind or an animal collision. Too loose, and it won't hold anything back."

Daniel took the fence stretcher, applying the new knowledge with focus. He found the rhythm of the work, the physical task coupled with the need for precise judgement, both challenging and deeply engaging.

As they moved along the fence line, repairing sections of wire and reinforcing posts, Lucy and Daniel fell into a comfortable silence, each lost in their thoughts but aware of the other's presence. The physical space between them was minimal, with their movements often synchronised as they handed tools back and forth, their hands occasionally brushing.

"This fence," Lucy said, breaking the silence as they stepped back to admire their work, "it's a lot like the boundaries we set in other areas of our lives—clear lines that help everyone know where they stand."

Daniel nodded, understanding the metaphor. "And like any good boundary, it needs to be respected and maintained," he added, glancing at Lucy with a smile that suggested he was speaking about more than just the fence.

Lucy met his gaze, her eyes reflecting a mix of appreciation and deeper affection. "Exactly. And it's easier to maintain when you don't have to do it alone."

The sun was higher now, warming the air around them as they packed up their tools. The fence stood firm and strong behind them, a testament to their teamwork and the morning's efforts.

As they walked back to the house, their shoulders brushed, and Lucy reached out to take Daniel's hand. The gesture was simple but held a wealth of meaning—partnership, support, and a mutual commitment to whatever lay ahead.

"Thanks for helping today, Daniel. Not just with the fence—with everything," Lucy said sincerely, her eyes reflecting the depth of her gratitude.

Daniel squeezed her hand gently, stopping in their path to face her. "There's no place I'd rather be," he assured her, his voice soft yet firm, conveying his deep commitment.

As they stood there, the distance between them lessened, drawn together not just by their shared work but by the growing bond between them. Lucy looked up into Daniel's eyes, finding there a mirror of her own feelings.

Without another word, Daniel drew her closer, wrapping his arms around her in a warm embrace. Lucy rested her head against his chest, feeling the steady beat of his heart matching her own. The morning's chill faded away, replaced by the warmth that radiated between them.

Slowly, Daniel tilted Lucy's chin upwards, and their eyes met once more, a silent agreement passing between them. The moment felt suspended in time, the air around them charged with anticipation.

Then, bridging the gap, Daniel kissed her, a kiss that mingled gratitude with passion, promise with affection. Lucy responded in kind, her arms tightening around him, both affirming their connection not just to the land they stood on, but to each other.

As they finally parted, their smiles were as bright as the clear sky above them, and they continued their walk back to the house, hand in hand, their hearts as aligned as the fence line that stretched behind them.

Water Wisdom

The Harding farm, nestled in the vast expanses of undulating fields and open skies, depended fundamentally on its water management system—a system that Lucy had been refining and perfecting since she took over farm operations. On a brisk morning that heralded the full flush of fall, she led Daniel to one of the farm's most crucial infrastructure elements: the irrigation system, powered by water from the farm's dams.

As they walked towards the first dam, Lucy began outlining the sophisticated journey of water from its source to the crops. "Our irrigation system is the lifeline of the farm," she explained, her voice carrying clearly in the quiet morning. "Every drop of water that we collect in these dams is directed through a meticulously designed network of channels and pipes to the fields."

The dam itself was a substantial body of water, contained by an earth-filled embankment and equipped with advanced sluice gates to control water flow. Lucy led Daniel to one of these gates, showing him how the manual controls worked. "We can adjust the amount of water that's released based on our current needs and the water level in the dam," she said, manipulating the heavy lever to demonstrate.

From the sluice gates, water flowed into a main canal that branched off into smaller channels, each strategically positioned to maximise the irrigation coverage across the vast fields of wheat and other crops. Lucy and Daniel followed the path of the main canal, the water's surface shimmering in the early morning light.

"Proper channel maintenance is crucial," Lucy continued as they walked. "Any blockage or breach can affect the entire system. We inspect these canals regularly to ensure they are clear of debris and structurally sound."

As they reached the fields, Lucy pointed out the large irrigation booms that spanned across the crops like mechanical giants straddling the land. "These are centre pivot irrigation systems, commonly known as watering booms. They are one of the most efficient methods of applying water to the crops."

The booms were impressive in size and reach, designed to pivot around a central water source, their long arms outfitted with nozzles that sprayed water evenly across the crops. Lucy explained the mechanics: "Each boom can irrigate up to a hundred acres per cycle, depending on the configuration. They draw water directly from our supply dams through powerful pumps that maintain a steady pressure."

Daniel watched, fascinated, as Lucy started one of the booms, the machine whirring to life. The arms began to rotate slowly, water cascading down in a wide arc, droplets catching the sunlight in a spray of tiny rainbows. "The booms are set on timers to run during the coolest parts of the day to minimise evaporation losses," she added.

As the boom continued its steady rotation, Lucy and Daniel walked along the edge of the field, observing the reach of the water. "Uniformity is key in irrigation," Lucy noted. "We want every part of the field to receive an equal amount of water to ensure even growth and yield."

Discussing the technology further, Lucy shared her plans to enhance the system's efficiency. "I'm looking into integrating soil moisture sensors that can communicate wirelessly with the booms. These sensors would provide real-time data on the soil's moisture levels, allowing us to customise the irrigation schedules more precisely based on actual crop needs."

The conversation then shifted towards the potential integration of LoRaWAN technology—a low-power, wide-area networking protocol ideal for connecting battery-operated sensors over long distances in remote farm areas. "Imagine sensors placed throughout the farm, constantly monitoring water levels, salinity, and even nutrient content in the soil," Lucy elaborated. "These sensors could send data directly to our main system, which could automatically adjust the watering schedules and quantities needed."

Daniel, impressed by the foresight of the plan, saw how such innovations could transform not just their farm but agriculture practices in similar environments. "It's smart farming, isn't it? Using technology not to replace traditional methods but to enhance them and make them more sustainable," he remarked.

Lucy nodded, pleased with his understanding and support. "Exactly. It's about making informed decisions that benefit the farm in the long term. We save water, reduce waste, and increase our productivity—all while maintaining the health of the land."

As they concluded their tour of the irrigation system, the sun had climbed higher in the sky, warming the earth and highlighting the vibrant greens of the surrounding fields. They stopped to watch the watering boom complete its cycle, the rhythmic sound of water mingling with the gentle rustle of wheat.

"This is what it all comes down to," Lucy said, gesturing towards the thriving fields. "Water is our most precious resource, and managing it wisely is perhaps the greatest responsibility we have as farmers."

Daniel took Lucy's hand, squeezing it gently, moved by her passion and dedication. "And you manage it brilliantly, Lucy. I'm continually amazed by what you're accomplishing here."

Together, they walked back towards the farmhouse, their conversation light but full of plans for the future—plans that would no doubt weave Daniel's growing role on the farm into the fabric of its continued success. Their partnership, both personal and professional, was blossoming, rooted deeply in the fertile soil of the Harding farm.

Reflections at Dusk

As the sun began its graceful descent toward the horizon, casting the sky in hues of orange and purple, Lucy and Daniel found themselves sitting side by side on the grassy bank of one of the farm's dams. The water was calm, mirroring the colours of the sunset and providing a serene backdrop to their conversation. They had spent a productive day traversing the farm, and now, in the quiet of the evening, they took a moment to unwind and reflect.

Lucy pulled her knees close, wrapping her arms around them as she looked out over the water. "It's moments like these," she began, her voice soft but clear, "when I feel both the weight and the beauty of this place. It's more than just land and crops; it's a legacy that's been passed down to me, and now... I hope to share it with you."

Daniel turned to look at her, his eyes reflecting the colours of the setting sun. "I feel honoured, Lucy. Working with you, learning about the farm—it's made me appreciate not just what you do, but who you are."

Lucy smiled, a gentle warmth spreading through her. "Since Dad's heart attack, everything about running this farm has been in my hands. It's been challenging, but having you here has made a world of difference. Not just for the help, which I'm immensely grateful for, but for the companionship... and more."

Daniel reached out, taking her hand in his, a gesture that spoke volumes about their deepening connection. "I've felt something growing between us, Lucy. More than just friendship. I'm here for the long haul if you want me there."

Lucy's heart quickened at his words. She had felt the shift in their relationship, a gradual deepening of their feelings that went beyond professional respect or friendship. "I do want you here, Daniel. Not just as a partner on the farm but as a partner in life. I imagine a future where we manage this place together, where our goals and dreams intertwine like the roots of the surrounding trees."

They both looked out across the water, letting the magnitude of their shared vision settle in. "I see us innovating, bringing new technologies and practices to the farm, making it a model of sustainable agriculture," Lucy continued, her tone infused with passion and determination. "But I also see us building a family, a life where we support each other through everything."

Daniel squeezed her hand, moved by her vision. "I see that too," he murmured. "Working beside you, learning from you, building with you—it's become the most important part of my life."

The sky darkened as the sun dipped below the horizon, and the first stars began to twinkle in the twilight. Lucy leaned her head against Daniel's shoulder, feeling an overwhelming sense of peace and rightness.

"I used to be afraid of what the future might hold," she confessed. "Taking on the farm, facing challenges like McRae, worrying about water and crops... But with you, Daniel, I feel like we can handle anything. Your strength bolsters mine."

Daniel wrapped his arm around her, drawing her closer. "And your strength inspires me, Lucy. It's a circle, a cycle that keeps us both going. Whatever challenges come, we'll meet them. Together."

As the last light of the day faded, leaving them in the gentle embrace of dusk, Daniel turned to Lucy, lifting her chin gently so their eyes met. In that moment, everything felt aligned—their hopes, their dreams, their hearts. He kissed her, a kiss that sealed their promises and commitments to each other and to the future they would build on the Harding farm.

The night settled around them, cool and comforting, as they sat together, discussing plans and dreams, their voices mingling with the soft sounds of the night. Here, on the edge of the dam, with the world turning dark around them, Lucy and Daniel found a profound connection that would guide them through the days and years to come.

42

Underground Operations

Expanding the Tunnel

The cool breath of the earth enveloped Lucy and Daniel as they stepped into the newly extended section of the underground mine. The excavation site buzzed with the sounds of machinery and the intermittent clink of metal against rock, a symphony of progress and perseverance beneath the Harding farm.

Lucy, equipped with her headlamp and geological tools, led the way with confidence. Her familiarity with the earth's secrets, gained from months of study and hands-on experience, made her an adept leader in this subterranean endeavour. Daniel, though less experienced in the nuances of mining, shared her enthusiasm and was quick to learn, his presence a constant source of support.

The goal was evident: to trace the path of the newly discovered vein of gold, a hopeful band of ore with abundant minerals that reached further into the Earth's crust than expected. The vein's discovery had been a turning point, not just for the farm's financial prospects, but for Lucy's vision of a sustainable and profitable operation.

"Watch your step here," Lucy cautioned as they navigated through a narrow part of the tunnel where the overhead light didn't quite reach. She pointed her beam towards the uneven ground before continuing her explanation. "We've shored up this section with extra supports. The rock face here is stable, but we're not taking any chances."

The tunnel ahead expanded into a wider chamber where the main excavation was taking place. The sound of a pneumatic drill filled the air, echoing off the rocky walls as a couple of her friends (now hired miners) worked diligently to follow the gold vein. Each section of rock they removed was carefully catalogued and set aside for later processing.

Lucy approached the rock face, her lamp casting a focused light on the vein. The gold streak was more pronounced here, a ribbon of shimmering metal intertwined with quartz and other minerals. She picked up a geologist's hammer and gently tapped along the vein, checking for depth and consistency.

"This is good, very good," Lucy murmured, mostly to herself but loud enough for Daniel to hear over the din of the drilling. "The vein widens here, which could indicate a larger deposit nearby."

Daniel, wiping sweat from his brow, watched her work. "How can you tell?" he asked, eager to understand more about the geological indicators Lucy seemed to read so naturally.

Lucy placed her hammer down and gestured for him to come closer. "See here," she pointed, "the colour and texture change slightly. Gold veins often follow pathways through the rock that can widen as you follow them. It's like tracing a thread through fabric. Sometimes the thread gets thicker."

Their conversation was interrupted by one of the miners signalling a shift change. Lucy and Daniel stepped aside, allowing the fresh team to start their stint on the rock face. This pause in their own labours gave them a moment to discuss the logistics of further expanding the tunnel.

"We'll need to extend the reinforcement beams another five meters by the end of the week," Lucy calculated, checking the plans on her digital tablet, which contained detailed maps and structural data. "That means more beams, more concrete, and more time."

Daniel nodded, understanding the scale of the operation. "I'll coordinate with the suppliers. We'll need everything delivered by Wednesday to stay on schedule."

Lucy smiled appreciatively, her trust in his capabilities evident. "Thanks, Daniel. I don't know what I'd do without you here."

As the new team of miners took over, Lucy led Daniel back to a small alcove where they kept their planning and safety equipment. Here, away from the noise, they spread out a large version of the tunnel map on a makeshift table. With her flashlight serving as an impromptu spotlight, Lucy traced their progress on the map with a gloved finger.

"Our next major step is to install a secondary ventilation shaft here," she pointed to a spot further along the proposed expansion route. "That will help us manage air quality, which is crucial as we go deeper."

Daniel, who had been taking notes, looked up. "And the water drainage system?"

"That too," Lucy confirmed. "We need to update our pump setup. Water ingress is minimal right now, but with the rainy season coming, we can't afford to take any risks. Flooding in these lower sections would set us back weeks, if not months."

The practicalities of managing an underground operation of this scale were daunting, but Lucy's expertise and Daniel's quick learning made them a formidable team. Together, they reviewed every detail, from safety measures to equipment needs, ensuring that their approach was as meticulous as it was ambitious.

As they wrapped up their session, preparing to join the others at the surface, Lucy paused, her hand resting on the map. The lines and numbers transformed under her gaze into a vision of what could be—a thriving, responsible mining operation that could secure the future of the Harding farm and contribute positively to their community.

"Let's do this, Daniel. Let's make this mine something we can all be proud of," Lucy said with a determined glint in her eye.

Daniel, inspired by her passion, nodded in agreement. "We will. Together."

With the map rolled up and their gear stowed, they made their way back to the surface, ready to tackle the challenges ahead with the same partnership and resilience that had brought them this far.

A Sapphire Surprise

The cool silence of the underground enveloped Daniel as he descended alone into the depths of the mine. It was Thursday, the beginning of the off days for the mining operation, a scheduling decision Lucy and Daniel had made to balance their focus between the mine and the farm's primary operations. With the wheat harvest approaching, Lucy dedicated these days to the fields, while Daniel took the opportunity to advance their exploratory work below ground.

As he made his way along the tunnel, the beam from his headlamp cut through the darkness, illuminating the rugged walls that bore the marks of their recent excavations. The solitude didn't bother him; if anything, it provided a profound sense of connection to the earth under him, a reminder of why he had fallen in love with the rugged, honest work of farming and mining alike.

Reaching the new section where the vein had shown promising yields, Daniel set up his equipment. The solitude allowed for a focus that was sometimes harder to achieve during the busier mining days. He started the handheld drill, the noise sharp in the enclosed space, and carefully extracted a core sample from the vein. As the drill bit deeper, the familiar glint of gold flecked within the rock brought a satisfied smile to his face.

It was during these meticulous explorations that Daniel stumbled upon something unexpected. As he extracted a section of rock, a sparkle caught his eye—something distinctly different from the glimmer of gold. He paused, setting the drill aside, and took a closer look. Embedded in the grey rock was a cluster of small, rough stones with a subtle blue hue. Sapphires.

Daniel's heart quickened with the find. Although not large or particularly fine, these sapphires were beautiful in their own right. He carefully removed them from the surrounding rock, considering the possibilities. An idea formed—a gift for Lucy, something special to mark the success of their shared endeavours.

Pocketing the stones, Daniel decided to keep the find a secret for now. He planned to have the sapphires cut and set into a piece of jewellery, a surprise to show Lucy how deeply he valued both her partnership and the life they were building together.

With the sapphires safely stowed, Daniel returned his focus to the task at hand. He spent the remainder of the day mapping the vein's path, taking additional samples, and noting areas for further exploration. His meticulous work would provide valuable data for their next major excavation phase.

Above ground, Lucy was equally engrossed in her duties on the farm. The wheat fields, vast expanses of golden stalks swaying gently in the breeze, required her attentive care. The farm, spanning hundreds of acres, was the primary income for the Harding family, and Lucy was determined to keep it thriving through sustainable practices.

Lucy's approach to farming was holistic. She integrated crop rotation, used natural pest control methods, and experimented with organic fertilisers to maintain soil health. Her long-term vision included expanding into other types of ecological farming, potentially introducing agroforestry or permaculture to diversify the farm's productivity and ecological impact.

These quiet days, while Daniel was underground, gave Lucy time to reflect on the balance they struck between mining and farming. She firmly believed that the farm should remain primarily an agricultural enterprise, with the mine serving as a financial buffer against the uncertainties of farming life, such as fluctuating market prices or the ever-present threat of adverse weather.

As the sun began to set, casting a warm, golden light over the farm, Lucy finished her rounds in the fields. She felt a deep, abiding satisfaction in the day's work, knowing that her efforts above ground complemented Daniel's below. Their partnership, spanning the depths of the earth to the sprawling fields above, was a testament to their shared commitment to the land and to each other.

That evening, as they gathered for dinner, the contrast between their day's environments was stark—Daniel's clothes bore the dust of the mine, while Lucy's were specked with the earth of the fields. Yet, their conversations seamlessly wove the underground and above ground together, discussing crop yields and ore veins in the same breath, their plans for the farm and the mine reflecting a shared vision for a sustainable and prosperous future.

Lucy listened intently as Daniel recounted his progress in the mine, keeping his discovery of the sapphires to himself for now, waiting for the right moment to reveal the surprise. In turn, Lucy shared her thoughts on the upcoming harvest and her plans for experimenting with new farming techniques next season. Their dialogue, rich with details and interspersed with laughter and shared dreams, continued into the night, under the vast, star-filled sky that blanketed their home—the Harding farm.

From Ore to Gold

The morning air was brisk as the Harding farm stirred with anticipation. Today marked a significant milestone in the mining endeavour—the first major processing of the gold ore extracted from their expanded tunnel. Unlike traditional operations that might employ methods like cyanidation, Lucy had insisted on an environmentally friendlier approach to separate the gold from the ore, one that minimised the use of harmful chemicals.

In the barn converted into an impromptu processing centre, Lucy, Daniel, and a team of their closest friends and workers gathered around the newly installed machinery, all eager to see the fruits of their labour. The setup included advanced electrostatic separators and sluice systems designed to recover gold through gravity and static charge without the environmental risks associated with chemical leaching.

Lucy explained the process to the group. "This system uses electricity to create a charge that separates the gold from other materials based on their conductivity and magnetic susceptibility. It's safer for us and the environment."

As the machinery hummed to life, everyone watched intently as the crushed ore was fed into the separator. Gradually, fine particles of gold began to accumulate in the collection bin, sparkling unmistakably against the duller earth materials.

Once the separation process was complete, the collected gold, still mixed with some natural impurities, was carefully gathered to be dried and weighed. Lucy arranged for a large digital scale to be set up in the middle of the barn, and one by one, they weighed the gold. The excitement was palpable as the numbers on the scale climbed—confirming that their efforts had not only been successful but potentially life-changing.

James, Lucy's father, watched from the sidelines, his face betraying a mix of emotions—pride in his daughter's accomplishments and relief at seeing the farm's future becoming more secure. Despite his recent heart attack, he stood steady, leaning slightly on a cane, his eyes rarely leaving Lucy and Daniel.

After the weighing, the gold totalled significantly more than they had cautiously estimated. Cheers erupted in the barn, and Lucy hugged her father, his eyes shining with pride. "You've done something incredible here, Lucy," James said, his voice thick with emotion. "You and Daniel have secured the future of Harding Farm."

With the exact weight recorded, the next step was to melt the gold down into bars. The group moved to a secure area of the barn where a small furnace had been installed. Under Lucy's supervision, the gold flakes were carefully placed into a crucible and then into the furnace. The melting process was a mesmerising sight, the raw gold transforming into a glowing, liquid stream that was then poured into pre-formed molds. "This could take some time." Lucy exclaimed. "I didn't think we would have this much to process, so I only have 4 molds!" The smile on Lucy's face said it all. They had achieved more than they had ever expected.

As the gold cooled and solidified into bars, the reality of their achievement settled in. Daniel, standing beside Lucy, squeezed her hand gently. "We did it," he whispered, his voice reflecting both disbelief and joy. After the first 20 bars had cooled and everyone there had congratulated each other and had a quiet celebratory drink, most headed home excited to hear the final count the next day. Daniel and Lucy continued to smelt the gold down and pour the molds one by one until, very early the next morning, they finished. "303 bars," Lucy said, smiling through her complete exhaustion.

After securing the bars in a lockable transport box and then further securing them in the safe room, they decided it was time for a shower and bed. Sleep, however, didn't come easy. With excitement for the future, worry about her dad's health and fear of what McRae might be up to, Lucy tossed and turned with a fitful sleep. Eventually, though, she did sleep.

A sleep in which Lucy was rudely awoken from the phone ringing. It was her friends, all on a group call, eagerly awaiting the news of the final count. "God, I must look awful," Lucy said, realising it was a video call. "You look beautiful to me!" Daniel said as he handed her a mug of coffee. "I don't want to discuss this on the phone, but I will tell you it was.... More than we had expected. Why don't you all come over for lunch and we can ... Show you" she said. "

Realising the time, Lucy quickly drank her coffee, had a shower, and got dressed. Realising her mum had her hands full looking after her dad, Lucy decided the quickest and most satisfying meal to prepare for her visiting friends and family was a ploughman's lunch. She gathered thick slices of crusty bread and arranged large cuts of sharp cheddar and creamy Brie cheese on a wooden board. She added handfuls of crisp, fresh apple slices and a few bunches of grapes for a touch of sweetness. For the meats, she chose thick slices of ham and a chunk of pâté, complementing them with a variety of pickles—gherkins, onions, and a small jar of home made tangy chutney. To round out the meal, she included a bowl of hard-boiled eggs, cut in halves, and a fresh green salad tossed lightly with vinaigrette. She set the table under the shade of an old tree, just outside the barn, where they could all enjoy the meal with a view of the golden wheat fields, feeling a sense of communal warmth and simplicity.

Lucy, Daniel, her family, and their close friends gathered around a large, rustic wooden table spread with a hearty lunch. The air was filled with a warm, congenial atmosphere as everyone took a moment to relax and share in the camaraderie. As they passed dishes and filled their plates, Lucy stood up, her expression a mix of pride and gratitude. "I have something to show you all," she announced, her voice carrying over the buzz of conversation. She led the group to a corner of the barn, where a heavy-duty transport case was secured. With a flourish, she opened the case to reveal neatly stacked gold bars—303 in total, each shimmering with the promise of security and new beginnings. The group crowded around, their faces alight with wonder and admiration. "Thanks to everyone's hard work and dedication, we've achieved something incredible," Lucy continued, her eyes gleaming with emotion as she looked around at the faces of her friends and family. "This gold not only secures our farm's future but also symbolises the strength of our friendship and what we can accomplish together." The revelation deepened the sense of unity and celebration among the group, turning the meal into more than just a lunch—it was a feast honouring their collective effort and success.

The following day, Lucy and Daniel drove into Perth with the gold bars securely locked in a transport box. Their first stop was the gold dealer, where they sold the bars at a premium, given the high market prices and the purity of the gold. The transaction was straightforward but thrilling, each 1 ounce bar exchanged for a significant sum of money.

Flush with success, their next stop was the bank. They met with the bank manager, who was more than pleased to settle the farm's outstanding loans. Lucy presented the cheque with a steady hand, a smile of satisfaction on her face. They paid off every debt, including those incurred by the new machinery and the upgraded security systems. The remainder of the money was substantial—enough to pay generous wages to their friends who had helped in the mine, with a significant reserve left to fund the farm operations for at least the next couple of years.

As Lucy and Daniel left the bank, they felt a weight lift off their shoulders. The farm was now completely debt-free, its future secure. They had enough capital to invest in expanding their sustainable and ecological farming practices, ensuring that the Harding Farm would not only continue but thrive and innovate.

The ride back to the farm was filled with plans and dreams, not just for their crops and livestock, but for their lives together. They discussed ideas for the farm, for expanding into new markets, and even for building their own home.

As the Perth skyline receded behind them, the couple looked ahead to their future with optimism and certainty. They had turned a venture fraught with uncertainty into a resounding success, cementing not just the legacy of Harding Farm but their life together.

Rewarding the team

Several days later, Lucy had organised for her friends to meet at the Barn. The atmosphere in the barn was one of elation and warm camaraderie. As everyone gathered around, still excited at the tangible results of their combined efforts, Lucy prepared to address her friends and family, all of whom had played pivotal roles in the mining operations.

"Everyone," Lucy began, her voice steady and filled with deep gratitude, "what we've achieved here isn't just a testament to our hard work or the riches beneath our feet—it's a reflection of your loyalty, trust, and unwavering support. Each of you volunteered your time without expectation of payment, driven purely by a desire to help and a share in our collective dream."

The group listened intently, their faces a mix of humility and pride. These were friends who had stood by Lucy through thick and thin, contributing their skills and labour to the mine, driven by friendship and a communal spirit rather than financial gain.

Lucy continued, "While your help was freely given, your contributions are valuable beyond measure, and it's only right that your efforts are recognised and rewarded appropriately." A murmur of appreciation rippled through the group, with some exchanging glances of surprise and quiet acknowledgement.

"I would like to offer each of you a casual job here at the farm and the mine," Lucy announced, her eyes sweeping over the faces before her. "The mine will continue to operate a couple of days a week, focusing on sustainable extraction and ensuring that we don't compromise the integrity of our land. For those days, I'll need a reliable team to manage the operations, and I can't think of anyone better suited than you all."

A wave of excited chatter broke out as Lucy's friends absorbed the offer. It was an unexpected turn of events, transforming what had begun as a voluntary help into a potential livelihood.

"And there's more," Lucy added, raising her hand to recapture their attention. "In addition to being paid for the hours you work, I want to extend a share of the profits from the gold we extract. This isn't just my success—it's ours, and it should be shared as such."

The room erupted in cheers and applause, the energy palpable. People came up to hug Lucy, shaking hands with Daniel, who stood by her side, smiling broadly at the joy and unity displayed. The offer was more than fair—it was a continuation of the communal ethos that had defined their work from the start.

One volunteer, an older gentleman named Tom who had known Lucy's father for decades, stepped forward. "Lucy, your dad is so proud today, not just of the gold, but of how you're looking after us all. You're true to your roots, and that's more precious than any metal we could dig up."

Lucy, moved by Tom's words, nodded, feeling a lump form in her throat. "Thank you, Tom. That means everything to me."

As the group eventually settled down, Lucy and Daniel took a moment to outline what the new work structure would look like.

They discussed safety procedures, work schedules, and profit-sharing details, ensuring transparency and fairness in every aspect of their operations. Daniel, who had been discussing his own preferences with Lucy, chose a different path. "I appreciate the offer for the cash bonus," he said when it was his turn to speak, "but I'd like my share in gold, if that's possible. I believe in holding onto the physical representation of our hard work."

The meeting ended on a high note, with everyone eager to start this new chapter. As the sun set outside, casting a golden glow through the barn doors, the group slowly dispersed, chatting animatedly about the future.

The decision to pay the volunteers not only for their labour but also a share of the profits solidified the bond among the team. Ensuring that the mine would be a source of sustainable income and community development. Lucy and Daniel, standing together amidst the fading light, felt a profound sense of accomplishment and hope, ready to lead their team into a promising future.

Commitments and the Future

The evening air was crisp as the last of the golden sunlight washed over Harding Farm, illuminating the wide, fertile fields poised for harvest. Inside the farmhouse, a serious yet hopeful meeting was taking place, one that involved not only Lucy and Daniel but also Lucy's parents, Emma and James. The room was filled with a sense of accomplishment mixed with the weight of future responsibilities.

Lucy stood before her family, detailing the final counts and the profits from their first successful gold pour. The numbers were more than promising—they were transformative for the farm's financial stability. "With the revenue from the gold, we can clear all outstanding debts," Lucy explained, spreading out the paperwork on the dining table for her parents to see. "This includes the loans for the new machinery and the security systems we installed last year."

James, still recovering from his heart attack, listened intently, nodding in approval at the figures. Despite his frail health, the pride in his eyes was unmistakable. Emma, ever the supportive spouse, held his hand, sharing in his emotions.

"We'll also have enough to not only cover our operating costs for the next few years but to invest in expanding our sustainable farming practices," Lucy continued, her voice steady with the confidence of a seasoned farmer.

Emma smiled, her expression one of relief and gratitude. "Lucy, seeing you take on so much and succeed is more than we could have ever hoped for," she said warmly. "You've turned what started as a risky venture into a lifeline for our farm."

The discussion shifted towards the distribution of profits among the mining team, all of whom had contributed significantly to the project's success. Lucy outlined her plan for ensuring that everyone involved received a fair share, not just in wages but also in profit participation, which had been well received.

As the family mulled over the details, the conversation naturally veered towards the future. Lucy shared her hopes for further integrating green technologies into the farm operations, reducing their carbon footprint, and possibly expanding the market for their produce.

"It's not just about sustaining us financially," Lucy explained passionately. "It's about creating a model of farming that's sustainable for the environment too—something that can be replicated and that makes a real difference."

James, who had been listening quietly, his voice softened by illness yet still authoritative, finally spoke. "Lucy, you've done more than just keep the farm afloat. You've set a course for its future—a future that looks brighter than I could've imagined when I first started this farm."

His words filled the room with a mixture of nostalgia and forward-looking optimism. The discussion gradually wound down as plans were made and tasks assigned.

Daniel, who had been a pillar of support through it all, felt a personal moment was nearing—a moment he had been contemplating for quite some time. Glancing towards James and then at Lucy, who was speaking animatedly with her mother about crop rotations, he knew it was time.

"James, could we have a word outside?" Daniel asked, his tone respectful yet filled with an undercurrent of determination.

James looked at him, sensing the seriousness of the request, and nodded. They stepped out onto the porch, where the cool evening air and the vast expanse of ready-to-harvest wheat fields awaited them.

As they stood there, watching the last rays of sunlight dance across the golden fields, Daniel took a deep breath. "James, I've been meaning to talk to you about something important," he started, his voice steady but filled with emotion.

James turned to face him, his expression encouraging. "Go on, son," he urged gently.

"I... I love Lucy. Deeply," Daniel confessed, his gaze firm and sincere. "She's become not just my partner at work but the most important person in my life. I'd like to ask for your blessing, James, to ask Lucy to marry me."

The old farmer studied Daniel, his gaze penetrating yet kind. After a moment, a slow smile spread across his face. "I've always liked you, Daniel, and I've seen how my daughter looks at you. There's a kind of love there that comes once in a lifetime. You have my blessing, and I suspect you'll have her heart without much effort."

Daniel's relief was palpable, and he extended a hand to James, who shook it warmly. "Thank you, James. It means everything to hear that from you."

"When do you plan to ask her?" James inquired, his tone now lighter, almost teasing.

"Soon," Daniel replied, a smile tugging at his lips. "I have a few things to plan out first. I want it to be special."

James nodded, his eyes returning to the fields. "I know it will be. And I know that whatever the future holds, you two will face it together—here on the farm and in the mine, but most importantly, together in life."

As they turned to go back inside, the night settling around them, Daniel felt a profound sense of belonging and purpose. The Harding Farm was more than just land and crops; it was a foundation for a future filled with love, commitment, and enduring partnership.

43

Showdown

The Attack Begins

The cool evening breeze that had once brought respite now carried with it a new, ominous threat. As the sun set behind the Harding Farm, casting long shadows over the fields, the first Molotov cocktail shattered against the dry wheat stalks, igniting a fiery blaze with a horrifying whoosh. The sudden eruption of flames sliced through the tranquil dusk, turning the night into a chaotic tableau of fire and fear.

Lucy stood frozen for a split second, watching in disbelief as another and then another firebomb arced through the twilight, each one igniting a new inferno upon landing. The peaceful evening had turned into a nightmarish assault in mere moments. The terror that gripped her was quickly supplanted by a surge of anger—a fierce, protective rage for the farm that had been in her family for generations.

Snapping into action, Lucy's first thought was for the farm's sophisticated fire detection system. Its alarm now blaring along with the red strobe light casting a red hue across the barn. Installed the previous year, the AI-powered cameras were designed to spot fires and trigger the sprinkler system automatically, a technological safeguard that should have minimised any damage. However, as she scanned the fields, waiting for the reassuring sound of sprinklers, her heart sank. There was nothing but the crackling of fire. The system had been sabotaged; the pumps destroyed, rendering their primary defence useless.

Daniel, witnessing the destruction from the barn, understood immediately the grave danger they faced. Without hesitation, he sprinted to the tractor, attaching a portable sprayer unit that they typically used for pesticide application. Filled now with water, it was their makeshift fire extinguisher. As he drove the tractor towards the first line of fire, his actions were precise and swift, an attempt to beat back the flames threatening to engulf their livelihood.

Lucy, meanwhile, grabbed her phone and dialed the emergency services, her voice urgent and shaky as she reported the situation. "We need help—now! The fields are ablaze, and our fire system's been tampered with!" The dispatcher promised that help was on its way, but Lucy knew that every second they waited could mean more of the farm lost to the relentless flames.

Back in the field, Daniel maneuvered the tractor skillfully, spraying water over the flames. Despite his efforts, the fire was voracious, fueled by the dry conditions and steady wind. He worked methodically, trying to create a break in the fire's path, but the situation seemed increasingly desperate.

Lucy, not one to stand by, joined Daniel with fire beaters from the farmhouse, tackling the smaller fires that the tractor couldn't reach. Her face set in grim determination, she fought the encroaching flames, coughing in the thick smoke that began to blanket the farm. The fear of losing their farm, their home, drove her, even as her lungs burned with the effort.

The night sky, once dark, was now a canvas of orange and black, the fires casting a hellish glow. As they battled the blaze, the sound of sirens finally cut through the chaos—the local volunteer fire department had arrived. Led by Tom, the firefighters jumped into action, quickly assessing the situation.

"We need to get water on these fields now!" Tom shouted over the roar of the fire. Seeing the tractor and sprayer setup, he nodded in approval at Daniel's quick thinking. "Good work! Let's hook up the truck's pump to the sprinkler system. We can bypass the damaged pumps."

Working together, they connected large hoses from the fire truck to the farm's sprinkler system. Within moments, water began to jet across the fields, the pressure from the fire truck's pump breathing life into the otherwise incapacitated system. Slowly, the combined efforts of Daniel, Lucy, and the firefighters began to turn the tide against the inferno.

As the fires dwindled, leaving behind smoldering earth and the acrid smell of burnt wheat, Lucy leaned against the tractor, her body shaking not just from the exertion but also from the rush of emotions. Relief mingled with lingering fear and anger. How could McRae go this far? The realisation that their opponent was willing to resort to outright destruction was chilling.

Amid the aftermath, as the firefighters checked for any remaining hotspots, Lucy and Daniel shared a brief, exhausted embrace. They had fought back the destruction together, saved much of the farm, but the night had revealed the dangerous lengths their adversaries would go to. The battle was won, but the war, it seemed, was far from over.

Confrontation

Amid the settling haze of the extinguished fires, an eerie silence began to fall over Harding Farm, broken only by the occasional crackle of cooling embers. However, the night's drama was far from over. As the firefighters began to pack up their equipment, a sudden commotion erupted near the barn where Lucy and Daniel were assessing the damage.

A large figure emerged from the shadows, his movements aggressive and intent clear. It was one of McRae's known associates, a burly man with a reputation for trouble. His face was twisted into a sneer as he advanced toward Lucy, who stood her ground despite the clear danger.

"What do you want?" Lucy demanded, her voice ringing out strongly despite the adrenaline pumping through her veins.

The man's sneer widened. "McRae sends his regards," he grunted. "Says if he can't have the gold, nobody can. He's not done with you yet."

As he lunged forward, attempting to grab her, Lucy instinctively dodged to the side, her reflexes sharp. She wasn't quick enough to evade his grasp, however, and his fingers clawed at her arm, ripping the fabric of her shirt as she pulled away. Enraged, she swung her fist in a wide arc, connecting squarely with his nose. Blood spurted from the impact, and the man stumbled back, shocked and even more enraged.

Daniel, who had been momentarily distracted coordinating with a firefighter, saw the altercation and ran toward them, his fear for Lucy's safety igniting a fierce protectiveness. Without hesitation, he threw himself into the fray, landing a solid punch to the man's jaw, which only served to escalate the situation. The thug recovered quickly, his face bloody and contorted with fury, and he pulled a knife from his belt.

The sight of the knife sliced through the night's tension like a physical force, and Lucy screamed out a warning. "Daniel, watch out!"

The fight turned desperate. Daniel grappled with the man, trying to avoid the slashing knife, his focus on disarming him rather than inflicting harm. They moved with brutal intent, the thug swinging wildly while Daniel used his body to shield Lucy, receiving a gash across his arm in the process. The struggle was messy and perilous, each man fighting not just for the upper hand but for what they stood to protect.

It was then that the firefighters, hearing the commotion, rushed over. Led by Tom, they surrounded the assailant with a practiced efficiency born of dealing with emergency situations. Together, they tackled the thug to the ground, pinning him despite his violent resistance. The knife clattered to the ground, kicked safely out of reach by a quick-thinking firefighter.

With the immediate threat subdued, Daniel, bleeding from his nose and arm, pulled Lucy close, checking her over for injuries. "Are you alright?" he asked, his voice thick with concern.

Lucy nodded, her own adrenaline fading, leaving her shaken but unharmed. "I'm fine, thanks to you," she replied, her voice trembling slightly.

As the police sirens announced the arrival of reinforcements, Daniel's father, who had been on his way to the farm to check on them after hearing about the fires, spotted McRae shouting orders from just beyond the property line. Recognizing him instantly, Daniel's father approached the police officers as they arrived and pointed out McRae, explaining the situation.

McRae, believing himself safe from arrest since he was technically outside the farm's boundaries, sneered at the officers as they approached. "You can't touch me; I'm not on their land," he called out confidently.

One of the officers, a seasoned sergeant, shook his head as they cuffed McRae. "Inciting violence and conspiracy don't need a specific location. You're in plenty of trouble," he stated firmly.

As McRae and his associate were taken away, the Harding family and their allies from the fire department gathered to assess the night's damage and their narrow escape from disaster. The threat had been neutralised for now, but Lucy knew this confrontation was a stark reminder of the dangers they still faced. Her resolve to protect her family's land and legacy was stronger than ever, bolstered by the community that stood with them against threats both natural and man-made.

Aftermath

In the aftermath of the dramatic confrontation and the night's fiery assault, the Harding farm was a scene of organised chaos. As McRae and his thug were led away in handcuffs, the Harding family and their friends began the process of recovery and regrouping. The sense of relief was palpable, mixed with the weariness of a battle hard-fought and won.

James, despite his recent heart surgery and the ongoing recovery process, had not stayed idle when the threat to their home became imminent. With a protective instinct that overrode his physical limitations, he had taken up a garden hose and was diligently soaking the ground around the family home. Standing with a firm grip on the hose, he directed a steady stream of water, creating a wet barrier to prevent any stray flames from reaching the wooden structures. His actions, though limited by his health, were a testament to his resolve to protect his family and their ancestral home.

Emma, equally driven by the urgency of the situation, had sprung into action with a different task. Understanding the potential need for a quick departure, she began implementing their well-rehearsed evacuation plan. Moving with efficiency, she packed a bag with essential items—important documents, family heirlooms that could not be replaced, a change of clothes for each family member, and necessary medications. Each item was chosen with care, reflecting the possibility that they might not return soon if the worst came to pass.

The car was loaded methodically, with Emma double-checking each packed item against the list they had prepared months ago, never truly believing it would come into use. Her hands moved with practiced motions, but her heart raced with the anxiety of the moment. She paused occasionally to glance at the horizon where the fire had raged, now subdued but still a haunting presence in her mind.

Once the immediate threat was neutralised, the local firefighters, who had remained on site to ensure that all hot spots were extinguished, packed up their equipment. Tom, the fire chief, made his way over to James, clapping him on the shoulder with a look of deep respect.

"You did good, James. We couldn't have asked for a better response," Tom commended him, nodding towards the hose still trickling water onto the charred earth.

James, weary but satisfied, gave a small smile. "Had to do something. Couldn't let this place go up in flames—not on my watch."

Meanwhile, Lucy and Daniel, who had been coordinating with the police and providing statements, joined Emma at the car. Seeing her actions, Lucy embraced her mother, understanding the fear and foresight that had driven her to prepare for the worst.

"Mum, thank you. For thinking of everything, even in the middle of all this," Lucy murmured, her voice thick with emotion.

Emma smiled weakly, her eyes reflecting the strain of the night. "We do what we must, love. I'm just glad we're all safe."

With the farm now secure and the immediate threats subdued, the family gathered around the porch. They looked out over the fields and the damaged areas, considering the work that lay ahead. It was Daniel who broke the silence, his voice determined.

"We've got a lot of rebuilding to do—both the land and our defenses. McRae might be gone for now, but we need to ensure no one can ever threaten our home like this again."

Lucy nodded, her expression turning resolute. "We will. We'll rebuild, and we'll make sure we're stronger than ever. This farm has stood for generations, and it'll continue to stand for many more."

Standing together, the Harding family experienced a revitalised feeling of unity and purpose. The challenges they had encountered had only fortified their connections and their dedication to their land and one another. They acknowledged that the path ahead would be demanding, but with the support of each other, they were prepared to confront any obstacles that lay in their path.

44

Resolution

Triumph

The golden hue of sunrise bathed Harding Farm in a warm, reassuring light, heralding a new day and, more significantly, a new beginning for the Harding family. After months of struggle, threat, and relentless effort, the farm thrived. The successful extraction of gold from beneath their land paid off. This allowed Lucy and her family to clear all debts with the bank and secure a robust financial buffer for the future.

Lucy stood beside her father, the warm sun bathing their land in a golden glow. The gentle breeze carried the sweet, earthy aroma of the nearby oak trees. She could hear the distant chirping of birds and the rhythmic buzzing of bees as they danced from flower to flower. The soft grass tickled her bare feet, grounding her in the present moment. James, now stronger after his heart surgery, looked out with a renewed sense of appreciation for the beauty that surrounded them. The fields of wheat, golden and ready for harvest, swayed in the morning breeze, a testament to their family's enduring commitment to the land. "You've done something remarkable, Lucy," James said, his voice laden with pride and a hint of emotion. "You've not only saved the farm, but you've set us on a path that'll keep the family legacy alive for many more generations."

Lucy's eyes greedily drank in the breathtaking sight of the expansive fields, stretching as far as the eye could see. The vibrant green of the lush wheat danced in the gentle breeze, filling the air with a sweet, earthy aroma that tickled her nose. It was a sight that symbolised their unbreakable connection to this land, a legacy that had been carefully nurtured and passed down through countless generations.

As she stood there, a wave of emotions washed over her, tingling her skin and making her heart swell with pride. The soft rustle of the wheat stalks in the wind mixed with the distant chirping of birds, creating a symphony of nature's melodies. It was in this moment that Lucy felt a deep sense of gratitude and love, a feeling that she couldn't help but share with her father.

With warmth in her voice, she spoke, her words carrying a mixture of joy and reverence. "We did it together, Dad," she said, her voice laced with the scent of triumph and determination. "Your unwavering strength and wise guidance saw us through the darkest of times. This victory, it belongs to all of us—yours, mine, Daniel's, and Mum's."

The journey so far was full of challenges. The farm was at risk of being taken away, facing legal battles and physical attacks from McRae and his gang, who wanted to exploit the hidden wealth of the Harding legacy. However, Lucy led the family through these tough times with unwavering determination and resilience.

James, leaning slightly on a walking stick but standing strong, looked out over the land with a contemplative expression. "You know, I always hoped to pass on a healthy farm to you, but what you've accomplished... it's more than I ever envisioned. You've expanded the very definition of what our farm stands for—not just in terms of crops, but in terms of innovation and resourcefulness."

The early morning sun cast long shadows on the ground, mirroring the long journey they had undertaken. The discovery of gold had been serendipitous, a saving grace hidden beneath the very soil they had toiled upon for years. With careful management and environmental consideration, they had extracted enough to pay off their looming debts and invest in advanced agricultural practices.

As they walked through the fields, checking on the readiness of the wheat for harvest, Lucy shared her plans for the future. "With the financial breathing room we have now, I want to explore more sustainable farming practices. We have an opportunity to make Harding Farm a model of innovation. We could look into organic crops, maybe even expand into agri-tourism. What do you think?"

James nodded thoughtfully. "I think your ideas are exactly what the future of farming needs. We started with traditional wheat, but there's no reason we can't lead the way in sustainable agriculture. And agri-tourism could introduce people to the beauty of the land we love so much."

Their conversation was interrupted by the arrival of Emma, who walked towards them with a tray of freshly baked muffins and coffee— her way of celebrating every small victory on their farm. "Thought you two might need a little sustenance," she said with a smile, handing out the warm muffins.

As they took a break, sitting on an old wooden fence overlooking the fields, the discussion turned to the broader impacts of their recent struggles. "It's been a harrowing time," Emma admitted, her voice a mix of relief and lingering concern. "But seeing how you've all pulled together, especially Lucy, it makes all the hard nights worth it."

Lucy reached out and squeezed her mother's hand, acknowledging the shared sacrifices and sleepless nights. "It was scary, but it brought us closer than ever," she said, gazing at the horizon where the sky met the golden fields. "And it showed us that when we stand united, we can face anything."

As they finished their coffee, looking out over the land bathed in morning light, the conversation turned to plans for a celebration. They wanted to host a gathering for the community—those who had stood by them through the turmoil. It would be a way to express their gratitude and reaffirm the bonds that had helped them protect their home and heritage.

This moment of reflection and planning was tinged with a bittersweet realisation for Lucy. The challenges they had faced had fortified her leadership and deepened her roots in the community. The Harding family, once on the brink of losing everything, had emerged stronger, more united, and with a renewed vision for the future. As the sun climbed higher, casting light over their fields, the Hardings knew they were not just surviving; they were setting the stage for a thriving future, built on the bedrock of family, community, and the undying spirit of resilience.

Secret Mission

Daniel's journey to Perth was a feast for his senses, a respite from the familiar sights, sounds, and smells of the farm. The bustling cityscape greeted him with a symphony of car horns and distant chatter, creating a vibrant backdrop for his excitement. The air carried a hint of exhaust fumes, mingling with the scent of blooming flowers that lined the streets, filling the atmosphere with a sweet, floral aroma.

As he checked into the small, quaint hotel on the outskirts of the city, the creaking wooden floors beneath his feet whispered tales of countless guests who had come before him. Vintage furniture adorned the reception area, giving it a cosy, nostalgic feel. The soft hum of the air conditioning provided a soothing background noise, complemented by the occasional clicking of keys from the receptionist's typewriter.

Daniel deliberately chose this location to immerse himself in both the industrial parts suppliers and the upscale jewellery district. The sight of towering buildings with gleaming glass windows reflected the city's prosperity, while the scent of freshly brewed coffee wafting from nearby cafes invigorated his senses. The vibrant colours of the storefronts, adorned with sparkling jewellery, captivated his eyes, igniting his anticipation.

Every step he took in this new environment carried a palpable sense of solitude, a mix of eagerness and nervousness. The touch of the cool breeze against his skin reminded him of the vastness of the world beyond the farm's boundaries. With each passing moment, the weight of his dual-purpose trip became more apparent. He felt the urgency to find irrigation repair parts juxtaposed with the deep emotional importance of creating a custom engagement ring.

In this unfamiliar city, Daniel's senses came alive, enveloping him in a sensory symphony that mirrored the complexity of his journey.

On his first morning in Perth, Daniel awoke with the sun, carrying the weight of his aspirations. After a quick hotel breakfast, he set out to meet different suppliers. He needed to find mechanical parts to fix the farm's essential pump system. With great care, he meticulously cross-checked the list of components, ensuring that each item met the precise specifications and quality standards. With the sounds of bartering, the scent of old warehouses, and the gleam of colourful gems filling the air, his thoughts sometimes turned to his journey's more thrilling adventure. He could almost feel the rough texture of the ring's metal against his fingertips, envisioning the intricate designs that would symbolise a fresh chapter for both himself and Lucy.

With the pump parts ordered and scheduled for delivery, Daniel shifted his focus to the more personal aspect of his trip. He walked into the jeweller's shop with a sense of purpose masked by a veneer of calmness. Inside, the shop was elegantly appointed, with soft lighting that cast a warm glow, creating a cosy and inviting atmosphere. The gentle hum of delicate music floated through the air, adding a touch of elegance to the ambience. The exquisite pieces on display sparkled under the soft lights, catching the eye with their dazzling brilliance.

As Daniel stepped further into the shop, the air carried a faint scent of polished wood and fine leather, mingling with a subtle hint of delicate perfume. The smooth texture of the polished counters invited a gentle touch, as if beckoning Daniel to explore the treasures that lay before him.

Mr. Clarkson, the master jeweller, approached Daniel with a muted grace, his footsteps almost imperceptible on the plush carpet beneath. The air seemed to hold a sense of reverence and respect, as if acknowledging Mr. Clarkson's renowned skill and discretion. Daniel felt a sense of reassurance, knowing he had come to the right place, where his needs would hold importance and met with utmost care.

He presented the sapphires and the gold to Mr. Clarkson, explaining their significance and his vision for the ring. "These sapphires came from our land, and the gold is from our first successful yield. I want to create something that reflects the beauty of the place we love and our life together," Daniel explained.

Mr. Clarkson's experienced eyes appraised the raw materials with expert precision as he listened intently. "We can craft something truly exceptional and personalised," he reassured Daniel. He sketched several designs, each weaving the sapphires and gold into an elegant pattern that symbolised the intertwined lives and shared destiny of the couple.

Daniel felt a thrill seeing the designs come to life on paper, each line and curve another step towards the moment he would propose. After settling on a final design, he left the shop feeling a mixture of relief and mounting anticipation. The ring would take several days to craft, a period during which Daniel planned his proposal in minute detail.

During the week in Perth, Daniel stayed occupied with planning and preparations, but evenings at the hotel were quiet, giving him time to reflect on his relationship with Lucy and their future together. Being away from the farm and Lucy gave him a new perspective. He realised the importance of what they were building together. It wasn't just about their business, but also their life as a couple.

As the day to pick up the ring drew closer, Daniel's anticipation grew. He imagined Lucy's reaction, her smile, her joy, and her possible tears of happiness. Picking up the ring, he was struck by its beauty and the craftsmanship. Mr. Clarkson had truly captured the essence of their love and the farm in the design. Holding the completed ring, Daniel felt a confluence of his past efforts and future hopes, all crystallised into the sparkling sapphires set in lustrous gold.

Having steadfastly tucked away the sparkling diamond and sapphire ring, its brilliance catching the sunlight, and meticulously packed the squeaky clean pump parts, Daniel's mission in Perth came to a close. As he checked out of the hotel, the weight of the ring in his pocket pressed against his thigh, a constant reminder of his commitment and love. The faint scent of fresh air mixed with the lingering aroma of breakfast from the hotel's restaurant filled his nostrils, as he eagerly anticipated the moment when the ring would be unveiled beneath the expansive, cerulean skies of their beloved farm.

Sunset

After the tumultuous events of the past months, Daniel and Lucy had made a conscious decision to set aside time for themselves amidst the relentless demands of farm restoration. This evening, marked as their 'date night,' was a precious respite, an opportunity to reconnect not just as partners in the farm's business, but as a couple in love.

Lucy carefully chose her attire for the occasion, slipping into a lightweight linen dress that danced and swayed in the gentle evening breeze, its fabric caressing her skin. The dress, with its natural, earthy tone, blended harmoniously with the golden hues of the surrounding fields, immersing her in the rural landscape. The soft, warm air carried the scent of fresh earth and blooming flowers, enveloping her in a fragrant embrace.

To shield her face from the lingering rays of the setting sun, Lucy adorned herself with a cream wide-brimmed sunhat, its brim casting a shadow over her delicate features. As the sun's warm, golden light filtered through the gaps in the hat, it illuminated the loose strands of her hair, creating a halo of radiant beauty.

Daniel had meticulously prepared a picturesque picnic near the harvester, carefully choosing a spot that offered an unobstructed view of the expansive wheat fields. The grass beneath their feet felt soft and inviting as they settled onto a cosy blanket. The air was filled with the delightful aroma of freshly baked bread, tangy cheeses, and ripe, locally sourced fruits. A chilled bottle of their favourite white wine stood beside a basket, waiting to be uncorked.

As Lucy approached the picnic spot, her eyes widened with surprise and delight, her smile illuminating the surrounding scenery. The setting sun cast a warm, enchanting glow upon her, enhancing her natural beauty and making her appear as if she belonged in a fairy tale. "This looks absolutely wonderful," she exclaimed, her voice filled with genuine joy.

The couple indulged in the delectable feast spread out before them, savouring each bite and relishing the flavours that danced upon their tongues. As they shared stories and laughter, the weight of their responsibilities lifted, replaced by a sense of blissful serenity. The sun continued its descent, painting the sky with vibrant streaks of orange, pink, and purple, creating a breathtaking backdrop for their idyllic evening, as if nature itself was applauding their love.

With the meal winding down and the sky deepening into richer shades of orange and purple, Daniel felt a surge of excitement and a flutter of nerves in his chest. The air was filled with the gentle hum of conversation and the distant chirping of crickets. As he watched Lucy, her eyes sparkling with contentment, she leaned back and took in the breathtaking sight of the painted sky. The sweet scent of freshly cut grass mingled with the aroma of the delicious meal they had just enjoyed.

Feeling a lump in his throat, Daniel cleared it and reached into his pocket, his fingers brushing against the smooth fabric of the small, elegantly wrapped box. As he knelt beside Lucy, the grass tickled his knees and the cool breeze brushed against his skin, causing goosebumps to rise. Lucy turned towards him, her expression shifting from relaxed contentment to surprised curiosity, her eyes widening in anticipation.

"Lucy," Daniel began, his voice steady but laced with a mix of hope and love, "this past year, through every challenge and joy, I've come to realise that there's no one else I want by my side but you. Will you marry me?" With trembling hands, he opened the box, revealing the ring that glimmered in the fading light, the sapphires catching the last rays of the sun, casting a mesmerising glow. The soft scent of roses from the nearby garden wafted through the air, adding a touch of romance to the moment.

Lucy gasped, her hands flying to cover her mouth as tears welled up in her eyes. She was speechless, overwhelmed by the sheer beauty of the ring and the depth of her emotions. Her voice came out as a barely audible whisper, choked with emotion. "Yes," she finally managed to say, her voice quivering. "Yes, a thousand times, yes!"

Daniel gently slipped the shimmering ring onto Lucy's finger, the cool metal sending a shiver down her spine. As their lips met in a deep, passionate kiss, the air seemed to crackle with electricity, their emotions bursting forth like fireworks. When they finally pulled apart, Lucy's eyes drank in the sight of the ring, her heart fluttering at its exquisite craftsmanship. The ring glimmered in the fading sunlight, reflecting hues of blue and gold, captivating her senses.

"It's beautiful, Daniel. How did you...?" Lucy's voice trailed off, overwhelmed by the moment. With a tender smile, Daniel began to explain, his words accompanied by the scent of freshly turned earth mingling with the crisp evening air. He spoke of how the ring was crafted from the very sapphires he had tirelessly mined, their vibrant colours symbolising their shared dedication and perseverance. And the gold, a testament to their unwavering commitment to the farm, to each other.

As the sun sank below the horizon, casting a warm glow on their faces, Lucy leaned against Daniel, feeling the solid warmth of his presence against her side. The whispering breeze carried the scent of wildflowers and the distant sound of crickets chirping. Her heart swelled with a profound sense of contentment, an overwhelming feeling of love and belonging. In this moment, under the sparkling canopy of emerging stars, their shared past and hopeful future merged into one.

Under the vast, open sky, they stood together, enveloped by the whispers of the night breeze. With the promise of endless tomorrows, they envisioned a life overflowing with not only challenges to overcome but also boundless love to share.

45

The Storm Unleashed

Trapped

As the sun gracefully descended below the horizon, casting a warm glow across the landscape, Lucy and Daniel strolled hand in hand towards the homestead. The air filled with a symphony of chirping birds and the gentle rustle of leaves, as if nature itself rejoiced in their newly affirmed commitment. The scent of cut wheat mingled with the sweet fragrance of wildflowers, creating a sensory tapestry that enveloped them. With each step, their hearts danced with joy, matching the vibrant hues of the sky painted in deep crimson and shimmering gold.

Anticipation fuelled their footsteps, urging them forward towards the welcoming embrace of the house. As they approached, Lucy's voice resonated with excitement, carrying through the air like a melody. "Mum, Dad, we have some wonderful news!" Emma and James, their faces instantly transforming into radiant smiles, emerged from the living room, their presence adding to the palpable sense of delight in the air.

Before they could speak, however, the joyful atmosphere was abruptly pierced by the shrill tones of emergency alerts emanating from their phones. Frowning, Daniel and Lucy pulled out their devices, their smiles fading as they read the urgent government warning flashing on their screens: a severe cyclone warning, predicting a storm more destructive than the infamous Cyclone Alby, was headed directly towards their region.

The room fell silent as the gravity of the situation sank in. James's face grew pale, the recent memories of their battles with both nature and adversaries weighing heavily on his mind. "We need to prepare," he stated gravely, his voice steady despite the worry that creased his brow.

Emma quickly sprang into action, her instincts as a caregiver kicking in. "I'll start packing some essentials—food, water, medications, especially for you, James. We can't take any chances with your health."

Lucy, still processing the swift turn of events from joyous celebration to crisis management, nodded in agreement. "Daniel and I will secure the farm as best we can. We need to protect the harvester and all the machinery."

As they divided the tasks, another piece of unsettling news came over the radio. The cyclone had already made landfall at a coastal town, causing significant damage, including at the local prison where McRae and other inmates were reported to have escaped amid the chaos. The broadcaster's voice was tense. "Authorities are currently unable to confirm the whereabouts of all escapees."

A chill ran down Lucy's spine as she exchanged a worried glance with Daniel. The threat of the cyclone was daunting enough without the added fear that McRae might be at large, potentially seeking vengeance.

With no time to dwell on this new threat, Emma and James began packing the car with their emergency supplies. According to their evacuation plan, Emma would drive James to a friend's house located 400 kilometres away, out of the expected path of the cyclone. It was a tough decision, leaving the farm and especially Lucy and Daniel behind, but it was necessary to ensure James' safety.

Lucy helped her mother load the last of the documents and essentials into the car, her heart heavy. "Be safe, Mum. Call us when you get there," she said, hugging her tightly.

"I will, sweetheart. Take care of Daniel and yourself. Don't take any risks," Emma replied, her voice thick with emotion.

As Emma and James drove away, Lucy and Daniel returned to the task of securing the farm. They worked with desperate speed, reinforcing the barns and securing loose objects that could become deadly projectiles in high winds.

As the sky grew darker, ominous clouds swirling above, the first gusts of wind began to whip around Lucy and Daniel, sending a shiver down their spines. They knew, deep in their bones, that they couldn't outrun the impending cyclone. The air was heavy with anticipation, carrying the scent of rain and fear.

Hand in hand, their fingers intertwined, they sprinted towards the mine, their hearts pounding in their chests. The deafening roar of the approaching cyclone filled their ears, like a freight train hurtling towards them from a distance. It was a sound that struck fear into their very core.

Sealing the entrance behind them, they felt the full force of the wind slam into the farm outside, the sound now muffled but still terrifying. As they descended into the depths of the earth, they could feel the vibrations of the storm reverberating through the walls of the mine, the ground trembling beneath their feet.

Huddled together in the safe room, the air was thick with the scent of damp earth and the coolness of the rock that surrounded them. Lucy and Daniel clung to each other, their bodies pressed close for comfort and warmth. They could feel the raw power of the storm raging just beyond their sanctuary, but within the safety of the mine, they found solace.

The sounds of the storm echoed through the mine shafts, a symphony of chaos and destruction. It left them wondering about the fate of their beloved farm, the danger that McRae might still pose, and the safety of their parents. The uncertainty hung in the air, mingling with the scent of desperation and the taste of apprehension.

But even in the face of the unknown, Lucy and Daniel found strength in each other's presence. Their love, unwavering and steadfast, became an anchor amidst the swirling chaos. They held onto hope, their resolve forged in the trials of the past months.

The story didn't end there. The door remained open, beckoning them towards the next chapter in the Heartlands Trilogy. It promises more challenges, adventures, and chaos, leaving them eager to face whatever lay ahead.

About the Author

Steven Goldsmith, a craftsman in both woodworking and the art of storytelling, hails from the heart of Victoria, Australia. His influences, the likes of Dale Brown, Rebecca Yarros, and Mike Bennett, have shaped his distinct voice in the world of fiction. Outside the realm of ink and paper, Steve is deeply committed to Search and Rescue, where his dedication to others mirrors the passion he pours into his writing. A lover of adventure, he crafts narratives as intricate as his woodworking, blending thrilling action with heart-pounding suspense. And yes, in his world, even an aardvark might find a place among the pages.

You can connect with me on:

🌐 https://books.by/sgoldsmith

www.ingramcontent.com/pod-product-compliance
Lightning Source LLC
Chambersburg PA
CBHW072045190726
48294CB00005B/1421